Alicia knew the proper kind of men.

GORDON SEARS had married her when she was still a girl. She had been too young to see beyond Gordon's fine Boston breeding and aristocratic good looks to the snobbish do-nothing he really was. Though he gave her a good name and the comforts of wealth, he left her feeling empty and wanting something more.

GRAHAM PARKER wanted to marry Alicia. A successful psychiatrist, a widower with two young sons, he offered her the sort of marriage she thought she ought to have. Yet she couldn't help worrying that she'd eventually be bored by Graham's solid, reliable, dispassionate nature.

With Tony, she learned the proper way to love.

TONY SPINELLI was everything Alicia might have considered vulgar. He was arrogant, hot-tempered and stuck on himself. He treated women like playthings, and never had to look far for the next one. But when they closed the door on their separate worlds, and gave themselves over to love, Alicia was swept by an erotic ecstasy that made her think twice about everything else in her life.

HIDDEN ASSETS

CHRISTMAS PETERSON

 AVON
PUBLISHERS OF BARD, CAMELOT, DISCUS AND FLARE BOOKS

HIDDEN ASSETS is an original publication of Avon Books.
This work has never before appeared in book form.

AVON BOOKS
A division of
The Hearst Corporation
959 Eighth Avenue
New York, New York 10019

First Avon Printing, October, 1981

AVON TRADEMARK REG. U.S. PAT. OFF. AND IN
OTHER COUNTRIES, MARCA REGISTRADA, HECHO EN
U.S.A.

Printed in the U.S.A.

WFH 10 9 8 7 6 5 4 3 2 1

For Maggie Starr and for Sylvia Burack

PROLOGUE

WHEN Tony strips, everybody watches.

All the lights are on when he's onstage at the Carousel Club. The rest of the time, it's a shabby roadside bar near Boston. On the weekends, it's crammed with women who come to see the male strippers. The other boys strip and dance in the smoky room under spotlights that hide flaws. They require elaborate trimmings to carry off their acts.

But Tony keeps the lights on. He has nothing to hide, and the women aren't allowed to retreat in darkness into their own private fantasies. He likes to see himself reflected in their faces, he likes to feel the throb of excitement that surges up when he appears at the end of the night's show. Tony is what they've been waiting for: luminous skin, rippling muscles, a narrow waist, broad chest and shoulders. He looks taller onstage than he is, and he moves with sensual grace born of endless practice.

All these women, all ages and kinds, love his cool arrogance, and each one goes away with the imprint of that body, those black curls framing a face like a fallen angel's, burned into her memory. Tony's the best male stripper around.

And soon, he's sure, he'll make the right connection; that's how good he is. Somebody, the lucky break, will lift him into the big time. Rich is what he'll be then, with the trappings of stardom, more love, more applause, more money, women, cars, clothes, houses.

He'll probably have to move to the Coast to be near Vegas, where his kind of act belongs. A big mansion in Beverly Hills. Or a ranch out in the desert, the right place for a guy brought up in the cramped alleys of Boston's North End. One of those big-name designers will do his costumes for Vegas, and he'll get a choreographer to fix up the rough spots in the act. A bodyguard to keep off the dames.

"Hey, Spinelli! You asleep? Barbara just intro'ed you, get your ass onstage."

Sid Gabel's weary voice cut through the backstage shadows. Tony dropped the edge of the curtain where he'd been checking out the audience for the last show of the weekend. He always did this, hoping to see the face in the crowd he knew he'd recognize; the connection, the dame who could pass a word on to the right man and get him out of the Carousel. The face wasn't there tonight, but hope endured.

Tony Spinelli heard his music cue over the club's crackly sound system. Then he went to work, doing what he did best—stripping to skin and a glittering G-string.

Tony immediately picked out a plump young woman in the audience. She had a round face behind too-big glasses and was sitting with a group of friends in the front row. She'd be his victim, his personal audience tonight; he'd play to her. And he did. The girl friends thought it was a riot, and after a moment of confusion, the girl herself got into it, licking her lips as Tony came down into the audience and let her unbutton the last two buttons of the slippery white satin shirt he wore.

Don't you love it, he thought, while he smoothly evaded her outstretched hands that wanted to touch more of him, hold him, the way they all wanted to.

And you, too, he smiled at the girl next to her, a nice little piece, with delicate features and a tumble of reddish-blond hair. She sat back and gave Tony a real long look, sizing him up with a practiced eye. She'd like to hang onto all of him, and she'd know what to do about it.

Tony flashed that one a special, glowing smile. He liked to be appreciated. He liked his work, and he loved himself when he was working. He was always aroused by his own performance, but it was better when he saw someone aroused by him, the way this redhead was. She wasn't caught up in the shared frenzy of women egging other women on. She was engrossed in the perfect, graceful body that teased with unattainable maleness and the fantasy of sex with him, a promise always out of reach.

When the act was over and his G-string was stuffed with cash—much more than the strippers who preceded him ever got in tips—Tony scooped up his discarded clothes and left the stage and the audience. Offstage, with his clothes on, he was just another good-looking young man. Then only he knew that he was the best.

But he knew that he had to find the way out, the way that made him as big offstage as on, and he knew he had to use whoever came his way to do it. The problem was, it had to be somebody with class, somebody he could trust, who'd believe in him completely.

"Tony . . . ," a soft voice called behind him as he exited the club by the back door into the parking lot.

He didn't recognize her voice, except that it was female, light, and young, a local accent with no class or quality. He almost kept walking, but headlights from cars speeding north from Boston along Route 1 revealed the red-gold hair and fragile features of the girl who'd looked him over during his act.

"Yeah?" He was tired and it was a cold February night, not made for standing around to shoot the breeze with an admirer. But he walked over to her.

"Uh . . . remember me?" she said, and put her hands on his chest against the soft wool of his coat.

"Yeah, sure," he said. "Who could forget you?"

Tony considered her briefly. Real cute, nice figure, young and eager. Probably trouble. A girl like this had to have a couple of jealous boyfriends somewhere, or a brother or two who wouldn't like the idea of Tony Spinelli one bit.

"I'm Cathie," she said. "I kinda thought you and me . . ."

"Could find a nice quiet place and get acquainted?" Tony wouldn't mind, not with this chick, but he could and did pick and choose women at will. He didn't need this one, a kid from Quincy or Billerica or Charlestown. A nobody who'd likely end up trying to tangle him up in a continuing relationship. That he didn't need at all.

"Get lost, sweetheart," he said. But kindly. "I got better things to do."

Cathie drew back and pouted. She didn't like getting

3

turned down. He wouldn't like it himself, if it should happen, which was about never. He headed for his car.

"Wait, Tony." There was a plaintive note in her voice. She really wanted it. They all did. Usually it was a housewife who wanted to even scores with her husband, or a single dame who was a little too old for her own good and yearned for an adventure before it was too late.

Sometimes he gave them the thrill they were looking for, bringing them home to his apartment in the South End for a tumble. Then he got rid of them fast. Often he walked away from the invitation, as he did tonight, when he thought they would give him more grief than he needed.

At his car, he looked back. Cathie was still standing at the back door. It seemed to him that her eyes still glittered with desire for him—for the naked man she'd seen onstage.

He knew his power. He knew women were all the same.

The girl hadn't moved or taken her eyes off him, willing him to call her to him.

He raised his hand, and until the moment it happened, he himself didn't know if it was to be a wave of farewell, better luck next time, or a signal to come to him.

She came at the signal. Fast.

He didn't have anything better to do for the next couple of hours, after all, was the way he looked at it.

1

Now, that's nice.

Alicia Sears took in the medical student leaning over Debbie Koulos's desk. A refreshing sight he was, after the eight hours she had spent with figures and dollar signs, and the unbridgeable gap between the financial needs of a major medical school and the available money. It had been a day of bickering academics and their complaints, mostly about money, mostly about not enough of it. The last one to see Alicia had been the worst and most wearying, the persistent and impatient Dr. Ostrava. She put him out of her mind as she pulled shut the old-fashioned dark wood door to her office. It closed on her professional life with its usual impressive thunk of quiet authority. She liked the sound. Solid and safe.

She liked Debbie's young man, too. She'd seen him before around the administration building. And no question about it, Debbie would sacrifice her blue Correcting Selectric to end up in the sack with him. She was having visible palpitations while she tried to explain something.

"Good night, Debbie," Alicia said. It was a few minutes before five. Debbie was too engrossed to notice Alicia's amused half-smile.

"The dean can't, won't—uh, good night, Mrs. Sears—see you . . ." Debbie surfaced long enough to call after Alicia: "Mrs. Sears, the meeting tomorrow's at eight-thirty."

5

"I remember, thanks."

Debbie had gone back to the boy. To Alicia's dismay, the kid was watching her. She turned away quickly, and kept walking.

He wasn't a kid, but a second-year medical student, which put him somewhere in his early twenties. He was very dark, with a small, compact body and devastating eyes. Not Italian, maybe Armenian or a Sephardic Jew or . . . She imagined his bold eyes still on her. The idea made her inexplicably nervous. She walked faster to escape his view.

For Debbie's sake, Alicia hoped his taste in women ran to young, elaborately coiffed and made-up secretaries. Debbie's own tastes were simple enough—men, but preferably not, she had once confided in Alicia, middle-aged Greek businessmen selected by her parents. Debbie fully appreciated that one of the fringe benefits of working at the Commonwealth University Medical School was all the young, soon-to-be-doctor flesh passing by her desk in front of the deans' offices.

Not for the first time, Alicia thanked her stars that she had moved beyond the age of sexual turmoil Debbie lived through daily. Not that having embarked on her thirties qualified Alicia for the trash barrel; she did all right for herself. Not that having failed once in marriage, not that having doubts about any long-term relationship meant her life was over. There was more, somewhere.

"I do all right," she said under her breath. "Graham is perfectly all right."

Still, if she were ten years younger, and a man like the one hanging around Debbie made a move in her direction . . . Alicia tried to wipe him out of her mind. No febrile fantasies. They only reminded her of nagging dissatisfactions about her life in and out of the office, about several things she wished Graham Parker were but was congenitally unable to be.

Alicia crossed the big hall of the administration building. It was nineteenth-century graciousness left over from the founding days of the medical school—if you ignored present-day intrusions like the strategically placed fire extinguishers, the efficient pressure bars on the exit doors, the bulletin boards covered with university notices.

If Alicia, as Associate Dean for Financial Affairs, managed to extract sufficient millions from Rockefellers or oil sheikhs or a big benevolent corporation, the still-lovely old building would be demolished and replaced by an efficient glass and metal high rise. More room, more labs, more classroom space and an air-conditioned, soundproof office for her. The portraits of deceased deans and professors that had looked down from gold frames at generations of medical students would disappear, and the curving double staircase to the upper floors, the polished mahogany table on a tasteful oriental carpet in the middle of the hall, the dark green leather chairs and sofas that no one ever occupied except for the staff Christmas party and Dean Barrow's open house during Commencement Week.

Alicia noticed that Elsa Morant, the dean's long-time administrative assistant, had decided that February was close enough to spring in Boston to warrant a vase of forced forsythia on the vast table. Elsa was a dreamer: true spring was at least two months away.

Alicia peered out the front door. It was dark already, overcast and threatening more snow to add to the two inches of two days before.

Dr. Graham Parker was nowhere to be seen.

She had expected to find his tobacco-brown Mercedes at the curb. His lecture finished at four, give him fifteen minutes to answer his students' questions, and where the hell was he? She buttoned up her nutria-lined camel coat and pulled her fox hat down around her ears before she stepped out into the cold. Graham Parker was going to be made to feel sorry for her.

George, the building super, vast in girth and height, dark beige in color, and aloof from staff and students alike, was scattering salt on the steps as she emerged. Alicia Sears was the only person George seemed willing to converse cordially with. It was oddly flattering.

"Hello, George," she said. "More snow coming?"

"Miz Sears," George said in greeting. "Weather in this city could send a man to his grave young." He tossed a handful of salt. "That damn storm trooper Mister Doctor Victor Ostrava say he came this far from breaking a leg jus' now. Could break his thick skull for all I care, but then he'd be suing the school. I hear the man likes his money. . . ."

George moved off along the sidewalk with his bucket, toward the circle of light cast by the ornate twin lampposts at the end of the walk. He had a way of conveying his opinions to Alicia obliquely. Victor Ostrava must have put

7

on his grand-man-of-science-speaking-to-the-lower-orders act for George's benefit. Typical of Ostrava; typical of George to resent it fiercely.

Directly across from where Alicia waited were the windows of the medical school research labs. Men and women in white lab coats were still hard at work, bent over experiments and microscopes.

"We toil for the good of humanity," was how Victor had put it that afternoon. "We are cramming purpose and science into every waking hour, and you, my dear Mrs. Sears, must do your part."

Translated, Dr. Ostrava's speech on his own behalf meant that he wanted more money for his research, which was complicated and expensive and, he claimed, the road to a major breakthrough in the treatment and prevention of cancer—"As my published papers prove, if you would take time to read them, Mrs. Sears."

"I'm not qualified to judge research, Dr. Ostrava," she had repeated for the hundredth time. "I am qualified to wheedle money from foundations, corporations, governments, and alumni. Nothing more."

He had a look that said he did not believe her, that he was positive she had a great deal more influence than she claimed. He had not been satisfied when he left her.

In the ten years she had been working her way up through the administration of Commonwealth Medical, few doctors had struck a deeper sense of antipathy than Victor Ostrava, and this in spite of his invariably courtly manner.

"Dean Sears?"

Alicia whirled around to face the attractive medical student, who had given up his attempt to persuade Debbie to grant his petition.

"Ah, yes. Mr. . . . ?" But she knew his name suddenly: Mike Tedesco. "Mr. Tedesco."

"Hey, I didn't know you knew me." He was gazing intently at her. Very long lashes. Very straight white teeth. Aggressive, inviting. He was one of those people who radiate sexual energy, even when the body is buried under layers of winter clothes. He was completely unsettling; Alicia tried to avoid people like Mike Tedesco for her peace of mind.

"We like to know who our students are," she said. Too deanishly. "And how are things coming, Mr. Tedesco?"

"Coming?" He made it sound like an invitation.

8

"With school," she said quickly. He must be only about twenty-three, she had a good ten years on him, yet he was able by his mere presence to reduce her to stuttering confusion. It must be a special gift he was born with, like being able to draw a horse or play the piano by ear. And he was not her type, not at all like her ex-husband, Gardner Sears, or her present attachment, Graham Parker. He was too dangerous, risky, sensual, not suitable. Young.

"This year's not bad," Mike said. "But you still got to hustle. Grades, exams, the competition, money. You got to keep an eye open for every advantage you can grab."

An old story to Alicia, but why was he still looking at her that way? And seeing what? Alicia was never sure that the way she saw herself and what others saw were the same. Graham naturally approved of her subdued facade. In Boston, middle-aged, widowed professors of neurology at a medical school with a history and reputation equal to Harvard's do not run around with flashy women. Her ex-husband Gardner had seen the same safe person; that was one of the few things about her of which he had wholeheartedly approved. But then, he was a broker, very old Boston and conservative. "Pretty," though. Both Gardner and Graham professed to find her "pretty." That meant they admired regular features, nice eyes, good nose, thick, dark hair that was always well cut, not a bad figure, formed by youthful Colorado summers on horseback and winters on the ski slopes, the ballet class she took twice a week.

Mike Tedesco did not look as though he were seeing "pretty." He was seeing "desirable," which was something else. Not the way one related to medical students. Not the way Alicia normally related to men, but then, she avoided coming on strong as being not quite the thing for a woman like her. She knew herself well enough for that, she thought.

Why was Mike still sticking to her?

"I'm looking for a part-time job right now," he said. "I can fit it in with studying, and I need the money."

"Student Affairs . . . they list jobs . . . I don't know . . ."

He smiled at her. "I wasn't asking you," he said. "Of course, if you hear of anything . . ." He looked to have strength and gentleness in him. He looked so . . . nice. "I can do about anything. Anything at all."

Alicia wanted him to stop drawing her into a warm circle

9

of intimacy. And she wanted him to stay, to touch her even. Why was Graham so damned late?

"I'll be seeing you," Mike said. "There's my wife."

A beat-up black VW pulled up in front of the building, with a young blonde woman at the wheel.

"Don't forget me," he tossed back at Alicia as he started down the steps.

"I won't," she murmured.

A wife, huh? Bad luck, Debbie.

Alicia was drained by the encounter. George rejoined her on the steps, and stood contemplating Mike and the blonde with his chin sunk on his chest.

"Now there's a lucky guy," he said finally.

"You think so? Why's that?" Alicia was thinking that the wife was the lucky one.

"He gets through medical school," George said, "he's going to make a million bucks, that one. Then he's got a pretty chickie shows up every time he pokes his nose out in the cold. That's good in a woman. Devotion."

"He says she's his wife."

"Ah." George watched the VW slide on the ice at the end of Hancock Place and turn around. "Wives is something else. I got three I can look back on. They always lookin' out for their investment. And such." He grinned wickedly. George had two very fine gold teeth. "This chappie ain't going to last with her much past . . . oh, first year interning. Take my word. Got an eye for women and intriguin', that one. And women—they got an eye for him."

"I know what you mean," Alicia said. She was beginning to feel the damp chill.

George paused at the front door. "He probably on the lookout for a real foxy sort of woman, Miz Sears. Say, a good-lookin' woman who could push him along. A lady dean or such. You take care now, Miz Sears, he don't tangle you up."

"I'm too old for that sort of thing," Alicia said, and regretted sounding so prim in response to George's teasing.

"Ain't nobody too old for nothin'. You just a young thing anyhow."

The Tedesco car braked crazily at the corner, barely in time to avoid a collision with Graham's Mercedes as it turned into Hancock Place. Graham pulled up to the curb and leaned over to open the passenger door for Alicia.

"Got a ride home," George said, lingering. "Good

thing." He had a knowing grin now. George didn't miss much that went on at Commonwealth Medical. He knew perfectly well that Alicia had been seeing Dr. Parker for the past year.

"That damned idiot woman in the black car nearly hit me." Graham started talking as soon as Alicia slid into the car. He leaned over abstractedly and gave her a small kiss on the cheek, but he was still fuming.

"It was a Mrs. Tedesco," Alicia said. "Her husband is a student here."

"You weren't waiting long," Graham said, ignoring her remark. He carefully, very carefully, maneuvered the car over the icy turnaround. "She nearly cut right across my right fender." He headed the Mercedes on its stately way to downtown Boston. It was, as always, too warm in the car, and it had never lost the scent of brand-new leather. "I said," he repeated, "you weren't waiting for me long."

"Right, Gray. It wasn't long."

Graham Parker seldom asked questions. He made statements in his soft, reassuring voice, and was seldom to be contradicted. This was fine for the Brooks Professor of Neurology, but it would be difficult for those involved in a personal relationship. Alicia knew that she was sometimes unfair to poor Graham. And lately, she was often irritated by his style. Once it had been comforting and appealing; he had taken charge when she had been floundering and given her a place at his side. Now she felt guilt because she wasn't sure she wanted to continue in that place. And guilt made her critical, of his assurance, his predictability, his even temper, his probity. He was too good.

"You're preoccupied," Graham said. "It was a difficult day."

"Some lousy academic politics. Faculty agitation about Dean Barrow's development plans, nobody wants to lose an inch of status. And then those sheikhs are coming next week, and I'm sure they want some kind of payoff in exchange for their money. Victor Ostrava came in to connive for more money, as usual. I know he assumes a Nobel is in his future, not that it wouldn't be a good thing for the school. . . ."

Graham sniffed. He distrusted "foreigners" equally, regardless of race, creed, or national origin. Although Victor was many years removed from Eastern Europe, to Graham, he was as outlandish as a sheikh in a burnoose, or anyone

11

who was not also a Boston-born-and-bred Parker or of that circle.

"I don't care for the way he promotes himself and his work," Graham said. "He's not careful about his data. Of course, it's far out of my field, but one hears things, not that I care for gossip. I hope you won't promise him extravagant funds."

"Unfortunately, unless we hook the sheikhs or that big endowment from California we've been promised, we won't have extra funds beyond our present budget. And besides, I can't make promises; that's Dean Barrow's job and the committee's. Although I must say, now that his wife is so ill, the dean has given me a lot more say in who gets how much."

"And you enjoy that." Graham had a slight smile on his face, and Alicia wondered if he were recalling the first time he'd said that to her.

"Yes," she admitted. "I do."

She'd agreed with Graham the first time, too. They had been going out to dinner and the theater for a couple of months during the previous winter and eventually they had reached her bedroom, some eight months ago now, to begin a quiet affair.

Graham had said, "You enjoyed that," from the tumbled bed.

Alicia had laughed out loud at the serene assurance in his words. "Yes, I did, Gray." She had never been more content with Graham than in that first sexual encounter. It had been nearly a year then since she had slept with a man, and that man had been Brett Handley, a lean, wind-swept pilot with a young face and a crooked grin topped by short grizzled hair. He flew between San Francisco and Boston for a major airline on a reasonably regular basis. Their sporadic affair, which Alicia had kept hoping would become something more, had been defeated by her reluctance to be a mere fragment of a "girl-in-every-port" lifestyle. Brett had cheerfully denied it, but had taken her at her word, and had ceased to call.

"Brett was not a man to pin a future on," Harriet Gould, Alicia's best friend, had remarked, wise in the comfort of her domestic nest. "On the other hand, Graham Parker is a Gardner Sears clone, no offense intended, and you know how that ended up. I wish you'd fall for the real thing for a change."

12

"I don't think I can afford the luxury of waiting for the real thing to come along," Alicia had said. "I think maybe Graham *is* the real thing for someone like me."

Harriet had since contented herself with observing the relationship between Alicia and Graham, and never hesitated to provide her own candidates for the real thing as they occurred. As far as Harriet was concerned, Graham's sole advantage was that he had two motherless boys, a ready-made family for Alicia. Alicia lately was hard pressed to find any advantages, beyond having a pleasant escort.

Now, as they drove toward Boston, Alicia watched the parkway lined with stark, naked trees give way to shopping malls, then houses built close to the road, nice neighborhoods with landscaping and lawns, and less nice sections with shabby, two-family houses. The news murmured on the radio, too low to make out the words. She couldn't push aside a troubled and restless feeling that had haunted the edge of her consciousness for days, and especially so this evening. She wished she could put it down to the stirrings of spring, but it was more than that. Perhaps, in part, it was due to her recent Christmas visit to her father in Colorado. Donald Bridges had been a widower for more than a dozen years, still living in the big house in Boulder where Alicia had grown up, but this Christmas had found him ardently courting a recently widowed neighbor, Vera Ormond, with an enthusiasm and joy Alicia seemed to have lost in her life. If it had ever been there, she thought glumly.

They had taken a route through Boston's Roxbury section, dark semi-slums inhabited by minorities, battered street-corner shops, too many ravaged, boarded-up buildings, clusters of dispirited black men deep in conversation under streetlamps in front of brightly lighted barber shops.

A few flakes of snow sifted down onto the windshield.

" 'The snow falling faintly through the universe, upon all the living and the dead.' "

"Pardon?" Graham said. He got tense when he drove through Roxbury. An alien territory, a place and a people to be feared.

"It's something from James Joyce," Alicia said. "Roxbury reminds me of it . . . the living and the dead. And the snow is falling on me, too."

"I don't care for the sound of that," he said. "It's not like you. These people . . ." He waved his hand toward

13

streets in the grip of poverty. "Death in life, is that what you're saying?"

"In a way." Alicia hunched down and stared gloomily at the tall Prudential and Hancock buildings that dominated the Boston skyline. Graham glanced over at her, suddenly concerned and aware of her mood.

"Cheer up," he said brightly. Kindly. They were stopped at a red light. He smiled his boyish smile that could be so appealing. Such a nice-looking man. Prematurely gray hair; he was only in his mid-forties. Distinguished, intelligent, successful. Prosperous, too, and affectionate when he chose to be.

"I've been thoughtless," he said. "I forget how tedious administrative work can be, and you do work hard. God knows those ambitious young men can be difficult."

She thought immediately of Mike Tedesco. Lots of ambition there. He would make a million bucks. From women patients.

"Somehow I must have sensed you'd need something to brighten this dreary day," he said mischievously. "So it's a good thing I did what I could. Look in the back seat, I have the doctor's prescription for February depression."

"Oh, Gray . . ." She reached over the seat and picked up a small Shreve, Crump & Low envelope. The long narrow box inside held an extravagantly long gold and lapis necklace. The light changed and they turned onto Boylston Street, but Alicia ignored Graham's pleas to let him drive safely as she kissed his cheek soundly.

"It's gorgeous," she said. "Oh, Gray, I love it!"

Graham looked highly pleased with himself. How could she not feel affection for him? He did come up with lovely surprises.

She didn't bother to wonder why today, of all days, he had decided to give her a present. Not right then, anyhow.

"Where would you like to have dinner?" he asked. "Locke-Ober's? The Ritz? Jimmy's? Maison Robert? Chinese, Greek, Italian?"

"Anyplace. Whatever you say." The necklace made a melodic cascade of sound as she passed it from one hand to the other.

"My preference," he said, "is dinner at your place, if you haven't used up those steaks Harriet and Mark sent you for Christmas."

14

"You checked them out in the freezer not four days ago," she said, "and don't deny it. Sure . . . why not?"

But she felt a sense of foreboding. Something was up. And she definitely didn't feel much like going to bed with Graham Parker tonight. The necklace was nice, but she wasn't going to be bribed into sex.

Mike Tedesco probably had no need to do more than crook his finger. Then she was ashamed of herself for thinking of him at all, but his impact refused to go away.

"Gray, do you think of me as desirable?" And she could have bitten her tongue for bringing up the subject.

"What sort of question is that? You're an extremely attractive woman."

"But not desirable." Some devil in her tongue made her persist.

"I'm afraid I don't understand what you're getting at, Alicia. It sounds like something your friend Dr. Catlett would start you brooding about."

"Billy?" Alicia was amused by Graham's not too well concealed hostility toward her friendship with Dr. William Catlett, who was a successful dermatologist as well as a lecturer at the medical school. He was also gay, which, in Billy's words, pissed Graham off so much he was likely to drown in it. All made worse because Billy wasn't disturbed by his sexual preferences or what people like Graham thought. "Yes," she said, "I suppose it does sound like Billy, but no, it was a thought that came to me while I was waiting for you."

While Mike Tedesco was looking at her. While she was hating that look, and deep inside, reveling in it.

If only Graham, somebody, looked at her that way, every time . . .

2

"LET'S stop at the Lenox for a drink," Alicia said suddenly. She didn't want to go home yet, and the bar at the Lenox Hotel, with its white piano surrounded by chairs and the dim Victorian nooks where out-of-town salesmen murmured to barely met young ladies carried strong memories of Brett Handley. He liked the dark corners and the earthy, middle-aged blonde waitresses always welcomed him back like a lost son.

It was too bad about Brett, that it hadn't worked out to be something real and lasting instead of an extended series of first dates. Brett had treated her as desirable, they had always ended up making love, and she had always believed that one day he would tell her he loved her and she would be able to make a real emotional investment in him.

She had once told him that the person who was assigned the task of thinking up enduring clichés had had Brett in mind when he came up with "Here today, gone tomorrow."

Brett thought seriously for a minute. "Yup," he said. "Right after he thought up 'A bird in the hand.' But he was never able to top 'Hot enough for you?' "

Brett had been funny and appealing, sexy in a wild-blue-yonder kind of way. She remembered that his eyes actually were the exact pale blue of the sky over the mountains near Boulder in the early morning. Not a bad person for a divorced assistant dean in her thirties to be seen around

16

with. Once she'd taken him to a school reception for some men from the Ford Foundation. He had spent the evening charming Dean Barrow, who was not easily impressed. And every now and then, he'd look around and lock eyes with Alicia. Promises of things to come. Memories of things gone forever. Until today, she hadn't thought of Brett in months.

"We'll stop for one drink, if you wish," Graham said. "The Lenox has never been the same since Gladys Troupin died. She must have been there with her feathered hats for a thousand years. Alicia! What is the matter with you?"

"Sorry. I was reminded of an old friend. Brett Handley."

"That pilot?" He managed to inject a note of disapproval. Brett was one of several subjects they did not discuss, along with Graham's long friendship with Alicia's former husband, with whom he shared a common prep school, Harvard, and various Harvard graduate schools, not to mention family connections. Although Graham never referred to it, she knew they met for lunch at the Harvard Club occasionally and played squash under the watchful eye of the club pro. Old-boy ties never die, even when the boys share, sequentially, the same woman.

"Hillie always liked the Lenox," Graham said sadly. The late Mrs. Parker had gone untimely to her heaven, leaving Graham with two boys of five and seven. That had been about five years ago, about the time Gardner Sears had entered his particular heaven, namely Beverly Farms north of Boston, with a new wife and now a sturdy offspring.

"Alicia." Graham was lucky as usual in finding a parking space near the hotel, across from the Boston Public Library. "One drink, and then home, okay? I have something I want to discuss."

"Won't you tell me now?" She fingered the necklace she still had in her hand.

"Here? In the car?"

"Why not? If it's good, we'll neck to celebrate. . . ."

"What has gotten into you?"

"If it's not good, you can go home to Weston, and I can go to the Lenox and pick up a salesman."

A flicker of . . . disgust? Puzzlement? Alicia found it hard to read Graham's expressions except to categorize them as positive or negative.

"I'd really rather we were somewhere else," he said. "It's quite important."

"Now," she said stubbornly.

He sighed. "We're a good couple, Alicia."

"Yessir, we are."

"You know how deeply . . . how much I care about you." He put his arm around her and pulled her over close to him. "And the boys are so fond of you."

Ah, the boys. Ten and twelve now, somewhat spoiled by their father, made to toe a strict line by Graham's mother, who had had them in her charge since Hillie Parker's death. Alicia had the strong suspicion now that this was leading to a marriage proposal, and the thought of it made her uneasy. She had no idea how she might answer him— yes, I will accept an affectionate but passionless marriage? No, I cannot accept a lifetime without desire? And what about love? What, indeed?

Kiss me, at least, she thought. Hard. Tongues. Passion. Promise . . . as though I were desirable.

He kissed her ear, touching flesh between the collar of her coat and the fur of her hat.

She knew how she would answer, if it came to an actual proposal. There was . . . something, someone else . . . somewhere. The fleeting fantasy of a Mike Tedesco, the memory of a Brett Handley, even the single-minded pursuit of Gardner Sears that had shaped her early years reminded her that there was that "something." A promise to which, she felt instinctively, Graham did not hold the answer.

"Let's go to my place, Gray," she said. "I don't want to go to the Lenox." She felt defeated, by Graham, by Mike.

Her apartment was three blocks away, on Marlborough Street, in an old four-story building that had once been a town house. She owned an apartment there, at distressing cost; three rooms and a parking space in the alley in the back where her Volvo was still snowed in and would be deeper in a drift if the snowfall continued. She was able to afford the apartment only because of her "friendly" divorce from Gardner; he had insisted on paying the taxes and part of the mortgage until she remarried or chose to sell. It was more acceptable than alimony, which she had refused to consider. But she knew perfectly well that the arrangement had been inspired by Sears pride: Gardner wished to have his former wife maintain a certain residential status as long as she remained a Sears and in Boston. Surface impressions were important to Gardner, and while Marlborough Street wasn't quite Beacon Street, it was an acceptable address.

"I understand your friend Sheila Conroy is getting married," Graham said suddenly. Alicia was surprised that he knew; he claimed never to listen to university gossip. Sheila was an administrative assistant at the Business School whom Alicia had known for several years. Sheila said laughingly that people referred to her as "the one who never married."

"I was holding out for big bucks," she'd said when she called Alicia to announce her engagement to "her Arab," an immensely wealthy man who had showed up from his native Beirut with endless millions. The combination of Boston Irish Catholic and Lebanese Moslem was unlikely, but Sheila had never been conventional, and she seemed ecstatically happy with Said.

"She called to tell me," Alicia said, as Graham, ever fortunate, squeezed into a parking space directly across from Alicia's building. "In fact, her fiancé insisted she have what is called a 'bachelorette' party. This Friday night."

"Ah," Graham said. "Well, I have tickets for the new Maggie Smith play at the Wilbur for that night. I wanted to surprise you."

So many surprises. And here was one for Graham.

"You should have told me," Alicia said. "I've already accepted Sheila's invitation, and I've offered to drive some of the other guests."

It was a lie, but in her present mood, she wasn't going to let Graham make blind assumptions about her availability. Now she would go in spite of certain reservations she'd felt when she heard where the party was going to be held.

"I did want to see the play," Graham said, almost pouting.

"You can take your mother."

"Mother prefers matinees. I really did want to see it with you, Alicia."

"Sorry, Gray. Sheila and Said have gone to a lot of trouble. It's being held at this place out on Route 1."

"Route 1?" He made it sound like unspeakable degradation, instead of a narrow highway lined with fast-food restaurants, dingy motels, and aluminum-siding salesrooms.

"It's a sort of nightclub or bar. Debbie Koulos and some of the other secretaries go there all the time." They mounted the steps to Alicia's front door. She tilted her head to see Graham's expression when she said, "They strip there."

"They—strip?"

He was visibly, satisfyingly shocked when she said, "Men. Naked, taking it off. You know about strippers. But these are *men*."

"See here, Alicia . . ." He followed her into the apartment. She was perversely pleased that he had instinctively sounded threatened. Graham was only human after all.

"Hey, Gray, don't look at me as though I were one of your prize schizophrenics." He opened his mouth to say something further, but Alicia put up her hand. "And don't brother to sputter. I know it's not quite proper, ladies don't, et cetera. But ladies do, including Elsa Morant and me and dozens of others. Elsa is dying to go."

"A woman of her age ought to know better," Graham muttered. "And you should too."

Alicia turned on the lights. "Me? Because I choose to have fun out with the girls, watching the boys?"

"Another notion you probably got from Catlett."

"I don't get notions from Billy, Graham."

What she got from Billy Catlett was moral support and generous, open friendship that encouraged her to remember that there were positions to be taken outside the boundaries of the restricting conventionality she had grown up in. That it was a matter of setting her own standards, and not giving up on what she aimed for. The choice of goals was hers alone.

What Graham believed you aimed for, as did Gardner, was occupying fixed niches defined by social position, background, class, acceptable occupations for your sex. Under their influence, Alicia had tended to go along with the idea, but if Billy could deal with a life partly out of the mainstream and partly conventional professional success, so could she. Tonight she felt obstinate enough to give Billy's philosophy a try.

"Let me get dinner started," she said. "Can I get you a drink?"

"Yes, but I'll fix it," he said. "Scotch for you?"

"Please. And I'm sorry about Friday. Really. I have to go for Sheila's sake."

Graham waved away her apology, his humor restored. "I understand," he said. "Still . . . well, never mind."

When she came back from the kitchen, Graham was studying her bookshelves as if he'd never seen them before. Interspersed among her books were odds and ends she'd picked up on vacation travels: a pottery dove from Mexico, some Venetian glass, a black wood box trimmed in brass she'd found in San Francisco's Chinatown (a short visit to Brett on his own turf, the only time), a shoddy miniature Eiffel Tower from that trip she and Gardner had taken to Paris, when it seemed that the marriage could be healed, a reproduction of Michelangelo's *David* from a stopover in Florence.

"I've always liked what you've done with this place," Graham said. Alicia drew the drapes of the tall windows facing on the street.

She liked the room, too. Big, with high ceilings. It had once been the front drawing room of the town house. Big, fat sofas—there was room enough for two—covered in burgundy velvet, the wall of bookcases, and a long, low table to one side that she used as a desk. It was a piece of solid 1930s oak she'd come across at the Goodwill thrift shop and had refinished herself. Facing one sofa was a fireplace, although Alicia reserved fires for special occasions; firewood was too hard to come by and too expensive to waste. But the logs were piled on the andirons, ready for a match, if the special occasion arose. It was not tonight.

Graham got himself another drink. Well, she thought, two drinks means he's screwing himself up for something, but given his earlier preliminaries, it was only to be expected. Graham did not give up easily on a path once taken.

"Did I tell you that Mother is thinking of moving to Florida permanently next winter?"

Graham spoke offhandedly, but Alicia had a feeling of foreboding as she settled herself on the sofa.

"Really?" she said, trying to sound offhanded too. "I shouldn't think she'd like it there for more than a month."

"So many of her friends are now wintering in the Palm

21

Beach area," he said. "It will be better for her health. She's not young enough to cope with two growing boys anymore."

The hell she isn't, Alicia thought. Graham's mother could cope with a swarm of killer bees without blinking twice.

"Of course, she'll be here until the fall, although she'd like to spend the summer on the Cape with the Comptons. You remember their nice house at Truro. And Graham Junior wants to go to hockey camp in Rhode Island for most of the summer, and Timmy's been asked to drive out west in July with the family of one of his classmates. . . ."

Graham, you are truly devious, she thought. Mother Parker gone to the sunny South, no more built-in substitute mother for the boys while Professor Parker makes his way to the top of the academic heap. The boys and Mom safely taken care of for the summer, a perfect time for a European honeymoon for the professor and his bride, the former Alicia Bridges Sears. . . .

"Alicia." Graham was standing in front of her. She put her drink on the table beside the sofa and folded her hands.

Here it comes, she thought. And what do I say?

"I want to marry you. I need a wife . . . you need me."

Do I? she wondered. She was exhausted now, by Graham, the day, the decision he was asking her to make. She couldn't say yes. Could she? But how could she refuse?

Then he angered her: "In my position, marriage is important."

"Your position? You're standing there with a marriage proposal, and you're talking about *your* position? Goddammit, what about me?" Alicia's eyes blazed.

"I've never liked crude language in my women, Alicia."

"Too bad, Graham."

"I'm sure you don't speak to Dean Barrow that way, or the gentlemen who are potential donors."

She held her temper. "We are talking about a marriage proposal, not a grant from the Ford Foundation."

It was a standoff, Graham looking down at her, Alicia looking up. A thread of tension between them.

"And marriage is something I'd have to think about, Gray."

Graham fell on her, suddenly, finding her mouth in an awkward kiss. Alicia, startled, tried to turn her head, but he forced her face back to his and held it as he pressed his body against hers. This was unexpectedly exciting, completely unlike the decorous lovemaking Graham usually indulged in. Alicia felt a burst of real, almost wild pleasure. Spontaneous passion consummated on the living-room floor was not Graham's style, but Alicia hoped . . .

She felt herself responding, and started to loosen his tie, unbutton his shirt. She could feel his heart thumping where she put her hands against his chest.

"He certainly did get on with it," she told Billy later that evening, when he called her around midnight. "Why am I telling you this?"

"It sounds as though you need to tell somebody, is why."

"Well, he sat right up like Mrs. Parker's big beautiful boy and said, 'We'll go to the bedroom.' God, I felt like a big balloon somebody stuck a pin into. Then he got up and marched into the bedroom, taking off his own tie. Didn't even look around to see if I were following."

"I suppose you were following."

"Oh, hell, yes. But I'm not proud of it. I kept hoping."

"But?"

"But it was like always. Lie down, dear, just so, and let me put this here; there, you liked that."

"Did you like it?" Quickly. "I'm not indulging in telephone voyeurism, honest."

"Like it? That's not the issue." She stopped for a moment, remembering the secret images she had summoned up to accompany her through the event. It had been a man very much like Mike Tedesco. "I liked it as much as I ever do with Gray."

"Meaning?"

"It was the most predictable fifteen minutes I've ever spent."

"*Fifteen minutes?* The man had just proposed."

"Well, you know Graham. Not a man to waste precious time. But, Billy . . ."

"I'm listening."

"He didn't even know . . . how bad I felt. It didn't occur to him. I wanted . . . I want . . ."

"What *do* women want, anyway?"

"Don't start. You stick to teenage zits and leave the female mind to Dr. Freud. We do know what we want. I

23

do. I want something real and alive. A perfect match. I want heaven, in bed and out of it. Forever."

"This is too much for me," Billy said. "I have such simple wants and needs."

"Great moral support you are."

"No, I do understand, Alicia. Really."

Alicia knew he did, off on the other end of the telephone, in his big apartment on Beacon Hill. He truly wanted a permanent relationship, a household, a person of his own. Although his vision was a man rather than the opposite sex, he and Alicia were reaching after the same kind of dream. It was probably why they were friends.

"So you're alone now?" he said. He sounded sad.

"Of course. We had dinner, Graham put on his coat and said, 'I lecture in Worcester tomorrow, we'll take the boys skiing on Saturday. I'll call day after tomorrow.' And then he made a note in his pocket diary, probably something like 'Do something nice for Alicia. She deserves it.'"

Billy said, "Oh, Alicia, old Graham isn't such a prick."

"Sometimes he is," she said. "But I reminded him that I couldn't see him on Friday, because I'm going to Sheila Conroy's bachelorette party."

"Jesus—*bachelorette?*"

She was amused by his reaction. Her first chuckle in hours.

"I think it's because," Alicia said sweetly, "instead of having naked women jump out of a cake like at stag parties, they have naked men."

Billy Catlett was briefly rendered speechless. Then he howled with laughter.

"Did you tell Graham *that?*" he asked.

"Enough so that he got the idea."

"But you're not really going, are you?"

"Yes, I am," Alicia said firmly. "And do you know something, Billy? You men are all the same." She hung up.

She felt badly used by the day. Safe in her comfortable home. Alone. Nothing had been resolved. Her life stretched on ahead along the same path as the one she had trod yesterday and the day before.

Graham had never once mentioned love. She was not so starry-eyed and romantic as to believe in grand passions that endured forever. Experience had taught her otherwise. But there had to be a bond, a touch or a look that superseded the practicalities of life. Some secret joy between a man and a woman that both recognized. Something that engaged the senses and the mind wholly, if only for the fleeting moment. Once, she thought she had it with Gardner Sears.

Tonight, for Alicia Sears, there was nothing.

3

ALICIA Bridges had known she was going to marry Gardner Sears the moment she laid eyes on him.

She was fifteen, going on sixteen, wholly in love with horses, and especially with a big chestnut gelding named Dewdrop, who inhabited the Ormond stables near Boulder, Colorado. Alicia went almost daily to ride him during the summer. One day she rounded the corner of an outbuilding, and there was a tall, blondish young Easterner, shy in his stiff jeans and plaid shirt, boots that had barely seen a day's wear. Alicia, dark-haired, slim, tomboyish, was suddenly aware of her grubby clothes and messed-up hair, as the golden youth looked her up and down with the aloof arrogance of the well-bred Harvard undergraduate. He was wonderful, perfect, nineteen (she later learned). And to her teenaged eyes, the sexiest boy she had ever laid eyes on.

She had discovered a new, grown-up emotion: true love.

"Would you be one of the Ormond girls?" he asked. "I was told to find you to be shown about."

"No, I'm Alicia Bridges. I come out here from Boulder to ride." Her mind was racing: the Ormonds owned the stables, while her father was merely a modest real estate broker. And agony. Both Kathy and Linda Ormond were older than Alicia and prettier and more sophisticated. . . . "Are you from around here?" she asked, knowing full well that he was not.

26

"No, we're visiting the Ormonds while my dad looks at some property."

"My father's in real estate, maybe he could . . . ," she began, but he was gazing over her head, chin up, considering the spectacular view with a touch of disdain. He seemed about to continue his quest for Kathy and Linda and it couldn't happen.

"Do you like horses? Want to see them?" Anything to keep him with her.

The perfect young man looked around. Not an Ormond girl in sight. "Yes," he said. "Why not?"

Alicia drew him along toward the stables.

"Are you from . . . ?" She tried to think of what wonderful place might have produced him. "New York?"

"No. Boston. Chestnut Hill, actually."

Alicia tried to look impressed. It was some years before she understood, after she had finally seen the grand Sears family home and the other great houses tucked back behind walls of trees on the winding roads of Chestnut Hill.

"What's your name?" she finally asked, since he hadn't offered it.

"Gardner Sears," he said.

"I never heard a name like that."

"Gardner? It's a family name, my grandmother's name."

"And I never heard of a lady named Gardner."

"It was her last name, before she married my grandfather."

For some reason, Alicia felt a thrill of humility, the willingness to grovel before his obvious superiority.

"This is Dewdrop," she said shyly, bringing him to the stall of the big gelding. "I love him." But today, she did not love him quite as much as she had half an hour before. "Dewy, Dewy," she crooned, and the horse tossed his head.

"I ought to be getting back to my people," Gardner Sears said. "My mother is making noises about going back East tomorrow."

Alicia was aghast. She couldn't lose him so soon. "You just got here!"

Gardner shrugged and grinned. Suddenly he was less a distant prince, more a living, lovely human being. "I don't think she likes all this space. Says it's too high up, the air's too thin. . . . My dad and I will hang around for a couple of weeks. He wants to buy investment property."

Alicia was so relieved she could have kissed him. Well,

27

not exactly. Kissing was for later, for the dream that must come true. Alicia's mother had often enough reminded her that kissing . . . and stuff . . . was better saved for the future. When you were engaged or married.

"Do you like to ride?" she asked. "I can show you some great places to ride."

"Oh, yes," he said airily. "Of course I ride."

A small lie, Alicia later found out. Gardner tried to blame his awkwardness on being unfamiliar with western saddles, but she could tell he was simply not used to horses. At the time the prevarication make him more human and lovable.

The Sears bought property, Alicia managed to catch a glimpse of Mrs. Sears before she bundled herself home (Mrs. Sears barely took in the somewhat unpolished teen-aged girl in the background), and, best of all, Gardner returned for the next couple of summers.

Alicia herself embarked on a campaign to be allowed to attend college in the East, preferably Boston. Pauline and Donald Bridges had always encouraged her academic interests, and finally they agreed to her going far away for college. Gardner was at Harvard Business School, and was then going into the Sears investment company in Boston with his father and uncle.

"I suppose," her mother said, when the acceptance to the Boston college arrived, "you're only doing this to be near the Sears boy."

"Oh, no, Mom." But her mother smiled. Gardner was all a mother could want for her daughter: money, position, a future.

"Good luck, dear," she said to Alicia. "Remember to hold onto your self-respect."

By now, Alicia knew perfectly well what she meant, and had managed through high school to avoid succumbing to the sexual advances of her high school dates. She was saving herself for Gardner, in any case, and the boys she went out with seemed so young and clumsy in comparison. It didn't trouble her greatly that Gardner, during his summer visits, continued to see her as a little girl, up until the summer before she went to college. That was the year her devotion paid off, and he began to take her out. Real dates, with kissing and holding hands, and sometimes passion that alarmed her. Those were the best days of Alicia's life so far, and when she set out for the East, she believed absolutely that it was simply a matter of time. As long as he didn't do something stupid like marrying somebody else first.

Luck or fate, Gardner was unattached, and Alicia set out to make herself a perfect mate for him. The attraction on his part got stronger, because she worked hard to be what he wanted. And as she made her way through her college years, she made sure she almost—but never quite—went to bed with him. Pauline Bridges would have been proud of her, and even though she died suddenly when Alicia was a sophomore, the memory of her mother's admonitions about nice girls' behavior carried her through. Along with maintaining "self-respect," Alicia absorbed a great deal in the way of proper Bostonian gloss because that suited Gardner and the circle he moved in.

And how very little she learned of Gardner really, so eager was she to accommodate herself to his life and background. How very little he bothered to know anything at all about her. How sad that she accepted his style uncritically and that he was never able to see that there was more to her than the surface contrived to match his preconceived ideas.

How very long ago it all seemed now. It was unsettling to think that she had had a continuous connection with someone not a blood relation for twenty years.

But Harriet Gould was right; Graham and Gardner were, underneath, almost interchangeable.

Alicia called Harriet the morning after Graham's proposal, before going to the school for the eight-thirty meeting.

"He proposed," Alicia said.

"And?"

"You got me. I think I turned him down. I think I'm going to Weston and then skiing with him and the boys on Saturday."

"Will you be back on Sunday?" Harriet asked anxiously. "I want you to come to dinner. You have to come to dinner."

"Oh, sure. You know I'm in love with your husband. We might get to hold hands while you're in the kitchen."

"I can spare that much of him." Harriet sounded pleased that Sunday dinner was settled.

"You're not coming to Sheila's party on Friday night?"

"I can't, Al. Mark and Joshua and I have to go to

29

Mark's parents'. I can't see explaining to my mother-in-law that I couldn't make it because I had to see a bunch of naked men prancing around on a stage. But bring me a souvenir G-string, will you? Do they wear G-strings?"

"I don't know," Alicia said. "I'm an innocent about places like the Carousel Club. I suppose Lenore's going."

"My sister is having orgasms thinking about it. Don't let her jump on any of those guys. You know, penis envy in Lenore's case means envying any woman who has access to one. Please, God, let her get married soon."

Alicia could hear three-year-old Joshua nattering away in the background.

"Go sit down, Josh," Harriet said away from the phone. "Read a book. Grow up to be a sleazy lawyer like your daddy. Sorry," she said to Alicia. "Why did I ever decide to have a kid?"

Because you have a wonderful husband and mutual adoration and Josh makes it perfect, was what Alicia could have answered, and contentment that fills every empty corner of yourself to the brim.

"Well, have a good time," Harriet said, "and tell me all about it."

"Lenore will wake you in the middle of the night to tell you first."

"I've heard it all before from her. She's been to the Carousel a couple of times. I want the report of a sober and sensible and refined woman like you. Hey, Al . . . it's none of my business, but don't dwell on the Graham thing. It'll work out. One way or the other."

"Like Gardner worked out," Alicia said bitterly. "I got to run, kid. The dean awaits."

And not only the dean. The first sight to greet Alicia inside the administration building was Mike Tedesco.

I am being haunted, she thought as she hurried past him, sitting in one of the leather chairs. They exchanged a nod, and she knew his eyes were following her.

He was either waiting for Debbie or . . . he'd heard Debbie remind her of the eight-thirty meeting. He couldn't be there because of her, though. That was ridiculous.

She went into her office quickly and shut the door. Her heart was pounding. How dare he do this to her, with his blonde wife and his youth. And his seductive, alarming beauty.

Alicia was distracted throughout the meeting with the

30

dean and three doctors on the committee who were trying to match aspirations for development with projected funding. When the meeting ended and the men scattered to their lectures and labs, she found Debbie sitting at her desk, gazing into space.

"Can you type my notes?" Alicia asked. "Hey, wake up!"

"Oh, yes," Debbie said. Her eyes were bright with some kind of happiness. "You know that guy that was here yesterday? Mike Tedesco?"

"Yes," Alicia said shortly.

"He's gorgeous," Debbie said.

"He's married," Alicia said.

"He was here this morning, about a lab assistant job with Dr. Ostrava," Debbie said, ignoring Mike's matrimonial status. "Dr. Ostrava asked me yesterday if I knew anybody. . . ."

Alicia felt haunted by Victor too.

"I think Mike sort of likes me," Debbie said. "He said he'd be seeing a lot of me."

Oh, boy, Alicia thought. But she was relieved that Mike was hanging around because of Debbie, and not her.

Relieved, and maybe just a little bit jealous.

"Are you going to Sheila's party?" Alicia asked. Debbie nodded, dreamily. "Want a ride? I've decided to go."

"Sure. Can we take Lenore, too?"

"No problem," Alicia said. The more the merrier. Protection.

On Friday, Alicia decided to wear her red wool jersey dress to the Carousel Club and Sheila's party. It was one of her best colors with her dark hair and eyes, and the dress flattered her figure. When she looked herself over in the full-length mirror on the inside of her closet door, she thought she looked okay. Not that it was important to look smashing for dinner with Sheila and Lenore Marks, Debbie, Elsa Morant, and other friends. Or for the strippers at this club. They, of all people, probably couldn't care less about clothes.

One thing both Gardner and Graham appreciated about her was the fact that she dressed well. Barbara Bridges had instilled in her the idea that young ladies were judged by the appearance they presented. Life in the Sears clan had reinforced the idea.

When she finally locked the door to her apartment behind her at 6:30 on Friday night, she had a sense that she was getting back at Graham and the rest by doing this one unsuitable thing. But she felt a tingle of anticipation in her stomach, the way she used to when she waited impatiently for a date to show up; the way she used to feel when waiting for Gardner Sears; the way she felt when Brett Handley had called her, literally out of the blue from time to time, to say he was in town overnight and on his way to pick her up.

"If you're free, hon," he would say in that soothing drawl all pilots seemed to acquire in midair, regardless of where they came from. She always made sure she was free.

"Damn!" On the other side of the locked door, her phone was ringing.

She could never resist a ringing telephone. It might be Debbie or Lenore, whom she was picking up. It had better not be Graham, she thought as she fumbled to unlock the door and stumbled toward the phone without bothering to switch on the lights. She winced at the sharp pain when the corner of a table maliciously dug into her right thigh.

"Ali," said the man's voice on the other end of the line.

Alicia knew the voice. Oh, so well. A slightly broad New England *a* mixed up with a retained prep school drawl and one or two too many tumblers of Jack Daniels.

"It's Gardner, Ali."

"I know, Gardner, I know." She especially hated the feigned intimacy of "Ali." It pretended to a warmth and friendship that didn't exist, hadn't existed for at least a year before the divorce.

"How've you been?"

"Perfectly fine. Look, Gardner, I'm late meeting some people . . ."

Gardner ignored the implied suggestion to hurry up. Perhaps, and not unlikely, he hadn't even heard it.

"I thought I'd check in, see if things were going well with you," he said.

Impatiently. "I really am late, Gardner. Could you get back to me tomorrow, or Monday?"

"I don't mean to keep you, Ali. . . ."

"Alicia." She couldn't resist. She blamed Gardner for the throbbing spot on her thigh that was sure to be an ugly bruise.

"Alicia, I plan to drop by next week for a chat."

In spite of her annoyance, she was surprised. He never called her more than once or twice a year, usually when he and Jack Daniels had spent a long evening together, and absolutely never initiated a meeting. There were occasional chance encounters at Symphony, the ballet, receptions at the Museum of Fine Arts where they were both members, now and then on the street. They served to remind Alicia that Gardner was getting a bit balder, a bit paunchier, older but not better. But to meet on purpose? Never. Even their private arrangement about the condo was handled through his office.

"I have something I'd like to discuss with you."

"You won't, I suppose, give me a hint."

Gardner laughed, too heartily for the circumstances. "You know you always liked surprises."

"What gives you that idea?" She responded sharply, and tried to see her watch.

"Don't be cross. I have to see you, and you do like surprises. I haven't forgotten . . . all those good times before the marriage broke down."

Alicia softened. Gardner could be a royal pain, but he had always had charm, and there had been good times, and what could only be called love's young dream. Sometimes the good times seemed better than they were, looking back. Way back.

"Okay, Gardner. I don't know when I'll be free. I've got to run a luncheon at the school, and some other things. Call my office at the beginning of the week."

"You seem to be keeping busy." For some reason, Gardner was unable to conclude the call. "Give my best to Graham."

Alicia refused to allow Gardner to hang up without making sure that he knew whomever she was late for, it was not Graham.

"I'll do that," she said. "I expect I'll be seeing him in the next few days. Good-bye, Gardner."

She hung up quickly and got out of the apartment.

When she got to Allston, where Debbie lived with her parents and brothers, Mrs. Koulos opened the door of the frame house on the first ring of the doorbell.

"Come in," Debbie's mother said. "Despina is getting ready." She spoke as if English were still unfamiliar to her, although Alicia knew she had come from Greece as

33

a young girl. She was a somber woman, dressed in black, with her hair drawn back in a bun. A weary face that still retained traces of beauty that might have served as a model for an Athenian sculptor thousands of years ago.

They sat in a formal living room crammed with dark furniture. A row of faded, posed photographs on the mantel showed men with fierce mustaches, girls in white, boys in stiff suits, a matriarch with an elaborate hairdo. Generations of Kouloses.

"Despina likes to work with you," Mrs. Koulos said. "Her father, the brothers wish her to stay at home as a woman should." She smiled wryly. "So many men in the world keeping watch on their women. As if that would stop them from doing what they wished. What we wish." Woman to woman. "We never are able to escape their eyes. Ah, Despina is young, soon enough she will be shut into a house with a husband and children. It is good for her to enjoy . . . something. I have told her father so."

Alicia remembered Mr. Koulos from a Greek Easter feast. Solemn, heavy-bellied, demanding. Once on that occasion he had rolled out a ponderous command to his wife—in Greek, so Alicia never knew what he had said. Mrs. Koulos's eyes had unmasked, and Alicia saw a flame of naked emotion, anger or hate, certainly not love. But the woman had then quit the room and it seemed clear to Alicia that Mrs. Koulos had obeyed him.

Alicia knew better than to expand on their plans for the evening. She suspected that the slightest hint of the true nature of Sheila's party, and Debbie/Despina would be incarcerated by father, brothers, and even her mother.

Debbie came quietly into the living room, teased, sprayed, arrayed, and ready. Subdued and demure as she said good night to her mother.

Mrs. Koulos said anxiously, "Do not be late. Your father will not like it."

"Yes, Ma," Debbie said.

"Honest to God, Alicia," Debbie said when they got into the car, "they're *always* watching me." Debbie was punctilious about addressing Alicia as Mrs. Sears in the office; outside it, Alicia had begged her to use first names, and from there, they had gone on to a series of confidences —almost exclusively Debbie to Alicia, although Alicia couldn't figure out why she represented wisdom. Maybe it was her age.

"I mean," Debbie said, "I'm twenty-one now, right? I can do what I want. I want to move out, but they'd kill me. Not until I get married. And you should see the turkeys they trot out for me. A couple of guys even older than my *father!* And there was this one time, I met this great guy, and I made the stupid mistake of going to a Greek restaurant downtown, thought I'd impress him talking Greek to the waiters, and there was one of these old guys my father wanted me to *marry*—I said no, of course, and threw a fit—but this man told my father he'd seen me out—" Debbie was breathless recounting her tale. "—and I thought my father was going to *kill* me. Really. With a strap. What a scene!"

"He hit you?"

Debbie shrugged. "I told him after if he dared to lay a hand on me, I'd kill *him*. Sounds real great when you say it in Greek. So I guess he believed me, but they still watch all the time. When I come in, where I'm going, who I'm going with. And men like my father, they want to run your whole life, right? Even if it's none of their business. I bet your father wasn't like that."

"Mine?" Mild, quiet, intelligent Donald Bridges would not have dreamed of raising his hand to Alicia—in fact, they still laughed over the time he had been required to spank a four-year-old Alicia, and he had taken her aside and whacked a leather chair while his mystified daughter looked on, and Pauline waited in the next room in agonies of guilt, listening for her daughter's tears. Yet Donald too had watched over Alicia with deep concern, making sure she kept to the straight and narrow.

"My father kept a close watch on me," Alicia said slowly. "In a different way."

Lenore's face appeared at a second-floor window in the converted one-family house where she had a floor-through apartment, and within seconds, she came flying out to the car. What she lacked in beauty, she made up for with her vivacity and youth, and a constant stream of racy patter.

"I'm starved," she said. "We're going to Stella's, right? A little fettuccine will be fine. Pasta makes me sexy, never had it when I was a kid, it wasn't Jewish food, but give me spaghetti and bread and I'm ready to come."

She ground to a halt.

"You ever think of anything besides sex and food, Len?" Debbie asked over the back seat.

"Oh, sure. Getting paid. Getting married."

"The same as sex," Debbie said.

"Naw," Lenore said. "It's a whole different thing. Sex is all those boys waiting for us at the Carousel. I can't wait, love the place. Even when they don't have strippers, you can meet some great guys hanging out. Me and Deb drop by all the time. Aren't you excited, Alicia? A show just for us?"

"Oh, yeah," Alicia said. "Sure. It's a dream come true." She headed toward the Boston waterfront.

At least, she thought, I'll have a good dinner.

4

Tony finished oiling his chest and inner thighs, and stepped into his G-string. He liked the act of getting dressed, the feel of the material imprisoning his muscles. It made him ache to take everything off. The anticipation of seeing and feeling his own body aroused him. Tonight was an extra chance to do his number. After the show in the main room of the Carousel, he was featured at the private party for some dame who was engaged to a rich Arab. He'd already been paid a two-hundred-fifty-dollar bonus by this Said guy for working the party. He'd put on a good show; there was no telling who the Arab knew in show business, with all the bills he was tossing around.

In the full-length mirror of the Carousel dressing room, Tony could see the other strippers dressing. Raoul, with his Valentino-slick hair and a cream-colored, elegantly defined body, was watching Tony dress. Raoul had come from a prosperous Argentinian family, he claimed, who sent him money to keep him in America. He was too much trouble for Buenos Aires.

"Eh, plenty of soldiers," he had told Tony, shrugging his smooth, muscular shoulders, "but you don't know whether they are coming for you for fucking or shooting or maybe a little . . . what is the word . . . kinky? . . . torture. And that is a surer way to dead or worse than shooting. So I stay alive at the Carousel."

Tony had few friends at the club among the strippers,

but he got a laugh from Raoul, and didn't hold it against him that he was the only gay stripper at the club. Sid, who owned the place, preferred it that way, said he wanted "the real thing" for the ladies. But Raoul was good—not as good as Tony, of course—and he certainly provided the appreciative backstage audience the strippers needed to psyche themselves up before going onstage.

Tony Spinelli never needed anybody but himself to get psyched up. As he rubbed down his arms, he enjoyed the look of his biceps. Lousy light, though. Sid ought to have better lighting in the dressing room. Sid ought to give him his own dressing room, since he was the star attraction that made weekends at the Carousel worthwhile. Not a chance, though, for a star dressing room in this joint, an old, once failing bar that Sid had revived by taking a hint from a newspaper story about male strippers. Sid had served his time in downtown Boston's Combat Zone, running a strip club with girls, in among the seedy bars and porno movie theaters.

"Dames is tough," he remarked to Tony. "They got to turn tricks on the side, besides stripping. I don't know, they can't seem to help it. Then you got their pimps to deal with sometimes, and the guys trying to muscle in on everybody's action. Hell, you'd know about that, Spinelli. Ain't you guys from the North End got the mob under every bush?"

Tony knew: the two-bit hoods he'd grown up with who'd stayed two-bit hoods now in their twenties, and would end up being buried that way. Well, they hadn't found the Carousel yet.

"All I ever wanted," Sid had said wistfully, "was to put on a nice, classy show, where the audience didn't think they was going to get rolled. I figured, dames that would come to see men strip, they're here for the fun, maybe get a little thrill and go home to their old men happier." Then he shrugged. "I betcha it was their husbands who were coming to see the girls at my place downtown. Life's funny."

The Carousel had become a modest success, and part of it was due to Tony Spinelli. He had a loyal following. A lot of them came back every couple of weeks, usually in groups, to scream and applaud and hand him money because he was naked and sexy and right there within the reach of their hands. A tease, since Sid made it clear he didn't want his acts making a point of getting involved with the audience. Tony was careful; his women were chance met—and he never saw them twice. It suited him, and avoided the trouble Sid didn't need: his silent partner was reputed to be a pol with a lot of clout at the State House who didn't mind having a profitable piece of a strip joint, as long as no irate husband with more clout could claim some stripper was balling his wife.

The dressing room was getting crowded. The new kid, Tito, had come in and was getting into his outfit. Tony hadn't seen his act, but Sid said he was going to be okay. He didn't look very relaxed at the moment. Probably scared shitless. Tony'd never had that problem—he'd been doing an act his whole life, although it was only in the past couple of years that he'd been a stripper. An entertainer. Born to be in the middle of the stage and everybody loving him.

Raoul had taken Tito aside, probably telling him how hot he was, how sexy, how much the señoras were going to tip him when they'd seen him. By the time Tito was ready to go onstage, he was going to feel like the stud of life.

Tony studied Tito's reflection as he listened to Raoul. There was something about Tito that grated on him, a kind of bullying arrogance, except right now when he was facing both the main room and the party as opening act. Tony wondered where Sid had dug him up, and why. Most of the strippers had some kind of experience. Tito was strictly a beginner, from what he'd heard. Tony himself had always danced, always made himself the center of attention. It was nothing to do it on a stage.

It sure as hell beat heaving crates of vegetables around for his Uncle Angelo.

Raoul looked up from Tito for a second and caught Tony watching them in the mirror. He winked at Tony and made a graceful Latin gesture with his hands: a man's gotta do what he's gotta do. Tony smiled. Yeah, he liked Raoul, and Raoul appreciated Tony, at a polite distance of course. No funny stuff except in a joking way. Raoul was careful about that. No special attachments to the other strippers, except for one: Jeff. And that was okay, because Jeff handled it.

"Hey, Raoul, you won't have room for them socks if you keep a-lookin' at Tony's cock." Jeff had arrived, late as usual, a big Midwestern stud with a shock of corn-silk hair and a smile that made the incestuous mother rise to the surface in all women. Jeff had come east from Idaho with a thousand dreams, a shoebox full of rotten songs he'd written, an old guitar, and an enormous appetite for sex. He might have done better in New York as a farmboy hustler, but he'd settled for Boston.

"They're like folks here," he said. "Real nice ladies."

Since he didn't have a mean bone in his body and always gave what was expected, he was a successful Boston farmboy hustler. One of his clients was a woman who must have something on Sid, since she got him a "regular" job stripping at the club, sometimes with one or two of his lousy songs thrown in for good measure. He continued to hustle on the side, because he just plain liked to, but if Sid found out, he'd kick Jeff's butt out—fast. The strippers who knew about Jeff never let on to Sid that they knew something he didn't.

Standing close to the door, oiling each other's bodies, were Cain and Abel, blue-black twins, identical down to the little mole that grew directly under each's left nipple. They had radial cable muscles and steel-roped stomachs and when they stripped, the dames responded like they were the ultimate black fantasy, savage and uncontainable. Tony couldn't see it himself, but the twins were going to make it to the big time, if the Carousel audiences were any measure. Still, they liked him a whole lot more, which was the way it should be. Tony never saw the twins outside the club. Inside they kept to themselves. No hand-slapping jive from "Mirror Image." Tony envied one thing: they didn't need a mirror to see themselves; they had each other.

Three or four other guys had arrived, and were dressing up in the fantasies they would strip off—leather, a sort of cowboy, your basic dude in a weird silver space suit.

The dressing room was smoky and smelled of flesh and unguents. The odors combined to form a kind of primal scent. Sexual and dangerous. Bottle it, Tony thought, and you'd make a million. A cheap thrill, just like the Carousel.

"This place stinks," he said out loud. He took a last long look at the trim, smooth body he worked so hard to keep perfect, and started to get into his costume, fastening the Velcro closures on the tight maroon velvet pants.

Raoul patted Tito on the ass and sent him off to finish getting dressed. He stood in the middle of the room and sniffed.

"It smells like men," he said. "I like him."

40

"*It*," Jeff said. He was applying body makeup and nipple rouge to his light skin. He had already brushed shadow on his pectorals and along his stomach muscles, which made his powerful body looked exceptionally defined.

"It?" Raoul circled around Jeff, flirting.

"Man, do I have to teach you English?" Jeff grinned impishly.

"You could teach me—what this *it* is?"

"You give me a minute, and I'll shove them socks of yours where they really belong."

Jeff walked over to Raoul and teased him with his eyes, while his hand slipped down Raoul's side. Quickly he grabbed Raoul's G-string and snapped it hard. Raoul yelped and rubbed the red welt on his thigh.

"Son of bitch," he said, "you give me black and blue mark for sure." But he was pleased by the attention. It was the only kind of relationship that was possible for Raoul to have with Jeff. Better than nothing at all, the way he let Jeff tease him. As for Jeff, he liked to see everybody happy. It didn't cost him a thing to include Raoul, and besides, he liked to hear Raoul telling him how all the women in the audience dreamed about his blond body in their beds. Just as Tony suspected he was doing now, to judge from the dreamy look on Jeff's face.

Tito was pacing, a toreador in a tight-fitting blue and gold costume. He was affected by the tension building in the dressing room, as it did before every performance, and Tony saw a line of perspiration on his forehead. Nerves.

"It ain't bad, kid," Tony said. "You get out there and get it up and the women ain't fussy."

"Mind your own business, Spinelli," Tito said. "I don't need any good advice from you."

Tony looked him in the eye and turned on his heel. Little creep. Maybe he'd fall on his ugly, sneering face.

"Okay, you guys." Irv, Sid's younger brother and another creep as far as Tony was concerned, came into the dressing room. Sid was one thing, pretty easygoing, tough only when he had to be. And smart. Tony got along fine with Sid. Most of the strippers did. Irv was different. He was weasely, secretive, a lurker behind doors, who liked to flash the gun he carried to prove he was a big man. He'd ridden on Sid Gabel's hardworking coattails since he was a kid. If Irv weren't now, at Sid's indulgence, second-in-command at the Carousel, Tony would long ago have walked right over him and never looked back.

But Sid had made it clear that he'd granted Irv a certain amount of authority, and that was that. It didn't mean he got treated with respect, or that anybody liked him. Tony couldn't wait for the day when he was on top, and didn't have to jump for a crazy person like Irv. Because he was convinced Irv was nuts. Every now and then, he'd seen him fly off the handle when one of the guys got smart. Not that it made any difference. They only had a laugh behind his back. Once Jeff had made up a song about Irv and the fact he was the world's worst gambler, which he was, and sang it in the act. You could hear Irv screaming from the club to Bunker Hill, and if Jeff hadn't been three feet taller and about a ton of muscle heavier, Irv would have killed him with pleasure. A lunatic for sure, but less dangerous than he sounded when he had one of his fits of anger. Still, Tony and the others made a point of keeping out of his way when he got mad, in case he decided to shoot off his gun as well as his mouth.

"Okay," Irv said again, louder, and this time all eyes turned to him. "The women for this private party will be coming in in a couple of hours, right in the middle of the show in the main room. You follow the lineup I'm going to give you and then you move on to the party. Is that okay with Mr. Big Star Tony Spinelli?" Irv's voice was loaded with his usual sneering sarcasm.

Tony moved his shoulders, hips, showing off the lines of his body. To let Irv know that in a million years he'd never have what Tony had.

"Tito, you're on first. Hey, you niggers."

Cain and Abel, with absolutely expressionless faces, turned to Irv in unison.

"You follow Jeff, who follows Tito."

"Aw, shit . . ." Jeff liked coming on late in the show.

"What are you complaining about?" Irv said. "You can sing them one of those godawful songs of yours, and strum your guitar with your dingdong for all I care."

Jeff brightened visibly. He loved the chance to sing.

"Then the others . . . then Raoul, then Spinelli, **Mr.** Wonderful."

Tony figured he was at least one up on Irv by not being drawn when he baited him. So he nodded and examined his reflection.

"The guy paying for this party, that Arab or whatever he is, wants a good show." Irv looked at his list self-importantly.

Tony looked at Irv, who was uncomfortable and tried not to show it. He knew that Tony always put on a good show, and not because Irv told him to.

Barbara, the big-busted six-footer with bright red hair who acted as emcee at the club, stuck her head in the dressing room door. She was the only person who called Irv a prick to his face and got away with it. First of all, she had five six-foot-plus red-haired sons at home in Dorchester who would rip Irv apart if he dared to hand her any shit. More important, rumor had it that the politician partner in the Carousel was actually Barbara's uncle.

"Hey, you pieces of meat," Barbara said. "I'm going to start the warmup for the main room. You getting yourselves all pumped up? Spinelli, you're not even dressed—how you going to send them home happy to their hubbies if you look like you just stepped out of a barrel of olive oil? Isn't that what you dagos take baths in?"

Tony grinned at Barbara. "Sweetheart, it's better than sleeping on a sack of potatoes. Isn't that what you Micks use for a bed?"

Barbara whooped with laughter. They always traded ethnic insults, trying to top one another. Nobody else needled Tony in quite the same way. Barbara closed the door.

"You'd better get dressed, Spinelli," Irv said, and went over to Tito, who actually appeared to have something to say to him.

Tony watched Irv steadily, thinking how much he'd like to bust that smug face.

"While I'm dressing," he said, "you ought to go call your bookie and find out how many bales of hay you bought for the nags today."

Irv hated to be reminded what a lousy gambler he was. Tony picked up the ruffled shirt he wore in his act and slipped it on, turning his back on Irv. In the mirror, he could see Irv staring at him in a blind fury. Irv took a step in Tony's direction, but Tito put out a hand and stopped him. He was saying something to Irv that calmed him down. Irv actually wore a thin smile, something you only saw when he was about to give you bad news. Tito was smiling too.

43

Little ass kisser, Tony thought. Have to be to want to talk to Irv.

Then he turned his concentration onto himself. His face, a great face. His body—perfect, the kind a woman would die over, and he always thought of the audience as just one woman. The pleasure he got from taking off his clothes, that was the best part. He deserved someplace classier than this joint, but that was a matter of getting known to the right people and he'd find a way.

But the pleasure—that was there, wherever he was, whether it was an audience of thousands or Tony Spinelli alone with himself.

5

LATER, when the night was finally over, and Alicia was safe at home, she knew she should have taken Gardner's call as an omen. She should have gone straight to bed as soon as she hung up, with the covers over her head.

From the moment she set foot in the restaurant where they were meeting Sheila and the others, Alicia was caught up in a barrage of sensual innuendo that finally resolved into actual physical intrusion on her well-guarded self. How could she have allowed it to happen? she wondered again and again as the minutes and hours passed. And she cursed her stupid eagerness to spite Graham by going to Sheila's party, her tasteless curiosity in wanting to see what a male strip show was like.

They reached the waterfront restaurant before the others.

"Hello, *there*," Lenore murmured, as they were seated.

Alicia followed her glance; Lenore had fastened on a young, dark-haired waiter three tables away. He had barely attractive features, but Lenore was not looking at his face.

"Do you think he could have gotten into pants that were any tighter?" Lenore asked rhetorically. It was clear that the black trousers he was wearing were about as tight as any man could manage and still be able to walk.

"He's got a great ass," Lenore added, surveying the waiter from head to toe. He could not possibly have heard her, but he glanced in their direction.

Debbie clamped a firm hand on Lenore's arm. "Don't

45

you dare wave to him," she said. To Alicia: "Len's a real burden when we go out. I'm always afraid she's going to grab some guy's crotch."

Alicia smiled thinly and wondered if there was any possibility of escaping—at least after dinner, if not before.

Lenore giggled. "I did once, remember? He asked for it."

"I thought I'd die laughing," Debbie admitted. "The look on his face . . ."

Alicia tuned them out. They sipped drinks and ravaged the bread and carrot sticks and olives and talked about men.

What, she thought, could Gardner Sears want to talk to her about? He couldn't be having marital problems and needed a shoulder to cry on. Gardner would never admit that the new Mrs. Sears was not precisely what he had always wanted and didn't get when he married Alicia. He would never admit that anything was amiss with him; he never had. He had gone through their courtship, marriage, divorce with the tacit assumption that if there were strains and unhappiness, the source was Alicia, never him:

If she had been one of the nice Windsor or Buckingham Schools girls who finished up their education at Wellesley or Radcliffe or Smith, someone the Sears family had known forever . . .

If she hadn't insisted on going on to business school after she graduated from college . . .

If she hadn't chosen to work for a time in the early part of their marriage . . .

If she had been what Gardner's Great-Aunt Lydia had neatly presumed her to be . . .

She had met Aunt Lydia at an engagement party for Gardner's younger sister, Muffy. Gardner disappeared into the crowd and Alicia was left to the bright-eyed examination of an incredibly ancient-appearing lady.

"Gardner's young woman, they tell me," the old lady said positively.

Alicia had long since ceased to count the glasses of champagne she had downed to get her through the party. She nodded and smiled idiotically at the tiny figure in mauve lace, with the face crisscrossed with wrinkles and topped with an untidy fluff of white hair.

"You know me, of course," the grande dame said. "Gardner's great-aunt Lydia."

"Oh, yes, ma'am."

46

"I understand," Great-Aunt Lydia said, "that Gardner intends to marry you. Eleanor intimates as much."

"You see, nothing is . . . I mean, we're not engaged or anything . . ." Alicia, glowing with the Moët, glowed a bit more. Gardner had informed his mother of his intentions. At the moment, it didn't matter that he had neglected to inform Alicia.

"I presume you'll have the wedding in Eleanor's rose garden." Great-Aunt Lydia ignored Alicia's confusion, but raised an eyebrow as Alicia grabbed another glass of champagne from a passing waiter. "No, that won't do. Church wedding. Church of the Convenant, Brimmer Street, reception in the garden. Next June."

"Actually, I'm from Colorado," Alicia said.

"Your mother's dead."

"Yes," Alicia said, taken aback. "For two years."

"You see?" A note of triumph. "And no family to speak of. Weddings have to be managed by a woman. Eleanor will take care of it. Then you'll settle down in a nice home and have some nice children."

"I'm starting graduate school in the fall, and I plan to work for a time when I finish," Alicia said.

"Sears women," Great-Aunt Lydia said ominously, "are highly educated, but . . . Sears women *do not work*. Sears women have duties. We have our charities, our cultural interests. We raise our children properly, and we supervise our households. That is enough. I suggest," she added, drawing herself up to her full five feet, "that you dismiss any other thoughts, if you wish to be a proper wife to Gardner." She looked at Alicia with an expression not unlike the Queen Mother discovering aphids on her prize rose bushes, then she turned on her heel and marched through the guests toward the bride-to-be, Muffy, who most certainly knew what Sears women and those of their circle did with their lives.

Looking back over the years, Alicia knew she should have paid closer attention to Great-Aunt Lydia, and either slipped into the reality she had summarized succinctly or given up her dream of life with a perfect Gardner then and there. But she'd stayed the person she was and had gone for the impossible ideal.

Garner's perfection was all in her eyes. The traces of the man for whom she had yearned for so long were faint indeed in their five years of marriage, and it was a toss-up whether things were worse, eventually, in or out of bed.

". . . And get him into bed," Lenore's raucous voice startled Alicia from her memories, along with the arrival of Sheila and Elsa Morant and a friend of Sheila's Alicia knew vaguely, Jennifer Newman.

"So sorry we're late," Sheila said. "It's all Elsa's fault, getting fancied up for the men at the Carousel."

"And why not?" Elsa said. Her short, gray hair had been given a curl, and she was wearing a dress rather fancier than the plain spinsterish clothes she wore at work. Elsa was in her late fifties, but her eagerness for the night ahead was written on her pink, cheerful face.

"I don't think they encourage the ladies to make dates," Lenore said, then looked slyly at Alicia. "It takes people like my sister to do that."

"What do you mean?" Alicia said.

"So, you're going to dinner at Harriet's on Sunday, I hear, and darling, she has a nice surprise, so you shouldn't be a lonely divorcee. A lawyer, yet." Lenore's eyes glittered with good humor and what Alicia read as lascivious speculation.

"She promised she'd stop matchmaking," Alicia said wearily.

Jennifer Newman said, "And they're always somebody's rejects, aren't they, the fixed-up dates?" Jennifer was a very tall young woman with short, curly hair and a wide, humorous mouth. "They're always four inches shorter than I am, as if my friends think a recently divorced woman doesn't care, as long as it's a man."

"Harriet's too happily married," Alicia said. "She wants me to keep taking a chance on the lottery—a winner's got to turn up eventually."

"Don't count on it," Jennifer said.

Elsa settled comfortably into her chair, looking at the menu with a drink close at hand.

"When you get to be my age," she said, "nobody thinks of fixing you up with a date. I suppose they think that after a point, men don't interest you." She smiled happily. "Frankly, they're wrong. I can't wait for tonight. I've never seen a man . . . well, naked. In public." She peered over the top of the menu at Lenore and Debbie, who were looking at her openmouthed. "When I was growing up, of

48

course, everything about sex was referred to as 'It.' Even the . . . sexual parts were 'It.' "

"No kidding," Lenore said, somewhat dazed.

"Personally," Elsa said as she ordered another drink, "I can't wait to meet 'It' face to face, as it were."

"Hey, Sheila," Debbie said, "you're the one who's going to get a lot of 'It.' Tonight will get you ready . . . for 'It.' "

Alicia smiled bleakly at Sheila across the table, but Sheila was caught up in the mild crudity of the conversation.

"I think there might be a certain satisfaction in sitting back and judging a lot of naked men to see if they're up to standard," Sheila said. "Talk about role reversal."

"I've been there," Debbie said breathlessly. "It's terrific, I mean it. You'll love it. Even Alicia."

Even Alicia? She was stung by the implication in Debbie's words, innocently spoken. Debbie had neatly slotted her with Elsa . . . no, somewhere beyond Elsa, perhaps with Great-Aunt Lydia, had she known her, and the ancients who frowned down at youthful exuberance. And "It." She answered defensively. Thoughtlessly.

"It's Sheila's night, and this club sounds like an amusing idea," she said with forced gaiety, "but I do rather feel I should be wearing dark glasses and a wig. Imagine the sort of woman who goes there."

Then she looked around the table at the women who were her friends, and who were looking forward to going to the club. They watched her in uneasy silence. Alicia was ashamed of herself, and proceeded to make it worse.

"I mean, who really cares about seeing . . . these men? It's—" She caught herself before she said "childish," at least. "It's something that would have shocked my mother," she finished weakly.

Sheila patted Alicia's hand. "Don't be so sure about *that.* But it's no big deal, this thing about men stripping. The funny part is how eager Said was to have me throw this party, have the same kind of stag party men do. Very un-Arab of him. He probably thinks of it as my last fling." Sheila looked very happy. "He's a constant surprise. And remember, Al, turn them upside down, and they all look the same."

Alicia grinned at her, the gaiety at the table was restored. For the others.

"I hope," Sheila said, "Sister Mary Joseph, up in heaven

49

with the saints, isn't looking in tonight. She used to bust my knuckles with that ruler of hers if I even thought of looking at Eddie Flanagan during catechism class."

Alicia glanced around at her companions. She still had a strong feeling that somehow she had missed the mainstream. Gardner was to blame for her mood; and Graham too, for that matter. Neither of them ever tried to touch her in the core of herself. Both of them always made assumptions about her needs, that they matched theirs, and there was no reason to look further than the surface. Of course, Pauline Bridges' warnings about "It" had shaped her attitude—her life. It was not quite the thing to demand sexual gratification, not for a woman like Alicia.

But why not? she wondered.

Because that's the way it is, she answered herself.

But around her were five women not so different from herself who didn't seem to share her disquiet.

"I hope they're hung." Lenore's gravelly voice filled up a moment of silence. People looked over at the table. Elsa was puzzled, then comprehending, and a bit shocked.

"Big, she means," Debbie explained to Elsa softly.

"I know," Elsa replied. "The sexual revolution may have come along too late for the active participation of the likes of me, but I do *read*. And, goodness knows, I see a lot—all those young men at the school. Some of them . . . well!"

Involuntarily, Alicia glanced at Debbie, who seemed to be examining her water glass with great interest. Lenore's favorite waiter insinuated himself between Lenore and Debbie, pencil poised for their orders. Lenore grinned wickedly at Alicia, then looked up at the waiter. As threatened, she wanted only spaghetti and decided on clam sauce. And more bread.

Alicia wasn't hungry, and ate her veal piccata without interest. The others seemed to be enjoying their meals. Even here, among friends, Alicia felt vaguely out of synch, as if nothing anywhere in her life approached serenity. Not Graham, who was supposed to be perfect for her in all respects. Not the distant Brett Handley, who might have been right, if he hadn't been so independent and elusive. She was jolted from her musings by the pressure of the waiter's body against her shoulder. She drew back as though someone had put a torch to her, and shuddered. It was the same sort of boldness one encountered on buses and subways, in crowds, the random sexual intrusions from anonymous

50

men, the not accidental pressure of their organs for what pleasure or need it filled.

"Forgive me," the waiter murmured and leaned forward to address the others on the matter of dessert.

Alicia fought the impulse to run outside for air.

"And for you?" he said to Alicia, and smiled. Confident in his masculinity, knowing exactly how she had reacted to him.

"Nothing for me," she said, and refused to look at him.

"Nothing?" She must be imagining the seductive overtones, she was being silly. And she couldn't wait for dinner, the whole evening to be over.

Finally, Sheila signaled for the check, and raised her hand as the others fumbled for their handbags.

"I'm the big spender tonight," she said. "Or rather, Said is. He will no doubt be eternally unfaithful to me with any available talent, but he does know how to hand out cash."

"So far," Lenore said. "Hey, he's not going to make you wear one of those veil things, is he?"

Sheila smiled sweetly. "Only in a bed, dear."

"No kidding?" Lenore was momentarily perplexed. "Won't it kind of get in the way, I mean, what if you . . ."

"We know what you mean," Sheila said, over Debbie's shriek of laughter. Alicia and Jennifer exchanged looks. Jennifer hadn't said much, but had listened in a detached way to the chatter.

Suddenly, Alicia couldn't take it anymore, the talk of sex, the waiter, the prospect of the strippers, "It" in all its manifestations.

"I'm going to wait out in the car, okay?" Alicia said, and stood up quickly.

"I'll go with you," Jennifer said. "I ate too much, I need some air and exercise."

When they got outside into the cold night, Jennifer said, "You look sort of overwhelmed. Are you all right?"

"Oh, sure," Alicia said. She took a deep breath and felt better. "I'm not a stuffy prude, no matter what Debbie implied. And I like men and sex and all of that, but lately, it seems that I've lost my perspective. And equanimity. God, they sound like the proverbial locker room."

"New freedom," Jennifer said. "But then, women have always talked about men and sex a lot more than men ever thought they did."

Alicia sighed and unlocked her car. The others were beginning to trail out of the restaurant.

Sheila divided up the passengers, then linked arms with Alicia. "I'm speeding ahead," she said, "so I can be there to greet the ladies. You're being a good sport, Alicia, and really, it will be fun."

"I know, Sheila," Alicia said. "And I promise to enjoy myself."

Sheila gave her a curious look, saying with it, "So you must promise to be entertained."

Aloud, she said gaily, "Ready for the men, everyone? We start at the Carousel and see what we end up with."

"There can't be anyplace *but* up from there," Alicia said to Jennifer.

Lenore and Debbie, caught up in the spirit of the adventure, were so talkative and animated that Alicia had no need to speak herself as they followed Sheila out toward Route 1 and the Carousel Club.

6

THE Carousel Club looked harmless from the outside: a blank building with a small neon sign in the shape of a merry-go-round and set in the midst of a parking lot already crowded with cars.

"They only have strippers Fridays and Saturdays," Lenore said. "Rest of the time it's . . . well, not a singles bar, exactly. Just a place where you can sort of meet people, not college kids."

Sheila had arrived ahead of them. They passed her parked car and stepped into impenetrable darkness. Alicia blinked to adjust her eyes, and knew immediately and with absolute conviction that she didn't belong here. The place was packed with women, sitting along the bar and in chairs close to a small stage. Speakers poured out loud, driving disco music, and a hundred female voices chattered on in counterpoint.

No one paid the least attention to her and Debbie and Lenore as they trailed a bare-to-the-waist youth through the main room. Alicia could feel the tension and excitement around her. The women, young and old, seemed to be straining toward the empty stage, and in the dim light, she could see they were figuratively licking their lips. As the young man opened a door with THE GREEK SUITE stenciled in gold, the music changed, and behind her, Alicia heard a united, high-pitched scream from those hundred women and a wave of furious applause. The show was going on in the main room. The fun had begun.

Only Alicia knew that what lay ahead for her would not be fun. Eventually, too, someone would catch on that she didn't belong there, and they would all rise up and drive her away....

Alicia had never felt so much an intruder, so out of place.

No, that was not strictly true. Once, a year or so before, Alicia and Billy Catlett had finished up a long evening of stunning food at a new French restaurant he'd discovered on the North Shore. They'd had a lot of wine and they'd talked about his life and hers. Then she managed to persuade him to take her to a gay bar in the city as a perfect way to end the evening.

"You wouldn't like it," Billy said.

"Oh, but I'm curious. It'll be fun."

"Let me put it this way. Not only wouldn't you like it, they wouldn't like you. It's simply not your place, and it's definitely not a place to go as . . . an observer." Billy was too kind to say that she sounded as though she were going slumming, although he did mutter something about her having lived too long with Mayflower descendents.

"I'm a grown-up lady," she said, willfully misunderstanding. "I can handle it."

The bar, tucked away on a side street between tall buildings, was so dark, even coming in from the night, that she'd had to shut her eyes for a second to be able to see the men sitting at the bar. Two or three couples appeared to be dancing to faint music, the talk was a low murmur.

All movement and talk ceased as she and Billy came through the doorway. Heads were turned toward them. The music played on. It wasn't hostility; it was a wall, and the men behind it had sensed she was an intruder. Billy looked at her quizzically.

"You're right, Doc," she said. "It's not going to be fun." They had departed immediately.

For the first time, too, she felt alienated from Billy. He had felt at ease in the bar. The women she had come with tonight were clearly entirely at ease at the Carousel.

Sheila, Elsa, Jennifer, and perhaps a dozen or more other women were already there, settled on individual chaises that were grouped around a low platform stage. Sheila was holding court, while the waiters took orders for drinks. Even as she walked over to Sheila, more guests were being shown into the room, including many familiar faces from the university. Dean Barrow would have been shocked to see them. Debbie and Lenore bounded off to find themselves good spots close to the stage. Sheila waved and indicated that she'd saved a chaise for Alicia between her and Elsa.

Jennifer, passing her on her way to the far side of the room, whispered, "Check out the statues. Maybe we should get one for the corner of our living rooms."

Alicia checked. Debbie and Lenore were pointing to one of the statues tucked into a niche and backlighted, a copy of a famous Priapus from Pompeii.

Too bad, Alicia thought, the management doesn't know the difference between Greek and Roman. But no one seemed to care.

On each chaise, she noticed, was draped a pastel toga to put on. Alicia thought not, although several women had thrown them over their shoulders. She sat down on the empty chaise beside Sheila.

"Good stuff, huh?" Sheila said. "I told you it would be a hoot. And we can take it like women, lying down."

Elsa tittered. She was holding a tall dark drink, and might have been slightly tipsy.

"This is going to be the talk of Commonwealth," Sheila said. "A suitably scandalous send-off."

"If anybody deserved one, you do," Alicia said. She managed to make herself comfortable on the chaise, using the toga as a buffer between her dress and the somewhat dingy and threadbare upholstery. She slipped off her shoes and flexed her stockinged toes. "I keep thinking I'm about as out of place as a nun among hookers."

Elsa snorted with delight. "That's the first time anyone's ever referred to me as a hooker. Have yourself a drink, 'licia, and join the rest of us ladies of the night." Elsa tossed back the last of her drink and signaled to a waiter. He was quickly at her side, smiling. He looked like a college student who had misplaced most of his clothes.

Alicia turned to Sheila with what she hoped was a cheerful face. "I've said it before, Sheila, but I'm awfully happy for you."

"Well . . . thanks, Al. I'm happy for me too."

"Look at my bad luck with marriage, with men. I've never been able to choose right."

55

"Graham is perfectly nice," Sheila said absently.

"And has asked me to marry him."

"You could do worse."

"Put it another way. I can't do better. You're lucky, Sheila. You're comfortable with everybody. I could never marry someone like Said."

Sheila raised an eyebrow.

"He's terrific," Alicia said quickly. "I don't mean that. But you know me, you know what I mean."

"He *is* terrific, and you're right. You couldn't possibly bend to the kind of benevolent despotism Said wields without breaking. I think," she said, and stopped. "Never mind."

"What do you think?"

"You don't need my advice. You know what you're doing."

"I think, Sheila, I need all the help I can get."

Sheila looked at Alicia, who was waiting to hear. "Don't worry so much. I think, well, I've known you quite a few years, going back to Gardner, right? You shape yourself too much to them, because you think that's right. It is, and it isn't. You have to find the happy medium, between them . . . him, whoever he is . . . and you." Sheila laughed. "I guess my training at the hands of Sister Mary Joseph taught me more than I thought. Adaptability in the face of discipline."

She managed to make Alicia laugh, then looked at her watch.

"At least you have your work. Hey, it's time to get the show on the road."

Right on cue, the lights went down, and Barbara, in a white satin jumpsuit, parted the back curtains and came out on stage.

"All right, ladies," she said, and the babble of voices stopped. She stood in a circle of white spotlight. "It's time for the start of an evening you won't forget." The thirty or so women in the room settled back on their chaises.

"I understand you girls are here to celebrate the coming marriage of one of you. . . . Now, how many of you told your husbands you were going to a bridal shower tonight?"

A few giggles and a couple of raised hands.

"Remember the good old days, when a shower meant buying a potato peeler for the bride? You're going to see some peeling tonight, but it's not the kind you do in the kitchen."

"I do!" said a voice from a far corner, and the women laughed delightedly.

"We're going to show you Tito, dancing to Latin rhythms, our Jeff, who's blond . . . all over; we've got all kinds of men, including the star of the Carousel Club, Tony Spinelli!"

Alicia heard some applause, probably from Debbie and Lenore.

"And ladies, remember these are poor working boys . . . you show them your appreciation, and they'll show you everything they've got!"

The warmup was having its effect. Many of the women were sitting up, leaning forward expectantly.

"And don't you let anybody tell you that ladies don't like the same kind of sexy bodies to look at that men do—it ain't so! We girls like sex as much as the next gal . . . or guy!"

Alicia remembered well how that point had started a row with Graham six months ago. They had left the theater after a play and had walked up Tremont Street to the parking lot, past the neon-lit strip joints and the bars that spilled the odor of stale beer out onto the sidewalks. It was sleazy and depressing, but it was noisy and busy, too. Alive. And an alien land. A young black prostitute with a kind of weary beauty behind her painted face had brushed up against him. She had muttered an obscenity, and Graham had grasped Alicia's arm firmly, marching up the street. It was as though the speedy departure would erase the existence of the woman, from both his and Alicia's consciousnesses.

"Have you ever gone to a prostitute?" she asked him.

"Of course not." Annoyed. "Not around places like that!"

"But other places, then."

"Alicia, the need to patronize prostitutes is a sign of a number of problems, the fear of growing old, the inability to form stable relationships, the need for illicit actions. . . ."

"I thought it was for sex. And all I asked was if you ever did." She remembered times with Gardner when they were married when she came on strong, sexy, exotic, experimenting, and he had shut her off with, "Only whores do that."

57

"Well, did you?" she asked again.

"Perhaps. In my younger days. It's the kind of thing young men do," Graham said. He was being especially difficult.

"And what did Hillie have to say about it?"

"Hillie! I would never dream of telling her something like that. Hillie was a lady!"

"Ladies are interested in all kinds of things."

"We never discussed it." In spite of the finality of Graham's statement, Alicia persisted.

"Well, what was it like?"

Graham was tight-lipped.

"I mean," she said, "was it different from your wife or me or what? I'm only asking because I'm curious. Women don't 'have to' do that sort of thing, when they're 'young.'"

"I should hope not."

"It's a good thing you don't see patients nowadays, Gray. I don't think you have a clue about what women are like."

She hadn't intended to speak so sharply or bitterly, and wondered why she was being so persistent. She chose to believe it was because she wanted to understand Graham as she had failed for so long to know Gardner.

Graham stopped and turned her to face him. He was calm, but hurt showed on his face.

"That was uncalled for, Alicia. You can be quite difficult yourself, as you may not be aware. And maybe you don't understand that according to my lights, there are matters which aren't discussed. Perhaps I am wrong in this, and I dare say I have as many imperfections as the next man, but I try to be consistent."

A lecture, and she pulled her arm out of his grasp and started walking. Graham kept pace with her, and kept talking.

"Sometimes I think we're well suited to each other, and then you do something like this, which suggests you don't have the perception I credit you with. You begin with what you call 'curiosity,' and end with rudeness."

"Stop it," she said. "I don't feel like arguing."

"I'm not arguing," he said. "I'm giving my point of view, which is what you asked for."

"All I asked is whether you had ever gone to a prostitute."

"No," he said softly. "You were asking for a kind of

intimacy I don't know if I'm capable of. And I didn't deal with it well. But then, neither did you. You are, you know, curiously inconsistent. Possibly that is why I find you so appealing. You're not boring."

"But you are," she merely whispered, and never knew if he had actually heard her words. She would have taken them back as soon as they were spoken. In any case, he didn't so much as call her for two weeks. Then she had given in, and called him, to apologize for being difficult. Graham had laughed and said he had missed her. Their relationship resumed, and Alicia tried to be obliging. Graham remained consistent.

The women around her in the Greek Suite applauded happily as the mistress of ceremonies wound up her warm-up, and the lights blacked out entirely, except for tiny pencil spots over the little tables between each chaise. A dozen speakers in the walls spat forth a sinuous music of a Portuguese fado, and there was Tito in a spotlight on the small stage.

He was dressed in his blue and gold bullfighter's costume that showed every contour and bulge of his body. As he moved his hips, the muscles in his buttocks tightened and relaxed, and the audience caught the mood. Somebody whistled—one of those rare women with the gift Alicia envied of being able to whistle with two fingers, sharp and loud.

After a few mannered turns to the fado, the music switched to a samba, and Tito started to strip. The ornate short jacket came off, and the wide sash. Some of the more demonstrative women shouted encouragement, a few clapped to the rhythm of the music.

Alicia had to admit that the stripper possessed a kind of crude grace, and he conveyed an earthy sexuality in his movements. It was sensual, but not terribly exciting, even when he had removed all his clothes except for the satin pants and suspenders.

By the end of the samba, his skin gleamed with a sheen of sweat. Next came the slow habanera from *Carmen,* for the last of his clothes. Now he was different, more grace-ful, seductive, desirable. . . . The sound of breathless and rushed breathing came from the circle of chaises. The lights had come up some, and Alicia could see that Lenore's hands were gripping the sides of her chaise. She couldn't see Debbie's hands at all, but she was leaning forward, biting her lower lip. Her eyes were glued to Tito.

When Alicia looked back to the stage, he had removed everything but his G-string.

"Oh, my!" Elsa's gasp of surprise struck Alicia as more entertaining than the boy on the stage.

Now he moved down into the audience, snapping his fingers to the music and swaying close to the ladies in the audience, not quite touching them, but teasing them with his nearly naked body and his smile. Sheila tucked a bill into his G-string; others followed suit.

There was a rush of applause as he went back onstage, picked up his scattered clothes, and left.

"He didn't take *all* his clothes off, though," Elsa said.

"Probably just as well," Sheila said. "I think he must have had something in that pouch besides himself, and I'd just as soon not know."

"You mean," Elsa said, wide-eyed, "something like *falsies?*"

"Something like that," Sheila said.

"I had no idea," Elsa shook her head, "that men were vain . . . that way."

"It's not just great big biceps they like to be known for," Sheila said. "Enjoying yourself, Alicia?"

"Yes, yes, of course." Alicia was beginning to relax. True, she could not quite enter into the group experience the others seemed to be enjoying, a commonality of emotion that roused each woman to greater excitement. But the show didn't make her as uncomfortable as she had feared it would.

Lenore came over, infected with what Alicia thought must be the orgy mentality of the evening.

"Oy, such a schlong we didn't get to see," she bubbled. "I *love* this place, I could come in my toga. I'm going to the ladies', don't let anything happen till I get back." She disappeared into darkness.

A blond boy ("our Jeff, the blond who does have more fun," the emcee had called him) came out to strip. Alicia began to relax, and even to see the humor in the evening. She found herself applauding along with the rest when Lenore put a bill in the neckline of her dress and dared the stripped-to-pale-blond-skin Jeff to take it. He leaned down and removed the bill with his teeth, and Lenore squealed and fell back on the chaise.

There followed a procession of strippers, wearing an array of fantasy costumes that were supposed to suggest wild and wonderful sexual adventures. Two muscular black men, who looked like twins, did a few bizarre things and were quite effective. A man with a Spanish name stripped off a tuxedo and ended up in a G-string covered with rhinestones and silver sequins. All of the strippers seemed wedded to the idea of the rhythmic pelvic thrust, in time to whatever music was backing them. The colors of the lights changed, and the room got smokier. Whatever the thrill the strippers conveyed to the rest of the audience, it missed Alicia. Mere nakedness didn't do it. It wasn't at all like the unsettling nearness of an electric man like Mike Tedesco. She wondered if there were something wrong with her, but Sheila seemed calm enough, although Elsa had a slightly glazed look.

Alicia decided that she had stayed long enough. As the rhinestone and silver G-string slithered offstage, she was ready to ask Sheila if she'd mind giving Debbie and Lenore a lift home. They wouldn't want to tear themselves away until the end, and she most of all wanted to go away by herself and not have to listen to postmortems on the way home.

"I have to go now," she said to Sheila. "It's been a lot of fun." And hoped she sounded sincere.

"Don't leave yet, Al. The star is next. You can't miss him."

"You know me. When it's time to go, I go. Can you bring Debbie and Lenore home?"

"Oh, sure, but . . ."

Alicia got up and found her shoes, slipped them on.

"Where are you going?" Elsa hissed. "You're going to miss something."

"I doubt it," Alicia said. To Sheila: "I'll tell Len and Debbie."

She made her way quickly around the chaises to the side of the room where they were sitting. In the half-light, she had no trouble finding them. They were sitting side by side, clapping to a driving disco tune while they waited for the next act.

Then the lights went out. Completely. The room was in total darkness; even the tiny lights over the tables blacked out. Alicia stumbled against a chaise, then tried to get her bearings to find the door out.

61

She got halfway across the room again in the dark, when the lights came on. All of them. Blazing, almost blinding.

Onstage was a dazzling Elizabethan highwayman.

Tony Spinelli.

He radiated sexuality like none of the other strippers. It seemed to roll out from him in waves and engulf the roomful of women.

Alicia hated him before she recognized the emotion.

She needed desperately to escape, from this place, from the man onstage. He was not simply another in a wearying parade of interchangeable strippers, but vital and individual. A man who had stepped forward to violate her, out of every secret fantasy she had ever spun.

Yet she couldn't take her eyes off him. She couldn't move. Tony had captured her, his victim, his special audience for this performance. His eyes locked onto Alicia's, out of all the woman in the room, and he forced her back to her chaise with a look that said, "You don't leave when Tony's on."

She hated him all the more, because she had to obey him.

7

TONY watched the woman in red who slid onto an empty chaise. She hadn't been able to take her eyes off him, even when the dame beside her leaned over and whispered to her. She thought she was leaving, did she? No chance of that now. She was going to love Tony. Everybody always did.

He knew how perfectly his costume showed off his body. High, soft suede boots, skintight maroon pants, a thick white satin shirt with a lacy collar.

His music blared out through the room, a rhythmic rock tune that was beginning to become one of those songs you couldn't avoid. He'd picked it when it first started getting play, and it was almost time to find new music. If only he had an arranger or somebody who could do that for him . . .

Tony felt the satin of the shirt on his bare chest as he started to move. He had grace; the only person to equal him there was Raoul. And he had trained hard, from the days when he was a kid at school dances to actual lessons his sister Teresa had urged him to take. Above all, he was sexy. He'd grown into that in the course of his twenty-five years. A promise of tantalizing pleasure that women had always found irresistible. He was his own fantasy, and the secret desire of anything female from ten to a hundred. Tony loved the person who was swaying, thrusting, teasing on that stage and watching the eager, breathless women in the audience through arrogant, narrowed eyes.

And he especially watched the woman in red.

While he stripped, he played a home movie inside his head. He could visualize every nuance of movement, every vein and muscle and inch of his skin. They were all imprinted on his memory from hours and days of practice in front of mirrors. The mirrored Tony was almost more real to him than the flesh-and-blood body he inhabited, and what these women saw and adored, he loved much more. The emotional, gut reaction to his performance was a pale reflection of his own gratification.

The satin shirt slithered to the floor, and the women screamed their approval. It was so easy to grab these dames.

Once he'd said to Denise, who was about the only woman he saw with any regularity, "Shit, those women are lucky to have me, even if they don't get to touch."

He'd been nettled when she had laughed, tossing her mane of blond hair like she was still on a stage stripping herself instead of retired to being a cocktail waitress.

"You mean, you're so wonderful, you wish you could fuck yourself. Man, you ain't ever going to get any place until you get over being Tony Spinelli. You're on the biggest, whaddya call it, ego trip I ever heard. And you ain't nowhere yet."

"I will be," he said. "A hundred dames hot as rockets for me in Boston, a million more out there who don't know what they got coming. It's a matter of making a good connection."

"Ya can't fuck 'em all, Tony."

"But I can, sweetheart, right in their little heads."

The second time she laughed, he'd put on his clothes and gone home to his mirrors.

The thing about these women in the Carousel audiences, they got to be like one big animal howling for him. They fed on each other's excitement, he could sense it growing and growing, swelling up and reaching out to him, and there wasn't any one woman who could give that kind of love.

"Take it off, take it off," the women chanted, and he kicked off the boots.

"Yes! More!" they screamed, and he peeled off the trousers.

Now he was free, Tony, with his glistening muscles and his smooth skin and cock hard in his G-string. Through it all, he kept the woman in red pinned to the chaise with only his look. Her mouth was slightly open and she was breathing hard, but not moving.

He moved. His hips thrusting and rhythmic; his shoulders, teasing, alluring.

In his head, he was saying to her, "You're excited by Tony, sweetheart, you're holding it all in, it's going to burst, I'm the best, can you feel me inside . . . ?"

He was playing hard to her, and dammit, he was going to get a reaction. The rest of them—they reached out to him as he came down from the stage, and he let them barely touch his arms, thighs, ass as he alternately teased and insulted them with his body. They pressed money at him, tucking bills into his G-string.

Somebody tossed him a key and shouted, "My husband's away on Tuesday." Tony laughed and blew her a kiss. Another called, "Forget her, I don't have a husband!" and he made his way in her direction. As he'd hoped, she was good for five bucks in his G-string.

Once he got into the audience, the act almost became a joke, this naked man throwing his prick and his ass around, but the dames loved it.

The one in red looked like she was praying he wouldn't move in her direction. Her hands were clenched at her sides, and goddamn, she was looking down at her lap. The woman beside her was the one the party was for, he recognized her, and when he got to her, she shoved a handful of bills into the elastic of his G-string.

Tony kissed his fingertips to Sheila, who applauded delightedly, and turned his attention to Alicia. She couldn't ignore the thrusting hips beside her half-bowed head. He gave everything he had, like when he was rehearsing his number for himself only, the most important audience in the world.

Slowly Alicia raised her eyes and met his.

She was feeling him, oh, yes. . . .

Tony smiled, urging her to add something to the money the others had shoved in his G-string.

She shook her head and pantomimed, "No money." Then she tried to look away.

Nobody looked away from Tony. He reached down and took her chin in his hand, forcing her to keep her face turned to him. No more playing. No teasing. No games. It was a struggle of wills that he was going to win. She looked panicked, even though she kept a fixed smile on her face. He noticed two bright spots of color on her cheeks.

He held her chin and rotated his hips in front of her face, demanding a response. She must be about boiling over inside, and dammit, he was going to make her show it.

With his free hand, he gathered up the bills that had been thrust into his G-string and made a fan of them, lightly brushing her cheek.

There was anger, maybe hate in her eyes. That was a start. He was a bit angry now himself.

Suddenly, he let go of her chin and pulled down his G-string. His cock popped out inches from Alicia's face, in such a way that only she could see it, and she flinched as though she'd been slapped.

She was enraged, humiliated, and Tony was satisfied. He adjusted his G-string calmly and smiled. The audience, only sensing that something out of the ordinary had happened, screamed its rapture.

Tony wasn't through with her. He took a bill from the handful he had acquired and offered it to her.

"Yes, take it, yes!" roared the women Alicia knew as sane and sensible friends and colleagues.

Tony's eyes dared her to refuse.

"Take it from Tony, Al!" A voice above the others. Lenore, of course.

Alicia could scarcely breathe, and her heart was beating so erratically, she thought she was having a heart attack. She felt as though she had been ravished and abused by this terrible man who had dared . . . dared . . .

Yet she was strangely excited. A whole different world of sexual aggression had been revealed, a different kind of erotic encounter, impersonal and terrifying.

"Take the money!"

Tony was still waving the bill in front of her.

She forced herself to look into his eyes. Dark, knowing eyes that saw only her. A heart-stopping look.

She took the bill.

The applause and shouts were deafening. Tony had conquered. He moved away, back toward the stage, waving, touching a hand, evading others. He never looked back at

Alicia, who was sitting stunned and unmoving at Sheila's side.

He went up onstage and scooped up his discarded clothes.

She hated him for refusing to look at her again, she hated the self-satisfied smile on his face as he glanced out over his audience. He stopped at the curtain, relaxed and easy with his nakedness, and saw Alicia watching him as if she were trying to imprison his image in her mind.

He winked at her and smiled, raising his hand in a half-wave, acknowledging her. Alicia tried not to, but she smiled back. It was a fraction of a second, that flash of strange intimacy between her and Tony. She almost waved, but dropped her hand to her lap, and crumpled the bill he had forced on her into a tight little wad.

Then he was gone, through the curtains, and the women crowded around Alicia and Sheila, flinging their togas aside, returning to reality.

Backstage behind the Greek Suite was crowded, with the men coming offstage from the main room. Tito was hanging around, dressed in street clothes. Tony ignored him, and quickly counted the bills he'd collected in tips. Almost as much as he'd made during the main room show earlier.

"That's small potatoes, Spinelli," Tito said as he passed on his way to the back door to the parking lot. "Too bad your brains are all in your prick."

Tito sauntered away.

Tony put his tips into a neat pile. A couple of tens, a few fives, not bad. Some ones and a couple of twenties, which had come from the woman the party was being held for. Nearly a hundred bucks for a few minutes' work. Better than the main room, and a hell of a lot better than the other strippers ever did.

"Spinelli." Irv shoved his way through the strippers. "You know Sid don't like you touching the women, even at a private gig."

Tony looked at him blandly. "So did I? I forget."

"Christ, you were throwing your dick around like it was the American flag. I was watching."

"And I bet you loved it, Irv. They loved me, now get off my back." He couldn't resist a last taunt. Irv always asked for it. "You'd give your mother to have a bunch of broads coming over you the way they do for me."

"You dumb wop." Irv sputtered.

Raoul passed them and ran his hand over Tony's bare buttocks.

"It's a good show, man," Raoul said. "They were hot for you."

"See, Irv? Raoul likes me, and he's a man who knows a man when he sees one."

"Wops and fags, the shit I got to put up with." Irv stormed off toward the cubbyhole that served him and Sid as an office.

Tony and Raoul grinned at each other.

"You be careful, man, Irv don't get so mad he shoot you with the little gun he carry," Raoul said.

"He don't worry me," Tony said. "He needs his gun—and I got the only gun I need."

Raoul went off to dress, and Tony paused to part the back curtain an inch. The women from the party were standing around in groups, talking excitedly, putting on their coats. He caught a glimpse of the dame in the red dress heading for the door with a couple of chicks in tow. He saw that she was a little older, but not bad looking, details he hadn't noticed in the heat of his performance. She had a classy look you didn't see all that much around the Carousel. She'd go home remembering Tony Spinelli, that was certain. How good he was.

Too good for this dump, he thought for the hundredth time that week. If only he could get a break that would take him to Vegas, someplace worth being. He thought about it all the time. When he rehearsed his new act at home, when he hung out places with his friends—they had no ambitions, though, and only made jokes about Tony the stripper. And always when he stood behind the bar in the downtown hotel where he worked the day shift during the week. His Uncle Angelo had gotten him the job, and he didn't ask what kind of strings got jerked. Especially since the manager never said a word if Tony called in to say he couldn't work. There was always the chance that one of the daytime drinkers would be Somebody. A producer or a guy somewhere in show business. The bar was where he ran into the woman from the women's skin magazine, who liked him well enough to use some shots of him. He'd repaid her well for that.

He wished Uncle Angie would use his connections to help his career, but he knew his mother, estranged though she was, wouldn't let Angie lift a finger. Ma hated everything about Tony stripping. Check that: she hated everything about Tony. He hadn't seen her in years.

"Hey, Spinelli!" Sid came out of his office. Tony could see Irv's scowling face behind him. "Some dame wants you on the phone."

"This ain't your answering service," Irv sneered as Tony took the phone from his hand. Irv sat down in one of the chairs and fiddled with the gun he carried—to protect him going to the bank, he claimed.

"Careful you don't shoot off your leg, Irv," Tony said. "I don't suppose you even got a prick."

He turned his back on Irv and Sid and spoke into the receiver.

"Yeah?" He was sweaty and he stank, and he wanted to get to a shower and then home. The last thing he needed tonight was a woman. Any woman. For any reason.

"Where are you?" It was Denise, querulous. He could imagine her pouting, twisting a blond curl with her thumb and forefinger.

"Hiya, sweetheart. What's up?"

"You were supposed to be. You were supposed to be at my place an hour ago. I took the night off, remember?"

He'd forgotten. And he'd forgotten to tell Denise that he was working the private party instead of just the usual weekend shows. But he wasn't going to admit that.

"Hey, hon. I got rushed into this private gig. I tried to call you."

"Fucking liar," Denise said peacefully. "So are you coming or not?"

"I'm beat. It was a hard show."

"I'll bet. Look, you better get here in an hour, or you don't have to bother. Ever."

"That's my choice, huh?" Irv and Sid were busy going over a ledger, but Tony knew Irv was straining to overhear. "Baby, there's plenty more where you came from."

"I could say the same about you." She slammed down the receiver. He looked at the phone, shrugged, and hung up.

"Dames," Tony said cheerfully. "Most of 'em have no class."

"What would you know about that?" Irv said sourly. Sid looked at his brother with rueful despair and almost affection. Tony couldn't undersand how Sid could put up with Irv.

"She'll come crawling back soon enough," Tony said. "They all do." His shoulders were starting to stiffen up in the coldish office. "See you tomorrow," he said.

"Can't wait for that pleasure," Irv said.

This time Sid intervened. "Shut up, Irv. You never know when to shut up."

Tony showered and dressed. Cain and Abel, looking like cat burglars in black turtlenecks and black pants, were leaving.

"Tomorrow," Tony said.

"Right, man," they said in unison.

Jeff tumbled into the dressing room, beaming his good-old-boy smile, as Tony was putting on his coat.

"Ooo-eee," he said, "I got me a nice little date. Stuck a note right in with the ol' pecker, she did, right there in the main room. Not one of the housewives either, spending the food budget out with the girls. A coupla rings I thought to blind me."

Jeff was hopeless. "Keep it quiet, will you?" Tony said. "Or you'll be out on that cute little ass if Irv hears you and tells Sid."

"I'm okay," Jeff said. And went off looking like an over-grown cherub.

By the time Tony reached the parking lot, Alicia, Debbie, and Lenore were long gone. Alicia had endured a lot of good-natured cracks from the rest of Sheila's party, and she hoped she hadn't let her humiliation show.

Jennifer Newman had the good taste to be sympathetic. "It was funny, but a lousy trick to pull on you. Let's get together sometime and commiserate."

"I'd love to," Alicia said. "Right now, I can't wait to get out of here."

A quick thanks and good-bye to Sheila, and they were on their way back into the city.

Lenore's excitement was still at a high pitch.

"Fantastic! What a body. And he picked you, Alicia."

"He didn't pick me for anything," Alicia said, sharply. Lenore finally calmed down and got off the subject of Tony Spinelli.

Alicia drove fast, too fast, to get rid of Debbie and Lenore, get home, close her eyes, blot out the image of the stripper, that glistening, insulting body, the dark-eyed face, the silky black curls, his presence. Tomorrow, she and Graham and the boys would drive north to Vermont into the cold snowy mountains and she would ski and ski until she dropped, and tonight would disappear.

She dropped Debbie off first. One of the curtains on a front window was slightly drawn back, as if someone were watching for her return.

"He really is something," Lenore said, watching Alicia out of the corner of her eye.

"Who?"

"Give me a break, Alicia. The stripper. Tony."

"Sometimes," Alicia said, "I never want to see another man as long as I live."

"I've seen him before," Lenore said. "I never saw him do what he did to you tonight."

"Oh, yeah?" She tried to sound disinterested, but she was curiously pleased that she'd been singled out. And there was the final wink and then the smile. He had almost apologized for taking her into his act.

Why had he? Because she was standing up when he came on, of course. She remembered her hate and had to laugh at herself. Ladies shouldn't be the object of special attention, it's bad taste. But she was to blame, for being there in the first place.

She didn't hate him now, and the sense of humiliation would pass. She'd never have to see him again.

Alicia had restless dreams, and while she was in them, the man who flickered through them was dark-haired and naked and no one she had ever seen, but she seemed to know him. He made love to her . . . or did he? She awoke with the shudder of a dream orgasm still throbbing through her body, and wondered what on earth she had been living through in her sleeping mind.

Then she slept again, feeling deep peace, as if she were enfolded in safe, loving arms.

8

ALICIA woke to a dazzling day on Saturday.

She was on the road to Weston and Graham by 9:30, pausing at home only to call Harriet to say yes, she had a good time at the Carousel (Harriet snickered; Lenore must have called already), and yes, she'd be back from skiing in Vermont on Sunday in time for dinner with the Goulds. "And your little surprise."

"Len told, what a brat," Harriet said. "Never mind, you'll like him. But don't let on to Graham that I'm still trying to break up his happy relationship."

"I do not belong to Graham Parker," Alicia said.

Today she was certain that nothing permanent could ever exist between her and Gray.

The snow was piled high on the sides of the highway, and the sky was a clear, pale blue. It would be glorious farther north in the mountains. The ski slopes and the air and the sunlight would cleanse her. She was already wearing her ski clothes, her overnight bag was on the back seat, they'd be on the road to Vermont in the Parker station wagon as soon as she pulled into the driveway.

It took her a second to connect with the music playing on the car radio. The stripper's music from the night before. And suddenly the evening came back to her vividly, sending an icy tingle through her. Then, as quickly, she felt hot and tense and uneasy.

72

How awful it had been. Lenore and the others were probably talking about it still.

She swerved back into her lane as a car passing her blared its horn.

Alicia could see his face, the wink and the wave at the end. She wondered what it would be like to plunge her fingers into his curls, and feel that body enveloping hers. A voluptuous surrender . . .

"Stop it!" she said aloud, and flicked the radio dial to a sedate classical music station. The sounds of Mozart's *Sinfonia Concertante* filled the Volvo, controlled and rich and wonderful.

I will not think of him, she repeated. An animal, a crude and thoughtless man. A *stripper*, of all things!

She drove faster, to get to safe, predictable Graham as soon as possible. Maybe she'd tell him about last night, slightly censored. It would put it in perspective, remind her how funny it could be made to sound. Graham did have a sense of humor, after all. He was supposed to be on her side. By laughing together about it, they would make it go away. The awfulness. The threat to her that she hadn't asked for, didn't want.

Then she remembered that she had carefully smoothed out the crumpled bill he had forced her to take and tucked it away in a book last night before she'd gone to bed. When she got home from skiing, she'd spend it or burn it or give it away to charity.

Alicia made her way from the highway through the winding roads of prosperous suburbia: houses widely spaced, lots of trees, expanses of snow-covered lawns where little Westonites had built snowmen and dragged Flexible Flyers. In front of one vast split-level, a huge St. Bernard frolicked with heavy-footed grace, churning up the snow in his manic excitement.

I should be so carefree, Alicia thought, as she pulled into the Parker driveway. She was surprised to see that the station wagon hadn't yet been loaded with the boys' ski gear. She had a flash of resentment about the delay it would cause in getting under way. Alicia rang the back door bell. She was not yet willing to allow herself complete freedom of the Parker house, not while Graham's mother ran the establishment.

Graham came to the door. She liked him best when he looked the way he did today: flannel slacks, a pullover, and

73

loafers. She could catch a glimpse of Graham Junior and Timmy engrossed in Saturday morning TV cartoons in the family room off the kitchen.

"You're not ready to go?" she asked, although the answer was obvious.

"We're not going," Graham said, as he kissed her lightly on the cheek. "Graham has a hockey game this afternoon. I completely forgot about it until last night."

"You could have called," she said. Crossly.

"You were out last evening," he said, pointedly. "Say hello to Alicia, boys."

Junior barely looked up and mumbled. Timmy gave her a big "Hi!" before he reimmersed himself in the cartoons.

"I guess I can handle a hockey game," she said, gamely, hiding her disappointment. She found hockey boring, needlessly brutal, even when played by twelve-year-olds.

She and Graham had coffee in the kitchen. Very domestic. Mother Parker was shopping at the Chestnut Hill Mall, then lunching out. One small blessing. Alicia was not up to her.

Graham studied her for a moment, then said, "Proud of yourself?"

Alicia had no idea what he was talking about.

"The play was excellent," he said. "Mother enjoyed it very much. I hope your evening was as pleasant."

Then she knew he was obliquely criticizing her night out. It seemed to bother him. She knew that tiny frown.

"I'm always proud of myself," she said.

"Why are you smiling?"

"I was thinking of something that happened . . . the other day. Nothing." It would definitely not be a good idea to tell Graham about the Carousel Club, or Tony Spinelli.

"Alicia, I'm sorry about the skiing. Am I forgiven?" Graham could, when he chose, cease to be professor and master and become boyish and vulnerable. "I'll make it up to you."

"Think you can?" she asked playfully.

"As a matter of fact, it crossed my mind that when spring recess comes round in March, we might go out to Aspen to ski. Just you and me. We could stop in Boulder to see your father."

"Oh, Gray, let's! He'd love it. The way his romance with Vera Ormond is going, we might be in time for the wedding." Then she wished she hadn't mentioned marriage,

74

because Graham got a Look. The last thing she wanted today was more marriage talk with him, not after—everything. "I want to, Gray, if I can manage the time. You'll like Dad's girl friend. . . ."

Graham, standing behind her, kissed the back of her neck. The gesture pleased her. It was warm and loving. Clean.

"It's nice to have a girl friend," he said. "Every boy should have one."

She turned around and looked at him. He gazed at her with affection. She could not tell, though, whether he was simply defending a possession from intrusions. It was an intimate moment, but was a handful of such moments enough to build a life together on? Alicia doubted it. There had to be more. . . .

"When's lunch?" Graham Junior's voice intruded on their intimacy. Ah, family life.

Alicia went into the television room. "What do you want? Anything in the world."

"Escargots," Graham Junior said.

"Nobody likes a kid who's too smart for his age," Alicia said, and Junior chuckled.

"Pizza!" Timmy said. "One of those big fat ones, like they make at D'Amico's. None of that fish stuff."

"One pizza from D'Amico's, hold the anchovies," Alicia said. "Anybody want to come with me?"

Timmy did, Graham Junior had to look over his skates, big Graham thought pizza wasn't quite the thing, but he was voted down. Finally he handed her some money. She was about to tell him that it was her treat, but realized it wouldn't mean a thing to the kids, certainly not to Graham. She took the proffered bills. Not quite the same as taking money plucked out of a G-string in a smoky strip joint, but still . . . cash was cash.

"How's school?" she asked Timmy when they were belted into the Volvo. Timmy seemed small for his age, and to her, almost too quiet.

"Yuck. Miss Morrissey is . . . is . . ." He searched for a word to describe either ecstasy or despair. "She's like a wicked witch."

"You always find a few of those as you go along. She won't be the last. I had a third-grade teacher who would probably put Miss Morrissey to shame."

"Oh, third. I'm in fifth."

"I know," Alicia said.

"You know most things." Timmy stared hard out the side window, working up to something. "Are you going to be my mom?" he finally said in a small voice.

"What gives you that idea?" she asked gently. He was still looking away, a tense ten-year-old faced with adult mysteries.

"I heard Nana and Dad talking about it."

Alicia resisted asking what side his grandmother was on.

"We're pretty good friends, aren't we, Timmy?" He nodded, still not looking at her. "So you can tell me whether you think that would be a good idea or a bad one, and I promise I won't tell anyone, not your dad or your grandmother or Graham. What do you say?"

"I don't know," he said. "I remember Mommy."

She pulled off the road to a cleared spot and turned to him.

"I know you remember your mother, and I would never, ever try to take her place. But I have to tell you a secret you have to promise you won't tell, okay?" He nodded, silent. "I don't know what your dad and I are going to do. I don't know what *I'm* going to do. Grown-ups have as hard a time deciding on things as kids do. But I promise if it looks like I'm going to be your mom, I'll come and talk things over with you beforehand, just you and me. No surprises, right?"

"Right!" He was relieved, and now looked at her, with Graham's green-flecked eyes. "I love you, Alicia."

She knew, thank goodness, not to make too much of that.

"That's about the nicest thing any man has ever said to me," she said. "And I love you, too. Now! Let's get that pizza."

It couldn't be easy for the boys, caught between their busy father and a grandmother like Mrs. Parker. Graham Junior was growing up, would be off to prep school in a year or so, but Timmy seemed so vulnerable. She wondered if he were like his mother, as Junior was like his father. She'd only met Hillie Parker once, years before, when she was still married to Gardner. Hillie was already beginning her decline into terminal illness. The Parkers had been living in St. Louis, where Graham was teaching at Washington University. He had moved back to Boston so that Hillie could die where she had been born and raised. Poor Timmy, who remembered her without understanding.

"Timmy, since we're pals, I want you to remember that you can always call me up if there's anything that bothers you, or you think I can help with. Any time at all. I won't tell anybody."

"I don't know your number," he said.

"I'll write it down for you, my house and my office."

"Okay," he said, happily. "Know something else? I don't like green pepper on pizza; Dad does, but do we have to get it?"

"Nope," she said. "We're in charge."

"He'll say something."

"Too bad," she said.

Graham did complain, when they got home with the pizza, that it lacked green peppers. Alicia and Timmy exchanged knowing smiles across the table.

The hockey game was interminable, but Alicia cheered the team lustily. Graham Junior's side won. Mrs. Parker was home when they got back, and the pleasant domestic tone of the day altered subtly. The boys escaped to their rooms. Mrs. Parker served tea. Alicia could have used a good stiff drink.

Mrs. Parker, who was in her late sixties, but looked younger, probably by pure force of will, fixed Alicia with a penetrating look, pleasant enough but sharp.

"You young women nowadays have such freedom to dress as you please," she said.

Alicia still was wearing her ski clothes from the aborted ski trip.

"I suppose," she added, "that if you have to get dressed up every day to work . . ."

Then Graham said, "Alicia can look very nice, Mother."

She was stung at both the tone and the content of that.

"We saw an excellent play last evening," Mrs. Parker said. "A pity you had another engagement. Graham would, I'm sure, have much preferred to attend with you. I understand you had unavoidable social obligations."

For a wild moment, Alicia wondered if Graham had told his mother precisely where she had been. He seemed to be doing a lot of confiding in her lately.

"Unavoidable," Alicia agreed. And then, a touch maliciously, for Graham's benefit, "But very enjoyable."

"Will you two be staying here for dinner?" Mother Parker asked brightly. "Or do you have plans in the city?"

"We hadn't talked about—" Alicia began.

Mrs. Parker continued, unchecked. "Although, of course, the boys have seen so little of their father recently, he's been so busy. You've probably seen more of him than they."

What an old bitch, Alicia thought, as she smiled pleasantly at Mrs. Parker.

"Naturally, you're welcome to join us, Alicia," Mrs. Parker said. "And stay overnight, if you wish."

Alicia never stayed overnight in Weston if she could avoid it. Mrs. Parker herself was ensconced in her own wing of the big house, but it was tacitly understood that there was to be no dalliance between an unmarried couple under her roof. The Parker house was not, to Alicia's mind, conducive to dalliance in any case; certainly not the cold, formal guest room she stayed in when it was occasionally necessary to spend the night. Graham was sunk in contemplation of some abstruse neurological concept. Or else he was being pointedly miffed still about her jollity about the previous evening. He neither encouraged her to stay nor signaled his willingness to accompany her back to Boston.

"I'd love to stay to dinner, Mrs. Parker," she said.

If she did ever marry Graham, would she be able to call this formidable woman anything but "Mrs. Parker"? She certainly wasn't anybody's "Mom."

"But I ought to get back to the city tonight," she continued. "As Graham knows, I was out very late last night with . . . the girls." She could be bitchy too, for all the good it did her.

"Of course," Mrs. Parker said. "One cannot keep up the same pace as when one was a girl. I mean, a *young* girl. Well, let me put a roast in the oven. I'm sure you two have a great deal to talk about." Mrs. Parker went off to the kitchen.

"Do we have something to talk about, Gray?" Alicia asked.

"Mother was only being polite," Graham said. "I certainly don't want to engage you in serious discussions if you're so tired out from your night with the 'girls.' And boys, if I understand your activities correctly." There was a tinge of contempt in his voice. "I hope it satisfied your

78

juvenile curiosity. Although how you could give up Maggie Smith . . . for *that*."

"Wait a minute," Alicia said.

Graham did not pause. "I ran into your friend who runs the box office at the theater; he was surprised you chose not to come. Naturally, I didn't tell him. . . ."

"Oh, Kenny would have thought it amusing, Gray."

"But *I* do not find it amusing."

At last Alicia understood. Graham was threatened by her adventure at the Carousel Club. So threatened that he had reverted, like his mother, to sly digs, refusing to ask her what it had been like. Refusing to talk about it, except around the edges.

"It was nothing, Gray. Really."

"To me, it seems somewhat perverted, this desire to look at men removing their clothes."

At this moment, Alicia saw Graham Parker slipping away and out of her life. She had failed in his eyes, as she had in Gardner's, to live up to the Parker standards.

And he had failed to meet hers, which were not half so complex: humor, serenity, trust, and understanding.

"I think you have taken leave of your usually sound senses. I assure you that going out with my friends to a place where men strip does not mean I've become a degenerate. Or my friends either. We had a good time. I *liked* it."

In retrospect, sitting in this house, she had. The realization came as a mild shock. She had had a glimpse of vibrant life, with no ponderous analyses required, no discussions, no present and inflexible standards to meet.

Graham said sullenly, "Since you're a woman, presumably you think you know what you're talking about. I find your behavior disquieting."

At least, she thought, he didn't apply further words of description, like appalling, unforgivable, disgraceful to God and country.

Dinner was not lively. She and Graham exchanged few words. Mrs. Parker carried the conversation, and Alicia thought she could detect one or two "I told you so" glances between mother and son. Perhaps she was being oversensitive.

She escaped from the Parkers as soon as she could, remembering to slip Timmy a piece of paper with her telephone numbers. Whatever was going on between her and

Graham, her commitment to Timmy couldn't easily be broken.

Only when she was well along Route 128 toward Boston did she realize that the promised trip to Aspen next month had not been mentioned again. The treat was offered if she was going to be good; apparently she had not been sorry enough for what she had done. The treat had been withdrawn, for the present.

Dammit, what have I done? she thought. He doesn't even know, except that it wasn't what he wanted me to do. I can go to Colorado on my own. I can do anything I want.

Maybe, who knew, she might end up going with the man Harriet thought she might like to know.

She hoped she was going to like him very much.

Flying through the night, back to the city, Alicia was determined she would like him if he had three heads and a mother to put Mrs. Parker to shame. For once, she was unreservedly grateful to Harriet for making the effort in the face of resistance to finding a suitable man.

The real thing. Wouldn't it be a laugh if that's what he turned out to be? Not another Graham, or another Gardner, but . . .

Tony smiled in her head. She saw him pausing at the curtain in sharp detail and looking back across the room to her. Virile and intense, the lines of his body clearer in her memory than they had seemed in the smoky club. She forced herself to blank him out in a rush of . . . guilt? Fear? Embarrassment was more like it. A boy who had passed through a corner of her life and had kept going.

9

MARK Gould flung open the door to Alicia on Sunday night, swept her into his arms, and bent her over backward in a simulation of passionate kiss.

"Excuse me," he said, when he set her back on her feet. "I was expecting someone else altogether." He pulled her into the living room, frantic with energy. "You look sensational, Alicia!"

She knew she looked very good. She'd put up her hair, and had worn nearly iridescent dark green Italian silk slacks and flowing overblouse. She felt silky all over, young and irresistible. She had also worn Graham's new necklace.

A faint greeting from Harriet floated in from the kitchen. Mark fussed around, never still. He was a collection of disparate elements—wild, frizzy hair, gangly arms and legs, big nose, bright, eager eyes—that somehow worked. Mark was so highly charged with energy that Alicia often wondered how Harriet stood it. But she knew: he was Mark—unique, charming, stimulating.

"Do we have a surprise for you!" He settled her into a chair.

"Would it be a candidate for man of my dreams?"

Mark's face fell. "She told you."

"Only the fact. Rumor had gotten around that Harriet had gone back on her word about no more blind dates."

"It was my fault, my fault. He's not here yet, called to

say he was held up, on his way. Jerry Godwin, new associate at the law firm, great mind—"

"That's what I need, a great mind."

"No, listen, Harriet's met him, thinks he's terrific, and . . ." Full of glee: *"Not Jewish.* Perfect. I couldn't believe Abe would hire him, but . . . Did I tell you how great you look? Just great!"

Harriet sang out from the kitchen, "I'm sending in a pathetic child to keep the two of you on the straight and narrow."

"Hey, come on, Josh!", Mark called. "Great kid, what a live wire. And this Jerry, now Alicia, you're going to like him, trust me? Good."

Joshua came cautiously into the living room, wearing his pajamas. Although fathered by a whirlwind, Josh was a shy child, who examined visitors seriously, even familiar ones like Alicia, before plunging into the social fray. He was alarmingly bright for his age. He was followed by Harriet, wearing a long, golden hostess gown from Alfred Fiandaca on Newbury Street and looking as happy as a rabbit in clover.

"Wait till you see him, you'll forgive me," she said.

"The only man for me is already married to my best friend," Alicia said, and Mark beamed his lopsided smile.

"Flattery will get you . . . what? A drink. White wine, you sit down, Harriet." Mark galloped out to the kitchen, grabbing some wine goblets from the dining room sideboard.

Harriet sat down with a sigh. Joshua crawled up on her lap and stared solemnly at Alicia.

"Hey, kid," she said, pinching his cheek. "It's your Aunt Alicia." She shook her head. "I can't shut him up from morning to bedtime when we're here together, and I bring in an audience to be impressed, and he's as verbal as a rock. So, how are Graham's boys, the skiing?"

"The boys are nice, and we didn't go skiing. I came back on Saturday night, after a tense evening, a boring day. The presence of Mother Parker didn't help."

"Ah," Harriet said. "If anything could prevent you from succumbing to Graham's proposals, that one could."

"It's not only her," Alicia said. "It's everything." She thought of Timmy Parker's sweet vulnerability that asked so much. A commitment beyond marriage she wasn't prepared to make. "Harriet, I can't keep drifting along with

Graham, but I simply can't marry him. What's wrong with me?"

"Not a thing, not one thing." Harriet thought a minute. "I think good sex is nature's way of making you forget how really dumb it is to get married. If you don't have it . . ." She looked closely at Alicia, seeing, understanding as only a very old friend can. "Am I right? It's not everything, but it gets you through a lot. Like Said and Sheila. I mean, putting an Irish Catholic and some kind of Moslem together without any common ground much . . ."

"Except for money," Alicia said wryly.

"Oh, sure, and once they get to Paris and Sheila starts cutting a swathe—but it never would have happened except for that *thing*, you know, pounding hearts and all that."

Mark came back with the wine.

"Alicia, are you acquiring billions for the medical school, along with saving a place for my son, the twenty-first-century doctor?" Even sitting, Mark never seemed to be in repose.

"We're pushing now for petrodollars—petromillions, I hope—from this tiny but rich emirate. The dean does most of the wooing. I've been relegated to woman's place: being charming and arranging luncheons. I don't trust them myself, they're going to want more back for their bucks than a polite thank you. But I know nothing. The boys don't tell the girls." Alicia thought of Victor Ostrava and his extravagant demands and the claims he made about his work. "Or else they distort."

"Men lie," Mark said. "Even when they don't need to. I do it myself."

"You ask why I love my husband?" Harriet said. "He's the only man I ever met who admitted that. And so cheerfully."

The buzzer sounded from downstairs. Mark went to answer. Joshua decided that Alicia was the same Aunt Alicia who brought good toys and read good stories when she baby-sat. He climbed up on Alicia's lap and examined the links of her gold and lapis chain with interest.

Alicia decided that between Timmy Parker and Joshua Gould, she had enough men in her life.

She thought so until she saw Jerry Godwin.

He wasn't the kind of man you immediately thought of as sexy, but then you looked again. And again. Six feet

83

tall, a swimmer's body and a dazzling smile. He had beautifully cut hair, and a habit of running his fingers through it, as if to brush it back. He had a deep voice, with a trace of the Southwest. Jerry was about Alicia's age, the faintest bit worn—he had wonderful laugh lines around his eyes—and he had a perfect nose. He was almost too good to be true. This man was nobody's reject, no matter what Jennifer Newman said.

He was charming, a wonderful storyteller, who made the saga of growing up in Midwood, Texas, in the deadly heat of summer enthralling and hilarious—"Biggest thing in life was finding a way to get to Corpus Christi for the movies, and then crowding into a picture-taking booth in Woolworth's, all six of us, to commemorate the event."

Dinner was an unqualified success. They talked about movies, theater, books. Jerry often went to New York to see new shows. They found they had a few friends in common in theater, mostly college acquaintances of Alicia's who'd gone into acting or production. It was so easy to talk to him, listen to him, watch him. Alicia knew he was interested in her. Not only because he listened when she spoke, and seemed to be speaking mostly to her, but why else would he keep looking directly into her eyes and accidentally touching her leg under the table? She wondered what would happen if she accidentally touched his? During coffee, she let her hand rest on the side of her chair, barely touching his thigh. Jerry smiled at her knowingly, nicely, and his hand brushed hers, pausing for just the briefest squeeze. It was all pretty much coy, high school stuff, but it seemed to signify what she thought was so. An attraction. The beginning of that "thing." Alicia felt she was beginning a great adventure, whose end she couldn't yet see.

"I've heard it all," Harriet said, "but Alicia, Mark is dying to get your account of the Carousel Club."

"Oh, no . . . it's all such a . . . a powder room joke."

"Carousel?" Jerry asked. "Haven't I seen ads for the place, um . . . men?" He raised an eyebrow.

"Right. A dark, smoke-filled room, sort of Greek statues, fig leaves omitted, a red-haired lady wrestler to emcee, toreadors, cowboys, and a . . . highwayman, Elizabethan, yet. You ought to ask Harriet's sister, who could tell you about every muscle, and vein, and sequin, and armpit." Alicia spoke mostly to Jerry, to amuse him, to excuse herself for having gone. He was interested, not threatened.

"I wish I'd gone," Harriet said. "It sounds like fun. I see so few naked men around this place."

"It was mildly entertaining," Alicia said. She smiled at Jerry. "Frankly, I find tonight much more fun."

Mark and Harriet, as if by prearranged signal, decided they would do the dishes.

"Mark's never washed a dish in his life," Alicia whispered as she helped Harriet carry plates to the kitchen.

"That's not so. He washed a plate, a fork, and a frying pan once."

"Hah. When was that?"

"Three years ago, when I was in the hospital having Josh. Then he discovered he could go out for all his meals."

"You're being obvious, you know that," Alicia said. "Not that I mind. In fact, I forgive you all the others."

Harriet beamed her pleasure. "If at first you don't succeed . . ."

"Don't try any more. You can't top Jerry."

"Go. Talk to the man. Enjoy. I've told you a million times to trust me."

"One out of a million ain't so bad," Alicia said, and went to join Jerry. Mark dutifully went to his wife in the kitchen, but Alicia doubted that he would ruin his record of three years without a hint of dishpan hands.

Jerry, she noticed, had beautiful hands, with long, strong fingers and a dusting of golden hairs on the backs. Nails probably manicured. Nice to hold hands with, nice hands to feel on your body, a gentle caress, skin on skin . . .

"We ought to sneak out while they're in the kitchen," she said. "It would serve them right for being so obvious." She was usually less forward, always trying to keep her take-charge self she needed at school in the background on social occasions. Not too aggressive, her mother had taught her, and let the men think they've done it all. Pauline Bridges had made it work: major decisions seemed to come from her husband, but Alicia knew they all originated with Pauline.

"I'd love to," Jerry said. "But I didn't bring my car. A friend dropped me off. I was planning to call a cab to get home."

"Don't be silly," Alicia said. "I can drive you home.

85

Unless you happen to live halfway across the state in Worcester or something."

"I guess I didn't say, did I?" Jerry laughed. In fact, he'd said very little about his present life, a lot about those long-ago Texas days. Very cagey. She wondered if maybe he were married. No ring, and if he worked with Mark, he wouldn't dare fool around, surely not so soon anyhow. "I live in Cambridge," he said. "I don't want to inconvenience you."

"No problem. Maybe we could stop halfway for a nightcap? The Hyatt on Memorial Drive has a bar on top—great view of Boston across the Charles River."

"Sounds good."

They didn't actually slip away unnoticed. But they left soon after. Harriet grinned contentedly. Mark told her she still looked sensational after a night of debauchery at the Goulds. It was like being seen off on a teenage date by her parents.

Alicia drove them through the back streets of Brookline, with Jerry talking about what he really wanted, a house outside the city, "Concord, Lincoln, lots of trees, a garden, plenty of green after years at two hundred feet above sea level in a hundred-plus degrees in Texas . . ."

Without thinking, she turned right onto Commonwealth in the direction of her apartment rather than crossing onto Storrow Drive for Cambridge.

"Oh, damn!" she said. And really believed she hadn't done it on purpose. Jerry stopped in mid-sentence. "I made a wrong turn. Do you mind stopping someplace downtown? Or my place?" He didn't say anything. "I didn't plan it, Jerry, I promise! I don't think that fast."

"I believe you. Sure. Your place."

She wasn't sure he did believe her, but he didn't seem disturbed by the turn of events. She promised herself she would go carefully with Jerry. He was too good to be allowed to slip away without a fight.

"Hey, I like it." Jerry looked around her apartment with approval.

"I've got to take off these shoes," she said. "How about starting a fire while I do?" If this wasn't a special occasion, she didn't know what was.

"I'm not the world's greatest Boy Scout," he said, "but I think I can strike a match when pressed."

"Help yourself to a brandy," she called from the bed-

86

room, as she unpinned her hair and looked at her makeup. Not bad for an old broad. She felt a flutter of excitement in the pit of her stomach. It wasn't that she wanted to hop into bed with Jerry, not then, not in a rush. But eventually, when she'd seen more of him. The Goulds would encourage that, she could rely on Harriet to arrange opportunities for the four of them to get together. Cambridge was a lot closer than Weston. And if he had a mother, he'd left her behind in Texas.

The fire had caught well, and Jerry was sitting on the sofa facing the fireplace with a brandy snifter when she came back. Alicia left one lamp burning in a far corner so that the light from the fire flickered on Jerry's handsome profile.

He's so damned attractive, she thought, and curled up on the sofa beside him. Close, but not too close. Let him make the first move.

"The Goulds are a lot of fun," he said. "I like to see that kind of solid relationship. And the kid's great. So often you discover people you thought were fantastic have managed to produce a little monster."

"Josh is wonderful," Alicia said. She watched him out of the corner of her eye. A little bit of Brett Handley there, in the laugh lines, in his easy charm. O that he would turn out to be even more like Brett in other ways. "You're sort of wonderful yourself, Jerry."

"Far from it," he said. "I have as many flaws as the next man. Please don't make any mistake about that."

"Surely you don't kick dogs and trip old ladies," she said in mock amazement.

Jerry chuckled. "No. Dogs and ladies are safe with me. And I pay my taxes and show up for appointments on time. Well, most of the time."

"Let me get you more brandy," she said, and reached for his glass, making sure her hand brushed his. She managed to look directly into his eyes, and liked the funny half-smile he wore. She wanted those lips on hers, those arms around her. She knew that the adventure was going to turn out all right.

"Do you ski, by the way?" she asked.

"I've managed a few beginner's trails without breaking a leg. I'm more the sun-and-sand type, though."

That's okay, she thought. I'm adaptable.

"Only a drop of brandy for me," Jerry said. "It's getting

late, and I have to be in court tomorrow bright and early."

"Sure." She hid her disappointment in walking away with the snifters: a drop for him, quite a bit more for her. Amber courage. The least she could expect was something that would bring him back.

She sat down closer this time, almost touching. Jerry didn't say anything, didn't move toward her clear invitation. He stared into the fire with the snifter in both hands. Alicia put her hand on his arm. He looked away from the fire, to her and back.

Alicia felt a moment of doubt. There was nothing that said desirable in his look and her confidence drained away. She wasn't attractive, she was too old for his taste, she was coming on too strong. . . .

"Jerry." She spoke softly, but her mind was shouting, "I want you to want me!" She drank down her brandy and put the glass on the floor. "I want . . ."

"You're a lovely woman, Alicia." He spoke before she could finish. "The kind of woman I like: pretty, smart, funny."

"Isn't that a coincidence?" she said. "You're the kind of man *I* like."

"What would you say if I told you there was someone else in my life?"

"I'd say," Alicia said, throwing all caution to the wind, "that since you're here with me, someone else will have to take her chances." She put her hand on his neck, and brought their faces together. He had to kiss her, and he did, a curiously passionless kiss on his part, deeply felt on hers.

"I would like now to work around to something more serious," she said. "Like bed."

"No, Alicia," he said and kissed her again, very gently, before he drew away. "If there were someone else in your life, wouldn't you be able to resist the advances of an extremely attractive and sexy person?"

"Maybe there is someone," she said, "but I'm not resisting you."

"I'm not the one coming on here," Jerry said. "Much as I dislike pointing it out to you. Alicia, please," he added quickly as she sat back with an injured jerk. "I don't mean to hurt your feelings, or burst your romantic bubble. Can't we simply leave it?"

"No!" she said vehemently. "I don't want to leave it, and I don't want to be considerate and ladylike. I want *you*."

Jerry sighed. "I have to be going."

Alicia felt stinging tears at the corners of her eyes. Humiliation again. Anger and rejection.

"Oh, don't," Jerry said. "Please don't cry."

"I'm not," she said angrily. "I feel so damned stupid for making such a fool of myself. If you don't find me desirable, you're probably right. But I don't know why you bothered to come to dinner if there's somebody else. You must have known the Goulds were fixing us up."

"I knew. But I had to accept. Listen, Alicia. You are desirable. You're a lovely, sexy woman. Very sexy. And I'm very gay."

She stumbled to her feet and looked at him, with the firelight dancing on his cheekbones, his eyes dark in the shadow of his brows.

"Gay! How dare you be gay! After all I've been through this week!"

Jerry looked resigned in the face of her anger. Alicia sat down abruptly and shook her head.

"What a silly thing to say," she said. "This whole thing is my fault. I apologize . . . for everything."

"It's I that should apologize. I moved to Boston to be with my lover who got transferred here from New York. I'm such a new boy at Mark's law firm, I didn't figure to let him in on that part of my life, not yet." Dryly. "After all, I'm not only gay among straights, but also goy among Jews. Usually I can manage to avoid a situation like tonight. Or I handle it better. I've had enough experience."

"So have I," Alicia said. "I have enough gay friends to have sensed . . ." She forced a laugh. "I guess I've endured so many kinds of sexual assault recently that I decided to try it myself. Oh, just games," she added quickly when Jerry looked startled. "But they can be as unsettling as attempted rape."

Jerry stood up. "I ought to be on my way."

"I'll drive you," Alicia said.

"No. I'll catch a cab down the street. I don't suppose you'd like to have dinner sometime?"

"Oh, sure," she said, knowing she wouldn't. "Who wouldn't want to be seen in public with you?"

"One thing," he said at the door. "If you wouldn't mind not letting on to the Goulds . . . ?"

"I'll keep your secrets like my own," Alicia said. "Good luck, Jerry."

"The same and more to you, Alicia." He kissed her on the cheek and went off into the night.

Terribly civilized.

The phone started ringing almost as soon as Jerry had gone. It had to be Harriet, curled up in bed beside Mark, wanting to hear about everything. She didn't feel like talking to Harriet. Let her think she and Jerry were tangled up in a wild embrace and couldn't be bothered with the phone.

Alicia had another brandy, then she went to bed, naked. At least there was imagination. That couldn't fail her.

Imagination brought her the mocking image of Tony Spinelli. She wrapped herself in his fantasy dance, stripping away his clothes, coming closer to her, pulling her against his naked body. She could feel him thrust himself between her thighs, she felt a burst of violent release as she moved to the rhythms of her dream lover.

And in the morning, she remembered but couldn't recall if the man had been Tony or Brett or some unknown incubus who had come to ravish her out of a hidden corner of her mind.

What she did know for a certainty was that she felt battered and abused, at the lowest point in her life for a long time. And helpless in the face of what had been occurring.

It had not been a good weekend.

10

TONY came off the last show of the weekend furious with himself, the audience, everyone in his path.

You always have the occasional bad night, the show when the women in the audience could have been dead bodies for all the response you got. But tonight it hadn't been only that. He'd been lousy. Like he had two left feet, like his mind was anywhere but on the stage of the Carousel. He hadn't felt any of his usual pleasure in stripping; there hadn't been a face in the crowd he wanted to play to, get that personal reaction from: the shock of realization that he was taking off his clothes for her and for her alone.

He was tired, that was part of it. He had been working hard on a new act, and keeping after the woman who was doing the costume to finish it so he could try out the act for a live audience. If it clicked—it had to—he was that much closer to the big time.

Of course, that bitch Denise thought the act was a riot. But what did she know? She'd spent her life stripping for a bunch of drunks and sailors downtown, and that was definitely not the classy audience he was aiming for. Not that Denise didn't have a couple of good ideas now and then, but she was nobody. The people she knew in the business were guys like Sid, small-time operators who barely got by and couldn't imagine anything more than what they had. Tony had—what did you call it?—a vision.

Tony thought of how easy it was for Jeff to latch on

to these rich dames who were willing to pay whatever he asked. But then, Jeff would screw a plate of spaghetti for a price and still enjoy every minute of it. Tony wasn't like that, just as he'd never had to pay for sex himself or wanted to be paid.

Still . . . if he could meet up with the right person.

He wasn't going to find her at the Carousel, that was a sure bet. But he wasn't going to be the hit of the place either, if he didn't get back his concentration onstage.

Tony counted the tips he'd managed to gather during the last show. Less than twenty-five bucks. Terrible.

That smirking little bastard Tito walked by Tony while he was counting. He looked pleased with himself. Jeff had reported to Tony that the audience had been really hot for Tito.

Stone cold for Tony.

He decided that he would make a point of getting to the club early enough next weekend to catch Tito's act, size up the competition.

"Tony." Sid was standing at the office door. Irv wasn't around tonight. "Before you leave, stop in, will ya?"

Sid was probably old enough to be Tony's father, if Vinnie Spinelli had managed to survive eighteen-hour days working at a hundred cheap jobs to keep the family going. But he'd died half a dozen or more years ago, a couple of years before Tony left home for good. But Sid and Tony were of a kind, out of near poverty, struggling to the top of the heap for as long as they could remember. Tony, though, was damned certain he wasn't going to be struggling when he was Sid's age. He was never going to be bald and paunchy, with bifocals on his beak. He wasn't going to get old and spend his life in a dump like the Carousel.

Sid was sitting back in the rickety swivel chair with his feet on the desk when Tony came in.

"Siddown," he said. He lit a rumpled cigarette, offered one to Tony. "Eh, I forgot, you keep that body of yours healthy for the ladies." He coughed. "Got to give them up myself."

Tony moved a ledger off the seat of the only other chair, a straight-backed wooden job with peeling paint.

"So." Sid didn't seem to know how to begin. "A coupla things. You know this Raoul kid pretty well? Yeah, I thought so."

Tony couldn't imagine where this was leading. Raoul

claimed to have had some wild times, but far, far away from the Carousel.

"Raoul and I are friendly around the club," Tony said cautiously. "I don't hang out with him, if that's what you mean. He's, like, got other interests I don't go for."

"I wasn't suggesting you'd turned funny," Sid said. "It's that I've been hearing some things." He looked at Tony over his glasses. "These foreign guys, you don't know. . . . Look, you know I ain't going to lean on any of you strippers if you want a little something to get you up before you go on. Grass and stuff, whatever you got privately like. As long as you don't mix me up in any kind of problems. Professional interests, if you get me. There's people don't want trouble because Barbara works here, and I don't want to get caught in the middle."

"No problem, Sid. No kidding. There's no dealing here, if that's what you're getting at. I ain't seen real dope here more than three, four times, and it's usually guys who come and go fast. And the rest . . . a little smoke and that's it."

Sid raised his hand. "I don't want to know. As I say, it's something I heard, and they suggested Raoul was mixed up in it." Sid looked away from Tony.

Irv. It had to be Irv who was telling tales. The only person he hated more than Tony was Raoul.

"Irv doesn't like Raoul," Tony said.

Sid sighed. "Yeah, I heard it from Irv, but he heard it from somebody else."

The pieces fell into place for Tony. Irv was tight with Tito. Tony wouldn't put anything past Tito, from what he was beginning to see of him.

"Raoul's straight, Sid. Well, you know what I mean. But I'd keep my eye on that Tito, if I were you."

Sid shifted uncomfortably, and Tony knew he was right about the source of the rumor.

"Yeah, I'll do that, kid." Sid seemed more uneasy. "There's another thing. We been thinking we should try a midweek show. Like, bowling night for the boys, strip night for the girls. One show, ten-eleven on a Wednesday. We do okay with the bar weeknights, but maybe we could try this. Men allowed only if accompanied by a woman. How's that sound?"

Tony nodded. He wouldn't mind the extra bucks.

"But," Sid went on, "we ain't going to have the whole

bunch do the show, not until we see how we draw. I figure one or two strippers to start."

"Who?" Tony was thinking that Raoul would be a good one to share the show with him. Or blond Jeff and dark Tony.

"I was thinking of Jeff, and . . . Tito. People seem to think he's pretty good."

"He's lousy." Tony didn't do well hiding his annoyance.

"You seen him? I thought not. Sounds like professional jealousy to me, sonny. I ain't been in the business with guys for long, but you're beginning to sound more and more like the dames. Bitching about who goes on first, second, star. Anyhow, Irv picked up the idea someplace."

Tony wanted to tell Sid his brother couldn't pick up an old cigar butt from the gutter. It had to come from Tito, since he and Irv were so cozy. Conversations in corners, and it was funny, the way Irv dropped his usual bluster with Tito. Like Tito had some unsuspected authority. Tony didn't like it.

"If it goes," Sid said, "we'll work something out for you if you want to do another show, midweek."

"Sure, Sid. We'll talk. When you planning to start?" He'd talk Sid around to using Tony before the thing got going.

"This week," Sid said blandly. "We had an ad in the paper today."

Son of a bitch, Tony thought. Little Tito works fast.

"By the way," Tony said. "I got a brand-new act I've been working on. I'll be ready to break it in pretty soon, if you're interested. Okay?"

"Great. And listen, Spinelli, if you hear of anything that's going to give me trouble, let me know, will ya? My protection only extends so far, you get me?"

"Got you, Sid. But don't worry. Look, I got to meet my girl. I can't stand her up again."

Tony went out into the cold. Cold, but you could smell a breath of something else, the turning of the seasons.

Fucking bastard Tito. He'd have to keep an eye on him, being so tight with Irv. What could it be? Jesus, it had better not be some kind of homosexual thing, Sid would hit the roof. Somehow, he didn't think it was; Raoul would have caught on and passed the word. But God knew what kind of miserable secrets Irv had that Tito knew and was using.

Tony couldn't figure still where Tito had surfaced from,

but he hoped he wasn't as good at stripping as the talk had him. Lousy little exhibitionist, was what he was. No kind of style; all he wanted was to have dames gaping at his body. There were guys who got off on that.

If his new act was a hit, Tito and the pricks like him wouldn't matter. Tony would be up and away. He'd already gotten some publicity, he had pictures, and even a small reputation. If things broke right, he'd have a bigger one. The important thing was to be ready, and being ready meant concentrating on his act. Not only the moves, but that power that went out and grabbed the audience. Tony knew it was something he'd been born with; it used to get him into trouble before he knew what he was doing, back when he was a kid on the streets in the North End. When he finally figured out that he was the only person he could trust, and the power was something he should use carefully, he straightened out. There'd always been temptations to get involved with the guys who ran the hidden life of a big city, the one that went on behind the law and the proper Boston front everybody liked to pretend was the whole pizza. But you couldn't trust those hoods most of all, even less than women.

Tony had no intention of meeting Denise; after she raised hell the other night after the private party, he'd decided to let her steam for a while. That party was more like it, alive while tonight had been dead. The look on that dame's face, he'd never forget it.

He was heading to his place to rehearse. He had his mirrors, who were a perfect audience if you wanted to concentrate. No screaming women, just reflections of Tony that told him everything he wanted to know. And never argued back.

11

How many medical students are there at Commonwealth, Alicia wondered. A thousand? More? Not many fewer, certainly.

Why, then, was the only one she seemed to see Mike Tedesco? He was strolling down Hancock Place Monday morning.

She bent her head so as not to catch his eye and got up the stairs to the administration building as fast as she could. Surely the boy must have classes to attend, studying to do. A wife to entertain.

She ran into George, literally, as he was coming out the door of the building.

"Sorry," she said. "Did I do any damage, George?"

"Not to me, Miz Sears," George said, and picked up her newspaper and the envelopes she'd dropped in their head-on encounter. "Don't get too many cuties rushing into my arms these days. So it's my pleasure. Besides . . ." George had a look of knowledge not to be revealed, ". . . you got worse facing you than a little collision."

George smiled blandly. He wasn't going to say more, and Alicia knew enough not to press him. She hoped he was, as usual, overdramatizing. The worst she could think of was that Dean Barrow's wife had taken a bad turn or a terminal one, and she'd be left to face the sheikhs on Wednesday without the dean's support, or have to cancel the luncheon.

Debbie, at her desk, signaled Alicia over and spoke in a half-whisper. "He's not moving until he sees you."

"Who?" She looked around, expecting to see Mike or Gardner Sears looming up behind her.

"Dr. Ostrava. I told him you were busy today. He said he'd wait in the small conference room until you were free."

"Give me ten minutes to look through the mail."

"Okay," Debbie said. "He means business. He's wearing his lab coat."

Alicia raised her eyes to heaven and started toward her office.

"My dear Mrs. Sears." Victor Ostrava stood in the doorway to the conference room. "If I might have a moment . . ."

Alicia and Debbie exchanged a hopeless look.

"I'm quite busy this morning, Doctor," Alicia said. "The luncheon on Wednesday . . ."

"What I have to discuss has reference to the occasion," Victor Ostrava said. "If you will permit me . . ."

He swept ahead of Alicia and opened the door to her office for her. George had been right. Ostrava was the last thing she wanted to face at the start of this week. He shut the door behind them and stood with his hands in the pockets of his long white lab coat—as if Alicia had pulled him from his test tubes at the brink of a major breakthrough in his research—while she composed herself to meet whatever he was about to lay before her. He had a thick folder under his arm, and she suspected that was going to be it.

"You do look charming on this gray morning," he said suddenly. He smiled, but it looked false.

"Mmm." She wasn't going to be suckered by compliments, not from him. Victor Ostrava fancied himself suave and engaging, irresistible to women. He probably believed he represented sexual magnetism, but to Alicia, all his gestures were calculated to charm. and the man himself held no attraction. He had broad, coarse features and light hair that he wore slicked straight back. She knew he was perhaps fifty, and had made his way to Commonwealth Medical and his well- (and self-) promoted career in cancer research and teaching from Eastern Europe. She was not sure if he were a refugee from some sort of oppressive regime or a dedicated seeker of personal fame and fortune. Victor retained a slight accent that crept in and out of his speech—it was most evident when he was being courtly and condescending. This morning, for example.

"What can I do for you, Dr. Ostrava?"

He placed the folder on her desk in front of her.

"The research data on my current project," he said. "My staff has completed the initial report."

Too confident, too arrogant, too convinced of his own importance in the scheme of things. He could be almost frightening in his single-minded egocentricity.

"I have told you that I'm not qualified to evaluate research," Alicia said.

Victor brushed aside her denial.

"It is so clear, so exciting. You will understand without difficulty. An intelligent and . . . perceptive lady like you will understand without difficulty. I beg you, read it before the luncheon on Wednesday. I wish you to be able to confirm the major significance of my work when you meet the distinguished gentlemen from the Persian Gulf. It will be to both your advantage and mine if they are made to understand the international acclaim to accrue if they directly fund my research."

"No," Alicia said. Victor Ostrava blinked, startled by her firmness. "You should take this to Dean Barrow, who does have the background and—"

"But my dear lady, in this time of his trouble, his lovely wife so ill. I could not disturb him."

Alicia was surprised to learn that the rumors of Mrs. Barrow's illness had gone beyond the bounds of the staff closest to the dean. But Victor seemed to know everything.

"My research, of course, relates directly to, what should I say? a hope for Mrs. Barrow. Surely, you would wish to encourage any possibility—"

"I don't see the direct relationship between your research, which may take years, and the immediate problem of the dean's wife."

Victor Ostrava was about to explain, when Debbie called Alicia on the intercom.

"A *Mr.* . . . um, Parker?" Debbie said. "He says he has to talk to you. Line one. Mr. Timothy Parker?"

"Ah." She turned her back on Victor. "Excuse me, Doctor." She picked up the phone, but she knew he was listening. She would have much preferred to call Timmy back when she was alone, but sensed that a call at nine o'clock on a school day, after she had given assurances that she was there for him when wanted, meant need at an intense level to a ten-year-old mind.

"Hi, Tim. What's up?"

"I had to stay home from school today. Nana says I have a fever." There was a tremor in his voice, a holding back of tears. "I don't. Honest. We were going on a field trip today. The Science Museum. The whole class."

"Timmy, honey, it's hard to face, but your grandmother knows best."

Alicia knew she was trapped between an unhappy little boy and the grandmother who never doubted she knew best.

"I know but . . . all the kids are going."

"Some things you can't argue about. I know how you feel." She remembered still the feeling of excitement of getting on a bus with your whole class in sight of the entire school and taking off for the day. "I tell you what. I'll see if I can take you to the Science Museum Saturday after next. The two of us, we'll leave Graham and your father at home. How does that sound?"

"Okay, I guess." The tears had receded.

"Let's keep it a secret for now, and you get well. I'll call you later in the week."

Timmy sounded more cheerful when he hung up. Alicia swung around to face Ostrava again. He wore a bland, knowing smile.

"I'm sorry for the interruption, Doctor," she said. "You were saying?"

"I am sure you will be greatly missed," Victor Ostrava said, wholly irrelevantly, she thought, as she tried to penetrate his meaning. "Surely you will not continue to work after your marriage."

"My *what?*" For a brief moment, she wondered if Graham had been announcing an event that seemed more and more unlikely ever to take place. Ostrava managed to look nonplussed.

"Naturally, everyone assumes that you and Dr. Parker . . . An ideal couple . . ."

Alicia struggled to keep her temper, although she was seething at his presumption.

"Dr. Ostrava, kindly do not make assumptions, and please do not refer to my personal life. Ever."

He narrowed his eyes. Victor Ostrava did not like being taken to task by a mere woman.

"And," Alicia added, "I'd be grateful if you said what you had to say so that I can get on with my work." She wondered if she had spoken too sharply, because Victor put both his hands on her desk and leaned toward her.

"What I have to say, as you phrase it, is this: You will pay close attention to the information in the file, and to the estimate of funds I will need for research in the coming year. You will then be able to persuade your colleagues in administration that I must have this money. You will make every effort to persuade the gentlemen from the East that their contribution would be enhanced if it were made specifically for my work."

"You cannot make such demands, Doctor," Alicia said.

Ostrava proceeded as though she had not spoken. "And let me assure you, dear lady, that these gentlemen are most susceptible to the charms of a pretty Western face. They would be so grateful for your very . . . special attentions. A woman of your experience . . . could provide diversions that would be highly appreciated to those from a culture where women do not mingle . . ."

My God, Alicia thought, as his meaning became clear, is he possibly suggesting that I go to bed with the entire delegation of sheikhs so he will get his money? She wanted to slap him for the insult, but to make an enemy of Ostrava was patently unwise.

He stood back, hands in his lab coat pockets again. "Nothing must stand in my way, Mrs. Sears," he said. "My work is important. In a very large sense, the responsibility for its success rests with you. You have a good deal more influence than you claim, and I intend to see that it is used for my advantage."

He turned on his heel and departed. His lab coat flapped behind him as he left the room.

Victor Ostrava had left her with a threat she did not doubt he fully meant, although she could not see how he could carry it through. The problem was, of course, that his research was generally acknowledged to be significant, in spite of Graham's hint that Ostrava was known to be careless. And there was no denying that success in a field like cancer treatment attracted dollars, and dollars brought more dollars. There were discussions going on now, too, heated ones, about whether it was justified for universities and researchers to enter commercial partnerships to market discoveries. Alicia shuddered to think of such an event if

Victor Ostrava accumulated both financial and administrative leverage. He had no special loyalty to Commonwealth, and probably none to academic integrity. Only to himself.

Alicia wished for an instant that she could turn her back on the Ostravas and the pressures and politics, and slip into an uncomplicated dream existence that consisted of pleasures and pampering, no responsibilities, a life of the senses. But was she not securely fixed here, in this office, for the balance of her working life? An inheritor of Elsa Morant's mantle, the gray-haired lady who selected flower arrangements for the hall table and watched ever-younger students in their tight jeans come and go?

"The caterer on line one." Debbie's voice startled her. "And when you have a minute, I need to talk to you."

"Sure," Alicia said wearily. "Would you ask Dean Barrow if I can see him when he's free?" She knew she had to put her encounter with Ostrava on record with the dean, although she knew how strongly he supported Ostrava's research, in a kind of hopeless hope that it would reach fruition in time to aid his wife.

Ah, men.

The caterer, at least, was on top of everything. French food for the sheikhs, the luncheon to be served in the small faculty dining room on the second floor of the administration building, an elegant, dark-paneled room seldom used.

Alicia saw Dean Barrow in the afternoon.

"I wish you could persuade Victor Ostrava that I have far less influence in granting his financial demands than he thinks," Alicia said.

Dean Barrow was polishing his round, gold-rimmed glasses. He looked tired and detached. She supposed that being a doctor himself, he was participating on the sidelines of Mrs. Barrow's illness with the same intensity as her physicians.

"You know what these dedicated scientists are like," the dean said. "Obsessed with their work."

"I'm afraid he intends to blame me personally if he doesn't get what he expects. Then when he picks up his research and goes elsewhere, the university will blame me."

"I think you must be exaggerating."

"Perhaps. But he seems to think that it's merely a matter of me going to bed with a bunch of sheikhs to have a few million fall in his lap."

Dean Barrow looked at her openmouthed. Alicia wondered if she had spoken too freely. Then he put back his head and laughed. "My dear Alicia! What a suggestion!" His eyes twinkled as he hooked his glasses over his ears. "I assure you, that particular activity is not a requirement of your job here at Commonwealth."

"I'm relieved to know it. By the way, what do they really want in exchange for their money?"

She had caught him off guard, and he fumbled for an answer.

"Well, I . . . there is no specific . . ."

"Does their government have some little favor we might grant, perhaps?"

"The sheikhs are not officially connected with the government; naturally they have certain interests. This kind of money seldom comes free of strings, but I assure you, we are considering most carefully . . ." The dean shifted nervously. He wished she would go away. Alicia knew she wouldn't get much out of him.

But he knows something, she thought. He wants that money for Victor and the new building and his development plans, and he'll do whatever he can to get it.

"I understand, Dean Barrow," Alicia said. "I'm sure everything will work out well." Didn't she hope.

He appeared to be relieved when she left.

"Alicia!" Debbie jumped up from her desk. She looked flushed and happy, as though she couldn't wait to pour out a joyful tale. She followed Alicia into her office. "It's that guy, Alicia."

"What guy?"

"Mike. Mike Tedesco. You remember. He asked me *out!*"

That was not a twinge of jealousy I just felt, Alicia thought. It was shock and disapproval.

"Debbie, he's married."

Debbie was momentarily downcast. "I know. But he's so terrific looking. I mean, wow. Lenore will die."

"I wouldn't go spreading it around, Deb. And I ought to add, I don't think you should get involved with Mike."

"I knew you'd say that," Debbie said. "But you don't know what it's like."

What? To be twenty-one and eager? To be singled out by a gorgeous man who leaves you panting from only a look? To be teased by beauty and the promise of sexual

102

delights, and never mind the arguments against involvement?

"I know what it's like," Alicia said. "Trust me. But I also know enough to wonder why he fixed on you. Not," she added quickly, "that you're not the kind of person any man would want to date. But I've talked to Mike, he's ambitious, he uses people. And if he's willing to betray his wife, he'd do the same to you."

"He said he'd talked to you. He was real interested in you." Now that had a note of jealousy too clear to miss.

"I'm sure he's interested in anyone who can help him along," Alicia said coolly. "You have to make up your own mind, but he's not the only man in the world."

Debbie looked as though she thought he was. True, men who looked like Mike Tedesco didn't land at your feet all that often. Alicia's own fleeting fantasies about him proved how great an impression he made.

"He wanted to know if it was true that you and Dr. Parker were engaged," Debbie mumbled.

"What! I hope you told him it was none of his business." Between Mike and Victor, she'd end up marrying Graham in spite of herself.

"I told him I didn't know."

"Good. I'm not engaged to anybody. And I see other men besides Dr. Parker."

The painful memory of Jerry Godwin returned. Well, if Harriet kept at it, sooner or later someone might turn up.

"I think I'll go out with him," Debbie said. "Just once, so I can say I did. For the fun of it."

Just once. What harm could there be? Love them and leave them: it was as simple for a woman to do as a man, or it should be.

"Be careful, Debbie," Alicia said. "There's no telling where 'the fun of it' might get you."

Alicia turned her concentration to her work, determined to put intrusions like Mike and Ostrava, the Parkers, Jerry Godwin, and even men who stripped for a living out of her mind.

12

NEAR the end of the luncheon on Wednesday, Alicia was wishing that Billy Catlett had been in attendance to bolster her, instead of off combining a medical meeting in Florida with a few extra days in the sun. He would have been a good antidote to the sheikhs and the doctors and the overbearing presence of Victor Ostrava. Elsa was the only other woman at the luncheon, and she and Alicia had been relegated to a small table with a few of the less important medical school faculty, apparently where they could be quietly ignored while the grown-up men discussed business.

Two or three of the visitors had worn Arab robes, but the man who was obviously the head of the delegation had on a Western business suit. Victor had made a point of introducing him to Alicia at the beginning. Sheikh Ahmad was a smooth number, cultured and gracious, who made polite conversation with Alicia on a variety of subjects, none of them relating to the purpose of his visit to Commonwealth. She was aware that he looked her over in a way that had more to do with the purchase of a slave girl for the harem than her ability to acquire and allocate funds for a major university, and she wondered if perhaps Victor Ostrava had been absolutely serious about exchanging her favors for six million dollars.

It's nice to know my price is that high, she thought, as she agreed with Sheikh Ahmad that the finest horse in the world was the pure-blooded Arabian (he owned three), and that one tried never to miss a Pavarotti performance at the opera (he often dined with Luciano in Italy), and that New England weather was a trial (he was fond of his little place in Beverly Hills; he enjoyed the climate at his villa at Juan-les-Pins at certain times of the year). She had the feeling that she was viewed as a mostly irrelevant occupier of space, but she buried her resentment.

She tried to turn the conversation toward matters of money and research. Sheikh Ahmad dismissed her opening gambit with, "My people have discussed that with your dean. I am sure that the matter of admissions can be worked out."

Before she could ask what admissions he meant, the sheikh said, "It has been a delight, Madame Sears. I see we are moving toward the luncheon table. I trust we will meet again."

He left her feeling that her price on the slave exchange was not worth the return in his opinion. She was secretly pleased that Victor had overestimated her value, but it was not so pleasing to realize that she had been rejected by the sheikh as surely as she had been by Jerry Godwin.

"Isn't this exciting?" Elsa said. "What a beautiful job you've done, Alicia."

"Mmm." Alicia looked around the room from the now cleared table. Everyone seemed cordial, everything appeared to be going smoothly. "Elsa, do you know anything about an admissions policy having to do with the sheikhs?"

"No," Elsa said, too quickly. Elsa had served the dean for so long as secretary, aide, comforter, friend, that to admit she knew nothing was almost laughable. "I mean," she said, "it's something you'd have to speak to the dean about."

Alicia did, catching him in a moment when his guard was down, and came away from the luncheon angered and helpless.

Billy Catlett, looking tanned and relaxed and, although he was about Alicia's age, like a blond teenager, was sitting at her desk with his feet up when she came back to her office. He was leafing through the folder of Victor Ostrava's research data, which Alicia had read and digested as best she could with her lay person's understanding of biochemistry.

"I just got in," he said. "Did you get the money?"

"Chancy at best, I'd say. Those sheikhs are devious."

"Don't I know. I got involved with one once . . . well, never mind, but they can be odd."

"What these fellows have in mind, as far as I can determine from the dean, is an open admission to the medical school for whomever they choose to send, in exchange for their millions. Dean Barrow seems almost willing to agree, but I think he's lost his perspective. I intend to do what I can to keep it from happening."

"They won't get away with it, Alicia. Academic types are deeply concerned with ethical questions."

"Except, apparently, when it comes to money," she said bitterly. "Consider Victor Ostrava."

Billy tapped Victor's folder. "This guy is something else. I'm not into this kind of research, but the conclusions appear to be made by leaps of faith rather than proven data. Maybe I'm a cynic, maybe he's a wishful thinker. Let's forget it. I'm sick of doctors."

"Billy dear, you *are* a doctor."

"Today I feel like a beach boy. Tell me about your adventure in striptease land."

"God, that seems years ago. It was fun. The star himself took a fancy to me. You'd probably love him. Tony Spinelli."

"Now, there's a name I've heard. . . ."

Alicia groaned. "Don't tell me he's gay. That would be one too many."

Billy looked at her questioningly.

"Nothing personal," she said. "There was this great-looking guy Harriet and Mark sort of fixed me up with. One of the best-looking people I've ever brushed thighs with." She laughed without humor. "He's keeping his tastes a secret, he says. For professional reasons."

"I'm sorry, Alicia."

"His words exactly."

"You deserve someone good, Al. Graham's not bad, but he's not for you." Billy stood up. "I've got to run, but how about a treat to cheer you up? Say lunch on Friday, upstairs at the Ritz? Table by the window. We can look down at the peasants slogging through the slush on Arlington Street."

Alicia was willing to have all her plans made for her today.

"Sure. Let me check my messages in case there's something . . ."

Billy slid a square of pink paper across the desk to her. "Sorry I'm so nosy," he said.

"Oh, God. Gardner. He said he wanted to see me this week. I'll call him tomorrow. I'm in no mood for him now. I'm leaving too. I've had enough today."

Debbie barely looked up from her typewriter when Alicia and Billy passed. She had a new hairdo, though, and bright new red nails, although she did not look happy. Alicia had not been able to ask whether she'd actually gone out with Mike. She didn't want to know.

George was standing outside the administration building surveying the melting slush.

"You turn up with a new man following you every time I see you, Miz Sears," George said.

"At my age, George, you got to take what turns up."

"Tut. Ain't so at all. What do you say, Doc?" George managed to tolerate Billy better than most of the faculty.

"I love her like a sister," Billy said.

George chuckled. He missed very little that went on.

On her way home, Alicia stopped to buy magazines at the corner of Massachusetts Avenue and Boylston Street. She needed mindless reading, matters remote from real life. She picked out *Town & Country, Vogue, People,* and was about to take them to the cashier, when a familiar face caught her eye. Next to the latest *Playgirl* on the stand was an imitation *Playgirl* of sorts, with an inset picture of Tony Spinelli on the cover. No one was paying any attention to her, so she quickly leafed through the magazine and found two pages of nude and seminude photos of Tony.

"Popular entertainer currently working in Boston," the caption said. "Soon to leave for an extensive engagement in Las Vegas."

Alicia stuck the magazine between *Town & Country* and *Vogue.* The bored cashier didn't blink as he rang up the total, but Alicia stuffed them all into her oversized bag and managed to get to her illegally parked car right before one of Boston's overzealous meter maids.

She felt a sudden rush of fear when she found that her front door was unlocked, and pushed it open cautiously, ready to scream or run if anybody was there.

Gardner Sears was there, sitting in her living room with a drink in hand, reading her address book.

"What the hell do you think you're doing?" she said far too loudly and angrily. She had been frightened, and now she was very annoyed to see him. "Give me that!" She grabbed the address book.

"Now, now, Ali. I told you I was coming to see you. When I couldn't reach you at the school, I decided to wait for you here."

"How did you get in?"

"Why, I used the key you gave me for emergencies after our friendly divorce, remember? I didn't think you'd mind."

"This is an emergency?" She was trembling with fury. "Yes, I mind. I mind very much. This apartment is mine, Gardner, and whatever you provide is a voluntary contribution, because you couldn't bear to have people suggest your former wife wasn't well taken care of. You're *such* a snob."

She threw her bag down on the sofa and tossed her coat over the back. Gardner watched her with his familiar fatuous smile; once she'd thought it sweet. He looked fitter than she recalled, although his hairline continued to recede, and his once slim form was now padded with the results of the good life in Beverly Farms.

"Say what you want to say and leave," Alicia said.

"I don't remember you having such a temper, Ali . . ."

"Stop calling me Ali, dammit!"

Gardner blinked. She wondered if he had more to drink than the one he held in his hand. He often did. "Whatever you say," he said.

"I've had a lousy day. Say what you want and then go."

Gardner avoided a direct answer. It was a technique he probably learned at Harvard Business School and refined in the investment house on State Street. Tell customers nothing.

"I'm going to speak seriously now, Ali—Alicia. For your own good." He got up and poured himself another drink without asking. "It's not good for a fine woman like you to go through life alone." He put up his hand to stop her protest. "We've known each other a good long time, since way back . . . way back. I know we had our problems, I wasn't always easy to get on with, you were young."

She glared at him.

108

"We were both young, I mean to say," he corrected himself. "Just one of those things. I'm lucky now, I've got a lovely wife and a lovely, lovely little boy. I want you to have the same chance at happiness that I've had. You deserve it."

"Everybody thinks I deserve something better," she said bitterly. "You might as well add your two cents' worth." But she didn't say out loud that she thought so too.

"Listen, Alicia. Graham Parker is a fine man. I've known him most of my life. He's a very, very good friend, and I know the two of you see a lot of each other."

An alarm signal in Alicia's brain told her not to listen too carefully, else she would smash Gardner with the heavy vase standing not twelve inches from her hand. He droned on, and periodically a phrase or two penetrated.

"Parker family money . . . position . . . ready-made family . . . good breeding . . ."

Then a phrase she reacted to: "He'd be so good for you."

"Gar, you don't know what's good for me. You never did. And you don't know now. If I ever marry Graham Parker, it will be in spite of his friendship with you and the rest of the Sears, *not* because of it."

"You don't understand, Ali."

"I understand plenty. I admit I don't see Gardner putting you up to this, but the way things are going, anything is possible. But if you two thought I couldn't resist the power of big strong men begging for me to get married, you're wrong."

"Graham loves you, Alicia. And you're still a desirable woman."

"Still! Love! Oh, please. The last and best person who said he loved me was ten years old. I think he's the only one of you who knows what he's talking about."

Gardner looked into his drink as though he were reading the future. "Did I mention that Diana and I are going to have another child? This spring. She wants a big family. And so do I," he added quickly. "But it's going to be a very large financial burden."

"Oh, my God, I should have figured it out. You want to pare down your expenses without ruining your reputation in your circle. All deals are off when I remarry, right? No more taxes on this place, no more mortgage payments."

"Now, Alicia . . ."

"And heaven forbid you should have to dip into capital to raise your little Searses. Isn't that supposed to be worse than turning to prostitution in Boston?"

"Diana thinks you . . . that I needn't spend . . ."

"Gardner, go home and tell Diana that I don't need your money. I never needed it. I make a good salary, and while I like this place, I don't have to stay here if it turns out I can't afford to. But I can. So you can get out of here and take your money and your marriage proposal from Graham."

He got out of his chair with difficulty. The several drinks he'd had showed in his unsteady walk. Alicia stood up quickly and backed away as he came over to her.

"It's not Graham's idea, Alicia," he said. "He does love you. I do want to see you happy. I hated it when you were unhappy."

"Then why the hell didn't you try to do something about it when we were married?"

"I tried. I didn't understand you, it seemed like enough that you cared about me so long." He was standing in front of her and looking down, blinking. "I've always cared about you, Ali. . . ." He grabbed her arm and tried to kiss her.

"You're drunk or crazy!" She pushed him away. Hard. He tottered as he stepped back.

"Come on," he said. "Where's the harm? We used to have a good time, remember? Remember we went to that place, Montego Bay, the two of us? And Paris? You loved it in Paris. It was like a second honeymoon. It was fun."

"It was *never* fun with you. None of it!" She wanted to wound him as deeply as possible.

He narrowed his eyes and focused on her.

"You're not getting any younger," he said thickly. "You should be grateful that Graham . . . that I still want you."

"Grateful!"

Gardner took another unsteady step toward her. Alicia reached down and grabbed her bag, as Gardner lurched at her. She swung the bag furiously at his head. "I'll be damned if I'm going to be raped mentally or physically by the husband *I didn't want any more!*"

Gardner blocked the bag with his forearm, sloshing his drink over his tweed jacket. The magazines she'd just bought tumbled out of the bag and scattered across the floor.

Gardner stopped in confusion. He looked down at his drink-soaked jacket, and tried ineffectually to blot up the wetness with a handkerchief. The imitation *Playgirl* was at his feet. He picked it up and nodded with half-drunken wiseness before he tossed it on the sofa.

"I see, I see," he said. "Poor Alicia. This is all she's got left. Naked boys in dirty magazines. Shame on you."

"You smug Beacon Hill bastard, get out of here! Now! Before I tell your very, very good friend Graham Parker how you came here to speak for him. And why."

"Poor Alicia." He picked up his coat and wound a scarf around his neck. Harvard crimson and white, of course.

Her face was hot, burning up, with rage—and, she hated to admit it, shame.

I will not say another word, another word, another word, she repeated to herself, as she stared Gardner down. And out the front door. He did look smug, as though he couldn't wait to tattle on little Alicia.

Finally he was gone. Alicia rushed to put the chain lock on the door. She felt as though she had been invaded, burglarized, violated by Gardner. By Graham. By the whole world out there who were trying to find her place in the scheme of things without bothering to consult her.

Alicia picked up the magazine with the pictures of Tony Spinelli. Even in the grainy photos, he looked smug and confident. Even Tony Spinelli, who picked her out of an audience and forgot her the next minute, he was out to manipulate her.

Methodically, she tore the magazine in half, and as her eyes filled with stinging tears, she tore the pages with his pictures again and again and scattered the fragments of Tony on the rug.

She wished she could tear up her life in the same way. Oh, yes, to the outside eye it was a better life than a lot of people had. A good job with responsibility, friends, even a lover of sorts.

And a ten-year-old who looked to her for friendship, if not mothering, and comfort.

Yet she felt trapped, without choices. Fixed in a pattern that held no promise of . . . what did Alicia want? The apartment darkened in silence as she lay on the sofa, too drained to get up, turn on lights, fix dinner, read a book, watch television.

Slowly it came to her that there were choices she could

111

make, if she were brave enough. She could entice a child like Mike Tedesco, she could tear up the ways of thinking and behaving that her circle and her profession demanded. The thought actually caused her to smile in the darkness. It was ridiculous, of course, but amusing to imagine herself taking any other path than the one she was on. You don't toss a respectable success out the window.

Then she thought of Gardner, who had once seemed the crowning success. What had he become, in her eyes? An infuriating failure. Gardner had not failed, though. He had been what Graham called "consistent."

Alicia was the failure.

13

IT was nearly nine o'clock when she called Billy.
"Are you busy?"

"I have . . . a few people here. What's the matter, Alicia?
You sound terrible."

"It's the dark night of the soul, nothing is well."

"You're not worried about those Arabs still, are you?"

"Them? No."

Gardner's empty glass stood on the table where he'd left
it hours earlier. The pieces of torn magazine littered the
floor. She surrendered to a vision of Tony, the dangerous,
unknown man, with his dark, almond-shaped eyes, those
long lashes, and cheekbones that seemed to have been
glazed by a sun not seen for centuries. A man of mysterious joy and energy, who found himself on the stage of a
cheap nightclub, who might have lived in a Moorish castle
in Spain or on a Sicilian beach between the sky and the
sea. She remembered how he moved, walking toward her
through the hazy lights of the Carousel, naked, as if he
were walking on clouds, somewhere out of time, coming
to his woman. . . .

"Gardner was here when I got home. The perfect end
to a perfect day."

"Jesus, what did he want?" Billy did not cherish his few
encounters with Gardner Sears, and in the way of friendship, he reflected Alicia's views of the man.

"He was here, my dear, and listen closely, to insist that

113

I marry Graham Parker. So he could save a few bucks on the mortgage he demanded he be allowed to pay, which I didn't want but gave in to. Which I can perfectly well pay myself . . ."

"Take a deep breath and explain."

"I told him that my marrying Gray solely to enable him to send his sons to Andover and Harvard was a bad idea. Then he suggested that he and I might get cozy, like old times. Is the whole world going crazy? Or just me?"

Alicia could hear voices behind Billy. Men laughing, and music. His private life, in which she had small part, nor did she want to. She sensed that his attention was not on her.

It was one occasion when she needed it, like a life preserver, and through no fault of his own, it was beyond her reach.

"I shouldn't be bothering you, Billy."

"Darling, it's perfectly all right. At least you call at nine instead of three in the morning."

"Give me a chance, and I'll be doing that, too, if things get much more depressing."

"Careful. Talk too much about depression, and Dr. Parker will send you into therapy."

"I don't need therapy. I need . . ." Alicia was sprawled on her stomach on the sofa. Idly she started to fit together the torn pictures of Tony Spinelli like a jigsaw puzzle. She focused on the picture and quickly scattered the pieces again.

"Look, Alicia. This is your doctor talking. Take a hot bath. Do you still have that little bit of grass I gave you? Smoke it, and forget. Crawl into bed, pull the covers over your head, and dream a little dream or two."

"Of you?" She giggled at the rhyme.

"No, dear. Not me, please, not me. I have enough to worry about, and so do you."

"I don't want dreams, Billy. I want something real."

"We'll talk about it at lunch Friday. Maybe you should call Harriet. She's a rock in the midst of storms."

"She'll also try to pump me about Jerry Godwin. I promised him not to tell the truth. Oh, hell . . ."

"I hate hearing you sound so low." A man's voice spoke behind Billy, close to the phone. "And I hate saying I've got to go, but I do."

"I understand, Billy." Good old understanding Alicia. "Day after tomorrow at one," she said. "In the Ritz lobby."

She hung up slowly. For the first time since she'd known him, years now, back to the time when he'd first become a lecturer at the medical school, she nearly hated Billy, for who he was, what he had. Something like a whole life.

"Let's be fair," she muttered and dusted off the Chinese box on her bookshelf. "He's got problems, too."

Some months before, Billy had given her a joint, calling it an "emergency kit." She'd put it away in the box and mostly forgot it, since she rarely felt the need for that kind of high. Tonight was different.

"Why not?" she said aloud. It might make her feel better, help her sleep, and maybe stop her from talking to herself, which she took as a bad sign. The joint felt dried out and brittle from its long stay in the box. A good thing Graham hadn't opened the box the other night when he was investigating her bookcase, she thought as she lit the joint and pulled in a big lungful of smoke. He'd have sputtered and complained about people who thought life could be supported by stimulants.

She coughed. The distinctive smell of the marijuana drifted through the room and the tingle of its effect spread through her body. It took very little to swing her up from her weary depression to a sense of peace, if not euphoria. It was nice. Billy had been right: sometimes the pain of living got too bad, and what were friends for if not to help?

Who else reached out a hand to help, when she was feeling lost at sea and everybody else had nice, safe lifeboats? Gardner Sears had been the safest boat of all before she realized what a selfish bastard he was. Of course, he hadn't been all bad, he'd been good enough to her in the beginning. There had been some wonderful times. Gar had mentioned Montego Bay, that had been their honeymoon because she'd wanted to go to the Caribbean, and he hadn't argued one bit. Not at all, and he'd even taken her back during the winter for the two following years. Then there was Paris, he remembered Paris. It had been as though they were brand-new lovers, like he was the shy, golden young man she had come upon at the Ormond stables.

She giggled. Humphrey Bogart saying to Ingrid Bergman, "We'll always have Paris." She and Gar used to make a pilgrimage to the Brattle Theatre in Harvard Square for the Bogart festival. Even when you could see all those old flicks on television. They both liked being in the midst of an audience who shouted out the lines before they were spoken, a group experience.

Group experiences like their Christmas party; Gar had loved big parties. The Sunday before Christmas every year, and no caterers for young Gar Sears, his wife was so clever in the kitchen, imagine doing the food for all those people, and she works besides. Such a pity, though, no children yet . . .

What was the point of having children if making them was no fun? But she might have gotten pregnant in Paris; she didn't do anything to prevent it, and it had been so . . . different. Gar had been different, ardent and free—and then they had had to come home, and she wasn't pregnant after all. It had been a close thing. That was when her dissatisfactions with Gardner and the Sears family began to press on her as never before, and she was certain besides that he was having an affair, someone from his office or . . . it didn't matter. Not now, not even then.

Alicia got up and walked around her living room. It was a good room, and she hoped she'd never have to give it up. Her head felt light, and the buzz from the grass was so . . . pleasant. She was too warm. Click! she flicked on the switch to the radio and found a rock station. Young music, she felt young. On her way back to the couch, she stripped off her blouse to the music, young music, and she didn't know the group. The velvet of the sofa felt so soft against her skin, soft as hands.

Brett Handley used to like to touch her body, inch by inch, with his hands, his mouth, his tongue, and he'd bring her to such a pitch of arousal, waves of orgasms swept through her. While he was there, and after he had gone.

He was always gone, Brett was. And each time he flew away west, she tried to shut her mind to him, to the hope that he would be back soon. He was never back soon, and finally she had shut him out for good.

She wanted him, someone like him, with her now, and there was no one. No one to love her. Brett had never said he loved her, not even when they were making love. He was annoyed when she hinted that he ought to say . . . something. No, not annoyed. Brett was too easygoing for that. Amused was more like it. But he liked her, or else he wouldn't have kept calling her.

If I ever get to San Francisco, she thought drowsily, but

116

I am going, I have to go in the spring, there's a whole pile of money out there some old lady is promising to give us. Unless Victor Ostrava and those funny men with their sunglasses and all their oil money got her removed because she'd tell them Commonwealth Medical wouldn't accept camel drivers, no matter what, they had to know how to read and write. . . . Imagine Victor putting his hands on her. Shudder . . .

The joint was a tiny, barely glowing roach, and she took one more deep mouthful of smoke and swallowed.

Brett Handley had been sitting in one of those hanging-plants-and-polished-wood-floor places that pretended it wasn't a singles bar but really was. She was supposed to be meeting Sheila, who claimed to want to check out the action for over-the-hill types like herself, but Sheila was an hour late. Then the tall man, with a kind of crooked smile and pale blue eyes, offered to buy her a drink, saying he'd been stood up and had no one to spend his walking-around money on, and unless a guy was going to turn up in the next five minutes and take her away, how about it?

"I'm waiting for a girl friend, to tell the truth," Alicia had said, "and I'm humiliated to say that she's stood me up."

"Then we're adrift together. I'm Brett Handley, and why don't we go someplace for dinner? I'm comparatively harmless, and I'm leaving town in the morning, so you're going to be abandoned, whether or not we ever get around to the seduced part."

They got around to it, to Alicia's delight and surprise. It was like an awakening, and only then did she realize how badly damaged her self-esteem had been by the divorce, and possibly by her marriage as well.

She had tried to explain it to Brett, and he had said, "Yeah, divorce is lousy, even when it's the right thing to do. I got through one myself, a good while back. You got to learn to lighten up, 'Licia. And don't go crediting me with more than I have to give."

"I didn't really love him," she said aloud to her white ceiling, with the molding of entwined vine leaves around the edges; you don't find that kind of elegant detail in new houses nowadays. . . .

"He was gone today, gone tomorrow. Gone for good."

She sat up. Her limbs felt light and good, but the effects of the grass had diminished.

117

"I've got to get out of here." The radio was still playing, the room was dark, and she was all alone. "Good idea, Alicia." She answered herself and stood up. She had stripped down to bra and panties and she felt a little silly. At least no one had been around to watch.

"Maybe I'll get lucky, turn up a winner."

Losers don't necessarily attract winners.

Where to go on a Wednesday night? At this hour, the crowded bars in the middle of the city had emptied and the young businessmen and the young women on the prowl for companionship had made their connections or gone home. The night spots, the discos and the true singles bars, were likely to be shoulder to shoulder with kids from the colleges of Boston and environs. Too young. Poor Alicia was too old for the too-young students she saw every day.

No, those students wouldn't be out on the town, those serious, ambitious medical students. They were home at their books or working at part-time jobs to make ends meet. She wasn't going to run into Mike Tedesco roaming the streets.

It crossed her mind to walk over to the Lenox.

Before she knew it, she'd washed her face, put on make-up, combed her hair. Put on a bright green turtleneck and black wool slacks. Graham's necklace for good luck or bad. A spray of Cristalle, like a breath of spring. She looked at herself in the mirror and what she saw pleased her: Her eyes were bright and her skin seemed to glow.

She put her hand on the doorknob and knew the Lenox was not a good idea. She wanted to find someone, or something, but her courage failed when it came to sitting at an ordinary bar, waiting to be picked up.

Maybe she'd drive north, to the sea at Gloucester or up into Maine, where the pine forests loomed along the highway and the snow was still deep. She'd be peaceful.

And alone. She didn't want to be alone.

Although she refused to admit it to herself, she knew where she was going when she backed her car out into the alley and headed for Storrow Drive, and across the Mystic River Bridge, with the lights of Charlestown below, the airport off to the right.

The small neon sign up ahead on Route 1 said THE CAROUSEL CLUB.

She could have kept going, on to solitude and the Maine woods, but it was easy to turn in, park the car, and get out.

118

Hadn't both Lenore and Debbie said that the place was just a bar where a lot of people gathered on the nights when the strippers didn't perform? There was no chance of running into someone she knew, as she might have at the Lenox or anyplace in the city. She would be safe among strangers, free to stay or go, and she might find someone to pass the time with.

Strangers rather than lovers, a new face, an adventure. And not a humiliation like the last time she had been there, no naked men, no laughter at her confusion from friends.

There are plenty of good reasons to be here, she thought. And I can stay a few minutes and move on, if I choose. Go to that big steak house somewhere along Route 1 for late dinner or back to Chinatown to one of those places that stay open forever.

She walked into the Carousel, wholly justified in what she was doing. She was not here because of an irresistible memory of Tony Spinelli and his mocking smile. Not at all.

Alicia was convinced she was making a new start, a bold, independent gesture. Only in later weeks could she admit that there had been something irresistible about the particular place she chose, and by then, she knew quite well what had drawn her there.

14

ALICIA was not sure what she expected to see when she stepped tentatively into the sudden darkness of the club, and tried to get her bearings in the gloom.

It was less crowded than she'd anticipated from Lenore's reports, and most of the people seemed to be seated in the chairs circling the stage, the way they had been when the strippers were on. A few couples were dancing to a jukebox, though, and others were scattered around at the tables.

She sat at the bar, feeling a bit uneasy and self-conscious. She wasn't used to going out alone like this.

"You here to see the new guy?" the young bartender asked.

"I don't . . ." Alicia tried to fathom his meaning.

"First middle-of-the-week strip show we've had," he said. "The boss thinks it'll bring in a lot of business."

Alicia's confidence plummeted. Her one bold gesture couldn't have had a worse outcome.

"I didn't know, I thought it was just weekends."

"Not the full show," the bartender said. "What'll you have?"

"Scotch," she said quickly. "Who's . . . um, performing?"

"This guy, Tito, and one other." He put the drink down in front of her on a cocktail napkin. She fumbled for money in her bag so she could drink her drink and depart.

"Would the other be Tony Spinelli?" she asked, and gulped down a good third of her drink.

120

"Naw. A kid named Jeff. You'll like Tito, though. He's supposed to be as good as Tony."

"Really? That's a hard act to beat."

The bartender smiled a professional smile and moved away. Alicia breathed relief. She was *not* here for Tony.

"You think so, lady?" said a man's voice behind her. "I'm a hard act to beat?" Alicia spun around on the bar stool.

Tony Spinelli was leaning against the bar with a grin on his face. He had heard her whole exchange with the bartender. The bartender had known he was there. Alicia felt herself blush. He looked considerably different tonight, in a jacket and vest, an open-collared white shirt, but he had that same magnetic attraction as that first shocking moment he had appeared onstage as a highwayman from the past.

"You've seen me?" he persisted.

He didn't remember her at all. Not the way he had used her, to her humiliation, not the way he had apologized with a wink and a smile.

"You've seen me, too," she said, looking away from him.

He reached over and turned her face toward him. Alicia pulled back from his hand with an aversion to his touch that appeared to surprise him.

"I wore a red dress. You wore very little."

Now he did look at her. "Hey, yeah. The lady in the red dress. The gig last Friday. Oh-ho. That's why you remember me so well. Look, it was all part of the act. Nothing personal."

"It seemed very personal to me," Alicia said. "I have to be going." She started to slide off the stool, but Tony put his hand on her arm.

"Wait," he said. He had an engaging, contrite smile. "Forgive me. And do me a favor. Stick around for the show."

She was taken aback. "You're forgiven, but . . ."

"Men aren't allowed unless they're accompanied by a lady. I want to see the new kid's act."

"That rule includes the help?"

"I'm not 'help,' " he said sharply.

"I didn't mean . . . only a manner of speaking . . ."

But he wasn't listening. Tito had come out onstage. The toreador. Alicia remembered him from Sheila's party. She glanced at Tony, who was watching Tito's every move through narrowed eyes. Alicia found looking at Tony and

121

feeling him standing so close to her gave her considerably more pleasure than watching the stripper. He looked softer and younger than he had onstage, perhaps not quite as flawless in looks. His nose might have been broken at some time; he wasn't quite as tall as she'd remembered.

"Like what you see?" he said. Although he hadn't taken his eyes off Tito, he'd been aware she was looking at him. He was smiling faintly.

"He's not as . . . good as you are," Alicia said, flustered.

"You're not looking at Tito, lady," Tony said. He turned to her. "But you're right, he's not. He's not really into what he's doing. It's all an act."

"And you're not?" She was beginning to feel more at ease, as if the memories and fantasies that had haunted her had been blown away by this encounter.

"It's different," he said slowly. "Tito don't mind if these dames fall in love with him because he ends up bare ass on the stage, but he don't care either. About them, about himself. I care. I care about me, I can do anything."

"So why do you strip for a living?"

"Hey, I like taking my clothes off. What are you doing? Writing a book?"

"No," she said. "I came here tonight . . . to find something."

"Me?"

"Hardly. I didn't know you'd be here. But it's not so bad, seeing you."

"You're only seeing part of me, lady," he said. "Is it the part you like best?" He gave her a long, considering look.

Alicia laughed. "You men are impossible egotists."

He looked hurt.

"Listen, Mr. Spinelli . . . Tony, maybe I did sort of wish I could run into you here." As she spoke the words, she realized that they were not the polite fiction she'd intended, but the truth. "But I didn't believe I would," she added softly.

"What's your name, lady?" Tony asked suddenly.

"Alicia. Alicia Sears."

"I'll call you Ali."

"Please don't." It was sharply spoken, and she saw her denial penetrate. He stopped smiling and thrust out his chin. She thought he looked like Timmy sometimes did, when his grandmother told him no.

"Sorry, Tony. My ex-husband used to call me that. He

122

was calling me that only tonight when he came around to bother me. I hate it!"

"I know these guys who never let up, like the two of you never split."

"He's remarried. It was something else."

"I'll call you Alicia, then. Tell me more about this book you're writing."

"I told you I wasn't writing a book." It was silly cocktail party banter. She was actually enjoying herself. Tony leaned back against the bar on his elbows.

"What do you do, Alicia? Secretary? Nurse?"

"I work at Commonwealth University."

"Oh-ho. A smart lady. A professor."

"Not quite. I raise money for the medical school. I'm nice to people. Rich, important people who have money to give away."

"What kind of important people?"

"Every kind under the sun. Doctors, lawyers, people who run foundations, people with guilty consciences about having so much money . . ."

"Ever meet up with guys in show business?"

"Now and then." Alicia was amused by his eagerness. She'd never met a performer who didn't have an eye on another step up the ladder. Strippers were apparently no different from ballet dancers and actors. "Unfortunately, they're usually looking for money as desperately as I am."

"Yeah, well . . . connections are important in my business, you never know."

"If any of my acquaintances are in the market for a male stripper, I promise to mention your name."

"Let's sit over there," he said and jerked his head toward the banquettes at the back of the room. "It's quieter for talking. I got bigger plans than stripping. . . ."

"I ought to be getting home." It had gone far enough. She'd almost forgotten who this man was, how he had humiliated her, how strong his presence had been in her mind the past few days. He ignored her remark, and took her arm. She had to slip off the bar stool and be guided by him across the room, far from the noisy audience near the stage. He sat beside her, and the face that was so close to hers was one she had seen in her dreams above hers as she surrendered to her fantasy. Her ease with him vanished, and she felt an unbidden surge of desire for him. Looking at him made her feel almost breathless. His hand was on

123

the table between them, and she wanted to touch it, feel his skin, have him hold her. Not in a dream, but in reality.

Stop it, she thought. Don't let him sense what I'm feeling.

"I'm working on a new act," he said. "I want to take it to Vegas or someplace classy."

"I read you were going to Las Vegas," she said absently. If she reached out to touch his hand, he surely would snatch it away. . . .

"You saw that rag with my pictures," he said. He watched her steadily until she was uncomfortable. His eyes glittered in the light from the stage and the back bar, and now there was a sexual undercurrent between them. Tony was playing to her, the way he had on Friday. There were only the two of them in the room, in the world.

"I—I happened . . . I'd just seen you here . . . it was in the magazine store." She tried to look away from that intense gaze, but he held her. Tonight, though, she didn't hate him or fear him. She wanted him, as she had seldom wanted any man.

"You don't have to explain, sweetheart," he said. "Everybody wants to fall in love with Tony." He covered her hand with his, and she let herself respond to the tingling excitement of his touch.

"*I* don't," she said. But desire spread through her body and left her weak. She fought against it; it could only mean trouble and disappointment. He was trained to be seductive and exciting, he was using her now to gratify his ego. He was talking softly, telling her about the people at the club. Simple, kind Jeff with his taste for hustling, the enigmatic black twins, his friend Raoul, Sid who ran the place and his crazy brother Irv, Tito who wanted to be a star like Tony.

She answered him, asked questions, and gave in to the strong and irresistible force that held her in her place with his hand stroking hers. As if they belonged together, lovers working through verbal foreplay to greater and greater intimacy. Desire so overwhelming that if he had pushed her down on the banquette and held her while he made love to her in the lights of the bar and the stage, she wouldn't have resisted. . . .

"I have to be getting home," she said, in the middle of his sentence.

"Your home or my home?"

"I didn't mean . . ."

"I know you didn't," Tony said, leaning toward her. "Or maybe you did, without knowing it." Their heads were almost touching. He leaned closer and touched her cheek with the tip of his tongue. "Lady, you came for me, whether you say so or not, and you found me. My place. I don't make the offer to every dame who comes looking for me. Only the ones I want."

"Why do you . . . think you want me?"

She couldn't penetrate his expression.

"Don't ask so many questions," he said. "A good-looking woman shouldn't have to ask."

He stood up. She got to her feet, and found she was unsteady. Nothing like this had ever happened to her before. It was not the way she led her life.

"I'm going to drive home now." He told her the address in the South End. "You can follow me in your car, or you can go home." He walked ahead of her toward the door, pausing to wave to the bartender on their way out. A couple of the women in the audience called out to him as they passed.

"My fans," he said to Alicia. "They wish they had the choice you have right now."

The ego in his words brought down her tension. Her head cleared and the desire she had been feeling slipped away. She would go home, of course. The idea of following Tony Spinelli to his apartment was ridiculous. But she was flattered that he'd asked. She was desirable.

"Where's your car?" he asked when they got outside. It was warmer than it had been for a long time. Spring really was over the horizon. Much of the snow had melted, except for high piles in corners of the parking lot where the plows had left it.

He walked with her over to where she'd parked, holding her arm, with his body leaning in against hers. A good feeling, a good way to end this foolish adventure.

They faced each other at the car.

"Tony, I've enjoyed talking to you." She would be kind and gracious, and never regret that she was too smart to go home with Tony Spinelli.

"Alicia. You're coming to me."

"I can't."

He rested his arms on her shoulders. "You are. You will. Lady, don't give me any arguments."

125

Before she could answer, he pressed her against the car and kissed her hard, forcing his tongue into her mouth and pinning her arms. She was kissing him back, violently, and felt as though she had been struck by lightning. He released her and walked to his car without a word. Alicia was trembling so she could barely turn the ignition. As she fumbled, the lights went on in a low white car a few spaces away. It backed out and roared out of the parking lot onto the highway in the direction of Boston. She followed, more slowly. She had twenty minutes or so to make up her mind.

But her mind was already made up.

Boston's South End, in the throes of redevelopment, was a combination of newly reconditioned three- and four-story buildings and shabby near-tenements. Alicia couldn't see Tony's white car as she drove slowly down the street, trying to catch a glimpse of the number he had given her. She reached a stop sign at the end of the block, and tried to decide whether she should keep looking, or . . .

The passenger door swung open and she gasped in fear. Tony got in.

"Lady, don't you know it's dangerous to drive around at night with your doors unlocked?"

"Tony," through clenched teeth, "you scared me nearly to death."

"I ain't kidding," he said. "Don't do it again." He reached over and ran his hand over the back of her neck.

"Yes, sir," she said, drained by her fright. Unbearably happy to see him. "I . . . didn't expect to see you."

"I expected to see you," he said. "Look, take a right up here, I'll show you where to park."

His white car was parked in an alley.

"Pull in behind. Good. Now, come on, Ali."

She didn't mind the nickname. Nothing about this evening now reminded her of Gardner. Tony led her through the alley, back to the street where he lived. He had an apartment that could be defined as a basement, since it was downstairs from street level rather than up. But the walls along the stairs had been stripped to brick and the paneling was new. The living room was a bit too much of everything, pillows, colors, pictures, some of which seemed to be sketches of Tony. He didn't let her pause to look.

"Come here," he said. Commanded.

He stood in the bedroom.

"Mirrors," Alicia said in surprise. Walls of mirrors. Some faceted, some flat, all around the room.

"What else?" They reflected dozens of Alicias and Tonys.

He flicked a switch on a console beside the bed and a flow of music spread out through the room.

"Too many clothes," he said softly, and helped her slip off her coat. She kissed the hand at her shoulder, and Tony stopped and smiled at her, a lazy, slow smile.

"Strip," he said. "Together. Slow and sexy."

"Like at the club?" she asked, wondering if her misguided passion had gotten her into something bizarre.

"Sort of," he said. "Only it's better with mirrors, and it's a lot better with just you and me. Trust me."

"I don't know how," she said.

"Then you'll have to learn. Now."

The music was soft rock. Alicia was shy now, with the edge gone from her earlier excitement, but she watched Tony watching himself in the mirrors, taking off his jacket, stripping off his shirt. Mesmerized by the image of himself on all sides. Onstage.

"Come on, Aliiii . . . ," he teased. He took her hand and pulled her beside him. They faced each other, and he slipped his hands under her sweater. They were colder than her skin, and she involuntarily moved her torso at his touch.

"Hey, that's a start," he said, and helped her pull the turtleneck over her head. "That's better, sweetheart. Ain't no stripper in the world who'd go on with that on."

He kept moving, dancing, the man in front of her and the hundreds of men in the mirrors.

"Nice tits," he said, and cupped his hands under her breasts so they rose over the top of her bra. "And I like black underwear, come on, move nice and easy. Tease me, sweetheart, dance, tease yourself, don't you feel it coming?"

He put his hands on her waist, and they danced together. Slowly, inches apart, not touching, and she began to feel.

"Touch me," he said. "Put your hands on me, on my chest, my back, I like it. Feel it, you like to touch me, you've wanted it since you saw me. Go on, move, you got a nice body, you can dance with Tony."

For a second, they were side by side in front of the mirrors, and their eyes met in the reflections. Tony was smiling. He moved around her, always dancing, and unhooked her bra. She slipped out of it, in time to the music, country-Western rock, love-yearning music. He grinned

127

with pleasure and moved in front of her. Always moving, dancing. He bent down and flicked his tongue across her nipples. She wanted him to stop moving, and take her then, but he danced, slipping out of his pants with a graceful movement born of long practice. He put her hand on his hard penis that rose in the bright bikinis he wore and started to help unbutton her slacks. Always dancing, thrusting his hips, near her, away. Teasing. She was breathing in slow, deep breaths, and when she stepped out of her slacks, he pulled her up against him and slipped his hand under the elastic of her panties and stroked her.

"Almost ready, Ali," he said.

"Tony, please . . ."

"Take them off, lady, nice and slow and together, and we stick together and move. . . ."

The music, the dance, the strip blended into a single movement as reflected Tonys and Alicias rushed in on them from all sides, surrounded them, held them in the center of the room. They were still dancing when they fell together onto the bed with Tony deep inside her, and Alicia knew she had never been so totally possessed and alive and responding. He was looking at her now, and not at the mirrors, and she cried out with him at the blinding shudder of climax that came finally for them. And she sobbed because it had happened, because it was over, because she wanted more and forever.

He pulled her close beside him as he lay back on the pillows and she clung to him to make him stay, make it last.

"You aren't bad, lady," he said. "Got a few things to learn . . . but you aren't bad."

"You are . . . fantastic," she said. She was elated and exhausted. So peaceful. Tony looked at them lying together, coupled still in the mirrors that surrounded them. He was in total agreement. He knew he was fantastic.

"I don't ever want another man. Ever."

He laughed. "Don't ask for the impossible. Course a classy type like you wouldn't bother messing around with a shit like that Tito, that's for sure."

He seemed to expect an answer. Instinctively she would have said no; she could tell by the way he waited that he wanted more.

"No, of course not!" she said. "He's so young, and not sexy. You're right—he puts on an act, and you're the real thing."

Tony breathed a contented sigh. "Yeah. Whether I just got me, or you, or a whole shitload of women watching and feeling it." Idly he ran his hand across the smooth skin of her belly. "The best," he said, and she didn't care if he were talking about her or himself. He was every fantasy made real, and if it never happened again, she didn't care.

She did care.

Tony ran his fingers over the large still-purple bruise on her thigh where she'd run into the table in the dark on Friday.

"Your boyfriend beat you up?"

"An unexpected contribution from my ex-husband. By long distance, I assure you. I was running to answer a phone call that turned out to be him."

The intrusion of that life of hers that existed outside Tony's room and would continue to exist long after he'd disappeared made her realize the folly that underlay the night's adventure.

"It's late," she said. "I wouldn't mind staying here with you forever, but . . ."

"Hah!" he said. "Don't get greedy."

"I won't," Alicia said. "It was just so . . . good."

The goodness she would remember, that was certain, but however much she might wish for Tony again and again, this particular pleasure was impossible to repeat. She had a position to maintain, she was at least eight years older, she was so different in every respect from this man leaning back against a pile of pillows, his eyes half-closed, naked and so wildly desirable.

She wanted very much for him to ask her to stay. He seemed to know what she was thinking.

"I like to sleep alone," he said. "Nothing personal."

"Are you so eager to get rid of me? Or is this the way you treat all the customers you bring home from the Carousel?" She was suddenly hurt by his attitude.

"Women!" he said and sat up. "You're pissed off all of a sudden because you *are* greedy. You fall in love with Tony and then you want to know who else is sharing the goodies."

"Well, do you?"

"Nagging bitch," he said good-naturedly. "I don't make a habit of bringing home women I drag out of the audience. I'm an entertainer. I sell sex at a distance. And I don't like jealous women."

"I'm not jealous."

"Sure you are. Now, move that nice ass off my bed and go home. I got to get some sleep. I got rehearsing to do before I go to work."

She was surprised. "Do you do something besides strip?"

"Yeah, sure," he said. "I work at one of the hotels."

But he didn't say which, and Alicia thought he sounded evasive. She picked up her scattered clothes. Tony went to a closet hidden behind a mirrored wall and slipped on a blue velour shirt and black pants.

"You don't have to walk me to my car," she said.

"I wasn't going to."

"Then why are you putting on clothes?"

He kissed the back of her neck as she combed her hair, facing a dozen reflected Alicias. "Because I like taking them off," he said.

"But—"

"You know," Tony said, "you smart dames are dumb sometimes. If my ma thought I'd let a woman walk out on the streets in the middle of the night alone, she'd nail my balls to the wall. And there goes my career."

Tony strolled out of the bedroom. Alicia looked at the phone beside the bed and prayed she'd remember the number. Not that she would ever call him.

"Come on!" From the next room.

He put her safely in her car. She rolled down the window.

"Should I say thanks?" she said. Hoping desperately that he'd say he would call her. She wanted to see him again, but only if he chose.

"If you want to, lady," he said. He leaned in the window and kissed her. She was elated and depressed by the night. Maybe that was the way the best things were: never to be repeated. He stood back as she started the car.

"Alicia."

She turned to him.

"If you . . . you know . . . like run into anybody like you said who could do something . . ."

"For you?" She didn't know whether to laugh or cry.

"Hey, that's not why I brought you home, you know."

"Do I know that?"

"You do. You leave your phone number under my pillow?"

"No. No, I did *not!*"

He was still standing in the alley as she backed out and sped up the street. In spite of her annoyance, the feeling that she had been used, she could not forget this night with Tony. She wished, in fact, that it was starting all over again.

Tony Spinelli wasn't much given to reflection.

He went home, to his mirrors, to watch himself take off the clothes he'd put on. Moving to the music. Stripping. For himself.

15

She was glad she had lunch with Billy to look forward to. He would understand.

That in spite of the sour ending, it had been the most exhilarating experience of her life. It didn't matter what Tony Spinelli's motives had been. Motives were irrelevant. Hers had been as self-seeking as his.

She wanted to see him again. Before she went to work on Thursday morning—wide awake and feeling vibrantly alive, washed in the memories of Tony's lovemaking—she looked long and hard at the number she'd scrawled on the back of an envelope when she got home. She would never call it, but it seemed like a talisman. Proof of what had been, a reminder that she could seek out a fantasy and make it real.

What hotel? What did he do?

Please, God, not the Ritz, she thought.

And to be sure, she called the Ritz and asked if they employed a Mr. Spinelli. They did not.

Dean Barrow congratulated her on the excellent luncheon for the sheikhs. "Sheikh Ahmad was most interested in your work," he said. "You made quite an impression, very important man."

"I don't approve, Dean Barrow," she said.

The dean was silent. He understood.

"Sometimes we have to make compromises, Alicia," he said sadly. "Bend a principle, give up a cherished notion about who we are. For the sake of something . . . more. I, no more than you, wish opprobrium on the university. Sometimes . . . ," he looked beyond Alicia to some scene of peace distant from the academic wars, ". . . it works best to go by instinct and not by preset standards."

"Even standards of our profession and class, Dean Barrow?"

"I will not do that, Alicia." He looked desperately weary. "In the end."

Debbie looked weary too. Silent and unhappy. A young woman with secrets. Alicia felt she had to say or do something.

"Are you busy right after work?" Alicia asked. Debbie shook her head but didn't look up from her typewriter. "We could have a drink or coffee."

"I know what you want to talk about," she said. "It's not important." Alicia waited. "Okay, why not? Lenore's no help because I can't tell her. At least you're all together."

That's how much you know, Alicia thought.

They went to a coffee shop near the university. It was a few minutes past five, so the undergraduates who couldn't face dining room food one more time hadn't yet descended to devour the hamburgers and chili and French fries for which the place was famous. A couple of earnest discussions going on in corner booths, a student and a teaching assistant in one, two young women ganging up on a young man in another.

"I'm not prying," Alicia said when they sat down, "but you look . . . terrible. I mean, unhappy."

"And you look happy."

"Do I? I guess I am. For no good reason."

There was a good reason, and its name was Tony, but Alicia was taken aback that the odd mix of turmoil and serenity inside her could be so obvious on the outside.

"I guess I have no good reason for not being happy," Debbie said. "I got what I wanted. Mike Tedesco. I've been seeing him. You're the only person now who knows."

Gently. "Do you suppose that maybe his wife knows too? It's hard for a man to keep that kind of news from the woman he lives with, even without putting it into so many words."

Debbie flushed angrily. "That's none of your business."

"True, but it's something you have to face. And believe

133

me, I'm not talking about moral issues. It's the future you've got to think about. What kind of mess is around the corner." As Alicia spoke those words, she realized the irony of having them issue from her mouth. There was a lurking sense of a mess around the corner in most people's lives; certainly in hers.

"Alicia, he's terrific, I mean it. You know what he looks like . . . and sexy, God . . . I mean, those guys at the Carousel, remember? they got nothing on Mike."

Debbie looked happy for once, a faraway happy, seeing intimate, stolen time with Mike Tedesco, a rumpled bed in the borrowed apartment of a single classmate, meetings in coffee shops like this one, chance encounters near the medical school. . . .

"I wonder, sometimes, why me?" Debbie said. "He says he feels relaxed with me. He says his wife—"

"Doesn't understand?"

"No." Debbie looked puzzled. "She understands, about medical school and all, and how he has to take some lab jobs evenings, even though she works. His wife . . . they were married when he was a sophomore in college, she thought she was pregnant, and they were going to get married someday anyhow. But he found out it was all a mistake. He likes her. He likes me too. I know I shouldn't be involved with him but I didn't talk him into anything. He did it to *me*. Why should I have to give up what I like?"

Debbie stared at her coffee cup. The two young women in the back booth got up and pulled the man to his feet. They linked arms with him and walked out, easy, laughing, friends.

"Mike won't last," Debbie said sadly. "You're so lucky."

Alicia was taken aback. "Me? Lucky?"

"Oh, Dr. Parker and all that. And you're old enough so you don't get mixed up in things like this."

"Nothing is as simple as it seems." And, she might have added, age is no insurance. Age? Alicia had honestly never brooded about her age, even when she passed thirty a handful of years back. She had always felt that not having children growing up by leaps and bounds before her eyes had enabled her to ignore the passage of time.

Once she had considered having children. Gardner had claimed to want children. Mother Sears accepted with ill-concealed disapproval Alicia's decision to continue her

134

education after marriage and to work for a time at Commonwealth University before filling the house Gardner had settled them in with little boy and girl Sears. Still, she had sent Gardner's sister Muffy to Alicia with her perfect infant Eleanor Anne. At the time, Alicia and Gardner had been married two years. Alicia was enjoying a stretch of peace and relief after her long pursuit of the man of her dreams.

"Really, it's such *fun!*" Muffy said, settling down with Eleanor Anne on her knee, and beaming at Alicia, who suspected that as a sister-in-law, she left much to be desired in Muffy's eyes. "I was going simply *crazy* at home with nothing to do. Well, there was the Chorus Pro Musica, and the Junior League, but you know how *they* are."

Alicia didn't, but nodded agreeably.

"Then itsy-bitsy Baby Ellie came along to fill up my days. You really ought to have a baby, Alicia."

"Right now, I don't spend much time at home," Alicia said. "I'm just getting into this new job, and I do keep house. Gar and I like to travel, and I like having a couple of years to devote to my husband." It sounded logical to Alicia, but Muffy was not to be convinced.

"But you feel so *important* when you're pregnant," Muffy said. "People pay *such* attention. Mummy said the same thing."

Alicia watched Itsy-Bitsy spit up her lunch.

"It seems to me a flawed way of achieving importance," Alicia said, "if that's the only way you can do it."

"Oh, you're such a women's libber." Muffy's too-jolly chuckle made Alicia wince.

"I don't think that's quite accurate, Muffy."

"You can't deny it, Alicia."

"I can certainly refuse to be labeled. By you or anybody else."

Muffy and Eleanor Anne departed in a huff. In a way, their visit had an impact: she thought enough about what Muffy had said to bring it up with Gardner.

"What do you think about children right away?" she asked Gardner that night when he got home. He had stopped for a cocktail or two on his way home from his Boston office. He had been doing it more frequently of late.

"If you're so hell-bent on going to school and working,

135

it would be kind of hard, wouldn't it? I'm not going to stay home and clean up after a baby for you."

"I wasn't suggesting that, and I wasn't talking about the day after tomorrow, Gar."

"Of course we'll have children," he said impatiently. "That's your job, isn't it? But if you're going to fool around . . ."

He went off to his den with another drink.

Alicia began to wonder then if there was something seriously wrong with her marriage. It took her several years to determine that there had been, right from the start. The dreams of youth had blinded her to the fact that Gardner wasn't going to detour happily from the path of his forebears. He was going to bend her to his way. Yet she thought for a long time that she was a good wife. She concluded that she was definitely a bad wife for Gardner, and she was living in mild misery.

There was no fun in her life.

"We aren't even friends," she told Harriet the day, after many long days of thinking about it, she decided to ask him for a divorce. "It's a genuine case of mental cruelty for everyone involved; me, Gardner, the entire Sears clan. Maybe if we'd had children . . ."

"Trust me," Harriet said. "Children can make something not so good perfectly awful. Don't feel too bad."

"I feel about as bad as I think I can," Alicia said, and it took her several years to overcome the sense of guilt and failure her divorce gave her along with her freedom. And no children, no fun. Except for the fling with Brett.

That was what she had missed along the way: fun. She'd observed other people's fun—Harriet and Mark's marriage, Sheila Conroy's adventure with Said, Lenore's erratic and amusing progress through life, Billy's pursuit of what he wanted, even Debbie's present dilemma. She had spent so much of her life cornering Gardner and then extricating herself from the consequences of her devotion (and how well she knew she was repeating old dreams and old mistakes with Graham) that she had missed out on the heart-stopping excitement, the peaks, the fun. Brett Handley was perhaps as close as she had come in his style and unpredictability.

And then there was Tony Spinelli.

Suddenly, as she sat in the coffee shop watching Debbie

fiddle with her spoon and project illicit meetings with Mike Tedesco, she longed to hear Tony's voice, see him, learn more, much more of his language of body and senses. Not be Alicia Sears, of decorous upbringing and responsible position, but simply a woman having fun. And pleasure. And love; simple, uncritical, physical love.

She didn't care what Tony wanted in return.

"I got to get home," Debbie said. "My father's been complaining. He gives me so much grief, but what can I do? He's my father. I'm glad I had a chance to tell you about Mike. But I still don't know what to do."

"I'm afraid I don't either."

"I won't be seeing him much nights," Debbie said. "He's been working with Dr. Ostrava's lab; he's taking a lot of new research people on, did you hear?"

"I can't turn around without that man showing up. I suppose he wants to put on a grand show for the trustees meeting in the spring. There are four new trustees who've never had the privilege of giving their blessing to Victor Ostrava and the glory he is going to bring to Commonwealth."

"Mike says it's a good job, and it pays well."

"And the money comes from me," Alicia said, gathering up her things.

Or did it? Victor's research budget didn't show excess funds for new lab assistants this late in the year. For all she knew, though, he might have private means.

"Alicia, don't say anything to Lenore about . . . Mike, will you? She doesn't know."

Alicia laughed. "I'll bet she knows something. How could you hide how different you are?"

"Am I?" Debbie grinned, pleased, and looked beautiful in the way her mother must once have been. Touched by an evanescent hope, the impossible man who might vanish tomorrow but who was, for this brief time, the absolute center of existence. "I guess I am different. I shut out a lot of things that could spoil it, I don't want to mix this up with—with—"

"Real life?"

Debbie looked sheepish. "You could call it that. But what's real about it? What's so different?"

"A double life isn't easy," Alicia said, and hoped she didn't sound like a preacher who was missing the point.

137

She knew what Debbie meant. A circle of mirrored Tonys, to shut out real life. Or close it in.

One aspect of Alicia's real life rang her doorbell that night. It was unlike Graham to drop by without calling. Alicia felt a wave of irritation when she saw him in her doorway. She hadn't spoken to him since the previous Saturday in Weston. She had not put aside her annoyance at the part she presumed he played in Gardner's unpleasant visit.

"I've been troubled," he said. "About last weekend."

"It was nothing, Gray. I've forgotten it."

He sat down, ill at ease for once.

"I haven't," he said. "I simply don't understand your attitude."

"I thought you mind experts understood everything."

"Don't be sarcastic, Alicia. It doesn't become you."

"And it doesn't become you to send your pal Gardner Sears around to beg me to marry you." She watched him closely to catch a reaction, but Graham had studied well the art of not giving anything away.

"You know I wouldn't do that," he said. "I can speak for myself. Alicia . . . let's agree to put aside the past few days. I know you've been under pressure at the school."

When Alicia opened her mouth to answer him, she knew she was going to say something that would alter the path of their relationship irrevocably. Events had nudged her along to a brink of sorts; she figuratively closed her eyes and jumped.

"I don't think we should see each other for now, Gray," she said. She wasn't prepared for the look of hurt that crossed his face.

He does care, she thought. Why did I say that? Because of a night with a male stripper whom I will never see again? The answer, she knew, was yes. Because of Tony.

"Why?" Graham said in a strained voice. "Because of what Gardner said? I assure you, I had nothing—"

"A lot of things," she interrupted. "I really don't want to talk about it."

Graham stood up. "That's unwise. I'm entitled to know, understand. We've been so close for so long."

Alicia couldn't look at him. What he was saying was true, if she wanted to be fair to him. There was a long, tense silence between them.

"Please remember," Graham said, "I have not abandoned you." He walked toward the door.

"Gray," she said. "I'm not abandoning you, I'm choosing a clean slate, because I . . . I feel I have to."

He looked back and smiled very sweetly. "Of course, my dear," he said. "The boys will miss you. . . ."

She thought of her promise of a private field trip with Timmy. She'd have to work it in somehow.

"I have a neurological convention in Dallas," Graham said. "I'll be gone for quite some time, but I will call you, if I may, when I get back."

She nodded.

When she was alone, she stared at the phone. Her heart was pounding, and she saw her hand was trembling as she reached out to dial.

16

It was just as well Tony hadn't answered, she thought. It would have been humiliating to have had to explain why she was calling.

But surely he would have known. Tony Spinelli was not dumb. Alicia Sears was, and she'd never do anything like it again. Chance had saved her. But chance, she later learned, had only been waiting in the wings to pounce on her when she least expected it.

She left her office on Friday morning before noon. She had spent two hours doing too little to justify her salary, and she was impatient to meet Billy, to spill out the tensions and events that had swirled through her life in recent days.

Alicia parked in the Berkeley Street garage, a few blocks from the Ritz, with an hour or more to spare before she had to meet Billy. She resolutely faced away from the streets leading to the South End. The abortive telephone call had closed off that aspect of life, however impertinently Tony hovered at the edge of her consciousness still. Instead, she headed down a side street toward Arlington and Park Square. She planned to kill time looking over the glittering cases of jewels in Shreve's, window shopping on Newbury Street. And there was also F. A. O. Schwarz up the street from the Ritz where she could indulge herself by buying an extravagant toy for Josh. She might even find an equally extravagant adult toy for Mark, who could get as excited about surprise packages as his son.

The shock of recognizing the jaunty figure strolling down Arlington toward her made her stumble. What she had desperately wanted was happening. And now that it was happening, she allowed chance to propel her toward Tony rather than away, although she could have ducked into the bank or the hotel or the airlines office close at hand.

"Hey, Alicia!" He looked pleased to see her, that was something. She was so flustered that she found herself babbling idiotically, explaining about her lunch date, how she was early, what was he doing here?

He laughed. "I'm going to work." He flicked his hand toward the hotel.

"Here?"

"I told you," he said. "I work in one of the bars, day shift. You sure you weren't hanging around to run into me, after that nice little tumble?"

She was indignant. "Certainly not!"

"Sweetheart, I'm teasing you. And you don't fool me. You're glad you found me."

She looked up at him and felt again the sensations that had been like promises of her life finally fulfilled.

"Yes," she said. "Yes, I am."

"Look," he said, "I don't, like, make a habit of seeing the same woman twice. No, wait, don't get off on your high horse. I could duck out of work today, we could do something, talk or . . . anything."

"I have to meet my friend," she said. "He's expecting me."

Tony shrugged. Alicia couldn't allow him to escape her.

"You could come to lunch with us," she said.

"I don't want to interfere with your boyfriends," he said. "Not my game."

"He's not exactly . . . He prefers men to women, actually. A doctor. He's . . . um, got a lot of friends in show business. Please? I'd like to have him meet you."

"Why?"

"I want you to. Need more reasons? I can think of some, good ones, bad ones . . ."

"Okay, okay," he said. "Why not?"

"It's the Ritz," she said. "Right up the street."

"Lady, I was born in this town. Never been to the Ritz, though."

"It's . . . quite formal," she said, suddenly aware of his casual clothes, and not quite knowing how to tell him

141

delicately that without a coat and tie he'd never make it through the doors of the upstairs dining room.

"I'd better change my clothes," he said. "What time?"

"One," she said. "But your job . . ."

"I ain't my uncle Angelo's favorite nephew for nothing. It's no problem. I'll be there. To meet your pal."

What am I getting myself into? she wondered as they parted and she made her way toward the Ritz. She was numb. Billy would be okay. He had a gift for bridging awkward social gaps. She only hoped Tony would be able to manage the pretensions of the place and the complexities of the situation she'd landed him in. She hoped she could handle it.

"There's going to be someone else for lunch," she said to Billy when they met in the lobby of the Ritz Carlton Hotel. "Do you mind? He's very good-looking."

"In that case, I don't mind at all. But *please*. Give me a hint."

"It might be awful, Billy. He's one of the strippers from the Carousel Club."

For one of the few times in his life, Billy Catlett was totally nonplussed.

"I sort of got . . . involved. Stupid of me, wasn't it? I couldn't help it. Really involved, I mean."

"Alicia, you surprise me." Billy looked at her closely. "You're happy, though. He was good for you." She nodded. "Then it's all right."

She was saying a silent prayer that it would be all right.

He appeared to know what she was thinking. "I'll be perfectly charming," he said. "And I'm fascinated. Not exactly like the Alicia I thought I knew so well. Let's go upstairs and get our table."

They walked up the graceful curved stairway to the second-floor dining room, and were seated with a flourish.

"We are expecting a third," Billy told the maitre d'.

The maitre d' was not amused.

Alicia kept looking toward the wide doorway into the big, high-ceiling room, where the maitre d' hovered.

"Calm down," Billy said.

"This is so dumb, it's not a place where he'll be comfortable. I mean, I'm a Sears-by-marriage, and even I'm not terribly comfortable all the time." She looked at Billy and grinned. "I'm always afraid I might mortally offend one of the waiters."

The room was fairly well filled with discreetly dressed and prosperous businessmen, well-off Beacon Hill and suburban matrons. Billy nodded to a couple of men he identified as distinguished doctors from Massachusetts General Hospital entertaining an out-of-town colleague. At one table, Alicia noticed a party of four or five focused on a man unmistakably a famous Broadway actor in Boston for the out-of-town tryouts of his latest play. The Ritz was a short walk across the Public Garden to the theater district.

Then Tony stood uncertainly in the doorway. It was the only time in their short acquaintance Alicia had seen him unsure. He was wearing, thank goodness, a suit and tie. Without them, the maitre d' would have turned him away without a second look. The overall effect, however, was noticeably unlike the prevailing tone of the dining room—au courant, tasteless to a degree, a look loudly at variance with the prevailing tone of proper Boston.

"Well," Billy breathed. "Well, well. We ought to find him a good tailor, but darkly handsome, indeed. I never dreamed. . . ."

Tony's dark beauty, in spite of the trappings, drew the eyes of all who noticed him. The woman seated next to the Broadway star had her eyes riveted on him, and she nudged the star, who also gave Tony an appreciative look. On the other hand, the dining room staff, themselves largely Italian and Hispanic but polished to a degree of snobbery possible only in a dining room like the Ritz's, knew Tony for exactly what he was. The signs were subtle, but they were definitely there. The young man who led Tony to their table (not the maitre d', not for a mere Tony Spinelli) wore a look of insolent amusement and contempt.

"The rest of your party, Dr. Catlett," the man said.

"Hope I'm not late," Tony said smoothly. He didn't seem troubled by his surroundings. "I must've passed this hotel a million times, and never been inside."

"Tony, this is Billy Catlett. Tony Spinelli." Alicia, suffering an agony of unease, reverted to her well-bred lady cover to mask her anxiety. "It was so good of you to be able to make it on such short notice. Dr. Catlett, Billy, teaches at the university and practices north of Boston. I've known Billy, oh, how many years now? Quite a few . . ."

Tony leaned toward Alicia and said distinctly, "Shut up, Alicia. And start over."

Alicia shut her mouth with a gulp. Billy winked at her, then scooped up the conversational ball.

"Alicia tells me you're in show business, Mr. Spinelli?"

"Tony. Yeah. Since you and her are such good buddies, she probably told you all about me." He addressed Billy with an excess of ingratiating charm, and Billy responded cordially. A waiter offered menus. A busboy poured water into the glowing blue Ritz tumblers that matched the blue in the chandeliers. Billy watched Tony with speculative eyes.

"She told me a few details," Billy said. "I didn't quite believe her when she described you, however. But she was amazingly accurate."

Tony looked at Alicia out of the corner of his eye. She pretended to be engrossed in the menu, but she knew he was watching her.

"So I live up to my advance notices, huh?" He opened his menu. He looked quite pleased, the necessary homage paid to Tony Spinelli. "What is all this stuff?" he asked, scanning the menu.

"It's all of it pretty good," Billy said. "In fact, it would be surprising if anything on the menu wasn't very good indeed. Tell me about your work, Tony."

"What do you want to know, Doc?" Tony gave Billy a long look from under his lashes. A tease. Well, that was his work. Alicia looked from one to the other, furtively. She was still smarting over Tony's command to shut up; in her world, the positions of the sexes were less blatantly expressed. It would have taken a serious conflict for Graham or Gardner, or even Brett Handley, to tell her to shut up so firmly and so confidently assuming obedience.

She could tell that Billy found Tony attractive, and she fretted inside because Tony's attention was directed away from her. A wave of jealousy was added to insult.

"I strip," Tony said. "That's what I do. Alicia knows, don't you, sweetheart? She likes my act, Doc, and don't let her tell you she don't. Doesn't."

"And do you, Al?" Billy asked archly.

"Tony is . . . an exceptional person," she said. "Shall we order?" She made herself too busy to look at either of them.

"Have the pâté to start," Billy said to Tony. "The Ritz has excellent pâté."

"And will I know what I'm eating? This pâté?" Tony said.

"Consider it fancy meat loaf, my dear," Billy said. "I'll order the wine."

"Which means I'll doze at my desk all afternoon," Alicia said. She and Billy decided to share rack of lamb. They persuaded Tony to try tournedos Rossini. Alicia was not hungry, in any case. She regretted her invitation to Tony because, selfishly, it was not the experience she wanted with him. She had too little control. The very fact of Billy altered her fragile connections with Tony.

"Did you grow up in Boston, Tony?" Billy was carrying on where Alicia had lapsed into silence.

"I've spent my whole life here. Well, I've done some traveling. Out to the Coast, to Vegas. I go down to New York for a couple of days every few months. My sister is married to this guy from New York and they live out on Long Island now. She's the only one in my family I'm still close to. Leo's a real bastard, but he's got dough. Italian, import-export business, so he's okay with my mother. She didn't care what kind of life the guy leads Teresa, as long as she's got a big house and a bunch of kids." He lowered his voice. "Me, I know he's mixed up with the mob, and one day they're going to bring Leo home to Terry in a cement block looking like a sieve, but I don't say nothing. I don't ask. I pick her up and take her out on the town, show her a good time for a change. She's only three, four years older than me, but sometimes I could swear she felt about a hundred. Four kids. I remember when Terry was a beautiful girl."

Tony finally seemed at ease, talking about himself and his family. Alicia even felt at ease, as if she were finding substance behind the shadow cast by that body she had encountered so briefly.

"I ain't ever going to do that to any of my women," Tony said. "And I ain't going to turn into a fat slob like Leo. I'm going to be just what you see. Forever."

Alicia thought that probably both she and Billy, at Tony's age, maybe ten years younger than they were today, believed that they would stay the same forever. A few years later, they knew they wouldn't, but Tony would hang onto it for as long as he could.

"Hey, this is good wine," he said, taking the bottle from the silver bucket beside Billy and refilling the glasses. A nearby waiter flared his nostrils at the sight. "And the food's not bad. I got to remember to make this place a regular hangout."

Both Billy and Alicia laughed. He had spoken without irony, but aware that they were laughing at him, he seemed to withdraw into himself.

He pushed back his chair. "I'll be right back," he said.

As he walked through the dining room in his unlikely clothes, presumably in quest of the men's room or perhaps just to regroup out of range of Billy and Alicia, the eyes followed him again. He walked with arrogant grace, with his head up.

"He's priceless," Billy said. "And fabulous to look at. Not to mention the . . . promise he holds out."

"Mmmm."

"I know what you were thinking, Alicia, before. He's a tease, but I wouldn't tread on your territory, even if he were serious, which he definitely is not. He's yours."

"He's not *mine!*" Alicia spoke almost violently.

Billy raised an eyebrow.

"He's not," she said again. "I don't know what he is to me. If he's anything to me. I don't know why I asked him today. I—had to see him again, after . . . after seeing him the other day," she finished lamely.

Billy patted her hand. "Don't try to explain. I know. It's happened to me, an obsession that needs a good dose of disillusionment to get over. Sex is the strangest thing, the physical attraction, that need, keeps getting interfered with by real life. You try to fight it. Then you give up fighting, let it happen, and on the other side of the river, you realize how silly it was. And how important."

"Will we manage to get through lunch?"

"We'll make it," Billy said. "He's doing a good job. You're the one who's uncomfortable and pouting like a two-year-old because he's not thigh-to-thigh under the table."

"Now, just a minute."

Billy put up his hand to silence her. "Alicia, I'm your friend, with no ax to grind and no designs on your boyfriend. I'm telling you the truth. And if you continue to huddle down in your chair and pick at your food, you're going to bore him to death. That boy isn't going to stand around waiting to be bored, believe me. But he likes you."

Alicia looked up sharply, hopefully. "He does." Billy indicated the doorway. "Here comes your hero."

Tony paused at the doorway, right behind a young, very young waiter. Short and slim, with a haughty look as he surveyed the dining room. The maitre d' was busy with the reservations book and a distinguished gray-haired lady with a tasteful dark mink coat who was demanding some special table. Tony, Alicia noticed, appeared to be speaking to the waiter from behind, and as she watched, the waiter's face dissolved into what could only be called a murderous expression. Tony, as far as she could tell, had a smile on his face; he seemed to be full of good spirits.

He walked jauntily back across the dining room, looking positively jubilant.

"I want to tell you," he said as he sat down, "they got some funny guys working here. See that kid over by the door, the one who looks like he's about to burst into tears? I pass him on my way out, and he's saying something in Italian just loud enough for me to hear. Something that isn't so nice, not if you're Italian. Now my old man came over here from Naples when he was young, and he spoke the dialect at home. I know it as good as I know English. So this kid is insulting me, but I'm not causing trouble in a fancy place like this. I just go along nice and peaceful and find the men's room, but when I come back, he's got his boss standing right in front of him. And I go up behind him and think up every Neapolitan insult I can remember. The kind of stuff people get knifed for and thrown into the Gulf of Naples, right? The kid can't do a thing."

Tony was in an exceedingly good humor.

"Right before that, this rich old dame who could barely walk, with all her furs and diamonds and her tired old legs . . ." Tony looked around the room. "There she is, over there."

It was the woman who had resolved her dispute with the maitre d'. Tony lifted himself slightly off his chair and actually waved to her. Alicia was horrified.

The woman waved back, beaming Tony a smile.

"Anyhow," he said, "she says to me, 'Young man . . .'" Tony spoke in a high-pitched voice that captured the Beacon Hill accent perfectly. "'Young man, your arm, if you please.' So I give her my arm and haul her up those last few steps, and I say, 'Lady, why didn't you take the elevator, ma'am?' And she looks at me, shocked. 'An elevator? To the *second* floor? One simply doesn't.' I bet she'd get her rocks off sitting in the front row of the Carousel watching me strip."

After that, everyone relaxed. Completely.

"We must do this again," Alicia said, suppressing the thought that this day was a special set of circumstances. It was not part of a continuing pattern. She didn't, if the truth be known, know if she would ever see Tony again, under any circumstances.

Billy shook his head imperceptibly, with a knowing that expressed a lifetime of the ins and outs of carrying on a life where pieces, big pieces, must always remain in the shadows. Tony, Alicia thought, might work in a combination with Billy, but where else? Not in her general circle, not if she wanted to maintain it. Totally absorbed in himself, among people willing to let him indulge in his self-absorption, he was amusing. Alone with her, in a bed surrounded by walls of mirrors, he was an experience that ought, if God were good, to go on forever. The meeting of the various elements of her life in Tony—impossible.

When Alicia perceived the distances between them, she breathed relief, cured of her infatuation. It had been madness to go with him the night before, but no harm done.

But she wouldn't forget it.

"Uh-oh," Billy said. "It's after three. I've got to see my patient at the General. Tony, if you ever get rushed to the hospital, use your dying breath to say, 'Take me to Mass. General.' And I hope," Billy said as they reached Arlington Street and he put his hand on the door of a waiting cab, "that we three shall meet again."

Tony shook hands. "Be seeing you, Doc."

When Billy kissed Alicia on the cheek, he whispered, "We made it, as promised. It wasn't so bad, was it?"

After Billy had driven away, Alicia said, "I've got my car over on Berkeley. Can I drop you someplace?"

"You're going back to work?" He grabbed her arm and turned her to face him on the windy corner of Arlington and Newbury. She was horrified to see behind him Victor Ostrava examining old silver teapots in the window of Firestone and Parsons, but observing her and Tony out of the corner of his eye. She hadn't noticed him when the three of them came out of the Ritz.

"What? Yes, I have to." She pulled her arm from Tony's grasp and started up Newbury. She glanced back over her shoulder; Victor was still watching them. Alicia hurried on, with Tony keeping pace at her side.

She hated Victor's intrusion, however innocent. He was a nagging anxiety in her professional world, and never more so than since the Wednesday luncheon, following which he had furiously blamed her that the sheikhs hadn't simply handed over their fortune to him. Seeing him now had spoiled whatever was good about the day.

"You mean you're just going to leave? It was just to *eat?*"

If only she could stay with Tony now, go back to the room full of mirrors and music and dim lights, where no sound or sight from the outside penetrated. Victor and the rest, from oily sheikhs to a dean harassed by personal and university problems—shut out.

"Yes," she said. "But I'm glad I saw you again."

They crossed Newbury, and were passing shop windows where the two of them were reflected against the faceless mannequins wearing drifts of pastel chiffon and impossible silver kid shoes.

"Wait!" he said, and stopped her in midstep. "If you go back to work now, what time do you leave?"

"About five."

"Huh, less than two hours."

Tony seemed to be surveying the window display.

"You ought to be wearing sexy dresses like those," he said. "But red or something. Okay, let's go. Your car in the garage?"

She nodded. He took her arm and rushed her along, past F. A. O. Schwarz. Josh wasn't going to get the toy of his dreams. At the corner of Berkeley and Newbury, she looked back again, and thought she saw Victor edging across the street through traffic, but she couldn't be sure. Tony didn't pause until they entered the parking garage and reached the third level.

"Give me the keys," he said. "Get in, I'll drive."

"But—"

"You can use a telephone," he said. "You call from my place, tell them you were poisoned at lunch."

"I don't want . . ." she began.

"Alicia," he said softly. "You do. Now, give me the ticket, and shut up. Do I have to spend my life telling you that? You want what you had the other night, and more. And better. Tell me."

"Yes," she whispered. She felt like a child offered a

tantalizing treat by a grown-up, but when she looked over at Tony, he was leaning against the wheel, laughing at her.

"You're okay, Alicia," he said. "I don't run into many dames like you. Class and connections, nice tits, and you're hungry."

"Hungry?" She felt wonderful.

"For me, sweetheart."

They sat together in her car in the silent garage, the only two people in the midst of rows of empty autos. It was different today, being with Tony. They had stepped beyond the casual pickup of Wednesday to another sort of intimacy, where they were beginning to know each other, what would happen when they reached his apartment and he shut them off in his room. He would be safe among his reflections and she would come into his arms.

It was easy to know what Tony wanted, how to slip out of her clothes to the music as he shed his, and to come together, naked and without shyness. Not Alicia, not today.

"Don't hurry," he said to the Alicia he saw in the mirrors. "We got time."

Standing behind her, he put his hands on her waist and brushed his lips across the back of her neck, her shoulders, her back. Their eyes met in the mirrors, and they both laughed.

"There isn't time," she said. "I want you now."

She knew she had fallen in love with some part of this dark and assured man/boy with smooth skin and tangled curls, and eyes that seemed to see himself in her. She was his hand mirror, who gave back to Tony the confirmation he demanded of his power to move and excite her.

Even as they spoke to each other in a silent language of the senses, she prayed it would not end, and she would be called back to Tony's room tonight, tomorrow, forever.

17

THERE was no tonight, no tomorrow, and by the Wednesday following lunch at the Ritz and the hours of lovemaking in the middle of the reflections, it appeared that there was no forever for Alicia.

She hadn't heard a word from Tony and she had suffered through five days of hurt pride and rejection with a short temper and restless discontent. In her mind, she went over and over the miracle of discovery their afternoon had represented, the sharp realization that she was learning how to please him. How to please herself.

Had he said he'd call? Or had he said only, "I'll be seeing you"? The man who never saw the same woman twice, he claimed. She clung to that half-promise until even the hope began to fade and she reluctantly admitted to herself that she'd been used and tossed aside.

It made her furious. It destroyed her composure. It made her cry in the privacy of her Marlborough Street haven, with her books and her furniture and the fragile mementos of other promises that had failed her. The model of the Eiffel Tower was a phallic mockery of her long-ago life with Gardner, but she saw the humor in her symbolic gesture of depositing it in the trash.

She could even see the humor in her guilty survey of the rows of magazines in the Out-of-Town newsstand in Harvard Square for another copy of the magazine with

Tony's pictures. Why else would she so eagerly have agreed to a prework breakfast in the Square with Jennifer Newman, who worked at the Harvard School of Education up Brattle Street?

Jennifer chatted about her job and the two children she was raising alone since her divorce and then said, "You're up to something."

"Me? What do you mean?"

Jennifer laughed. "If you ever feel like telling me, feel free. If you think I can be of use, use me."

"I don't feel like telling, but thanks. Later maybe."

She didn't feel at all like sharing Tony, not even with Billy who knew or Harriet who didn't.

The second time with Tony had been more and better. It hadn't mattered that she knew that afternoon that the most intense level of their communication was purely physical. He had begun to instruct her in a new kind of language, sexual and sensual, and she wanted to know more, learn it fluently, hear and feel it spoken as only Tony could speak it, of all the men she knew. She had no one else to communicate with on this plane, except Tony. And Tony, it seemed, wasn't talking.

"It has to be a man," Jennifer said. "I had the same glassy look not too long ago, until it finally sank in that I was reverting to adolescence over somebody not worth it."

"Are they always not worth it?"

"If I said yes, I'd be lying. There's always one or two who are worth it. Is yours?"

"No," Alicia said between clenched teeth. "I've got to get to work."

Yet in spite of herself, she flew to the phone every time it rang in her apartment. When she saw the light for an incoming call flash on her office phone, she waited and prayed for Debbie to tell her it was Tony Spinelli. It never was. It was as if he had washed up on the shores of her life for a brief encounter and had been swept away again by the tide. At least she understood what someone like Debbie must suffer in her desperate infatuation, although for her, it must be easier. Mike Tedesco was evident in the vicinity of the administration building at least once a day.

If I were any kind of friend to Debbie, Alicia thought,

I'd tell him to let up on her. But it's not my business, and I'd hate to have him decide to turn his attentions on me.

Besides, Debbie looked awfully happy, with a freshly styled hairdo and a new shade of nail polish every morning.

Even Sheila, engrossed in her coming wedding, was so overwhelmed with her man and her future that she was no one to give advice and counsel.

The one thing she did do with regard to her personal life was write a formal letter to Gardner Sears, requesting that he terminate the financial arrangement regarding her apartment.

Alicia was surprised at how quickly, after that afternoon with Tony, she managed to isolate herself, and to dwell in a private world where, much to her distress, the boundaries seemed to consist of Tony Spinelli. She was irritated and unhappy, all the more so because for a few hours she had been supremely and unexpectedly happy with him.

She was shuffling papers on Wednesday afternoon when Billy stopped by her office after his weekly lecture at the medical school.

"Busy?" He was looking at her closely.

"Not terribly. Well, yes, I should be, but I can't seem to concentrate."

"You've been rather abrupt on the phone," Billy said. "Thought I'd better check you out and see what was wrong."

"Nothing's wrong." Spoken somewhat too sharply.

"Tell the doctor. I insist."

"It's nothing, really. I'm distracted. All this fund raising before the end of the semester, it's hopeless. The Arabs aren't going to come through as we hoped, I know it. I've got to plan the trustees meeting. And I have spring fever."

As March appeared, Boston's false spring had arrived with a vengeance. People were, as usual, predicting a blizzard for the St. Patrick's Day parade. For the moment, however, it was unseasonably warm, with the heartaching loneliness spring brings if you don't have a man's arms around you. It was a teenage feeling Alicia could remember from long ago as the winter withdrew from Boulder.

"What do you hear from your boyfriend?"

153

"Uh . . . not much."

"Aha! I knew it. He's moved on, left you behind. Alicia, you're a dear friend, and you're going to listen to some advice. More than that, you're going to follow it."

Impatiently. "Really, Billy, it's nothing. A little fling. You know about little flings, don't you? You seem to suggest that you do, anyhow. I don't want to hear about it. Or anything."

"Nevertheless, you're going to." Billy sat down beside her desk. "There's an unwritten code for this sort of situation: You screw around with them, but you don't *ever* care about them. And this kid—he really is a kid, Alicia—he's the kind that assumes if you have yourself, you don't need anybody else, except when it suits you. He brings in somebody to reflect himself, he doesn't worry about other people needing reflections as much or more than he."

"Funny you should mention that." She didn't sound as though it were amusing.

"What?"

"Reflections."

Billy shrugged his incomprehension. Alicia had never mentioned Tony's mirrors. Or the stripping, the dancing.

"Never mind," she said. "You were saying?"

"What I'm saying is, get hold of yourself, have some people over, go out, see your friends. What does Graham think about all this?"

"All what?"

"Don't play obtuse with me, my dear. I know the signs. You don't have to marry Graham, you don't have to do anything, but you do have to pull yourself back to where you were."

Alicia looked down at her desk.

"I don't want to go back, Billy. That's the truth."

"All right, not backward. But back somewhere near the person you are."

"Maybe this is the person I am. Maybe I'm different. Anyhow, I told Graham I didn't want to see him any more."

"Oh, nonsense!" Billy threw his hands up in the air.

"You're right. Half right, anyhow." Alicia relented. "I've been waiting for Tony to call for days. Five days. He hasn't. That's that." She stood up. "In fact, Billy, you're absolutely right as always. Are you free for dinner tomorrow? My place. I'll get Harriet and Mark, and Sheila. I'll even ask Graham before he goes to Dallas." Billy looked doubtful. "He'll come; he didn't believe me. And I'll cook up a storm, and you and I will pretend that nothing ever happened." She looked at him anxiously. "Don't hint anything, even, about Tony. Promise?"

"I promise. Good girl."

So they had all come to dinner, even Joshua. She couldn't help but notice Graham's pleasure at being there. In fact, he had been positively charming the whole evening, the way she had first seen him and been attracted to him. He was cordial to Billy for a change, and the two doctors with Mark listening in had discussed the possible effects of Dean Barrow's projected development plans for the medical school. Alicia, Harriet, and Sheila gossiped about the wedding, movies, books, the school. Very civilized and nice. Homey and familiar. Tony's influence had receded, as Billy had predicted. It was a relief being with people she belonged with, who, if they didn't arouse her to unexpected peaks, at least were dependable, intelligent, safe.

By about ten, Harriet was making noises about getting home with Joshua, who had gone to sleep on Alicia's bed, fenced around by pillows to keep him from tumbling off.

"I don't understand you, Alicia," Graham finally got around to saying. "Why did you ask me tonight, after what you said?"

"Billy convinced me I acted hastily." Graham winced at the name. "I didn't mean to suggest that we resume . . . where we left off. Maybe it was mistake."

"No," he said gently. "I always enjoy being with you."

The phone rang. Alicia was paralyzed for a second, and her eyes met Billy's, which showed amusement, questions, understanding.

"I'll get it," Harriet, who was close to the living-room phone, said.

"It's okay," Alicia said quickly. And got to the phone first.

"Alicia," Tony said. "I've been waiting for you to call." Her heart actually stopped and fluttered at his voice.

Cool. "Sorry. I've been busy."

"Alicia, I was looking at my mirrors and thinking of you." Teasing. Not to be resisted.

She was lost. Damn him.

"I can't talk right now," she said. "There are people here."

Billy was watching her carefully, half-listening to Graham, who continued to talk, but who was, she could see, straining to overhear her conversation.

"Get rid of them," Tony said. "Meet me."

"I can't."

"Why do you keep saying that to me?"

"I mean it. I can't. Not right now."

"Don't put yourself out, lady. I never ask more than once."

"Wait. They'll be leaving soon. My friend has to get her little boy home."

"You're kidding. I thought you had some guy there."

"Oh, Tony."

Billy heard the name. His eyes brightened to awareness. Graham was still keeping his attention on Alicia, and Billy made a great effort to divert it—he said something that must have been highly controversial, because Graham turned his whole attention to arguing Billy down. Alicia winked at Billy. Tomorrow she'd tell him what a prince he was.

"I could meet you in half an hour or so," Alicia said softly into the phone. "At your place?"

"No," Tony said, surprising her. "Haymarket. Right by the flower market near Faneuil Hall, you know it? It's open late. You can't miss me."

"But I do."

"What?"

"Nothing. Half an hour, forty-five minutes at most, okay?"

"If you're later than eleven, I won't be there."

"Now, just a minute—"

But Tony had hung up.

"Sorry," she said to her guests. "I guess I'm going to have to throw you out into the cold. I . . . I have to do something for a friend. A sort of emergency."

Harriet came out of the bedroom with a sleepy Joshua flopped over her shoulder. Everyone accepted her story with equanimity. Graham looked concerned.

Billy whispered, "I told you that you weren't supposed to care."

"But I do," Alicia said. "I've got to meet him."

156

"I know the feeling," Billy said, as Graham edged his way between them, making it clear he had something to say to her privately. Billy retreated graciously, and joined the others in a flurry of going-home activity.

"Will you be long?" Graham asked her. "What sort of emergency? Medical?"

"Emotional," Alicia said dryly. "I may have to stay overnight."

"Now, Alicia, you can't go running off. Is there something I can do? I'd be glad to come with you." She couldn't tell if he was trying genuinely to be helpful or was trying to find out where she was going.

"It's Jennifer Newman, you don't know her," Alicia said. "I'll be fine. And you have a good trip to Texas."

It had been a mistake to have him.

Graham retreated at that, not graciously. Alicia looked at her watch. The minutes were slipping away.

"Good night," Billy said loudly, and managed to herd them out the door. Graham, frowning, still wanted the last word with her. Harriet got it.

"It's not Jennifer Newman," she said. "She doesn't have emergencies, she's too smart. Is it Jerry?"

Alicia, in the many years they'd been friends, had never lied to Harriet. The channels of intimacy between them had always been open. So it was with a pang of guilt that she half-nodded, not quite saying yes, not quite denying it. She simply couldn't let Harriet in on Tony, not yet, and Tony, in the end, might evaporate, so tentative was his involvement in her life.

"I get you." Harriet smiled knowingly. "You're not saying."

Alicia was determined to use Jerry again in the future if the need arose. One hand does indeed wash the other. Her guests were finally gone. Alicia changed quickly. She hoped Graham wouldn't do something out of character like follow her.

Traffic at nearly 10:30 was light, but it seemed to take her forever to get around the Public Garden on Boylston and Charles, up Beacon Street and down the other side of the Hill to Government Center. She parked in the first space she found near the massive new City Hall. It would save her time to walk across the City Hall plaza and down

157

the steps on the other side to Faneuil Hall and Quincy Market.

The preservation of the old market district that centered on Faneuil Hall where patriots had met in Revolutionary days had been a success. Quincy Market had been built from an old warehouse and had become a long arcade of shops and cafés that attracted local residents and tourists day and night. The flower market, outdoors, with the coming of Easter and spring was busy late into the night. Pyramids of pink, crimson, and white azaleas glowed in heated, glassed-in greenhouses. Rows of Easter lilies still in bud lined the borders of the market area. A few people strolled through the greenery.

Alicia scanned the market from the back steps of City Hall, but she couldn't see Tony. She descended the stairs and crossed the cobblestone square with a sinking heart. He hadn't waited. It was another tease, and he was very good at that. Why had he bothered to call? Why had she agreed to meet him? Why hadn't she listened to Billy and worked on trying to reestablish with Graham the kind of relationship they'd had when they first started to see each other? Then he had been lonely and vulnerable, coming out of a couple of years of mourning for his wife and trying to deal with his two sons. That had softened her up: that and the fact that he was so much like Gardner in so many ways, the Gardner she had fallen in love with those many years ago. The problems came as she saw Graham as more and more like the Gardner she had finally fallen out of love with.

And now there was Tony. Or rather, there was no Tony. Nowhere in the whole market area.

I will be philosophical about this, she thought. I can withdraw with dignity. Stood up, and he can go to hell. She could go home and call Billy, and they would have a laugh about it, and he would tell her she should have listened to him in the first place.

Across from the flower market, where some of the old Haymarket buildings were being torn down, she saw what she thought was her worst fantasy come true. But it couldn't be Mike Tedesco. When she tried to fix on the man that seemed to look like him, she couldn't pick him out of the shadows. Her mind playing tricks. Then Tony emerged from one of the greenhouses, with a too-wise smile on his

158

face. A short, dark-haired woman followed him, looking anxiously from Tony to Alicia.

"You giving up on Tony so fast?" He pulled the woman forward and pushed her toward Alicia. "Meet Lina Davio. She was like a mamma to me when I was growing up."

Lina bobbed her head, smiling broadly. She was middle-aged and plump, and wearing a beat-up jacket and boots.

"She works here," Tony said.

"He's a good boy," Lina said. "A real nice boy."

"I think so too," Alicia said. "Sometimes."

She met Tony's eyes. And knew that he had been watching her all the time, coming down the steps, walking across the square, looking for him. He was pleased that she wanted to find him, that she had been disappointed when she had not.

She shook her head as if to say, "You bastard, I know your game."

"We got to move along, Lina," Tony said. He put his arm around Lina's shoulders and gave her a squeeze. Lina beamed up at him.

"Such an artist, Tony is," she said. "I always thought he should have been an artist instead of a dancer, if he wasn't going to go into business with his uncle Angie." Lina was examining Alicia covertly while she talked, sizing her up. "You ever seen him dance?" Alicia nodded. "Why he wants to waste his life working in a place like that."

Lina shrugged eloquently. "A stubborn boy, don't listen to anybody."

"I like my work," Tony said. He seemed embarrassed by Lina's comments.

"Some work." Lina obviously adored him. She murmured something in Italian to him, and Tony laughed. The hard, assured quality in him softened, and he looked young and lovable.

"You have Tony bring you around sometime for good Italian cooking," she said. "I move to a new house, out of town, in the spring. Take care of my boy, now."

Alicia looked at Tony standing beside the plump little woman who was gazing up at him as though he were the only and best man in the world. The lights of the market made him look the way he did onstage. So handsome that Alicia's heart leapt at the very sight of him. She wondered if the longing she felt for him, the need to be able to reach out and touch him to reassure her that he was real, meant she was truly falling in love, not with a sexual experience but with him.

"*Ciao, caro,*" Lina said, behind them. "Come back to me soon." There was yearning adoration in her voice.

Lina loved Tony, too.

18

Instead of heading for one of the small bars in Quincy Market, as she assumed they would, Tony moved her along toward Haymarket itself, the old produce market. In midweek, late at night, the streets that circled the cluster of buildings housing butchers and cheese stores and a few eating places were empty. Here and there in the light of the streetlamps, Alicia could see wooden frames of stalls and piles of empty cartons.

The area was alive only on Friday nights and Saturdays, when the sidewalks and roads were filled with people, buying, selling, and the rickety stands were transformed into an open-air produce market. The butchers opened their shutters and stood in the doorways to lure customers with promises of extraordinary bargains. Sidewalk entrepreneurs sold grilled sausages and cartons of cold shrimp and hot sauce. Alicia remembered that there was a shop, barely a room, where passersby could buy great wedges of pizza. The contrast between the market alive and crowded and this night was startling.

"Why are we here?" Alicia said. "It's strange at night with nobody around." She was uncomfortable passing the silent ruins left by demolition and reconstruction, and she expected to come upon Mike around every corner.

"It's home," Tony said. "The low-rent district."

They passed the old Union Oyster House, shabby, tilted buildings that had existed since colonial days.

"Home," he said, waving across toward the elevated ramps of the expressway, toward the Italian North End. "Just like every mick in Boston calls Southie home, whether they were born in South Boston or not."

Tony stopped at a corner, surrounded by the empty tables and frameworks of fruit stands.

"I got an uncle in a lot of businesses, one of 'em is wholesale produce. Romantic, huh? We had a stand right here on this corner, selling off the surplus. I hear Mamma still keeps it going, with my kid brothers."

"Don't you know?"

"I ain't seen my mother in a few years," he said shortly. "My old man died. He was worn out from working at shit jobs and beatin' up on his kids. Five of us altogether."

"Why—what split you up from your family?"

"My ma didn't like the line of work I got into. Other things. She always liked the two girls, and the other two boys. Never had much time for me, I was in the middle."

He surveyed the corner with his hands on his hips.

"Man, when I was about thirteen, fourteen, I used to come out here on Saturday mornings, and I used to *sell*. I ran that stand like General Motors. These ladies, I swear they used to come here to buy just to see me. They loved me, like they wanted to scoop me up and take me home. And they used to give me tips—can you imagine that? Tips for a kid selling tomatoes and eggplant. All of 'em did it. Old black ladies from Roxbury, they all came to do their shopping here, and didn't they love to hear me talking sweet to them and telling jokes. And the ladies from Beacon Hill, students, young girls, even tourists. They all loved Tony, like I was the star of Haymarket."

He looked around, seeing something Alicia couldn't, hot summer mornings maybe, with the crowds so dense they could scarcely move along the sidewalks with their brown shopping bags overflowing with the day's purchases. All of them stopping to buy from little Tony Spinelli with his big brown eyes and his wisecracks.

"I ain't ever going back to that kind of life," he said. "Anybody can sell rotten eggplants. Only Tony can sell . . . Tony."

He guided her toward the dark spaces under the expressway ramps where a few cars were parked, toward the bright lights of Hanover Street, the Main Street of the North End.

"Were you poor?" It sounded to Alicia like a typical poor boy's story.

"The Spinellis? Naw. Not real rich, but we did all right. He worked hard, he was from Naples, you know. But my old lady, she's *romana*, a Roman. Thinks she's a princess, took a step down marrying my father. Always looked down on him. Me, too. She said I was just like him."

They made the dangerous crossing through traffic funneling onto the expressway, and paused at the end of Hanover Street.

"Where are we going?" Alicia asked.

"Just looking, sweetheart. This is Tony, the one that used to be, where I used to be."

"Who's Lina?"

"Ah . . ." He made a very Italian gesture. She interpreted it as "Never mind." They walked past restaurants, pastry shops, cafés with crowds of men talking, gesturing. Pharmacies, shops with windows crammed with plaster saints and lamps with multicolored decorations, pots and pans for purposes hard to imagine.

"She took me in like a mother," he said suddenly. "Lina. I was about sixteen, right? I was going to school still, running with the boys. I had a lot of girls crazy for me, but strict families. My mother's sister came to live with us, a lot younger than Mamma, but older than me. A good-looking dame, and she thought I was something." He nodded at the memory. "Yeah, good-looking and wild. She got me into bed, see, and she thought she had something she could hold onto, me a kid and all. But I was . . ." He laughed. "It was some sort of experience for me, I can tell you, but I thought I was in love with this pretty little girl at school, what the hell was her name. Laura Petrocelli. I used to pray she'd be at the same Mass I was at, my old lady made all of us go to nine o'clock. And there were some other girls. I was young. I didn't know how lousy women can be."

"I'm not."

"Not yet. Anyhow, Auntie Marie wanted me all to herself, no Laura Petrocellis. So she tells Mamma that I attacked her, she couldn't help herself, I was a bad, bad boy. My mother shut the door on me then, and never heard my side. How do you like that? So Lina took me in."

"She said you were an artist."

"Oh, yeah. I like to draw, the outfits I could wear for my act, only Lina always thought I was some kind of

163

genius." He looked down at Alicia. "Don't go thinking I'm some kind of genius nobody ever discovered. I'm not—it's only what Lina wants to think."

"Curious," Alicia said.

"Me?" Tony bristled.

"No, a curious story, not you. How did you get to be . . . what you are? I mean, how did you pick stripping?"

"I dunno. Teresa was married, living in Brooklyn then, and I spent time with her, in spite of Leo. I used to go up, hang around Time Square. But if you're from there, from some Brooklyn gang or something, it's one thing. If you're not, you're just another out-of-town guy, so I came home to Boston. I seen enough dames stripping to know what it was. Teresa, she pushed me into taking dancing lessons, for a while, so when the Carousel started, I got into it. Sid I knew already, I went around with this Denise, from his place in the Combat Zone. Now I practice a lot."

"I bet you do," Alicia said. "With Denise?"

"Jealous, like I said. Never mind about Denise."

"I take ballet class, you know," Alicia said.

"That's why you're in good shape." He looked at her out of the corner of his eye. "For everything. Think you could teach me anything I don't know?" She didn't have a chance to answer. "Let's stop for something. Cappuccino? Canolli?"

He turned abruptly into the Paradise Café through a cluster of men who looked her up and down. Only a few blocks away, the spire of the Old North Church, where Paul Revere had looked for lighted lanterns, poked its white steeple up above the accents of Sicily and Naples.

"Tony, *paisano* . . ." There was a murmur of greetings.

He sat her down at a small, round marble-topped table. Someone came with a coffee and a pastry, and Tony disappeared into the circle of men.

A small, skinny man came up to her table and spoke to her in Italian. She half-understood—he thought she was a pretty lady, why was she sitting alone? She shook her head. He went away. She caught sight once of Tony, but he was absorbed in the talk. She couldn't make him look toward her.

Alicia concentrated on drinking her coffee and eating the pastry she didn't want very, very slowly, to make them last as long as possible.

She was furious.

The skinny man brought her ice cream.

"Gelato," he said eagerly. He had few teeth and a dusty air about him.

"No, grazie," she said carefully.

"Ma, Tony . . ." He gestured toward Tony, who raised his hand to her in a half-wave.

"Tony?" She pointed to him and the ice cream. The little man understood and nodded vigorously.

"Sì, signora," he said. *"Che bella signora . . ."*

She shook her head. The man hung about for a time while she concentrated on eating the ice cream. She wondered what would come from Tony the next time.

The next time, it was Tony himself.

"Ti piace?" he said, sitting down. "You like it?"

"Very nice," she said. "Thank you." She looked at him, and was touched by the way he seemed to be asking for her approval.

"Next time we come here, I'll have you meet some of the guys."

"Why not now?" She didn't care about meeting people, but she was curious.

"I . . . well, I wanted to show you off a little, but they don't have too much to say, not to somebody like you."

"You do; why not them?"

"They're different, they can't see farther than their noses. They got no . . . vision."

She laughed in spite of herself.

"Stuck-up bitch," he said, but pleasantly.

"What next, Tony?"

"I'm beat," he said. "I rehearsed and I went to work, and tomorrow I rehearse and I work and I do three shows at the club. Let's go home."

"My home or yours?"

"You women, you're too much. You can't get enough of a good thing."

"I was teasing. You know about teasing, don't you?" But she was disappointed. She wondered if she would spend the rest of her relationship with Tony desiring him desperately, wherever they were, whatever the circumstances. It put certain restrictions on their relationship as far as she was concerned.

"I didn't drive," he said. "You got your car?"

"Near Government Center."

"We'll snag a cab to your car, you can drop me."

She stared at the table, the empty ice cream dish.

"Hey, Ali, don't look so glum. I got to treat this body right. It supports me."

"Yeah. Sure. Only . . ." She could scarcely bring herself to blurt out what she was feeling. He wouldn't understand, or he wouldn't want to. Not Tony Spinelli.

"Only what? You can tell me." He spoke softly, almost into her ear. He was so close she wanted closer still, to slip her hand under his shirt and feel his heart beating in his chest. . . .

"When you leave me, I won't know if you'll be gone for a while or for good." She was almost ashamed of her desire.

"I called you tonight," he said, and stood up. She followed quietly, while the men at the café watched them.

When they got to her car, he said suddenly, "Can I see your place? I want to see where you live."

"Sure, except there's dirty dishes and leftovers."

She didn't care, as long as she could keep him with her. She parked in her alley, and they walked around to the front, arm in arm. She wanted to take him in through the elegant foyer.

"Not bad." He was looking it over carefully. It was so different from his place. Alicia tried to look at her home through eyes like Tony's, and was impressed with her own restraint and elegance. He strolled around the living room.

"A lot of books," he said. "What you'd expect from a professor." He walked over to the tall front windows and pulled back the drape. "I could get used to this." He studied the street in front of the building. "Alicia, you got a jealous boyfriend?"

"What do you mean?" She rushed to his side. Could Graham have stayed around to see what she was up to? There was a man standing a short way down from her building looking up at her windows. It wasn't Graham certainly. The suspicion that it was Mike Tedesco she suppressed. She made Tony drop the drape. "Nobody I know." She hoped she sounded convincing. Tony flopped down on the sofa, the man outside forgotten.

"Yeah, I like this place," he said.

"You ought to see Billy's apartment. Two floors in an old house on Beacon Hill. Mount Vernon Street. Garden, too."

"I wanted to ask you something," Tony said, "you and the doc. Like to come to the Carousel soon? I got a couple of surprises."

"For me *and* Billy?"

"I got a new act. Real Vegas stuff. If it goes over—who knows?"

"I'm *sure* Billy will love it."

"Don't turn into a sarcastic bitch," he said. "You have that tendency. I want you two to see the act. And I got something else for the doc." He stood up.

"I'll ask him." Alicia walked over to Tony and put her arm through his. "I'll come, Tony, even if Billy can't."

She was resigned to having him slip away from her until Saturday. He was restless, unwilling to stay.

"Great. Ten o'clock show. We'll have to sneak Billy in —no guys until the late show. Tell the kid in the main room you're my guests, he'll send you around to the side."

"Have you been planning this all along?"

"I've been thinking about it, want a sneak preview now?"

"Save it for Saturday," Alicia said. "I really am too tired. . . ." She wouldn't risk another rejection, although she wanted to keep him there with her, to be held by him through the night. Would they ever come to that? Permanency was a frightening, impossible idea.

Tony detached himself from her and prowled around the living room. Then he went into the bedroom while she peeked out the window again. The man had gone. Certainly not Mike.

"Hey!" he called.

She followed him into the bedroom. She loved her bedroom. Not fluffy and feminine, but so comfortable. A green velvet chair with a footstool, a big double bed, dark blue walls. Since little light came in the one window onto the alley, she'd made it a dark, cozy nest.

Tony put his arms around her.

"I like your style," he said.

He kissed her.

"I like everything, Alicia."

"Thanks."

"I got to ask, though . . . how do you do it without mirrors?"

She tried to suppress her laugh when she saw he was absolutely serious. And hurt. Because she'd laughed?

"I've got to go," he said, and headed toward the living room.

"Tony." He stopped at the bedroom door without turning. She was desperate to make it right, narrow the gulf that had opened up between them in an instant.

"I didn't know about mirrors until I met this stripper," she said. "He has this great body, and he's a terrific dancer, and he's been showing me a thing or two about a few things. But I haven't had a chance to get to the mirror store yet."

"Okay," he said. "Have your joke." His good humor was restored.

"Come here," she said. He was startled by the commanding note in her voice and went back to her. "Hey, it works as well for me as it does for you. Now, Tony Spinelli," she said as she started to unbutton his shirt, "I don't care how tired you are, if you think I'm going to let you out of this house tonight . . ."

"You trying to make that boyfriend jealous after all?" he said. Then he held her face in his two hands and looked searchingly into her eyes. "Or are you maybe in love with Tony? The lousy Italian stripper who doesn't know anything except how to take off his clothes?"

"You know a lot more than that, Tony," she said. "More than I knew existed. And you know perfectly well I'm in love with you." She tried to make it sound offhanded.

"Yeah," he said softly. "I do that to women. But you're something else, Ali." He put his arms around her and pulled her close to his chest. "I got to ask you about something, though."

"Hmm?" He could ask for anything, as far as she was concerned.

"How *do* you do it without mirrors?"

"I'll show you," she said.

"You'll show *me?* That'll be the day."

They fell into a perfect embrace, suddenly overcome with breathless passion. There was no time for the refinements of a slow strip. They tossed aside garments in their haste and need for each other, and when Tony clasped her to him, she was trembling with the intensity of her response. More than she had ever felt, even with Tony. He was speaking her name, as if the words could bind her closer than the union of their bodies.

It seemed to Alicia that her life had begun anew that night, which had started with doubts and a sense of loss, and ended in quiet joy and the peace of expectations fulfilled as Tony went home through silent streets.

She would see him again on Saturday.

She would not think about how long their relationship would or could last. About the fact that he was so much younger, uneducated, different by worlds from her friends and colleagues. About the profession he worked at, if indeed stripping could be called a profession.

Alicia put all those misgivings aside, because all that mattered was that she was happy, and the source of her happiness was Tony. Instead, she ordered a full-length mirror from Jordan Marsh as soon as the store opened on Friday morning and resolutely forgot that she wasn't a woman who slipped easily into a double life.

She wished she could as readily forget her promise to Timmy, but it was not fair to betray his trust simply because her own life had been altered by her emotional entanglements.

When she called Weston on Friday, Graham had already departed for the Dallas medical meetings.

"I promised to take Timmy to the Science Museum tomorrow," she said to Mrs. Parker.

"Indeed?" Mrs. Parker's voice over the line sounded hollow and surprised. "Did Graham know about this?"

"I mentioned it, I believe," Alicia said. "If it's all right with you, I'll come out to Weston about eleven to pick him up, and have him home by late afternoon."

Time enough to get ready for the Carousel. Billy had agreed to come with her.

"Certainly it's all right with me," Mrs. Parker said. "Timmy is so fond of you. I do hope we'll be seeing more of you when Graham gets back from Texas."

"Oh, I hope so too," Alicia said mendaciously.

When Saturday arrived, Alicia concentrated on Timmy, but Tony and the night ahead was never far from her thoughts. They went, by Timmy's choice, to the top of the Prudential Building for lunch, and he gazed down fascinated at the toy streets lined with tiny trees, and the curving bands of highway radiating out of the city. On one of those streets, Tony lived; on the edge of one of the highways was the Carousel Club.

They saw everything at the Science Museum. Twice.

"It's better coming with you, Alicia," Timmy said contentedly. "Not so regi . . . registered?"

"Regimented."

"Yeah. And the kids had to *bring* lunch. It must be a million floors up to that restaurant."

"Not quite." She was amused by his excitement over everything they saw and did.

"Wait till I tell my brother; he'll be jealous."

"Don't rub it in. He won't let you get away with it."

"You're almost like a mom, Alicia."

Don't rub that in either, she thought, and drove him around by the Boston Garden to show him where the Bruins and the Celtics played. In the maze of streets around the Garden, she missed a turn and found herself heading toward the North End, through the crowded streets where she and Tony had walked two days before.

It looked shabbier in the daylight.

Timmy stared wide-eyed at the children and men and women overflowing the sidewalks, loaded down with shopping bags and baskets, gesturing and laughing. It was Old World and foreign to both Alicia and Timmy, bred and raised in spaciousness and comfort.

She was almost relieved when they reached the end of Hanover Street and she was able to get onto the Expressway that would take them to the Massachusetts Turnpike and Weston.

"I had a swell time," Timmy said.

"So did I, Tim," Alicia said.

She knew that the two halves of a double life didn't always fit together well. She knew that the half Timmy belonged to was the one she would sacrifice.

For Tony.

19

TONY got to the Carousel early on Saturday night.
His new costume took a lot of preparation, that was his
excuse to himself, but in reality, he was too restless to stay
in his apartment, too restless to seek out the friends he
played cards with or wasted hours with in idle conversation.
He stopped for a while at a truckers' bar on the fringes of
Chinatown where he liked to shoot the breeze with men
coming into Boston from distant points across the country.
It was mostly empty; the truckers got there in the middle
of the night. He moved on to the club.

He hated to admit it, but his unrest had to do partly with
Alicia Sears, as much as with his new act. He figured she
and Billy could probably do him some good with their connections, but more, he wanted her approval, and he wasn't
comfortable having a woman exert that kind of power over
him. In spite of himself, he was entangled with her. He
wasn't sure how it had happened. He could drop her in a
minute, of course, if she got too attached to him, but these
smart dames were as easy to run as any of the others he'd
known. He could manage her; there was no chance that
she'd start to run him.

He wondered how Teresa would like her if they ever got
together. Lina seemed to think she was okay, but Lina
thought anybody who liked Tony was a saint.

The doc was something else. Tony had lined up a way
of showing his appreciation for getting him through that

goddamned lunch at the Ritz with all the snobs looking through him as if he wasn't there. If he really had important connections—and those guys always did—and Alicia was around to push it along for Tony's sake, he might just get his break.

Barbara was standing outside the closed door of Sid's office looking glum when Tony turned up. She dropped her cigarette on the floor and ground it out viciously with the heel of her white boot.

"Heard the news?" she asked.

"What happened? Irv run away from home, I hope?"

Barbara sighed and shook her head. She was as tall as Tony, the only woman he knew who could look him in the eye. "Jeff," she said. "Sid canned him. He found out about the hustling. Jesus, that kid's okay, not the brightest bulb in the lamp, but a sweetheart."

"Come on, Barb. Sid made the rule, but he's got to know Jeff's no angel."

Barbara frowned. "Somebody made an issue of it. Actually I know it was Irv who did the telling. He did it at the top of his lungs; I thought he was going to have a stroke. Sid didn't say much. But Irv—you'd have thought somebody raped his mother. The man's a fool or worse. I don't like to be in a room with him."

"I don't like anything about him. I had a cousin like him, ran over his girl with a car, he got so mad. A little prick, wanted to be a big man. Who told Irv about Jeff?"

"Don't ask me," Barbara said. "But there's a lot of new guys around, looking out for themselves. You know."

"Like Tito, you mean."

Barbara shrugged. "I'm not saying it's so, but . . ."

"Pushy little bastard. I saw his act from out front the other day. Not bad; not as good as he thinks he is."

"He's tight with Irv, and I couldn't tell you why. Nobody else in the world is, except Sid, and he's got the perfect excuse. You don't dump your family."

"Hah!" Tony said. "Don't you believe it. Look, Barb, there's a lot of rumors goin' around this place." He told her about the drug story somebody handed Sid. "It came from Tito, it had to."

"Aw, shit," Barbara said. "That's all we need."

"I don't like that Tito," he said. "For a lot of reasons."

Barbara jerked her head toward the door. "He's in there

with Sid right now. Sid told me to hang around to get the new lineup of acts for tonight."

"New?" Tony shifted the bundle containing his new costume from one arm to the other. "That fucker'd better not try moving up into my spot. Barbara honey, I got a new act, wait till you see it. Real Vegas material."

Barbara gave him a wry smile. "You two-bit turkeys and your big-time dreams. All you know how to do is wave your prick around in time to music, and you think you're a star, for Chrissake. Thank God, my boys like the simple things of life."

"Like tearing telephone books in half with their teeth . . ."

"Or beating up on loud-mouthed dagos." Barbara looked at Tony with something like affection. Tony smiled back. He regretted that he'd never made it with Barbara, even though she must be somewhere in her forties, but she'd made it clear she stuck with her husband, who crisscrossed the country in an eighteen-wheeler and would cheerfully demolish anybody who messed with her.

"Good luck, kid," she said. "Give me a rundown on the act before you go on, and I'll talk it up for all those hungry dames in the audience."

The door to Sid's office swung open and Tito came out with a self-satisfied grin on his pretty face. Sid was right behind him, looking serious. He handed Barbara a scrap of paper with a penciled list, and she started down the hall to the cubbyhole she used as her dressing room.

"Tony, baby!" Tito was pleased with himself.

Tony looked at him with distaste.

"Tony," Sid said, "Tito's moving up into Jeff's spot, one of the new guys will do the opening."

Barbara shook her head, as if to say, "I told you so," before she disappeared around the corner.

"Moving up fast, Tito," Tony said.

"Worrying about the competition, Spinelli?" Tito said.

"It's not the competition that bothers me, it's the smell."

Tito's expression turned ugly. "You ain't talking about me, I hope."

Tony glanced at the impassive Sid and back to Tito.

"You know I am," he said. He put his costume down carefully on the flaking radiator next to the office door and walked over to Tito. "Want to discuss it?"

Tony was a couple of inches taller than the other stripper, but Tito was muscular and quick. Dangerous.

Tony spoke softly. "I don't like the smell, Tito. There's a real stink to a man who uses what he knows about a guy to kick him in the nuts."

Tito bunched his hands into fists at his sides, and took a step toward Tony.

"Or even what he doesn't know," Tony added, watching Tito's movements warily. "It's not hard to figure out who's been ratting on people standing in the way. It ain't my job to worry about poor dumb fuckers like Jeff or anybody else, but I start worrying about me when the slime starts to collect."

"Okay, you two," Sid said, and stepped between them. He put a hand on each of their chests and shoved them apart. "Get lost, Tito."

Tito started to say something, but Sid stared him down coldly. He turned on his heel and headed for the strippers' dressing room.

Sid turned his cold look on Tony.

"You knew about Jeff," he said.

"Hey, Sid. It's no big thing. So he makes a few bucks from broads. We all got to live."

"It's more than that," Sid said stubbornly. "He's a hustler. I ain't going to have this place get known for that. Some of the other strip places with guys, it's a different story. Not here. I had to get rid of him."

"Christ, Sid. It's like kicking a big blond puppy."

Sid didn't look like he was softening any, but he sighed. "Irv made an issue of it. What could I do?"

Tony held back on offering his opinion of Irv.

"I been trying to keep Irv straight since we were kids. Those fucking nags . . . and the man couldn't win a poker hand if he had five aces. I know you couldn't say anything about Jeff," he said. "Or the rest of the boys that know him, Raoul and the niggers."

"Yeah, man. Except, I wouldn't trust that little . . ."

"I know, I know." Sid looked dejected. "I thought when I got rid of girls, I got rid of all my problems. I guess bare asses mean trouble whenever. You ain't going to stir up my ulcer none, are you, Spinelli?"

"Not me. Besides, I got a new act for tonight."

"New act? Do we need a new act?"

"You will when you see it. And I got a couple of people

174

coming to see it, a woman of mine and this guy . . . my doctor. You think I can fix them up with a couple of chairs in the wings?"

"What the hell, why not? I ain't seen Denise for a long time."

"It's not Denise. It's a classy dame from one of the colleges. She's crazy about me."

"How does a dumb wop stripper get hooked up with a classy dame? I'll believe it when I see it. Okay, put 'em in the wings if you want. This once."

Sid went into his office, shaking his head and talking to himself. Tony's anger with Tito dissipated as he began to concentrate on his coming performance. He felt a familiar sexual excitement—like he was coming on to a new woman and she was going to be knocked out by what Tony Spinelli was showing her. The woman, the audience were going to love him. Alicia hadn't seen anything like it.

The dressing room was strangely subdued. The strippers were drifting in for the show, and giving Tito a wide berth. Word about Jeff had gotten around fast. Cain and Abel were dressing as far away from Tito as they could in the cramped room. The few new guys Sid had taken on didn't know what was happening, but sensed the undercurrent of hostility.

Raoul looked terrible. He'd been too fond of Jeff.

"You'll see Jeff around," Tony said. "And there are good things going to happen. Later."

"It makes me like . . . *homicida*. I like to kill. . . ." He trailed off with a string of Spanish words. Tony got the drift. Well, it wasn't as if they'd had anything real going.

Tony started to get ready for the show. Tito took the hint, got into his costume quickly, and left the room.

"Spinelli." Bob, one of the college-boy waiters, was standing at the dressing-room door. "I got a couple here, a man and a woman, who say they're supposed to ask for you."

"Jesus, is it that close to ten?"

"Nine-thirty. Barbara's getting ready to warm up the audience. What do you want me to do with those two?"

"Sid said it was okay to fix them up with chairs in the wings. Wait, I'll come with you, I got time."

Alicia and Billy were waiting in the hallway. Alicia glowed at the sight of Tony, and squeezed Billy's hand. Billy smiled. It was evident that Tony was equally pleased to see her.

175

"Glad you made it," Tony said. He didn't touch Alicia, but there was an almost visible electricity between them. "Bob will give you a couple of chairs offstage, do you mind? No men in the audience," he said to Billy apologetically. "It won't be too comfortable, but you can see it all, and Bob, their drinks are on me, okay?"

"Aren't you going to tell us about your act?" Alicia was stumbling for conversation.

"You'll like it, don't worry. And you're going to like what I have especially for you, Doc." He winked at Billy, who looked sidelong at Alicia and gave a tiny shrug.

"I hate surprises, Tony," she said.

"I don't believe that, lady. I never met a woman yet who didn't like surprises." Tony gave her a little shove in Bob's direction. "Sit. I gotta get into my costume." He was gone without a backward look.

The waiter unfolded two wooden chairs and set them down in the wings.

"It's the best I can do," he said. "I think you can see everything."

"It's fine," Alicia said. "Thank you so much."

"Can I get you something to drink, ma'am?" It sounded odd to hear polite prep-school words coming from a bare-chested boy wearing little more than bikinis.

"Scotch for both of us," Billy said. "No hurry."

"But I——" Alicia began and Billy stopped her. The waiter went away. "I wanted——"

"You don't need or want anything, Alicia. And calm down, you're beginning to make me nervous too."

"This is such an *awful* place, Billy. Do you think he'll do all right? It's so important. . . ." Billy hushed her again.

From the angle of their chairs, they could see dim figures in the audience and the haze of cigarette smoke hanging over the semi-darkened room. Barbara was onstage, joking with the audience. A man in black leather jacket, jeans, boots came up beside Alicia and Billy, and watched Barbara intently. He had a coarse face, but he moved his shoulders in time to the music. One of the strippers Alicia hadn't seen or didn't remember. The music thundered out, Barbara dashed offstage, and the stripper leaped into the spotlight. The women in the audience screamed.

"You aren't supposed to be here," Barbara said. Her silvery jumpsuit glistened in the light from the spots.

"Tony." Alicia was flustered by the confrontation. "He

176

said it was all right . . . his new act." Barbara looked doubtful.

Billy stood up. "I'm Dr. William Catlett, this is Alicia Sears." He turned on his most charming smile. "Mr. Spinelli invited us to watch from here."

"It's okay with me," she said. "I'm Barbara." She winked. "I keep the boys in line." She looked more closely at Alicia. "Don't I know you from somewhere?"

"I don't think so."

Barbara was sure now. "You've been to the Carousel before, out front. So Spinelli's picking up chicks from the audience, tsk tsk."

"It's not quite that way," Alicia said. "I mean, we're acquainted otherwise."

"Sure you are," Barbara said. She was smiling knowingly. "He's not a bad kid, don't get me wrong." To Billy, then. "Oh, sit down, Doctor William. Enjoy the show."

Barbara faded into the backstage shadows. The stripper had tossed aside his jacket and jeans and now wore very little. In a second, he had gone down into the audience and was lost from sight. Barbara came back with Raoul, in costume, ready to go. As he passed Billy, he glanced down and their eyes met. Then he walked over to the wings and watched the stripper grab his clothes from the stage and exit. The stripper pulled out the bills that had been tucked into his G-string and counted them greedily.

Barbara rubbed her hands and ran them through her red hair. "Okay, Raoul. Short intro for you, they're hot, don't need any patter." She slapped his ass and bounded out onstage. Raoul glanced back over his shoulder at Billy, then made his entrance.

Billy watched Raoul perform, his mouth slightly open, as if he were having a hard time breathing. Raoul seemed more seductive and alive than she remembered, and she realized with a jolt that the audience he was playing to in that blue spotlight wasn't the women, but Billy. Who leaned toward Alicia without taking his eyes off the now nearly stripped Raoul.

"That's the kind of surprise *I'd* like," he whispered.

Tony leaned down without warning between Billy and Alicia, a hand on each of their shoulders.

"Surprise, Doc," he said. "That's reserved for you."

"Do you mean what I think?" Billy watched Raoul.

"I thought you'd get along," Tony said. "You know, the

177

same . . . uh . . . interests, like." He walked around to Alicia's side, wearing a wicked grin. He had a robe on over his costume, and he'd outlined his eyes with a dark line and had highlighted his cheekbones. He looked strange and wild, like an animal, or a primitive hunter. Alicia found it exciting. It was exciting too when he rested his hand on the back of her neck, massaging it gently, possessively.

Raoul came offstage, out of breath, gleaming with sweat. He had a handful of bills which he used to fan himself.

"Doc, meet Raoul."

Billy stood up and put out his hand. They touched fingers. Alicia knew at once that each had found something he liked. How simple Billy's life was.

"We're going out on the town after the show," Tony said. "The four of us. I want to celebrate the act." Billy hesitated. "Don't worry, Doc. Raoul looks like a cheap spic stripper in this light, but he's the best."

"I am," Raoul said. He bowed to Alicia, who had no recollection of having a naked man behave to her in such a courtly manner. She thought she managed it well.

"Alicia, this is Raoul."

"*Señora,*" he said. He was not interested in her.

"I got to get around back for my entrance," Tony said. "You get acquainted." He went away, Bob came finally with their drinks, Raoul and Billy seemed to have drawn a transparent wall between themselves and her.

"Doc. Is that a name?"

"Doc is what I do, Raoul. . . ."

Raoul shivered. "I must change." He rubbed his arms. "They do not give us much heat." He turned to Alicia. "The *señora* is not cold?"

"No, not at all."

"But I am. And I stink of sweat and those women's hands. I come back . . . in time to see Tony's act, if I am quick." He glided away, moving for Billy's benefit.

"Whew," Billy said.

"What do you know?" Alicia said, "A double date."

"It'll be all right. I think."

They half-watched the next strippers, but Alicia found the sameness of them did not touch any emotional or erotic strings. She was convinced the frenzy of the women in the audience was aroused by the fact they were in the company of friends who both justified their presence and fed their excitement. There was certainly little stimulating about the

178

anonymous naked men, gyrating and thrusting, teasing and barely touching as they moved through the outstretched hands. How many real fantasies were being fulfilled, she wondered, by the touching of a thigh or a chest? The true fantasy fulfilled was, perhaps, being carried away to a mirrored room by Tony Spinelli and finding out he was more than you dreamed of. And he was hers.

Hers. Had she really allowed that word to surface in her mind?

Raoul, sleek and clean and dressed, put a folding chair down beside Billy, and rested his hand on Billy's thigh as he sat down in a gesture of immediate intimacy that startled her. The lights onstage were low as Barbara told the audience how lucky they were to be seeing the first public (hah-hah, they giggled obediently) performance of Tony's Las Vegas act.

Hers. The word came back. Native drums began to play softly but urgently in a complicated rhythm. The drums beat louder and more insistently, and the lights came up on Tony.

20

Tonight, Tony was a jungle hunter. Behind him, the lights played on the back curtain like tongues of flame, while the drums continued to beat out a primitive rhythm.

Alicia tensed. Too obscure; the audience needed something more obvious. He couldn't pull it off, she was sure.

The strip began much like all the others, although Tony moved more like a dancer, turning the hip-swinging, pelvis-thrusting movements into an intricately choreographed performance. She knew she was viewing him through the overlays of her personal, physical relationship with him; she was more responsive to him and at the same time, more critical.

The audience was reacting as they always did for Tony. The shadowy figures in the front rows reached out, the noise almost drowned out the drums.

As he dropped his clothing with practiced grace, Alicia saw that Tony appeared to be wearing a skintight, patterned leotard over most of his body.

The drumming stopped suddenly, and as suddenly, the voice of the audience dropped. In the silence, music began —not strippers' music but, to Alicia's shocked awareness, Debussy's "Afternoon of a Faun." Delicate, floating notes curled around the still figure of Tony, who was standing with his back to the audience. He was not, she saw, wearing a leotard after all. His body itself had been painted with swirls of color that made him look half-man, half-animal. As he turned to the music, his eyes glittered, and he was so convincing and arresting as a man-beast, the audience held its collective breath, fascinated by the faun who danced toward a climax and, as in the ballet, attempted to masturbate.

Alicia couldn't believe what she was seeing. She wondered when and where it would end.

The lights went out. A sigh escaped the audience. It hadn't been what they'd expected, but Tony had held them.

Then a string of tiny firefly lights flickered on in the darkness. They were attached with invisible wire to Tony's body, and they showed a perfect outline of his body, including two horns glowing on his head. Alicia glanced at Billy and Raoul. Raoul was enthralled; Billy, with his head tilted and his chin resting on his hand, wore a slight tight smile.

Unexpectedly, the music shifted to Ravel's "Bolero." It was almost too much for Alicia. Even Billy sighed, as he watched Tony's lighted figure, the electric faun with its penis erect and outlined in multicolored lights, move across the stage in time to the driving, monotonous, familiar music. Surely everyone would realize that this was too much of an interesting, if not good, thing. It was all wrong. It made Tony look ridiculous.

Alicia stood up.

Billy hissed at her to sit.

"I can't bear it," she whispered, and caught Raoul looking at her sternly.

She couldn't explain then and there what agonies she was suffering, the juxtaposition of Debussy and Ravel and a strip show with body lights. She gulped to catch her breath, and pushed her way past Billy and Raoul to get away from the stage. Behind her, she heard a thunderous cheer from the audience.

They had liked the act. Alicia felt drained with relief. She turned around to see Tony coming offstage. He had noticed she was gone from her chair. He went back onstage for another bow, and when he came off this time, she had returned to Billy's side. Tony barely looked at her. Raoul stood up. He swept Alicia with a poisonous look and followed Tony to the dressing room.

"Alicia dear, that was stupid of you," Billy said. "Your Tony didn't like it."

"It was too much, Billy. Debussy *and* Ravel *and* the lights. Maybe I'm being too sensitive. . . ."

"Whatever," Billy said gently. "We must assume that you hurt Tony's feelings by leaving. I'm sure Raoul will offer an opinion, as well."

"Don't lecture me, William Catlett." Alicia was righteously indignant that she had been misunderstood. "I was suffering for him."

"No need, though. It was an effective performance in its way. It certainly pleased the audience. Too bad you failed to share their enthusiasm."

"I did! Well, I was paying attention to different things."

"I bet you were," Billy said. "You can make it up to him. Use your womanly wiles, not that I have ever quite understood what a wile was."

Billy stood up and looked impatiently back into the shadows.

"Don't worry," she said. "Your new boyfriend will be back, after he's finished destroying my character for Tony." She instantly regretted the bitchy tone. Billy looked her up and down coolly.

"Tsk," he said. "Unworthy of you, Alicia, that naughty petulance. One can only hope Tony will beat it out of you."

"Why, Billy . . ." He patted her arm kindly. She couldn't be sure still whether Tony had been truly upset by her impulsive rush from the wings to spare herself further anxiety. She sensed that Billy was not wholly sympathetic tonight. Possibly because he was absorbed in contemplation of the gift of Raoul, and what it portended. Billy, she knew, saw a great many men, but she and he had tacitly agreed that there was no point in discussing his conquests, except in the most general terms. She was acquainted with one or two of his intimates, but she had never been out in this manner when Billy was newly smitten, as he apparently was tonight.

The object of his interest returned. Raoul headed straight for Billy, and she had to admit they made a fetching couple: the sleek Latin and the fair doctor.

"Tony will be here soon," Raoul said. "There is no late show tonight, I think there is some difficulty with the sound." He turned to Alicia. "I see you pay close attention to Tony's act, *señora*. But perhaps not close enough."

She was damned if she'd ask him what Tony had said

after leaving for the dressing room. Surely Billy had been overstating Tony's annoyance with her. But she remembered the expression on his face when he passed her.

"Tony is good, *señora*," Raoul was saying. She seemed to catch a subtle suggestion in his words that perhaps Tony was too good for Alicia.

Raoul guided Billy pointedly away from her, and the two men spoke together in an intimate undertone, out of her hearing. She thought fleetingly: Raoul doesn't like me because he thinks I didn't like the act. He doesn't like me because I'm a woman. He has already expressed his lack of liking to his friend Tony, who had needed only that to confirm his own displeasure.

She was suddenly gripped by an icy fear that she had alienated Tony beyond recall. She would not be able to explain her actions. He would refuse to understand.

I can live without his look and his touch, she thought. I don't need to arrange my life to go to bed with any man.

She felt as though she were fighting a lone battle against a stubborn adversary who had become the only man she wanted for a lover.

"Let's go," Tony said. He had joined them quietly, dressed in black and looking blacker than a storm cloud. He didn't meet Alicia's eyes, but walked toward the side door behind the stage that led to the parking lot.

Barbara was standing outside the door with her fur coat thrown over her shoulders.

"Great act, Tony," she said. "Loved it; so did the women. That asshole Irv said it was too smart for the Carousel, but Irv wouldn't know smart if it was wearing a sign. It was really great."

"Thanks, sweetheart," Tony said. "If you weren't such a mean old broad, I'd kiss you."

"And thanks for nothing, Spinelli," she said cheerfully. "By the way, it wouldn't surprise me if Irv or Tito screwed up the sound system so you wouldn't have a chance to do it all over again."

Alicia saw Tony tense.

"Hey, I was only kidding," Barbara said. "They don't have enough brains between them to think of that."

Tony relaxed. "You want a lift someplace?" he said. "Ah, this here's Billy Catlett and . . . uh . . . Mrs. Sears."

"We've met," Barbara said. "And no lift. Dennis, the

youngest kid, just got his license. He's picking me up if he hasn't totaled my heap. Aha! Here he is, first time he's ever been on time."

Barbara's "heap" was a gold Lincoln the size of a battleship. Behind the wheel was a freckled, red-haired teenager, who rolled down the electric window and grinned.

"How was the old lady's car?" Barbara said.

"Fan-fuckin'-tastic," Dennis said.

"Watch your language, kid. You're not at home." Barbara turned to the others. "It's not easy being a mother." She got into the passenger's side and Dennis roared out of the parking lot.

"Doc and Raoul are meeting us at this place we're going to," Tony said to Alicia.

Billy waved encouragingly to Alicia as he and Raoul went to his car. Tony headed across the lot to his car without waiting for her. She caught up and got in as he started the engine. They drove several silent miles along the highway toward Boston before he spoke.

"What was so fucking funny about my act?"

He kept his eyes on the road.

"Watch your language, kid," Alicia said, and immediately regretted her feeble attempt at humor. Tony glanced at her briefly, unamused. "Tony, I wasn't laughing."

"You got up and left. Didn't you like it? Wasn't it classy enough for a snob like you? Did you have a good laugh for yourself?" He was in a suppressed fury.

"It wasn't funny. I was nervous, and the idea of a ballet and a strip, Debussy and Ravel . . . I couldn't help it, it wasn't you."

"It was all me, out there. Nobody else was 'nervous.' They loved it. And I don't know about no Debussy. I saw this movie about some fag dancer, Nijinsky, but he did this thing, man and animal, it was like me, how I feel, and I knew I could put it over, and you've got to have, you know, sexy music to get those dames hot. It's a great number," he said fiercely. "No matter what you think."

Alicia couldn't see how she was going to reach across the big, deep gulf that had opened up between them. In a bed, maybe, if they were ever to end up in a bed again after tonight. But he cared so much what she thought, that was something. She had a thin thread of hope to buoy her.

184

"If they loved it in Boston," Tony was saying, "they'll love it in Vegas. I'll get an agent, you'll see. . . ."

He sounded like the kid who was going to grow up to show the class bully he couldn't mess around with Tony Spinelli.

"And I expect better treatment from my women."

Abject apology was the only possibility.

"I'm sorry, Tony. I loved your act. But it was like I was out there myself, that's how nervous I was. Forgive me?"

"What? Oh, sure." He wasn't totally convinced, but Alicia caught a glimpse of something that might have been the ghost of a satisfied smile.

It might have worked, the apology, she thought. How difficult he was. Unpredictable in her terms, unmanageable compared to someone like Graham. And entirely self-centered.

They went to a dim, crowded disco on a side street near Kenmore Square in Boston. Billy and Raoul parked two cars away and they all walked in together. There were the usual flashing lights and crowded dance floor, and disco music, with slow dances mixed in. The couples were various combinations of male and female, the age young, as befitted a city overburdened with institutions of higher learning. They found a tiny unoccupied table; Billy and Raoul joined the dancers. They seemed to be enchanted with each other.

"I'll be right back," Tony said. "Get yourself a drink."

He disappeared into the crowd. Raoul had tossed a pack of cigarettes on the table, and although Alicia seldom smoked, she fastened on them as a thing to do when one felt alone and out of place. She managed to get the attention of a bored waitress as she lit a cigarette.

"These tables are for more than one person," the waitress said belligerently.

"There are four of us. I'd like a beer."

"That's *all?*"

"For the moment." She tried to see past the waitress to the point where Tony had vanished.

"You aren't going to order for the others?" the waitress said. "It's a lot of trouble going back and forth with all these people."

"Just a beer." The waitress shrugged and went away.

Now Alicia could see the dancers, and catch glimpses of faces, hands, arms, as the lights flashed. She saw Tony once, before the crowd closed around him. He was dancing with a tall, dark-haired girl in a T-shirt and jeans, and he was smiling at her. She was smiling at him.

The music changed to a slow song. The dancers became couples. She caught sight of Tony. His arms were wrapped around the girl and they were dancing very close.

Alicia stubbed out her cigarette in the square cardboard ashtray and stood up. She hated Tony Spinelli.

"That'll be one seventy-five," the waitress said, slamming a beer bottle and glass on the table. Alicia sat down abruptly and fumbled for her handbag. Enraged at being drawn into adolescent jealousy situations by a—a— The waitress pocketed the two singles Alicia handed her and slouched away.

I can leave, she thought. I can walk home from here in fifteen minutes. I can find a cab in Kenmore Square. If I didn't have ten grant applications to finish before spring vacation, I could get on a plane and go home to Daddy in Boulder tomorrow. I could get on a plane and fly to the West Coast. To Hawaii. To Japan. I don't have to wait around to be humiliated by Tony Spinelli.

"You're not dancing, Al," Billy said. He looked serene and happy. "Great place, a bit young. I've heard about it, never been." He sat down.

Raoul, looking cool, Latin, and in charge, signaled gracefully, and the waitress was at his side.

"How ya doin'?" she asked.

"Excellent, señorita, as always. My friend and I will have . . . ?" He looked questioningly at Billy.

"Anything. Scotch, I guess. You okay, Alicia?"

"Fine. Super. Terrific. Happy as can be."

Raoul sat down. "And where is Tony?"

"Tony appears to be dancing," Alicia said.

"Not with you, however," Raoul said. He had a knowing look that Alicia didn't like. "There's a saying I learn here—boys will be boys?"

Billy read Alicia's annoyance and jumped in. "Raoul has some terribly interesting things to say about life in Argentina. . . ."

"I'll bet he has," Alicia said.

186

"Let's dance, Alicia," Billy said. "You don't mind, Raoul?"

"Not at all," he said.

"No," Alicia said. "I'm sure Raoul would prefer to have us listen to his tales of the pampas."

"Yes," Billy said firmly, taking her hand and pulling her to her feet.

The music was still slow, a sad, sweet song. An old Neil Diamond song from long past. Billy danced well, weaving them in and out among the other couples.

"Ow, you are in a foul mood," he said. "No need to take it out on Raoul, because you didn't settle things with Tony."

"I'd like to go home," she said icily. "I've had quite enough for one evening."

Suddenly, Billy had steered them to a spot beside Tony and his partner.

"Well, well," Billy said. The music abruptly changed to disco. He glided away from Alicia between Tony and the girl and danced away with her. Tony and Alicia faced each other while the dancers swirled around them.

"I'm going to kill you," Alicia said.

Tony looked at her through half-closed eyes. "And I'm going to fuck you tonight so you aren't going to remember you were going to kill me."

Alicia was overwhelmed by a sense of capitulation to his powerful presence. She surrendered to the reconciliation willingly. Indeed, as she stood there in the middle of the dance floor facing him, she experienced relief and release in knowing that he had instinctively manipulated her into submission, and she was glad.

"You bastard," she whispered. "You've been punishing me."

"Me?" Tony looked at her in mock surprise. The ghost smile of satisfaction flickered on his mouth. "Why would I do that?" He put his arms around her, and they danced slowly, to the much faster music. He kissed her ear, her eyes; he held her so close it seemed he commanded nothing to pull them apart.

"Who was that girl?" she murmured into his chest.

"Never saw her before. Not bad-looking, though. She was waiting around for action when I needed her."

Alicia leaned back in his arms and looked up into his eyes.

"I might kill her, too, if I see the two of you together again."

Tony laughed, pleased by her vehemence. "You're okay, Ali," he said. "Even if you're too goddamn smart for your own good."

They did not stay long at the disco. Billy and Raoul decided to go on to other places, and Alicia was impatient to leave the crowds and find the privacy of Tony's mirrored room, where the interfering world could not touch them.

Each experience with Tony was different, with new words and phrases in her expanding command of the language of the senses. Tonight, it was not gentle discovery or the shock of novelty. It was not desperate mutual passion. Tonight Tony was a demanding lover, as though he wanted to confirm his ascendancy over her, to deny that she had the power to hurt him. He made her feel young and helpless, desirable and desiring. It seemed there was nothing she could teach him, and she had no choice but to follow where he led.

"Strip," he said, disengaging himself from her arm around his waist. He kicked off his shoes and fell back on the bed. She made a move toward him.

"I can't, not without you. . . ."

In answer, he turned on the stereo and music poured into the room. She suddenly felt as shy as the first time, awkward and foolish. He fixed her with a look that permitted no denials.

So she stripped, allowing her inhibitions to fall away with her clothes, and feeling the rising sexual excitement overtake her. The naked Alicias in the mirrors moved around the man lying on the bed, watching her. Then Tony was on his feet in a strong graceful step, pulling off clothes even as he grasped her arm in an unbreakable grip. His expression recalled the half-man, half-animal she had seen onstage, primitive and frightening.

He had not spoken, did not speak as he pressed her down on the bed and forced himself on her. She tried to elude him, following some deep instinct that required ritual escape and pursuit. Tony pinned down her arms, and the face above hers before their bodies were joined was triumphant. Alicia's surrender to him was total, joyful. She knew she could go on forever, exactly this way, possessed by this man.

Later, after she had drifted into exhausted sleep, filled with content and still stirred to the depths of her physical self by the frenzy of their lovemaking, Tony nudged her in the ribs.

"Wake up," he said. There was a pale light in the room from recessed lamps above the mirrors.

"I wasn't asleep," she said drowsily, automatically. She struggled up through mists of sleep and remembered pleasure.

"You gonna spend your life denying what's really happening?" he said. "You were snoring."

"I was not. How awful. Really?"

"Really?" he mimicked. He pulled her close to him and she curled up in the curve of his hard, strong body. "You like your man," he said. It was not a question.

"Mmmm." She started to slip back into a doze, safe and protected with Tony's encircling arms.

He reached out and pressed a remote-control device beside the bed. A black-and-white picture flickered palely on the screen of the small television set on the night table. Ginger Rogers in satin and feathers was being swept across a bridge to a balcony on the arm of Fred Astaire.

"*Top Hat*," Alicia murmured. " 'Cheek to Cheek,' " and she hummed along as the fantasy seduction on the screen proceeded in decorous dance. "If you want to know what class is, it's them."

Tony sat on the edge of the bed, his back to Alicia. She could see his face reflected in the mirrors, totally absorbed in the film. He shut her out and studied Astaire in his black tails guiding a shimmering Rogers across the white floor, somewhere in a Hollywood-contrived Venice, to cinematic consummation.

"Tony . . ."

He patted her thigh abstractedly. "Go get me something to eat," he said. "Anything. There's stuff in the kitchen."

She didn't move. He looked around over his shoulder. "Well?"

She hesitated, then got up.

Indulge him, she thought. It's worth it. Then she had a sharp memory of a lifetime of various indulgences to please the men in her world.

But this is different, from this I'm getting something wonderful back. No uncertainties. Tony has defined our positions, and I have accepted them.

189

She looked at his powerful shoulders, his arms, the dark curls at the nape of his neck. The serious, brooding face, to her eyes a perfect face of surpassing beauty, seen in the mirrors as Tony concentrated on the dancers.

Hers.

21

ALICIA marked the night as the true beginning of her relationship with Tony. Her connection with him was no longer a matter of fantasies that might or might not come true; rather, it was the new reality of her life.

She was aware of the curious division that had taken place in a very short time. The routine of her work went on as before but it was detached from her association with Tony. At the same time, she seemed to be working harder and more efficiently. The lurking presence of Victor Ostrava, for example, no longer troubled her. She felt she could deal with him effectively when he again (and he would do so again) should press his demands. The spring trustees meeting a few weeks hence would undoubtedly inspire him to fresh onslaughts. Dean Barrow, however, would be less help than even before, but she was confident in her ability to outmaneuver Victor. The problem of the sheikhs' demands was, she knew, subject to intense discussion among various faculty members, and it appeared that academic integrity would triumph over the lure of mililons.

The one matter that puzzled her was the continual intrusion of Mike Tedesco. He no longer had the power to unsettle her as he once had, but he popped up in the most unlikely places, and she wondered if there actually were some truth to George's contention that he was on the lookout for an attachment that could bolster his ambitions, preposterous as it seemed.

191

There was no reason why Mike should not attend a late season Boston Celtics basketball game while the Celts were fighting hard for a place in the NBA playoffs. It happened to be a game Tony and Alicia went to themselves, caught up in citywide sports mania. The three of them came face to face in a crowded corridor, and before Alicia remembered Mike's connection with Debbie, she had introduced Tony. She hoped he would not mention Tony to Debbie, in whom she had not confided.

Mike looked Tony over carefully and then gave Alicia one of his gleaming smiles. There was knowledge behind it that gave Alicia pause. She realized she didn't trust him.

She forgot Mike in the mindless excitement of a Celtics win, with Tony hugging her, and the fans streaming onto the floor at game's end.

Breathless, they left the Boston Garden for a round of encounters with Tony's friends in the North End.

"I used to follow that team day to day," he said. "In the days of Bill Russell and Havlicek and Sam Jones," he said as he bustled her down a narrow street with shabby, dark buildings leaning in and shutting out the sky. "Me and this pal Gino Cantalupo, great guy, wait till you meet him, we used to go to a lot of games."

"How about Laura Petrocelli?" Alicia asked. "She go too?"

Tony stopped in the middle of the street and spun her around.

"How do you know about Laura?" He was completely taken aback.

Alicia laughed. "You told me, you turkey."

A big black Cadillac had edged down the street and blasted its horn at them. She and Tony jumped to the sidewalk, and the car squeezed past. The man driving leaned out, grinned and shouted, "Still chasing dames, Spinelli? Tell him no, lady, whatever he asks." The Cadillac kept moving.

"Just a guy I've known forever," Tony replied to her questioning look. "You know what we're going to do some night this week?"

"I don't dare imagine," Alicia said.

"We're going shopping. I'm going to buy you the sexiest dress you ever owned."

"Why?" The idea intrigued her.

"Because that's the way I like you to look." He took her

192

arm and they rounded the corner. A woman in a heavy coat, with her head down, met them. She looked up and Tony stopped in his tracks. She was thin, sad, tired, but her eyes flashed with . . . surprise? Anger? Alicia couldn't tell, nor could she understand the torrent of Italian that came from her mouth.

But she did understand Tony's stuttering response: *"Mamma . . . prego . . ."*

The woman glared at Alicia and then again at Tony and pushed past, disappearing around the corner they had just turned. Tony started walking fast.

"Your mother?" Alicia caught a glimpse of his stony face, and ached at the sight of hurt in his expression.

"Forget it," he said. "Nearly ten fucking years, and she's never forgotten anything. Not Marie, not what I do for a living. Nothing. And she doesn't forgive."

"Tony . . ."

"What?" he snapped. Then he looked down at her watching him anxiously, but he seemed not to be seeing her. "If I were famous, doing what I do, if I had money, then she'd forget fast enough. Women . . ."

Alicia was helpless to ease his bitterness.

They walked without speaking, and aimlessly. He seemed to have forgotten that they had been heading anywhere. It began to get dark, and they found themselves far from where they had begun in the North End. They had reached the waterfront, where the parks were empty, the shops closed, the lights on in the wharf buildings that had been turned into expensive apartments with boat slips at the front doors.

Tony leaned against the huge cement pilings joined by thick iron chains and stared down at the water that lapped the wall several feet below them.

Alicia took a deep breath.

"You know I love you," she said. "Maybe it doesn't mean anything to you, but it does to me."

"It means something, sweetheart," he said. "Let's go, it's getting cold."

Without him saying so, she knew that in his way, he loved her too.

Perhaps it's only for a little time, she thought in the nights when she stretched out under her own velvet comforter in her bedroom alone, when Tony was leading his separate life. I am the concentration of the admiration he craves, his necessary reflection, but he cares.

He bought her the dress he promised, making her try on a dozen before he saw the one he liked. It was dark red, a clinging, backless, bias-cut satin dress that she was almost afraid to put on.

"It's not *me*," she protested. "Where will I ever wear it?"

"You look beautiful," Tony said. "Great-looking ass in that dress. We buy it."

"No, Tony."

"Yes, Alicia. If it ain't 'you' now, it will be."

She thought that probably wasn't true, but she let him buy it, as he let her buy clothes for him from time to time, and listened to her reasons why some things were right and others were not. It was as though he were carefully examining the mysteries of her life and attitudes, while gently forcing her to absorb something of his. It was a symbiotic relationship, whose character was still very much determined by their continuing physical enjoyment of each other.

It's the kind of thing that goes away, she thought at other lonely times. It cannot last, but now we need each other.

She certainly needed him. She was content to lie around his place, making love in the mirrored room. She liked to have him sketch her or the two of them, naked and reflected from all sides.

"I wish I had one of those pictures," she said wistfully one night, as he tore up the sketches.

"You got me," he said. "You don't need pictures. I never did one good enough anyhow. I don't have the time."

Sometimes he let her watch him rehearse for the club, but now she never went to the Carousel to see him perform. She was jealous of sharing him with a hundred other women. She was increasingly impatient with his need to be onstage, and with the fact of his work as a male stripper.

"You don't need to do that, you know," she said. "You could do something else."

"I like my work, and I don't need a stuck-up dame with a big university job telling me what I can do."

"Don't speak to me in that tone," she said, and then had to give in and apologize for talking back to Tony. She did so because he expected it; she suspected that it would one day be less easy to do after her still growing ardor began to cool off.

194

"You got to know somebody," he said late one Sunday afternoon when she had walked over to his place at his command. He said he felt like sketching her, and he had posed her nude on the bed and concentrated on the sketch pad.

"Know who, for what?" she asked, but she thought she knew what he was getting at. "For your career as a stripper?"

He kept drawing.

"Billy knows more people than I do," she said.

"Doc says he hardly speaks to you nowadays," Tony said.

She sat up. "How do you know that?"

"I was over to his place with Raoul the other day," he said. "Nice pad he's got. Maybe it takes more than just knowing somebody."

"What else did Billy say?" Alicia had a nagging sense of guilt that she had so thoroughly separated herself from old friends. Harriet she spoke to rarely, claiming that she was frantically busy planning for the trustees meeting. Work in the past had occupied her to the exclusion of all else for brief periods; Harriet was understanding. She didn't even ask if Alicia had seen Jerry Godwin again. Maybe the Goulds had caught on to Jerry's tastes.

"He didn't say anything much," Tony said. "Get back the way I posed you. Good girl. This is gonna be a picture worth saving."

"Mmm. Is Billy seeing a lot of Raoul?"

"Lady, I don't mix myself up in other men's business. I got worries of my own. Tito, remember that kid? He's acting like he owns the Carousel. Irv's loonier than ever, and Sid's plain tired."

"I'm getting tired myself, kid," Alicia said.

"Jesus, listen to the old broad," Tony said to one of the multiple Tonys in the mirrors. "I ain't no kid."

"Come here," she said. "I don't like you so far away from me for so long."

Tony grinned at her. "You like telling me what to do, don't you?"

"Not half as much as you like telling me," she said.

But he put down the sketch pad and came to her.

The only flaw in her happiness was that guilt about her abandoned friends, that worry about the persistent Mike

Tedesco, the sense that Victor Ostrava had not withdrawn contentedly into his labs. Her future with Tony.

There are several flaws, she corrected herself. I am poised on a highly peculiar tightrope, and any way I fall means troubles I don't want to think about today. The good old Scarlett O'Hara philosophy comes to the rescue: I'll worry about it tomorrow.

"Tomorrow" was a Monday morning that put a tremor in the tightrope.

Debbie said, "Mike wants to make an appointment to see you."

"Mike *Tedesco?*" Alicia said stupidly.

"Yeah, Mike Tedesco."

Alicia couldn't tell if Debbie knew things she wasn't saying, but she was watching Alicia speculatively.

"Are you . . . uh . . . still seeing him?" Alicia asked.

Debbie pursed her lips, considering her answer. "I do, some," she said finally. "He said he's seen you around places. He's really not a bad guy, Alicia. Honest."

"I never thought he was."

"He works real hard, with his studies and—and for Dr. Ostrava. He spends an awful lot of time going places for Dr. Ostrava."

"I don't get you," Alicia said. "I thought he worked in the labs."

Debbie shrugged, but she seemed uncomfortable. "He's never really said what he does. But he gets paid a lot. Alicia," she blurted out. "Be careful."

Alicia was taken aback by the reversal of roles. Not so long before, she was warning Debbie to be careful.

"I'm always careful," Alicia said. She spent the morning finishing a major report for the trustees on projected grants for the coming year. She had not been able to bring herself to ask Debbie what she was referring to. She thought she knew: Mike had mentioned Tony Spinelli, and Debbie had understood right away that Alicia must be involved with him.

As if fate were reminding her that all seas were not forever smooth, Victor Ostrava turned up in the afternoon. He was jolly and expansive today.

"I thought I might invite you to dinner some evening," he said. "You must be terribly fatigued with planning the trustees meeting; what with the dean so preoccupied with

196

the unfortunate Mrs. Barrow, and Miss Morant, a fine woman but scarcely able to take on official burdens. . . ."

"I truly can't, Dr. Ostrava. I hope you understand."

"Surely you have time for relaxation, Mrs. Sears." He was both ingratiating and commanding. "A lovely young woman like you needs . . . friends."

"I think I must refuse," Alicia said. "Perhaps when I have less work."

"I encountered your friend Dr. Parker the other day," Victor said suddenly. "At the Bay Tower Room. I didn't recognize the young lady he was with. We did not speak, naturally, since he was obviously deeply engrossed in conversation."

Having conveyed the information that Graham had been out to dinner with another woman, Victor bowed his way out of her office, failing only to click his heels and kiss her hand.

She loathed him. She was thankful that at least he had no knowledge of her relationship with Tony Spinelli. She could not have borne the smirks.

Oh my God, she thought in a panic, as recollections of chance encounters and apparently random remarks rushed together.

Mike. Victor Ostrava. Alicia and Tony.

How dare he spy on me! she thought, and then tried to convince herself that she was being ridiculous. No one was that determined to get leverage in any way he could to influence the medical school's financial decisions. Her double life must be making her paranoid, but she decided to be even more discreet about Tony. Fortunately the spring break was coming up next week, and she would have a few days away from the office.

"Do you know what Mike wants to see me about?" Alicia asked Debbie before she left for the day.

"He didn't say."

"I don't know if I can fit him in before Friday," Alicia said.

She didn't want to see him at all, she realized, because of what he might have to discuss with her.

"Or after spring break," she said, hoping to put it off as long as possible.

"I'll tell him," Debbie said. "I talk to him almost every day."

And I see him almost every day, Alicia thought. I've got to get away from all this.

In the middle of the week, she contrived to fix up an errand in downtown Boston so she could stop at the hotel where Tony worked in the bar decorated like a ship's cabin —full of red and green signal lights, cute life preservers, buxom wooden figureheads.

The place was nearly empty, it being mid-afternoon. Tony was leaning on the bar, doodling on a napkin. He was pleased to see her, although she sensed he felt this job was farther beneath him than she believed stripping to be.

"What are you doing loose at this hour?" he asked.

"I had to deliver some papers, get a signature at the head office of the bank. And I wanted to see you."

"You saw me two days ago. You're too greedy," he said. He waved toward the gloom of the bar. "And you came at a bad time. It only gets interesting when the married guys who are screwing their secretaries sneak in at lunchtime to convince the girls they're really getting a divorce."

"It's always a good time to see you," she said. "You're so much nicer than anybody else I know."

"Is that so? What about all these friends of yours you're always telling me about?" He walked away to refill the glass of a lone patron at the far end of the bar. When he came back, he seemed detached and thoughtful.

"I wonder about this Harriet you mention. Your best friend, didn't you say? I don't recall shaking her hand. Or any of the others you hang out with."

"I only hang out with you," she said. "Is something bothering you today?"

"Nothing. I ain't getting anywhere, is all. This lousy job; I could die of boredom. Nothing's happening with my act. I'm getting tired of it all."

Good, she thought.

"Tony, could we go somewhere next week for a few days? Away from Boston? Could you leave this place for a couple of days?"

She'd been thinking about something like this for a long time. They had never had two whole days and nights together.

"Like where?"

"The Cape?" she asked tentatively. "The snow up north is bad, and you don't ski. . . ." She was thinking that they'd go skiing next winter, if they had a next winter together.

"You're crazy. It's too cold still for the beach."

"I didn't mean the beach. I meant the Cape, the country, no people. You and me. Walking on the dunes, all that ocean."

"Not my idea of fun."

"Please. It is fun."

"Why not?" he said. "Yeah. I've lived my whole life in Massachusetts, and I've never been to Cape Cod."

She left him feeling full of anticipation.

Only to come upon a cloud on her horizon.

When she saw Mike Tedesco studying an almost empty bank window across the street from the hotel, she knew that what she had suspected was true: whether for Victor Ostrava or for his own purposes, Mike was keeping track of her and Tony.

The distress was infuriating. The comfort was that she and Tony would be escaping from prying eyes for a couple of days. The latter was so inviting a prospect that she actually had a long, chatty conversation with Harriet late that night after she'd spent an exhausting hour and a half at her much-neglected ballet class. She felt as though the pieces of her life were beginning to settle into more comfortable grooves. There was nothing much to worry about.

22

A WEEK later, Alicia and Tony drove to the Cape. It was warm and sunny, and Alicia felt as if she and Tony were the only people in the world as they headed south from Boston to the Sagamore Bridge over the Cape Cod Canal. She planned for them to drive the length of the Cape all the way to Provincetown and double back to New Seabury to stay at the inn for a couple of days. The Mid-Cape Highway was almost traffic-free, and they passed quickly through the Cape towns—Sandwich, Barnstable, Cummaquid, Yarmouth, Dennis, Harwich. Alicia detoured them to Nauset Beach, where they stood near the lighthouse on the cliff and looked out over the Atlantic and the breakers rolling in on the long, empty beach far below. A family with a scattering of small children in windbreakers was visible far up the beach near a breakwater. Otherwise they were alone.

They drove past hundreds of souvenir shops at crossroads, some closed, others open to catch the first trickle of Cape visitors. Cranberry ice cream, cranberry jelly, cranberry pies and cakes and bread. Past the town of Orleans, the road was completely empty, except for an occasional car speeding down from Provincetown. When they reached Truro, Alicia had a pang of guilt about Graham. She had visited the Comptons there with him in their low, cozy house right on the beach. She remembered his long-ago suggestion that they spend spring break in Colorado for late-season skiing. How distant those days with Graham seemed now.

Provincetown was unhurried and serene in the March sun, slowly getting ready for the summer onslaught of tourists from everywhere by land, sea, and air. People were painting shutters, opening blinds, counting future profits. Tony and Alicia walked out on the pier. A small local boy was fishing with his grandfather. Most of the commercial fishing boats were out, but a few were tied up in port, being worked on by the predominantly Portuguese fishermen who manned them.

Tony hadn't said much, and Alicia was afraid he might be bored.

"Do you want to go look at the art museum?" she asked.

"I don't like museums," he said.

"It's not that kind of museum. It's a place where they show paintings by local artists. A lot of writers and artists live here. Eugene O'Neill used to live here; his first plays were done by the Provincetown Playhouse."

"Never heard of him," Tony said. "Yeah, we'll go take a look at the museum. Let's stop here first."

He pulled her into a small restaurant-bar, not a fancied-up tourist spot, but apparently a gathering place for fishermen. A Portuguese bakery next door sent out the heavenly smell of fresh bread. She bought some to take back.

Tony slipped easily into conversation with an old man, weatherbeaten and tanned, and a younger version of himself. Two or three other men came in and joined them and talk went on without Alicia, who might have been invisible. It was talk of the sea, the hardships of the fishing business, competition from Russian trawlers, the prospects of the Red Sox, the high cost of living. Strong opinions about everything. It was an hour later when she and Tony walked out into the sunshine, with Alicia feeling as though she'd visited a foreign country.

"Interesting, aren't they?" she said.

Tony shrugged. "I don't know anything about fish, but they sound like my old man and my uncles. Complaints and living a hard life for peanuts. That's not for me."

There were quite a number of cars parked near the building that housed the display of Cape artists. Alicia and Tony walked in on what appeared to be an opening of an exhibit. A group of people holding plastic glasses of wine were standing around one big room, an odd combination of

201

artistic types and city folk in country dress. Alicia steered them away from the room—a placard announced "New Paintings by Leif Einarssen"—and into a hall hung with watercolor land- and seascapes, the dunes in autumn when the sumac had reddened, the salt marshes, breakwaters of tumbled slabs of stone, the sea at rest and storm-tossed, quaint old houses. Tony examined them carefully, a quizzical expression on his face, as though he were trying to connect the pictures in front of him with the scenery they had passed along the way. He stood for a long time in front of a watercolor of the Nauset lighthouse.

"I like that kind of picture," he said. "A picture of something." He put his arm around Alicia and they walked slowly along to a big room at the end of the hall where big, bright abstract oils covered the walls. The light from the lowering sun through the windows near the ceiling gave the room a strange glow that was echoed by the vibrant primary colors of the abstracts.

"This is shit," Tony said.

"Now he's an art critic."

He laughed. "Maybe it's not to the mother of the guy who painted them."

"I think," Alicia said, leaning down to read the label beside a canvas that covered almost an entire wall, "the artist is a woman."

"Oh, well . . ." Tony dismissed the woman, whose name Alicia recognized as a person of some repute in artistic circles. "What are you laughing at?"

"Art critic *and* male chauvinist. I love it."

"I don't know much about art," he said, "but . . ."

"Don't tell me—but you know what you like."

"No. I know that for people like me, this doesn't mean anything. But this thing over here . . ." He walked over to a complex welded-metal sculpture on a block of polished wood. "This doesn't look like anything, first time you see it, but see, it's like a tangled-up life, with a woman in the middle of it."

"I don't see it," Alicia said.

"You don't know anything about art," he said loftily. "Take another look."

She looked, and she saw what he had seen, a shape that might be a woman in the middle of the web of tangled steel.

How unexpected he could be.

"You're terrific," she said. "I love you."

He kissed her, suddenly and surprisingly. A long kiss that was almost an answer to "I love you."

They walked out of the room with their arms around each other's waists, and into the icy stare of Mrs. Parker.

Alicia stepped away from Tony and dropped her arm. The room was full of people. They had come by a back door into the Einarssen opening. Tony wandered off to look at a brilliant nude that caught his eye. Alicia was left to face Graham's mother and the Comptons of Truro who were standing behind her.

"Alicia, my dear. *What* a surprise." Mrs. Parker shifted her eyes toward Tony and back to Alicia. "You remember the Comptons, of course."

"Indeed," Alicia said, praying to be transported to the other side of the world. "How nice to see you again."

The Comptons were old Bostonians who had retired to live year-round on the Cape; he was bald and hearty and rich, she quiet and unprepossessing, which probably made her an ideal friend to Mrs. Parker.

"You've come up for the opening?" Mr. Compton said. "Sound painter, Leif is. You take a good look, you'll like what you see." He seemed to be trying to herd the two women toward the exit, but Mrs. Parker was not to be moved. Not yet.

"I understood you felt you weren't able to take time off during the spring break," Mrs. Parker said. "Graham . . ." she glanced again at Tony, ". . . was terribly disappointed not to be able to go to Colorado for the skiing."

"I'm sure he was." Apparently Graham had not informed his mother fully of the break with Alicia.

Mrs. Parker shut her mouth with a snap, and looked at Alicia through narrowed eyes. Alicia could practically see her name being expunged from the Parker visiting list.

"Do drop in on us in Truro," Mr. Compton said. "Anytime."

Tony was drifting back in their direction.

"I will," Alicia said quickly. "Don't let me keep you."

"We do have to be going," Mrs. Compton said. "People coming by. Ladies . . ." He managed to get them moving, and Mrs. Parker merely nodded in farewell as she swept out, but Alicia coud sense the mental wheels turning. At least she hadn't had to introduce Tony.

Tony said, "Who's the *strega?*"

"*Strega?*"

"Witch," he said. "My mother used to tell me if I wasn't good, the *strega* would turn the evil eye on me. She had a look like that's what she was doing to you."

"Fair assessment," Alicia said. "She's the mother of a friend of mine. Never cared for me much."

"I notice you didn't like to introduce me," he said off-handedly. Then he looked at her. "Did you?"

"You don't want to know her," Alicia said.

"How do you know? Do you think I'm going to start peeling off my clothes or something when I meet a person?"

"Tony . . ."

"Don't whine," he said. "I hate that in a woman. Let's get out of here."

He took one last sweeping look at the room. Leif Einarssen's paintings were bold and vivid: nudes, landscapes, even some abstracts.

"I like these," Tony said. "I could do it, you know, maybe not so good, but I could."

"Why don't you try?"

"Not me. I don't have the patience. You got to put too much of yourself into pictures, and I don't waste me on things you stack up in a corner and nobody sees."

"What an exhibitionist you are," Alicia said. "You want everybody looking at the outside of you, and never mind the person inside."

"Maybe it's the same," he said. "What are you complaining about, anyhow? Don't you like looking at me?"

"I love it, you know I do."

"I know," he said. "I sort of like looking at the two of us. Maybe I'll do a picture of us, as good as one of these."

They drove back quickly to the big inn where Alicia had made reservations. Mrs. Parker was nearly forgotten, Tony's ruffled temper at her failure to introduce them faded. The inn was quiet and luxurious, and they had the two days and nights Alicia had wanted.

They were precious days, an idyll that came to her once and would not come again in quite the same way, with quite the same perfection and intensity.

The spring bloomed around them, the fragile haze of pale green on the dunes' edge, a golden sun, the sparkling waters of Vineyard Sound at their feet, the long, private expanse of Poppanesset Beach. They drove to Hyannis to satisfy Tony's curiosity about "all those Kennedys" and the compound where they found their haven.

Tony and Alicia were far more alone than they were even in his apartment, or hers. The world of strippers and Commonwealth University was a million miles away.

Mostly, they turned away from the sea and the dunes, and to each other. It was again different, eating out like a honeymooning couple, and going back to a strange room with no mirrors to speak of, no connection with familiar surroundings, to find each other in passion at times, in new gentleness and whispered endearments at others. Perhaps it was the very unfamiliarity that made Tony so loving and attentive, the city boy thrust into the midst of the spaces defined by sea and sky.

The first morning Alicia woke in the gray of dawn and watched Tony sleeping, with a dark stubble of beard on his chin and his curls tangled on his forehead. She was gripped by such a yearning for him that she could barely keep from waking him with a touch to see his thick lashes flutter open to see her, to know how much she loved him.

"What you looking at?" Tony's voice startled her.

"You. Just you." She felt shy at being caught in contemplation of him.

"What time is it?" He still hadn't opened his eyes.

"Early. Go back to sleep, darling."

"Come," he murmured, and stretched out an arm in her direction. She slipped easily, willingly, into the curve of his arm. He turned toward her and untied the loose knot that held her silk robe together. His touch on her naked skin electrified her, and now their eyes did meet.

"My Ali," he said, and Alicia did not, in their lovemaking, have the faintest memory of other voices speaking that name. It had become Tony's alone, as she had become his.

On the morning of their second day, Tony shouted at her above the sound of the shower, and then came out of the bathroom wearing a towel and running another through his damp hair.

"Did I hear you ask if I brought that outrageous red dress?" she asked.

"I asked if you brought the dress that shows off your ass," Tony said with a mischievous expression.

"As a matter of fact," Alicia said, "I did, for no reason I could think of. This isn't exactly the place for it."

"But New York is."

"New York is a long way away."

"Not far. We'll be there in a few hours. I already called Terry. We can stay there a couple of nights, or in the city at a hotel if you want."

"I can't. I mean, I don't have the clothes with me. . . ." Alicia saw her idyll evaporating.

"They got clothes in New York, sweetheart, I promise you. Get dressed. We'll do the town and be back in Boston Saturday night in time for my show."

"I can't, really. I—I have something to do on Saturday."

"More important than being with me?"

Alicia stared at her empty coffee cup and the crumbs of the Danish room service had delivered half an hour before when her life did not present her with the dilemma she now faced.

"More important, in a way. I'm supposed to go to a wedding on Saturday."

Tony dismissed weddings with a wave of his hand. "Weddings happen all the time."

"It happens to be one of my closest friends." She watched Tony get dressed, and wondered how to deflect him from the trip to New York. "She was the one who gave the party where I first saw you. Sheila Conroy."

"Hey, the guy she's marrying is loaded, right? Maybe I should go with you, get to know him better. He probably hangs out with a lotta big types."

"No," Alicia said slowly. "I don't think a joint appearance at Sheila's wedding would do you much good."

"No problem," Tony said. "Let's move, Alicia. I told Teresa we'd be there early afternoon."

"I cannot miss the wedding."

"Okay, okay. I hear you. But *I* want you to come with me."

"Maybe I could fly back to Boston on Saturday morning."

"Listen," Tony said. "You go with me, you come back with me. That's the way men and women do things. You don't run out on me. Unless you don't want to see me again."

"Is that a threat?" The idyll was vanishing with a rapidity she didn't believe possible. Even the weather appeared to have sensed it. The view from their window was a misty overcast, with no promise of the sun breaking through.

"I don't threaten, Alicia, I tell you the facts."

Silently, Alicia got up and put her clothes in her canvas bag. The red satin dress was still folded at the bottom, packed on a sentimental impulse.

Sheila will understand, she thought. Sheila knows what being in love is like. In love with a man like Tony who works out of a strict framework of how men and women behave.

Forty-five minutes later, they were well on their way to leaving Cape Cod behind, on the road to Providence and Route 95 that would take them straight to New York. Sheila's wedding was not mentioned again.

"You're gonna like Terry," Tony said, as they pulled up in front of a sprawling suburban house a few miles from New York City on Long Island. They had passed by the familiar Manhattan skyline in the distance and had turned onto the Long Island Expressway to Teresa and Leo's place. "Leo ain't going to have anything to say, if he's even home, so you don't need to worry about him."

"I'm not worried about Leo," Alicia said shortly.

"And would you mind not putting on that big Boston lady voice? This is my sister you're meeting."

"Yes, Tony."

What had happened in so short a time to shift their relationship again, and this time not to something better but to a delicate balance fraught with perils? Maybe it had been too idyllic on the Cape, and when the real world slipped in, Tony had reacted by heritage and instinct to prove once more that he commanded and she followed.

The young woman who opened the door to them had the look of Tony, dark and slim but worn-looking. Her face lit up at the sight of him, and she threw her arms around her tall brother with true Italian passion. Alicia could hear a baby crying in a distant room of the big split-level house.

"*Caro*," Teresa crooned, and Alicia thought she had tears in her eyes.

"Hey, Terry. You're lookin' good," Tony said.

Teresa stood back and looked at him, but she still held both his hands.

"You think so, Tony? At least I haven't gotten fat." She laughed nervously, and smiled shyly at Alicia.

"This is Alicia, I was telling you about," Tony said.

"Pleased to meet you," Teresa said. "Come on in, I got

to shut that kid up before he drives me crazy. You got any kids?" she asked Alicia.

"No, no I haven't."

"I don't know what I'd do without them," Teresa said. "Even if they never shut up."

Teresa led them into her house, grossly overdecorated to Alicia's eyes, although obviously very expensive. But her taste had never run to elaborate glassed-in fireplaces, golden wall sconces, mirrors and pictures in ornate gilded frames, and cumbersome matched living-room furniture covered in plastic.

"We got some new furniture, Tony," Teresa said. "You like it?"

"It's beautiful, Terry. *Bellissima.*"

"I told Leo it was stupid to buy a lot of stuff while the kids were so little, but he wouldn't listen, said he had the dough, why not spend it."

The baby was still crying.

"Take care of the kid," Tony said. "Is that Nicky?"

"Yeah. The other two little ones are taking a nap, thank God, and Anthony is next door. Look, Tony. I fixed up the two guest rooms for you and . . . Alicia. Leo's kinda funny, you know him." She seemed embarrassed about dealing with her brother's relationship. "But they're like, next door to each other. . . ."

Tony put his arm around her. "You got enough to worry about, Terry. Don't bother about us."

Alicia wished they were staying at a hotel in the city, if they had to be in New York at all. She felt she was intruding, and more: completely out of her element.

"We're only going to stay tonight," he said, and Alicia breathed her relief. Maybe he'd changed his mind about staying until Saturday. "Then we're going to be in Manhattan on Friday night. I got to be back in Boston for a show Saturday night."

Teresa, too, seemed relieved they were staying so short a time. Alicia was merely disappointed that Tony wasn't going to get her back in time for Sheila's wedding.

"You two get to know each other," Tony said. "The TV still in the den? Good, I'm beat from the drive."

And he walked off and left them.

"The baby's out back," Teresa said. "And I'll show you the garden. This is the first year I've had a chance to work on it. And I fixed some food, in case you're hungry."

She led Alicia out to a huge, orderly, spotless kitchen. It smelled wonderfully of sauce and spices.

"It must be hard to keep everything so nice with four children," Alicia said. There were only occasional reminders of the presence of children.

"Leo likes it that way." She went off to fetch the crying infant.

Alicia remembered what Tony had said about Teresa's husband, and wondered at a woman's willingness to defer so completely to a man who, by all reports, had little to recommend him.

Teresa, the fat and now cheerful baby Nicky, and Alicia toured the backyard. At one side, fenced off, were swings and a tricycle; nearby was an elaborate brick barbecue, a picnic table, and benches covered with plastic. The rest of the space was garden: neat furrows of dirt, some already showing a fuzz of green. The newly planted trees looked weak, but Teresa assured her they would be covered with cherry blossoms next spring, the maple would be taller, gladiolas would be massed at the back of the yard by summer's end, and the irises would come next year.

"The roses will bloom this summer," she said. "I got a special hand for roses." She'd started a grape arbor and had put up a statue of the Virgin Mary in a corner.

"It's going to be lovely," Alicia said.

I want to go home, she thought.

The other two children, little girls whose names Alicia never remembered, woke up; Anthony came home and gleefully disappeared to see his Uncle Tony.

"I'll put the food out soon," Teresa said. "I made ravioli, the way they do it in the old country, as soon as I knew Tony was coming. Sit, please."

She set the baby in a canvas seat and busied herself at the stove. The little girls stood at Alicia's side and observed her with bright, curious eyes.

"You like Tony," Teresa said, her back to Alicia.

"Why, yes. Yes, I do."

"He's a boy compared to you. No offense. I wish he were settled down, a wife and children. He's too wild, he's always been that way, trying to reach for things he ought to forget about." Teresa came away from the stove and sat down across the kitchen table from Alicia. The girls climbed up on her lap. "Tony likes to be the center of attention. The star. So he takes his clothes off for women. It's not a good life."

"I agree," Alicia said. "But I'm afraid he doesn't listen to me."

"That'd be the day, him paying attention to a woman. He knows better. And he's stubborn. He could have made up with Mamma. . . ." She looked at Alicia, who nodded her knowledge. "But Mamma is stubborn too. They're alike. I wish he had some kind of real work, Uncle Angie could get him into anything." Teresa sighed. "I love Tony, like nobody else, but he won't listen."

The ravioli, at least, was superb.

Tony and Teresa spent the evening reminiscing about unknown friends and relatives, while Alicia listened with mild boredom and sipped the glass of red wine Tony kept refilling to keep her busy. The mysterious Leo did not appear before they went to bed, although Alicia heard an unfamiliar male voice late at night, as she lay alone in her guest room. Tony had kissed her good night at the door, and had not suggested they share a bed. She had been very unhappy, but had not dared press him.

The morning brought her into Leo's presence, and after he had looked her up and down and had decided she was nothing that interested him, he had moved his hefty self out of the house and away to whatever his business was.

At last, she and Tony left Teresa at midday to spend Friday night at the New York Hilton. She still felt guilty about Sheila. As they drove away, Alicia looked back to see Teresa standing in the doorway of her immense house, holding Nicky and surrounded by the other three children. She looked forlorn and abandoned.

Another surprise in this surprising week: she put on her backless red dress and they had an amazingly good time, rushing to dinner at a northern Italian restaurant (while Alicia calculated the calories she had been consuming), to the bar at the top of the World Trade Center far downtown, back uptown to a famous disco whose name appeared frequently in the papers as a hangout of New York's Beautiful People, to another night spot with a view of Manhattan's lights, to the Brasserie in the very small hours because Tony decided he was hungry.

"I told you that dress would turn you into a new person," he said. "Isn't this better than all that sand? Man, I could live like this forever. I will."

They went to bed, too exhausted to make love, but Alicia was content to be close to him again.

"Do you love me?" he asked sleepily.

"You know I do," she said. But she felt a stab of apprehension, as she fell asleep in his arms.

There were cracks in her little world that she felt helpless to mend. Tony did not understand who she was; perhaps he would never want to see beneath her surface and the physical attachment that meant so much to her.

Perhaps he wasn't capable of seeing more than what was before his eyes, in his bed, at his side when they drank wine with Gino Cantalupo. In this, he was remarkably like both Gardner Sears and Graham Parker, however different the contexts in which she dealt with them.

It was much, much later that she realized Tony had learned to see more than any of the others.

She had fewer misgivings in the morning, although she had to repress thoughts of Sheila's wedding as they drove back late to Boston.

"This was great," Tony said complacently. "Good idea, lady."

Alicia was determined that they would do something similar again soon.

It was the sort of fun she supposed other people had always. Never mind the occasional bittersweet incidents. She'd have to learn to stop thinking and worrying about matters that had little bearing on the immediate moment.

Which was being with Tony.

23

BILLY looked at her quizzically from the deep armchair covered in apricot silk that was his preferred seat in his living room. His Abyssinian sat on the arm, staring.

"You haven't been talking much," he said, "but I take it you've been seeing quite a bit of Tony these past few weeks."

"Not really," Alicia said quickly.

"Mmmm. Want more coffee?"

Billy had requested her presence for Sunday brunch; he'd fed her on quiche and croissants and orange juice with a fizz of champagne; he'd chatted about people and events, and only when they settled in the living room did he bring up Tony.

"Not really, you say." Billy poured coffee at Alicia's nod. "You must be terribly busy with something. I never see you these days. And your best friend Harriet Gould saw fit to call me last week to ask what was wrong with you. You don't call her or see them, you're . . . how did she put it? . . . distracted, cold, uncommunicative."

"You didn't say anything, did you? About Tony?"

He looked at her curiously. "Of course not. It's none of my business to gossip about your sexual adventures. Oh, don't look so offended. It's the truth, isn't it?"

Alicia looked up from her coffee cup and away.

"It's also not my business to gossip about you with Graham Parker. God, it must have cost him a lot to sit down

212

in comparative public with me; I ran into him at the Faculty Club—"

"Graham's been asking *you* about *me?*"

"Don't shriek. A ladylike tone will suit. Yes, he hemmed and hawed and asked what you'd been doing in a round-about way. You know—'Mother and I are worried . . . seems so unavailable . . . Mother and I feel she must be overworking. . . .' "

"The old bitch must have mentioned seeing me and—"

"Yes?" Billy leaned forward, interested.

"You are a gossip." Alicia's humor improved. "Oh, Tony and I went to the Cape for a few days, and Mrs. Parker was at an art show in P-town with her friends from Truro. She happened to encounter us in an intimate moment."

"You're kidding!"

"We were just holding hands. No big thing. Naturally she was interested, to say the least. I managed to avoid introducing her to Tony. Fortunately."

"*That's* a relief." She blinked at his sarcasm. "Is Tony also to blame for your missing Sheila Conroy's wedding? I hear from Harriet that you didn't make it. No explanation."

"I—I had to go out of town."

"Alicia, you can be straight with me. It's Billy, not Graham Parker's proud and proper Mum."

Alicia looked slightly ashamed. "It was terrible of me, but I knew Sheila would understand. We could have come back, but it . . . wasn't that simple."

Billy looked at her, waiting for more.

"I couldn't exactly bring him to the wedding, could I? 'Happy wedding, Sheila, you remember Tony Spinelli, he took his clothes off for you.' "

"You haven't convinced me."

She sighed. "Billy, it's the first time in years that I've wanted to be with a man so much, I don't want to miss any minute he's there for me. I don't know why I care so much; there's not much intellectually to recommend him, I know, but he can be funny and interesting. I have fun with him." She couldn't admit her misgivings of the week before to Billy.

"I'll bet it was fun knowing you stood up a friend on her wedding day."

"Billy, please."

"I'm sorry, Al. That was uncalled for. But I'm worried about you. I like Spinelli. He's okay, in his way, but he's got to be out for something. Kids like that are on the make, and he's obviously totally in love with himself."

Alicia threw up her hands to stop Billy's flow of words.

"He likes *me*, I know he does. I don't care why, but why is it so hard for you to believe that he must care, or he wouldn't see me."

"Maybe what he likes is the fact that you like him. I don't imagine he knows many women like you."

Alicia set her chin stubbornly. "You don't understand. None of you do. Ooooh, how dare Graham ask you about me!"

"I think Graham cares about you, Alicia, more than you choose to see. I admit that I find him sometimes a pompous ass, a prisoner of his background and even his profession. He's full of opinions I don't agree with, although when it comes to medicine he's a sound man. He's not adept at showing warmth in his human relations, perhaps, and maybe he's a typical selfish, demanding man. But he does care."

"Don't tell me Graham has enlisted *you* to plead his cause. Gardner Sears I could see, but you!"

"He hasn't enlisted me to do anything. I'm offering an opinion. I don't want to see you fuck up your life, to put it simply, and I can see that happening if Tony Spinelli gets too involved in it. You have a good job, important work. I'd be the last person to tell you not to have a fling, but you have to be sensible."

"I don't want to be sensible. And I'm doing my job. In fact . . ." She stood up. "I brought some work home from the office that I ought to be finishing right now. Thanks for brunch. And the good advice."

She went quickly to the door, to keep him from asking more. To keep him from noticing that her indignation covered a vague insecurity that had wormed its way into her existence.

"You didn't take a look at the garden. It's going to be fabulous this year. I—I found someone to help out."

"You *did?*" she said. Billy looked at her sharply but she was gazing out the open front door down Mount Vernon Street where the trees finally were in leaf and the mellow bricks of the town houses glowed in the spring sunshine. "I suppose your gardener is a real winner, somebody like Raoul."

Billy didn't reply, and Alicia spun around.

"It *is* Raoul?" She was completely surprised. "And you're lecturing me about Tony Spinelli? Has he moved in as well?"

Billy nodded. "He was looking for a place; it's not permanent. . . ."

"You're a damned hypocrite," she said cheerfully. "I hope you know that. I suppose Raoul's the reason you know so much about me and Tony. Pillow talk."

"It's different for me, Alicia. I've been walking a tightrope with my personal and professional lives as long as I can remember. You have to admit that gay isn't precisely mainstream. I can handle it."

"And I can't? Well, maybe you're right. Frankly, I don't care."

"I think you do. Or will."

"We'll talk about it when it happens." She swung off down the hill toward Charles Street and the Public Garden. With Billy's revelation about Raoul, she didn't feel so guilty about the lie she had handed Billy. She wasn't going home to work, she was going to meet Tony. She had scarcely seen him in the two weeks since they'd come back from New York. He had been "busy," he claimed, but then so had she.

The Public Garden looked its best in the spring. The grass neatly clipped and green, the formal flower beds arranged with masses of tulips, hyacinths, and begonias; Alicia paused on the ornamental bridge over the little lake in the center of the Garden to watch a brand-new family of mallards paddle their way toward the tiny island refuge in mid-lake. The fringes of the pond were decked with people lying on the grass to catch the first tans of the season. The swanboats were lined up at the dock.

It was peaceful and urban escapist, this tiny plot of ground closely shadowed by increasing numbers of tall office buildings on two sides. Alicia headed for the big equestrian statue of George Washington that guarded the main gate on Arlington Street. It would take her ten minutes to walk to Tony's apartment in the South End.

She passed the hotel where he worked, although he had talked incessantly of late of devoting all his time to his "show business career." He had been restless, impatient when she mentioned anything about her work at the school, as if it were irrelevant. He didn't tell her what he had been doing with himself when they weren't together, except that

215

he'd been rehearsing "with some people who were giving me pointers."

She had bitten her tongue before she asked how many pointers a stripper needed, if he already knew how to undo buttons.

She had to admit that she was sometimes impatient with him. She hated having stupid arguments with him. She feared the possibility that he was getting bored with her. Alicia still needed him.

It took a while for him to answer her ring.

"Late night," he yawned. "What time is it?"

"Nearly two-thirty."

He rubbed his unshaven face with both hands. "I'll get dressed. You want to drive out to Winchester to see Lina?"

She didn't. She wanted Tony to greet her joyfully, pull her into the center of his life, talk and listen.

"If you want to go, I don't care," she said. "Why was it such a late night?" Alicia strayed around the living room, picking up pillows from the floor, gathering up sheets of discarded sketching papers. Tony was apparently dreaming up a new costume.

"Leave that stuff," he said. "It was a late night because I got friends you don't know. Oh, well, Jeff who used to be at the Carousel and some other people stopped by. Then we went out, he's going around with this rich old dame. You wouldn't have liked it."

"How do you know? I like being with you."

"Yeah? Well, you got plenty of friends of your own, even if I don't know them."

"I've told you a hundred times, you'd be bored by my friends." She put the sketches on a table beside the sofa.

Tony stopped at the bedroom door and came back. He gripped her arms. "Sweetheart, don't pull that shit on me. I don't know your buddies because you don't want me to know them. You don't want them to know you go around with a stripper. But it's an honest job, and I'm good at it. You wouldn't like it any better introducing me as a bartender, but I'm good at that too."

"You're in a great mood. Who've you been talking to?"

"Nobody," he said sullenly. "I got to shower and get dressed. Make me some coffee."

Alicia was bewildered by his attitude.

"I wish you'd be honest with me, Tony."

"Honest!" He laughed without mirth. "I guess you're honest with me, though, is that it? Bullshit."

"I am, and you know it."

"I suppose you think I don't know about your professor boyfriend."

"I don't have a boyfriend. If you're referring to Dr. Parker, he's not my boyfriend, and I haven't even laid eyes on him for weeks."

Tony did not look as though he believed her. "If you say so."

"Why are you being difficult? And how do you know anything about Graham Parker anyhow?"

He didn't answer.

"Billy?" It had to be Billy, at least by way of Raoul. She felt betrayed.

"Doc's okay. He wouldn't say anything against you."

"Against me?"

"You know what I mean. But I pick up on things, put two and two together. I may be a dumb wop from the North End, but I ain't stupid. Would you get that coffee going?"

He went into the bedroom, and then she heard the shower turned on full force.

She went out to his small kitchen, a cramped space into which the redevelopers of his building had managed to fit sink, stove, and refrigerator and little else. He liked very strong, black coffee, and she had made an effort to learn to brew it to his taste.

Was he jealous? Of Graham? It didn't seem possible, but who knows what interpretation an unfriendly Raoul might put on a perfectly straightforward comment by Billy. She sat alone in the living room while she waited for Tony and the coffee. She knew that some of what he said was true: she still didn't allow him to step over the line into her other world, and if she professed to believe it was because he wouldn't be comfortable, she also knew that it would be she who was uncomfortable, she who could be affected professionally and socially by her relationship with him, no matter how bold a face she put on it.

A part of her was a coward. The fact that he was a male stripper was only one aspect. There was his age, his background, his ambition.

At least, she thought as she picked up the pile of sketches, Mike Tedesco hasn't had much to see lately. She

217

had kept postponing the meeting Mike wanted, although Debbie had mentioned it again a few days before.

Alicia was suddenly stopped cold by a sketch she hadn't noticed before. The man in the sketch looked like Tony, but the semi-nude woman didn't look at all like Alicia. Tony had a gift for catching facial likenesses, even though his technique wasn't polished. She searched through the other sketches. The same woman was in several of them.

Now Alicia was afraid. She had never really thought of him being with another woman. She quickly piled up the sketches again, and when Tony came out to get his coffee, she asked no questions, because he might give her an answer.

"At least you know how to make coffee," he said. She took that as an oblique apology for his surliness. He was more cheerful. "If you don't want to go to Lina's . . ."

"I didn't say that."

"Sweetheart, I can read you like a billboard. I was thinking we could drive down to New York. I didn't see enough of Terry, she's got a lousy boring life. Stay a few days with her this time. Leo's out of town."

"I can't."

"You can't. Why not?"

"The trustees meeting is coming up in a few days; I have to have a ton of paperwork ready. Then I'm supposed to be giving a cocktail party on Tuesday for the trustees and people from the school. Before the opera; it's a big benefit thing. Therefore, I can't go to New York."

"Cocktail party, huh? All your fancy pals, I suppose."

"Very few pals. Mostly people the dean has invited on my behalf, since his wife isn't well enough to be the hostess. It's part of my job."

"I want to come. If I'm good enough for you, I'm good enough for them. Or do you think maybe I'm not good enough for you?"

"Of course you are. It's that they're people who would bore you. You wouldn't enjoy yourself."

"You don't want me there."

"It's not that. . . ."

"What is it, then?" He was demanding an answer, and her emotions got the best of her good sense.

"All right, then. You want to hear it? I *don't* want you there. It would be impossible to have you there. If you had a decent job with one of your uncles or cousins or whatever, that would make it more possible. If you knew that world and felt comfortable in it, that makes it more possible still. As it stands, however, it is *not* possible. It has nothing to do with the fact that I'm in love with you."

He set his mouth in a hard line.

"Don't you understand, Tony?"

"I understand that if I weren't a stripper, which is something I do well and get paid good money for, if I was a bank president throwing people out of their houses 'cause they can't make their payments, or if I was a painter slinging paint on a canvas any old way and pretending it was a real picture, then I'd have the great privilege of meeting your friends. Is that what you mean?"

He was impossible.

"Not exactly. Look, I don't want to get into a fight with you right now."

"I ain't fighting," Tony said. He sipped his coffee. "Not me."

She went home soon after. He had said little more. His silence had been ominous, and he hadn't said he'd call her or see her.

Alicia knew she was right about Tony and her circle. The two halves of her life could not mix. What she couldn't bear to think about was that the part that mattered most, Tony Spinelli, the Carousel Club's star stripper, might be the one she'd be forced to give up.

24

"WE don't have many evenings like this," Graham was saying wistfully, as Alicia made sure that her guests—the medical school's guests, in point of fact—were circulating, drinking, being served hors d'oeuvres by the uniformed maid the dean had sprung for. He'd also consented to a bartender and a couple of limousines to convey out-of-town trustees and spouses from Alicia's apartment to the theater.

"All dressed up and off to the opera?" she asked absently. Old Mrs. Nelson, whose husband had been a world-famous member of the Commonwealth medical faculty, appeared to be working on her third martini. Alicia feared she'd fall asleep or worse in the middle of an aria.

"I meant, being at a nice gathering like this together."

"I'm sorry I've been so involved with things, Graham. You understand. How's Timmy doing in school? I've been meaning to call him, but I've been swamped at work."

"He's fine. Working harder at school, so he won't risk missing that trip out West this summer. That's still on."

"Wonderful." Alicia was less than half listening. She liked to entertain, but her own choice of guests. Most of the people there were comparative strangers. Fortunately, she had managed to include Harriet and Mark, partly out of guilt for not having seen much of them recently. Graham had been put on the guest list by Dean Barrow in the blithe assumption that she would want him, and Mrs. Parker had been brought along by Graham since he, unlike the dean, had reservations about where he stood with Alicia. Mrs. Parker had been chilly, but made no reference to the Cape. Instead she surveyed Alicia's new dress with a raised eyebrow. It was not Tony's red satin, but Alicia had bought it remembering what he approved of. Black but daring. Graham seemed to like it.

"Would you like to drive out to the Cape with me on Saturday?" Graham said, and Alicia almost choked on her wine. "The Comptons have opened their house at Truro; Mother was up a few weeks ago."

"I'm not sure I can," she said. "I might be tied up with last-minute details of the trustees meeting."

"I wish you'd try. It's a nice drive. We used to have quite good times, Alicia."

He missed her, she knew it.

"You've always been awfully good to me, Gray," she said. "I promise to see if I can make it. I'll let you know later in the week, okay?"

"That would be wonderful," he said.

"I'd better behave more like a hostess," she said. She put on a social smile, but turned back to Graham with something warmer. She could afford a bit of affection, since she had Tony. They had tentatively made up after their quarrel on Sunday. He'd see her soon, after he got back from Teresa's.

"Mrs. Nelson," she said, "how lovely that dress is. I want you to meet Dr. Kilburne, one of our new trustees." She guided Mrs. Nelson away from the bar that had been set up on one side of the room toward the distinguished cardiologist from Chicago. She wished Billy had consented to come tonight. He was so good at social events like this. But he claimed a strong aversion to *La Traviata*, a sentiment shared by Dean Barrow, who would join the group after the opera for supper at the Beacon Hill club where he was a member. Alicia wondered if Billy's refusal had more to it than dislike of an opera. Their brunch the previous Sunday had actually included some prickliness on both sides.

"Alicia, I have some bad news." Harriet came across the room to her. "Mark is divorcing you, on the grounds of desertion."

"And he'd get a pile of alimony," Alicia said. "I've been terrible lately. I'm sorry."

"Josh is growing up believing the only aunt a boy has is a lunatic named Lenore."

"I haven't seen her in ages either."

"Not surprising. She's been dating the same guy for about four weeks, which occupies her totally. It's left her speechless. She can't believe anyone would tolerate her that long."

"Please, God, let him be a Jewish doctor."

"He's a dentist. You can't have everything." Harriet added slyly, "But you seem to be making a try for it."

Quickly. "What do you mean?"

"You have to be up to something terrific, I can read the signs. Even that dress—oy, is that telling me something!"

"Let's have lunch this week, Harriet. I do have a dilemma of sorts. Male."

"Hooray, at last." She nudged Alicia. "Don't look now, but Mrs. Parker is skewering you with her intrepid glance. Shall I send Mark to intercept?"

"No," Alicia sighed. "I'll go talk to her."

"Lovely party," Mrs. Parker said, without an ounce of conviction. "You're very adept at this sort of . . . affair."

Alicia wondered if she had chosen the word on purpose. Mrs. Parker was capable of it.

"Graham tells me we three will be sitting together at the opera," she went on. "How nice. Of course, I was a last-minute replacement. Suzanne couldn't make it."

"Suzanne?"

"An old friend of Graham's. I thought you knew her, Suzanne Benton." Mrs. Parker smiled like a barracuda. She'd gotten it across that Graham was seeing another woman. Scores were even, and Alicia discovered she minded only a little. Gray had been hers for so long, it was a minor shock to think he could be interested in someone else. She doubted if his mother had mentioned seeing her on the Cape; but anything was possible. How confusing. He didn't seem at all remote; if anything, more attentive.

"We ought to be getting these people on their way to the theater," Graham said into her ear. "Early curtain."

"Mmmm. Could you start herding them toward the door? See if anybody needs a cab? The limos are hovering outside."

"I can fit in a couple of people along with you and Mother. I'm sure the Goulds can take one or two." He surveyed the room. "If I can manage the intricacies of the human brain, I think I can manage transportation for this group from here to the theater."

How nice he's being tonight, Alicia thought. Extra effort gives extra points.

The sidewalk outside the theater where the opera was being performed was crowded with dressed-up types, quite a different scene from opera in New York, where well-pressed jeans outnumbered evening gowns. All of Alicia's guests arrived in good time; Graham dropped off his mother and Alicia and went to park. Mrs. Parker swept in, claiming a dislike for standing about the lobby making small talk. Alicia could hear Mrs. Nelson's piercing voice behind her, with rumbling responses from Dr. Kilburne, as she entered the lobby.

Directly in front of her was Tony.

He was wearing a sleek tuxedo, he looked handsome and assured, and he was talking to Dorothea Stanforth, whose husband was assistant to the Chancellor of Commonwealth University on all university fund raising. Alicia blinked. It couldn't be him, but someone who looked like him. It was Tony. He caught her eye, and smiled. Dorothea Stanforth saw her at almost the same moment, and waved her over.

"My dear, we were just speaking of you." Dorothea was a hefty, middle-aged Concord matron, who, many claimed, was the brains and power behind Robert Stanforth. She was nobody's fool, but apparently she and Tony were fast friends.

"Isn't it amusing. Anthony overheard Robert and me speaking of Commonwealth, and he mentioned his acquaintance with you."

"Ah . . . yes. Anthony. How nice to see you," Alicia said.

Tony smiled graciously.

"Robert has nothing but praise for the way you're able to persuade contributors to give the medical school money," Dorothea said. "But you mustn't moonlight, the university needs you."

"Moonlight?"

Dorothea waved a finger at her. "Anthony told us all about how you advise his mother on charity fund raising. . . ."

"Ah," Alicia said. She glanced at Tony, who rocked back on his heels and looked smug. "Anthony's mother."

"Robert is getting impatient," Dorothea Stanforth said.

223

"Perhaps we'll meet again at intermission, Anthony. Delightful to meet you."

"And you, Mrs. Stanforth," Tony said. He actually bowed, and Dorothea fluttered coyly in response before she went away to join her husband.

"What the hell are you doing here?" Alicia asked Tony through clenched teeth. "Anthony."

"Why," he said, "Italians grow up with opera. I thought you knew that. And this is a public place, isn't it?"

"How did you manage to get a ticket?"

"Hey, my uncle has a lot of connections. It's not all tomatoes and olive oil and the Boston Celtics."

"And how did you dare speak to the Stanforths?"

"Dare? People talk to people. Look, I'm talking to you, and you could be any kind of big, important lady. . . ."

"Tony . . ." she said warningly.

"Shall we join Mother?" Graham said, coming up behind them. He looked questioningly from Tony to Alicia. "If I'm not intruding . . ."

"Not at all, Graham. Ah, this is . . . Anthony Spinelli. Dr. Graham Parker."

"Yes, of course," Tony said. "I've heard so much about you." He shook hands with a flourish.

"I'm sure I'll be running into you again soon. Anthony." Alicia glared at him. "I thought you'd be giving your dear sister advice tonight. Unless you're here to get it from me."

"Your advice is always very good," Tony said. "Classy."

Alicia realized, when she took her seat between Mrs. Parker and Graham, that she had been thoroughly shaken by the encounter with Tony. She didn't dare look around to see where he might be sitting, and prayed that the lights would go down quickly.

"He seems like a nice young fellow," Graham said.

"He's not," Alicia said shortly.

"I beg your pardon?"

"Not so young. In many ways."

The prelude began, the curtain went up on the ornate red and gold first-act set where Violetta's supper party is in progress, and the lovelorn Alfredo is waiting to be introduced to her. The first act seemed interminable, and Violetta's "Sempre libera" aria at the conclusion ironic. Freedom and pleasure, loving and being loved. The worlds of the courtesan and the proper young man in love with her.

"I think I won't go out for intermission," Mrs. Parker said as the principals took their first-act bows. "Too much of a crush."

"We'll stay with you, Mother," Graham said.

"If you don't mind, I want to see if I can catch Robert Stanforth," Alicia said, and edged her way out into the aisle.

Tony was drinking wine near the mobbed refreshment bar when Alicia found him.

"Pleased with yourself?" she asked.

"Oh, sure. What a bore this is."

"I thought you grew up with opera."

"I didn't say I like it. Let's get out of here, Ali. Now."

"I can't, and you know it." She started to walk away, and he held her arm. As he did so, she caught sight of Harriet and Mark heading toward them. Alicia tried desperately to warn them off with the tight smile that says, "Don't ask, I'll tell you later."

"What is this 'can't'?" Tony said.

The Goulds had not been deflected.

"How many glasses of wine have you poured down?"

"Not many," he said. "And it's lousy wine. Do you know this dame heading for us?"

"This dame is my best friend, Harriet Gould." Nervous.

"Ease up, lady. 'Stripper' isn't burned into my forehead; nobody faints when they see me. And I'm gorgeous." He put out his hand to Harriet and drew her to him, kissing her on the cheek. "You must be Harriet, Alicia's told me all about you."

"This is her husband, Mark," Alicia said.

"Tony Spinelli," Tony said, putting out his hand.

"Do I know you? I mean, I wish I did," Harriet said.

"He's my demon lover," Alicia said.

"No kidding?" Mark said. "Never knew what one looked like."

"Alicia's such an amusing girl," Tony said.

"She hasn't told me all about you," Harriet said, "Mr. . . . ?"

"Tony. She will." He turned on every bit of glossy charm he possessed, and Harriet loved it.

"I seem to know the name . . ."

"Can we talk about it later, Harriet?" Alicia interrupted. The bell for the second act rang.

"Sure you can," Mark said, taking Harriet's arm. "Let's go, I hate stepping on people's feet."

The Goulds went away, and Tony said, "Let's go back to how you can't leave now."

"I have obligations. That's part of my world, and if you want to be in it, you have to understand that."

"Jesus, it's only an opera."

"I'm with people, I have to make sure they all get to this supper afterward, I have to stay with them. . . ."

"Who's that guy? That your boyfriend?"

"Mark?" But she knew he was talking about Graham.

"Forget it," Tony said. He turned away from her and started to push his way through the people still standing near the bar.

"Wait, Tony." He stopped. "Okay, as soon as everybody gets to this place after the opera, I'll say I'm not feeling well or something." For the first time in years, she missed her mother saying, "If you don't want to do something, blame it on me. Tell them I said you had to come home." Dean Barrow wasn't likely to go for a splitting headache, but what could she say?

"There's a new place in Cambridge," Tony said. "Inman Square. The Morocco Star. A pal of mine is running it."

"Not your darling Uncle Angelo?"

"Sometimes you're too fucking amusing."

"I'll be there," Alicia said.

Tony smiled. "I like the dress, sweetheart. Great ass."

Alicia's last straw came on her way back to her seat. Victor Ostrava loomed in the distance, probably furious that he hadn't been invited to either her cocktail party or the supper after the opera. He had hinted that he was eager to meet the new trustees informally; she had explained that the dean was compiling the guest list. He had suggested that even if she had no influence over how millions of dollars were apportioned, she surely could invite whom she chose to her own house.

"It's impossible, Dr. Ostrava. Truly."

"Nothing is impossible for you, Mrs. Sears. But please do not think I am begging. That is the last thing I would do. But you must also not assume that I have not learned through many difficult years how power is wielded, in public or in private. I have."

Victor Ostrava, more than anyone, made her realize how much her life was shaped by forces over which she had

226

no control. He constantly threatened her in subtle ways, and he gave nothing away. Nothing. He was impenetrable, wrapped up in himself and his work.

At the opera, she had no intention of speaking to him about anything, and hurried back to her seat. She refused to leave for the two subsequent intermissions, finding silence from Mrs. Parker and stilted comments from Graham preferable to anything that might be happening in the lobby.

"I'm getting a terrible headache," she managed to say to Graham. "I don't know how I'll get through supper."

He was sympathetic and she was both guilty and pleased with the smooth way she had planted the lie that would take her to Tony. She watched Violetta expire at the end of the opera. At least Alicia had her health.

The audience surged out of the theater after the curtain calls. She searched the crowd for Tony, and was relieved not to find him waiting for her.

"I don't think I'm going to be able to stay for the supper," Alicia said to Graham.

"You do look pale," he said. "Shall I drive you home after I drop Mother?"

"Oh no," she said sweetly, weakly. "I'll take a cab after I've seen the dean. Don't trouble yourself."

Dean Barrow was kind and concerned, when she handed over the school's guests to him at the club and made her apologies. Since lying was alien to her character, she was certain everyone could read her falsehood on her face, especially the dean who knew her well, but no one suspected that her departure was not for a bed of pain, but to Cambridge, the Morocco Star, and Tony.

That he had made such an effort to prove his worth and acceptability in her circle must mean, she thought, that he still cared about their relationship.

And she would make an effort too: to be what he wanted, to work out this silly problem, to ease him into part of the life from which she had excluded him.

Tonight was the beginning of making things all right again.

25

WHEN Alicia left him, Tony let the rest of the audience drift back to their seats until only he and the bartenders were left.

"Ain't you going in?" one asked.

Tony looked at him coldly, the Italian prince addressed by a peasant.

"I just asked," the bartender said. "It's starting, is all."

"So it is," Tony said, and walked out of the theater to the street, loosening his tie. He had borrowed the tux from one of the new strippers, who was about his size, but not quite. The waist was a little too tight, he hadn't dared take too deep a breath in case the jacket went. But he liked the way he looked. He needed a tux of his own if he was going to end up performing in Vegas. And he would. The act was in good shape, and he had a hundred new ideas, thanks to Denise, who knew the business of stripping like nobody. Lucky she had no hard feelings about the way he'd dropped her right when he met up with Alicia. But Denise had always been easygoing, more so than Alicia, who took things so seriously. Him, especially. For that very good reason, he sure as hell wasn't going to mention to her that Denise was helping him out.

Tony hated to admit to himself how much Ali had gotten herself into his life. It made him wary. There weren't many women in the world he trusted. Experience had been a good teacher, but Ali maybe was different. He did like knowing how completely she was his. It made him want success like he'd never wanted anything.

Then she wouldn't be so snobby about her pals.

He decided to leave the tux back at the club, since he had time before meeting Alicia at the Morocco Star. It was something the way she could talk about "responsibilities" and then jump when her man called.

Tony was smiling about that when he went into the Carousel. The place was dead tonight. The kid behind the bar was watching television, three or four couples were sitting at the tables, and an old guy who must have found the place by mistake was sitting on a bar stool, half asleep over a beer.

"What's happening?" Tony said to the kid.

"Fucking cemetery," the bartender said, not taking his eyes off the television. "Maybe things'll pick up later."

"Anybody around?"

"None of the guys. Oh, yeah. I saw Tito a while ago. Sid's coming in, I think. Irv's out back somewheres. Probably marking the liquor bottles in case I should drink any of this rotgut."

The bartender squinted at Tony in the dim light.

"Aren't you Mr. Sharp Dresser tonight."

"I was trying out a new act," Tony said.

"How'd it go?"

"A hit," Tony said, remembering the gleam in that dame's eye, Mrs. Stanforth, when she looked him over. "They really went for me."

Tony went around in back of the stage. One faint bulb lighted the hallway outside the dressing room. It was quiet. He had his hand on the knob of the dressing room door when he noticed a line of light under the office door. Irv. The last person he felt like running into. The firing of Jeff still burned Tony, even though Jeff seemed to be making out okay. It showed what a menace Irv was, especially with Tito apparently running him.

He opened the dressing room door, and switched on the light. He had a nice little surprise for Alicia. He'd actually finished a picture of her that was pretty good. If she behaved herself tonight, he was planning to give it to her. He had it out in the car.

The dressing room was a mess, piled with cartons of liquor that must have been delivered and not put in the storeroom yet. There were also cans of paint in the middle of the floor. Tony remembered Sid had said something about redoing the Greek Suite, since private parties were starting to get so popular. Tony surveyed the disorder, and decided to raise a little hell with Irv.

He went down the hall toward the office.

Voices. Irv wasn't alone. He heard Irv's whine and another voice, louder and angry. Tito. Tony despised him so much he avoided him as much as possible. He didn't want to risk letting himself go at the little shit, and he would, if Tito said one cross-eyed word.

Tony would have turned around and gone back to change clothes, except that when he heard his name, he froze. He couldn't have gone away now if they paid him a million bucks.

"And if you don't get rid of Spinelli, and feature me," Tito was saying, "Sid's going to hear how deep you are in with the sharks."

Irv, pleading. "Tito, you don't have to do that, tell Sid anything. I had a bad streak with the horses, and things, but I'm not behind with the money I owe them, you know that."

"That ain't so, Irv. I happen to know you got to come up with a bundle in six days. Or you're as good as dead."

So Irv was in over his head with loan sharks. That didn't surprise Tony, nor did the fact that Tito seemed to know all about it. There was a long silence on the other side of the door, then Tito spoke again.

"I could fix it, Irv. These guys owe me a favor. I could buy you some time."

"Could you?" Desperation and forlorn hope in Irv's voice.

"You already skim from the club. You could do better, pay off the boys and a cut for me," Tito said.

"I can't do it, Sid would know." Irv was babbling. "Jesus, I didn't know when you put me together with that guy; I needed the money, I had some hot tips at Suffolk. . . ."

"Shut up, Irv. I don't want to hear about it. I introduced you as a favor. It's your business if you can't pay off."

Tony was disgusted. He'd grown up surrounded by petty loan-sharking and crime and he knew the men Irv had gotten in deep with at a hundred percent interest. Tito was one of their boys. Just what he'd expect. And he wanted

230

everything besides, a cut of the skim and the star spot, for what good it would do him. Rotten little hood.

"I like my work here," Tito said. "And my friends want me to have the featured spot, they want me in solid here. Get rid of Spinelli, and I'll see they take the heat off you. For a while."

"Sid likes Tony," Irv pleaded. "I can't throw him out. Sid would never understand."

"Raoul said something about him banging some fancy dame; you could maybe put some pressure on her. . . ."

Tony had heard enough. It wasn't so much the blackmail of Irv or the mention of Alicia as the idea that scum like Tito wanted to replace him. He kicked open the door. Irv must have thought the hit man for the loan sharks had arrived, because he tumbled off the desk chair and cowered behind it in one motion. Tito whirled around, and before he could make a move, Tony landed a right on his chin and a good kick in the balls. Tito reeled back and doubled over, cursing.

"Tony, hey, Tony . . ." Irv was terrified.

"Shut up, Irv," Tony said. "Sid isn't going to like this. Especially if you're going to end up behind some warehouse with your hands wired up behind your back and a bullet in your head. All because Tito here couldn't get the big spenders to wrap a twenty around his prick."

"I'm gonna see . . . you're . . . dead, Spinelli." Tito managed to gasp out the words.

"Big talk, Tito. You worry about getting your dough back from Irv here, and forget about me."

"Tony, hey, what could I do?" Irv said desperately "You ain't going to tell Sid . . . ?"

"No, man. *You* tell Sid. If you weren't so fucking dumb, you'd know he'd bail you out and you wouldn't have to deal with this . . . hoodlum."

Tony turned on his heel and walked out of the office. There was silence behind him. He was sorry that his heroics seemed to have split a couple of seams on the guy's tux. He went quickly to the dressing room and changed into his own clothes.

"See ya, Tony," the bartender said as he passed on his way out.

"Yeah," Tony said. He was shaking with fury that Tito could think he was good enough to replace him—a real entertainer, not just a lousy stripper. He was better than that. Everybody knew it. He didn't need this joint.

Tony was surprised to see Barbara's gold Lincoln at the far side of the parking lot. It hadn't been there when he arrived, so he must have missed her while he was in the dressing room. Her parking lights were still on. He went over to shut them off. The doors were locked. He thought about going in to tell her, but he couldn't face another encounter with Irv and Tito. He'd kill them.

He sat in his car for a couple of minutes, thinking over what he'd heard. The more he thought, the madder he got. How many times had Alicia said he didn't need to be a stripper? He certainly didn't have to be one here. He could do anything. He waited a while longer, hoping Barbara would appear so he could give her a rundown on the night's events. She didn't come out. Tony remembered what he was planning to give Alicia—he opened the glove compartment and took out a rolled-up sheet of paper. Unrolled, it was the sketch of Alicia, lying back naked on a pile of pillows on his bed. He thought it was pretty good, better than anything he'd seen in Provincetown. He'd written across the bottom: "Alicia Sears does her best work lying down." Suddenly he knew what he had to do. He had a responsibility to himself.

Barbara still hadn't come out of the club. The parking lights still glowed across the asphalt lot. He tossed the drawing of Alicia on the seat and got out of the car.

He was going to quit. All the better if Barbara were there to hear what he had to say. He could imagine the explosion from Irv: first Tito pressuring him, then Tony quitting, and then he'd have to face Sid with the news. If Tony happened to let drop the fact that Irv had been taking money from the club to gamble and pay loan sharks, Barbara could pass it on to Sid, and Irv would get what he deserved. Tony felt pretty good as he walked back into the Carousel.

Alicia got to the Morocco Star a little after eleven. It was tucked away in the basement of a building off Inman Square, underneath a restaurant called the Morocco Sun, which appeared to be closed. She recalled reading a review of the place in *Boston* magazine or the *Phoenix*.

When her eyes adjusted to the darkness, she saw quite

a few people were sitting around the room on fat pillows set around low brass tables. The air was redolent with grass and a mixture of sweetish spices. Tony was not in sight. Alicia was still in her opera-going clothes, but Cambridge was accustomed to anything, even women alone in evening dress. No one turned a head to look at her standing beside the latticework screen at the entrance. Voices were low and Arabic music wound its way through the background, on the edge of hearing.

A young man with slicked-back hair and darkish skin made his way over to her.

"Yes?" A faint accent, possibly Moroccan, for all she knew.

"I'm meeting someone. Maybe you know him? Tony Spinelli?"

"Oh, Tony. He's not here, I think. I haven't seen him for a couple of weeks."

She was disappointed; he'd had plenty of time to get from Boston to Cambridge. One thing about Tony, he was usually on time.

"I'll wait, then. He should be here soon."

"This way," the man said, and led her to a corner table with a clear view of the entrance. "It's not really a place for singles," he said. "Couples, groups."

"And I am really waiting for Tony."

He looked her up and down, insolently. Tony had lovely friends, she thought. So warm.

Alicia collapsed in a heap on the cushion, with her dress tucked around her, and kicked off her shoes, as most of the other patrons had done. She felt uncomfortable being alone, as the minutes slipped by. Her neighbors were snuggled up close, smoking joints not too surreptitiously, and sipping on multicolored drinks. A waiter came by and suggested Moroccan mint tea or coffee or . . .

"I'll have tea," she said. She was starving, having missed Dean Barrow's post-opera supper as well as most of the hors d'oeuvres at her place. "Can I get anything to eat?"

"Sorry, the dining room's upstairs, and the kitchen's closed anyhow," the waiter said. "I might be able to find some almond cookies if there are any left."

"Anything," she said. "Please."

He brought back a silvery teapot and a small glass along

233

with a plate of crescent-shaped cookies. She nibbled them slowly, to make them last.

By quarter to twelve, Tony hadn't appeared.

At twelve, the music came up, and two musicians walked out into an open space at the end of the room. They began to play flute and drum, and a heavy-breasted woman in veils and bangles came out. The audience shouted and clapped. A belly dancer. She might have known. The woman began to dance, and Alicia admired her ability to control unexpected muscles. Maybe, she thought, she ought to take belly dancing lessons. Tony might be amused.

Alicia avoided looking at her watch, and she pretended to herself that she was interested in the movements of the dance, the swirl of her veils, the clink of her bangles and finger cymbals. She wasn't. She was thoroughly depressed at being stood up by Tony Spinelli.

"What a surprise. Mrs. Sears."

Alicia was jolted back to the reality of the Morocco Star. Victor Ostrava, looking somewhat like a trade commissar from a remote Iron Curtain country, was standing beside her table, beaming at her with an oily smile. Sitting on a low cushion, shoeless, put her at a distinct disadvantage.

"You're alone?" Victor said, taking in the single glass and the empty cookie plate.

"I'm expecting someone."

"But your . . . ah . . . escort appears to be much overdue. I have been observing you for some time. More than an hour. I did not know that Dr. Parker was so—hah-hah—irresponsible."

"I'm not waiting for Dr. . . ." She winced at being drawn into an admission she didn't choose to make to this man. It was too late. "Dr. Parker."

"Your friend, Dr. Catlett, then?" Ostrava was determined to discover whom she was waiting for. "I shouldn't think this place would be to the taste of either doctor. Ah, but Dr. Parker no doubt is attending Dean Barrow's gathering—as naturally I assumed you would be. Yet you came away to this . . . peculiar spot." He wore a faint smile.

Alicia felt a clutch of annoyance. Her white lie to the dean about a splitting headache to get out of supper was going to come home to roost. Victor Ostrava wouldn't hesitate to insinuate the fact of her presence here into Dean

Barrow's consciousness. And, God, if Tony walked in now . . .

Ostrava said, "Since you are alone for the moment, perhaps I might join you."

Before Alicia could speak, he had sunk down on the cushion beside her.

"Just for the present," he said, "until your escort arrives."

"How is it you happen to be here, Dr. Ostrava?" she said, keeping a watch on the entrance, ready to spring up and depart the minute Tony appeared, no matter how much he might protest.

"I come here from time to time," he said. "I spent some years in Rabat, and while the atmosphere is not precisely authentic, the cooking is distinctly North African. They serve an adequate *bstilla*. Although one hopes the pigeons therein are not the oafish residents of our Boston parks."

She ignored his attempt at humor, because she was seized with the conviction that he had followed her here. It was not at all a chance meeting. Now she wanted very much to escape him. The belly dancer had finished, loaded with bills in her waistband or tossed at her feet. Shades of the Carousel, or the other way around. The patrons were beginning to leave.

"I fear this place doesn't remain open late," Victor said. "I fear you have been . . . abandoned."

"Not at all," she said quickly. "It was a tentative arrangement, meeting here."

"Ah, yes. Of course." He eyed her knowingly. "I have been hoping that you might find a few moments—in the morning perhaps?—to go over with me again my needs for research funds. Before the trustees meeting."

Alicia sensed a threat in his words. His next ones confirmed it.

"I shall, naturally, say nothing of our meeting tonight. It might sound odd to Dean Barrow . . . this place. However, if the matter should arise in conversation . . ."

"I ought to be going," Alicia said. "Perhaps my friend had difficulties with the car."

Victor Ostrava leapt to his feet. "The car! Certainly! Why else would one ignore the charms of such a lovely lady? Now, Mrs. Sears, you must allow me to drive you home—Marlborough Street, is it not? Not out of my way at all."

"No. No thank you, I'll manage." She got up and found her shoes, shuddering when Ostrava reached out to steady her as she put them on.

"I cannot allow you to take a taxi," he said, and took her arm firmly.

The young man who had seated her was standing beside the lattice screen.

"Spinelli didn't make it?" He still had an insolent smile. "Should I tell him you were here if he shows up?"

Alicia didn't answer, but Victor did, in a jumble of foreign words she couldn't understand—except the name "Spinelli." Victor and the man laughed, and as Victor escorted her up the stairs to the street, he had an unpleasant smirk on his face.

"I imagine," he said, "that you found the belly dancer here tonight somewhat . . . different from what you are accustomed to? I presume you prefer . . . men? Yes. Dark Italians perhaps."

She pulled her arm out of Ostrava's grasp.

"I can't ask you to drive me home, Dr. Ostrava," she said. He did indeed know something of Tony.

"Please do call me Victor. And I insist. You'll not find a cab easily." He guided her toward a row of parked cars. "It's right along here."

Alicia glanced back over her shoulder, one last, desperate look for Tony and his white car arriving in the nick of time like the cavalry. There was no sign of him. He had truly stood her up. She should have guessed he had something like this in mind when they met at the opera.

It was a short ride across the Charles River to Boston. Alicia felt like crying, but she was determined not to show Victor Ostrava any emotion. She knew he must know a great deal about her private life, and he was prepared to use it to gain leverage with her in regard to his research money. It didn't matter how much she protested that her influence was minor. His last words as he pulled up in front of her building confirmed her suspicions.

"I shall stop by your office—when? Afternoon, I think." He was grinning like a shark when he turned to her. "I want to assure you, Mrs. Sears, that I am playing for very high stakes, financially and professionally. I am dedicated to my research, you understand, but I want far more. I need the backing of Commonwealth for the present, and I intend to have it."

"I must tell you again that I cannot influence . . ."

"The actual disbursement of funds? I understand that. But I think your positive or negative opinion of me carries a great deal of weight. And you, I assure you, are not the only person I have made my approaches to. In your case, however, I will not hesitate to . . . oh, shall we say, exert pressure because of information I have had gathered about your . . . social activities. I would not hesitate to inform my several contacts in the local press, for example. The resulting embarrassment to the university . . ." He didn't need to finish. Alicia understood him perfectly. "Good night, Mrs. Sears."

Alicia felt battered as she got out of the car. Now she did have a headache, and all she wanted to do was get into her apartment and call Tony. Forget about Victor Ostrava and find Tony. Have him there to hold her and make love, draw strength and contentment from his body . . .

She called. No one answered. She was empty, alone, miserable. She needed him, and he wasn't there. No matter how many reasons she could fabricate for Tony's non-appearance tonight, it always ended with one simple fact: he had failed her, suddenly and unexpectedly.

She tore off the dress she had brought so happily to please him, not knowing the circumstances under which he'd finally see it, and threw it on the bedroom chaise.

In her mind she went over and over the possibilities for his failure to meet her. The worst was that he had showed up at the opera, had forced her to agree to meet him, and had planned all along to stand her up.

But Tony, self-centered though he was, was not cruel. If anything, he was kind beneath the obligatory macho exterior, caring about his sister, his nieces and nephews, Lina Davio. About Alicia. He felt deeply the estrangement from his mother. He was so young and vulnerable, a little boy, really.

Perhaps that was the problem: his age and hers, although she resolutely tried to ignore the eight years between them. In those years, she'd married, divorced, worked at an increasingly responsible job. Eight years in the passage of time; immeasurable years in experience.

But I love him, she thought. And he, in his way, loves me. I know it.

It couldn't end this way.

Then, of course, she was certain that something terrible had happened to him. Even the thought of what Victor Ostrava was capable of doing to her because of Tony seemed unimportant.

26

ALICIA tried Tony again, early the next morning after a bad night.

A woman answered. She sounded young.

Alicia hoped in asking for Mr. Spinelli she sounded like somebody's secretary or a polite bill collector rather than a badly rested, slightly panicky lover.

"He's not here," the young woman said.

"When do you expect him?"

"I couldn't say." Surly. She hung up.

Now Alicia had more reason to feel as bad as she had ever felt. Jealous, furious, depressed by turns. Her mirror gave back the bad news: her hair looked terrible, her eyes had dark circles under them, she looked old and miserable. She didn't want to go to work; Dean Barrow would probably accept the idea that she was still ill, but there was Victor Ostrava to consider. He had obviously known whom she was meeting the Morocco Star, as he knew too much about her. She tried to suppress the sense of violation Victor aroused in her. He and Mike Tedesco, she did not now doubt, had conspired to invade her privacy, and if she didn't show up at the office today, she knew Victor would make sure Dean Barrow was made aware she hadn't been home nursing a headache.

It was also a certainty that when she saw Victor in the afternoon, he would proceed with his psychological blackmail.

" 'O what a tangled web . . .' " she said out loud to the mirror that hated her this morning.

And where was Tony? Why . . .

She almost fell running for the phone when it rang.

"Alicia?" It was Graham, sounding solicitous. "I called to see how you were feeling. I tried you last night and got no answer. I was worried."

"I unplugged the phone as soon as I got home," she lied. "I'm all right now. Needed a night's rest."

For a moment, Graham seemed like a haven. Good and kind, safe and reliable.

"Are you free for lunch?" she asked impulsively.

Graham hesitated. "The fact is, I'm not. And I'm afraid I can't break my date."

"Suzanne Benton?" The words slipped out before she thought about what she was saying. "I'm sorry, I don't mean to pry."

"As a matter of fact, it is Suzanne. I didn't know you knew her." He sounded surprised.

"I don't. Your mother mentioned her last night." Alicia got some pleasure from involving Mrs. Parker.

"She's fond of Suzanne," Graham said vaguely. "Well, we will get together soon. As long as you're all right. You are all right, aren't you?"

Something in his voice told Alicia that he had some inkling of the new path of her life, the one that had led irrevocably away from him.

"I'm fine," she said, and remembered the long night of tears behind her. "Don't worry about me, Gray."

She did not know how she would manage to begin, let alone get through, the day ahead.

Two people she did not care to be reminded of were sitting on the granite bench at the end of Hancock Place when Alicia arrived, somewhat late, at the administration building. Victor Ostrava—did he never rest? Mike Tedesco —did he never go to class? She thought they had not noticed her. Victor was speaking urgently to Mike, who appeared to shrug off what the doctor was saying. Then Victor stood up and, as Alicia pulled open the door with a backward glance at them, he headed for the laboratories.

"There are messages," Debbie said immediately, but instead of handing them to Alicia, she got up and followed her into her office, closing the door while Alicia took off her coat. "Harriet Gould called, and Dr. Catlett. . . ."

"I'll call them the minute I can." Harriet probably wanted to gossip about Tony.

What had happened to Tony? Why had he decided to end what they had had in this way?

Stop it, she said to herself. You've gone over that a hundred times.

Debbie was watching her with a puzzling expression. Speculative, worried, concerned.

"Alicia, a newspaper reporter called."

She sighed. "Everything about the school is supposed to come from the University News Office."

"It wasn't about the school. It was about you."

"Me? What about me?"

"What you did, where you were from, everything . . ."

"What did you tell him?"

"I told him your title, Assistant Dean, blah, blah. I hope that was all right. But nothing else, because I didn't know. Not really."

"Didn't know what?" Alicia felt the cold hand of trouble touch her.

"He wanted to know whether you knew a Tony Spinelli," Debbie said miserably. "I said I didn't know. He's going to call back. The reporter," she added quickly, because Alicia jumped at her words.

Alicia sat down and tried to look calm. Something was wrong, she knew. Something a reporter would call her about, and she wouldn't put it beyond Victor to have involved his "contacts" in the press.

"I know you know him," Debbie said. "Tony."

"Because Mike knows?"

Debbie looked more miserable. And guilty.

"But he never said why he . . ." Debbie was flustered on top of misery and guilt.

"He's been following me?"

Debbie nodded. "But I think it has something to do with Dr. Ostrava." She was unable to meet Alicia's eyes.

"Forget it, Debbie. I know. The reporter didn't say why he wanted to know about me and Tony?" Debbie shook her head.

She now firmly believed that Tony must be dead.

"Tony is . . . was a very good friend. But I don't want you to say anything to anybody, okay? Especially not any reporters. I'll talk to them."

241

Debbie was staring at her as though Alicia were a stranger. Alicia knew she must look awful.

"Ah . . . Mike wants to see you. Today."

"Dr. Ostrava is stopping by this afternoon. After I've dealt with him, I'll see Mike. And I've got to see Dean Barrow right away. Debbie, please. Stop looking at me as though I were a monster. I'm an old lady dean with funny friends. Ask the dean when he'll be free."

To Alicia's relief, Debbie went away without further conversation. A minute or two later, she called on the intercom to say that the dean could see her in half an hour.

Thirty minutes to consider Tony, the reporter, the shambles of her life. It had been such a short time she'd had with Tony, less than two months from her first sight of him, in his highwayman costume. From the moments of thoughtless humiliation he subjected her to at Sheila's party to his wonderful, ridiculous appearance last night at the opera, proving he could fit in if he wanted to.

Was he truly gone?

He couldn't be dead. Someone would have told her. Harriet or Billy . . . The two message slips, one from each, stared up at her from her desk. They had tried to tell her something. She made a move to call Harriet, then thought better of it. The school came first, and she had to concentrate on what she wanted to say to Dean Barrow.

It was only fair to prepare him for what might come, what Victor Ostrava might be plotting. She pulled herself together and went across to the dean's office.

Howard Barrow didn't look too happy this morning himself. Distracted and nervous.

"Sorry you were too ill to join us last evening," he said. "All right today?"

Alicia took a deep breath. "I have a confession, Dean Barrow. I didn't have a headache. Something came up which, at the time, seemed more important than being at the supper. I hope you'll forgive me. It was extremely irresponsible of me."

The dean considered. "Yes," he said. "But I accept what I take to be an apology. However, I wonder why you are bothering to mention it. I doubt I would have discovered your little lie."

"Because I believe that . . . Victor Ostrava, who ran into me when I should have been home with my headache, is going to use the information to put pressure on me for more money."

"That's ridiculous. The worst part of it was that I had to spend the entire meal talking to Mrs. Nelson. She had a bit too much to drink. If you'd been there, you could have deflected her."

"He might also suggest that the company I keep is not suitable. It's untrue," she added quickly, praying that Tony hadn't done something disgraceful. "But I wouldn't put it past Victor to embellish his comments."

"I understand," the dean said wearily. "I'm glad you told me, and I think I can trust you to handle Victor. Much as I hope that he is on the brink of success with his work, and much as I want him to have the facilities he needs to bring it to fruition, I also know that he has some . . . unsavory aspects to his single-mindedness. You do as you think best. I have to be leaving shortly anyhow. My wife took a bad turn, and I'm going home to be with her."

Alicia got to the door before the dean added, "The most important consideration with regard to the medical school is the avoidance of scandal. Nothing that would injure our credibility and distinction as an institution. I know you understand that. I doubt that Victor Ostrava sees further than his own self-interest. Which may ultimately be for the benefit of mankind, but his vision is basically limited to himself and his advantage."

"My feelings exactly," Alicia said.

She returned to her own office feeling that she had exaggerated what Victor Ostrava had the power to do. An unpleasant man. Possibly a great scientist. Graham had expressed some reservations about his work, but Graham was not above professional jealousy.

No scandal, the dean had said.

She'd exaggerated that possibility too, with respect to herself and Tony, whatever he might have become involved in. Victor might know she was having an affair with a male stripper some eight or nine years her junior, but what could he do with the knowledge? Everything could be denied to a reporter.

If she had followed her first impulse and had refused to attend Sheila's party at the Carousel Club, none of this would be happening.

If she had followed the impulse, she would not have had

Tony. She would have stayed asleep like a Boston Sleeping Beauty. . . .

She could never regret him.

"It's Mrs. Gould again," Debbie said about eleven. Alicia still hadn't brought herself to calling Harriet, but now the bad news couldn't be postponed any longer.

"Where have you been?" Harriet sounded frantic. "Did you hear the news? It was on the radio this morning. About your friend Tony . . ."

Alicia felt her stomach plummet, like an elevator dropping fifty floors.

"Is he alive?" she asked weakly.

"Yes, so far. Mass. General. There was a fire last night. At that place, the Carousel. Listen, it's in the morning paper. A possible gangland involvement . . . a man named Tito died."

Alicia groaned. "Does it say how?"

"He was shot. But wait, then it says there's Tony Spinelli's *mystery* woman, someone prominent in the academic community. I almost *died!* At least they didn't mention your name."

Remembering Tony's antipathy toward Tito, Alicia felt a wave of panic.

Harriet went on. "He was shot by the brother of the owner of the club. And Tony Spinelli saved this Irv and a woman named Barbara something. . . . Oy, Alicia. A *mystery* woman. You."

"You don't know that, Harriet."

"Alicia, I'm not so dumb. I harassed Billy until he told me a thing or two about you and Tony. I've known for ages. But if you didn't want to say anything, I wasn't going to make an issue of it. We're good enough friends to keep secrets as well as share them."

"Here's one I'll share. I think the press is on to me. A reporter has been trying to reach me."

"Say nothing. Refer him to Mark as your lawyer."

"I won't say anything, but I'm not ashamed of Tony." I don't think, she added to herself.

"Please tell me all about it," Harriet said wistfully, "when you have something to tell. And you know we'll stand behind you, whatever happens."

That was a small but welcome comfort.

"Dr. Ostrava's here," Debbie said while Alicia tried to absorb all that Harriet had told her. As soon as she got rid of Victor, she'd go to the hospital. She wanted to see Tony. He hadn't stood her up.

Ostrava came in looking like the wolf who had feasted on all three of the little pigs. He stood in front of Alicia's desk and leaned forward on his hands. Absolutely confident. He had a newspaper under his arm.

"Let us get down to business, my dear Mrs. Sears," he said. "I'm sure you have had time to think over how you might be of help to me. I have forgiven you your failure to persuade the Middle Eastern gentlemen—I understand it was because of your obstinate refusal to allow the dean to consider their desire for admission for their chosen candidates."

"It wasn't me, Dr. Ostrava. That would be totally against every policy of the university."

"Nevertheless, I blamed you. Now. I have determined that perhaps four million dollars over the next two academic years will be sufficient."

"Impossible. You haven't produced research data to support such a demand."

"I will," he said airily. "And not impossible. Not in return for what I might do for you. I have, you must by now understand, taken it upon myself to keep . . . a close watch on you. You are well respected in the academic community, but I might suggest that you are vulnerable to having your activities in certain areas . . . um . . . misinterpreted? The company you keep? Your sexual adventures?"

She had been expecting this, and didn't react.

Victor Ostrava persisted. "Your friend, Mr. Spinelli, for example . . ."

"Why would he be of concern to Commonwealth?"

Victor looked gleeful now. "A day or two ago, it might simply have been a matter of a questionable relationship. To give Dean Barrow and your social circle pause. Today, however, matters have altered somewhat." He watched her closely. "As you may be aware."

Alicia's knuckles whitened as she gripped the arms of her desk chair. She hoped the smile on her face gave nothing away, but she was thinking hard. Victor Ostrava had seen the papers, he knew she was the "mystery woman." No matter how vehemently she and everyone else refused to comment, the press knew something, and Victor could tell them more. And would.

"I think you are trying to blackmail me, Dr. Ostrava."

245

He feigned surprise.

"However, I am not ashamed of anything I've done," she said.

I will be strong, she repeated to herself. I won't let Ostrava get away with it.

"Ah, well," he said. "Because of the unfortunate circumstances your young lover finds himself in . . ."

"I understood he was a hero."

"And an artist as well."

Alicia was puzzled by what he was getting at.

"There is in existence," Victor said, "a certain drawing . . . um . . . unclothed, shall we say? It is clearly labeled as you, done by the young man."

"Not possible," she said faintly.

"It exists. I make it a point to maintain friendships with the ladies and gentlemen of the press." He drew a folded sheet of paper from his pocket. It was a Xerox of Tony's nude drawing of Alicia, complete with inscription. Unmistakably her. "Mrs. Sears, I could do considerable damage to your reputation. I have information to give . . . or withhold. Remember, too, the peace of mind of Dean Barrow. Scandal, tsk. It has a deleterious effect on contributions. I understand the dean is hoping for a large gift from a distinguished lady on the West Coast, for example."

"How do you know so damned much?" Alicia said. "And why?"

"I have learned to protect myself and my interests," he said. "Mine has not been an easy life."

Alicia sighed. "Dr. Ostrava, I don't know how to answer you. Your work, as you have said, attracts attention and funding to the medical school. The dean is interested in your research. I will do the best I can for you, but do not ever believe that I am bowing to your threats."

"Believe what you wish, Mrs. Sears. For the moment, I undertake to keep my knowledge of you to myself. If it becomes necessary to make it public . . . I expect decisions in my favor at the trustees meeting. Good day, Mrs. Sears."

He departed. Alicia loathed him. When he had had time to get out of the building, Alicia got her coat. She had to get to the hospital to see Tony. There couldn't be a picture of her. He'd always torn up his sketches of the two of them.

Mike Tedesco was hanging around Debbie's desk.

246

"I can't see you today, Mr. Tedesco," she said. "I have to leave." She never wanted to see Mike again.

"It'll only take a second, Dean Sears." He gave her his most ingratiating smile. "Please?"

"All right." He followed her into her office. "I suppose you want to explain why you've been behaving like a third-rate James Bond. Loathsome behavior, even for money."

He laughed, perfectly at ease.

"I know I'm a bad boy in your eyes," he said. "I suppose I am, but that has nothing to do with why I'm here." He took an envelope out of his inside jacket pocket and tossed it on her desk. "I've also been doing some lab work for a certain doctor. I've made a few notes you might find interesting. I haven't put my name on them, and I'll deny everything if asked. Do you know what he's doing?"

"I know he's trying to blackmail me, thanks to you."

"I mean his work."

"I know about the research, naturally," she said cautiously. "People seem to think it's one of the soundest directions for curing and preventing cancer. I don't pretend to understand the biology and chemistry and gene splicing that goes on."

"You don't need to," Mike said. "As far as this doctor is concerned, it's a lie."

"A *lie?*"

"Let's say that the published conclusions the doctor has arrived at are based on manipulated data. The papers he's had in journals, the stuff he's doing now. Phony data. Not that the direction isn't right. He knows a lot; he chooses to ignore the things that don't support his desired conclusions."

"How do you know this? Why doesn't somebody else?"

"I'm one of the few lab assistants who move around to different experiments. He trusts me, or he did; I did a lot of . . . checking up for him. But people told me things, what they suspected. I guess people . . . like me." Then Mike looked a little shamefaced. "Look, Dean Sears, I need the money, so I work a lot. I needed money enough so that I hinted around to him that I knew what was going on. . . ."

The place was a hotbed of blackmail.

"He said if I let out one word, I'd be out of the school so fast I'd think I was flying. I've always wanted to be a doctor, that's one thing. And I wouldn't put it past him to

247

go ahead and do it to me no matter how I promised to keep quiet. It was dumb of me to bring it up. The other thing is, if this faked stuff gets known, a lot of good guys are going to have ruined reputations because they were associated with him. So," he said guilelessly, "I want to do Ostrava in first."

"And the scandal would be very bad for the university," Alicia said, half to herself. "Worse than almost anything."

"Pretty nasty," Mike said. "Look, Dean Sears, about the checking up on you. I didn't think it would do any harm."

"It did, but it's too late now. I'll see what I can do with your report. I'll have to get some expert opinions, but I won't mention your name."

"Thanks."

"I ought to thank you. You saved me a bit of trouble. I think. I guess you're not such a bad boy after all."

He was so intensely handsome, standing there. She didn't blame Debbie one bit.

"But Mike, I don't want to see a good friend get hurt."

"She won't, Dean Sears. I promise."

Alicia wondered if Mike's information would forestall Victor, in the end. Somewhere that picture of her existed, and Ostrava wouldn't give up easily.

She hurried downtown to the hospital with mixed emotions. None of this was precisely the kind of fun she had in mind, when she thought that fun was what her life lacked.

She was ashamed that in the end what mattered most to her was that Tony hadn't stood her up.

27

TONY was in a semiprivate room, with a plump, motherly nurse hovering and Lina in a chair beside his bed. He was lying back with his eyes closed, looking boyish and innocent. He had a dark stubble of beard, but no marks on his face that Alicia could see, although his left arm had dressings on it.

Lina put her finger to her lips and got up to lead Alicia into the hall.

"I tried to find you," Lina said. "Didn't know the number to call. But that nice Dr. Catlett was around first thing."

"What happened? I only found out that Tony was here a little while ago."

"Eh, it's nothing. A couple of burns is all, and maybe some broken ribs. He'll tell you when he wakes up. Are you staying?"

Alicia nodded. "If it's all right."

"I think he was kinda waiting for you to show up. Denise came around, brought some things from his place. She's the one who used to go around with him." Lina looked into the room. Tony was still dozing. "I got to get back to the market," she said. "As long as you're here."

"Okay, Lina. Does his family know?"

"I phoned up his mother. She said it didn't matter none to her, as long as he wasn't dead and she had to pay to bury him. And Teresa knows. She's coming up from New York if she can."

Alicia went back into Tony's room. Someone had sent yellow roses. There was a screen drawn between his bed and that of the person sharing the room, and Alicia could hear a murmur of voices behind it. She sat down beside the bed in the chair Lina had vacated and picked up the newspaper on the floor beside it. The story was on page three: Fire destroys Carousel Club . . . suspicious origin . . . one dead . . . male strippers . . . Anthony Spinelli, 25, of the South End, featured performer in the strip show, credited with saving the life of Dorchester woman and brother of owner . . . police investigating possible loan shark connection . . . Spinelli reportedly closely associated with unnamed woman prominent in area academic community . . .

He was a hero of sorts, with a lot of unanswered questions.

"I'll be damned," Alicia said under her breath.

A small movement on the bed caught her eye. Tony's eyes were open and he was grinning at her.

"So you finally showed up," he said.

"More than I can say about you." She hid behind playfulness, to keep from crying from relief. "Are you okay?"

He shifted his shoulders and winced. "Hurts some. Ribs, from playing like a stuntman. Some burns, but not bad. No scars. Billy said I'd be all right."

"Good old Billy."

"He showed up this morning. You probably didn't think about me at all."

"I didn't know. I tried calling you, when you didn't meet me."

"Oh, Jesus, you must've been crazy sitting there in that dive. . . ." He laughed and winced.

"Me? Not at all." She, after all, had had Victor for company.

"Lying bitch, come here. Easy how you sit on the bed."

"I thought you'd . . . had enough, after that performance you put on at the opera. Gone forever. I had a bad night. Not such a great day." Victor had pursued her to this room.

"At least you didn't worry about me."

"Of course I did! Half the time I was furious and the rest I imagined you were dead."

"One thing you don't have to worry about is me being a stripper for a while. The Carousel's gone, and I ain't going

250

to show this body until it's perfect again. And besides . . ." He closed his eyes. "I was going in to quit when the fire happened. For you."

"Tony." She leaned forward to kiss him, and he grabbed her, whooping with laughter and pain, and pulled her down on top of him.

"Gotcha!" he said. "Ow-wee, that hurts."

The conversation behind the screen halted abruptly, and a gray-haired woman in a flowered hat peered around it at them. Alicia struggled to her feet and straightened her dress. The woman withdrew.

"By the way," Alicia said. "Who is this Denise?"

"Nobody." Impatiently. "A pal. Do I ask you who your pals are? Or your boyfriends?"

"There's nobody but you, Tony." The relief she had felt at seeing him alive and comparatively unharmed began to be pushed aside by other anxieties. "Tony, where did the drawing you did of me come from?"

"The one of you bare ass on the bed, yeah." He closed his eyes again, but opened one slightly to take a furtive look at her. "I was going to give it to you."

"How do you suppose a copy of it got into . . . unfriendly hands?"

Tony appeared to be considering one of the bandages on his arm.

"It's important, Tony. You have to tell me." She instantly regretted sounding like a teacher berating a recalcitrant schoolboy. "I mean, it could cause me trouble at the university."

"Screw the university. This whole thing is going to be great for my career. Publicity. I need it."

"*I* don't."

"Look, here's what happened. I went back to the club to leave the tux I borrowed. I had a little run-in with Irv and Tito. Irv's gotten mixed up with loan sharks, thanks to that shit, not that he wouldn't have on his own . . ."

"The 'gangland connection'? *Loan* sharks?"

"Those guys are not nice, Ali. Anyhow, the more I got thinking about it after I left, the madder I got. So I went back into the Carousel to quit, get that slime out of my hair. Barbara had showed up while I was changing my clothes, and when I went back, what do I find but Irv gone crazy, waving that cap gun of his around. . . ."

Tony was enjoying the retelling of the tale.

251

"You should have heard him, screaming like a maniac at Barb and Tito. He was going to kill them, he couldn't let Sid find out about the sharks, people were always out to get him."

"And then?" Alicia wanted him to get to the picture, to the way his connection with her managed to reach the newspapers.

"Eh, then he shot them, and came through the door into me. Tito he'd blown away, Barb got hit in the shoulder. I went after Irv, but I was hoping he'd gotten the hell out of the club and kept running."

The drawing, she kept thinking, and me. Get to the point.

"Well, he hadn't. Christ, I never saw anybody so out of his head. He went to the dressing room, you know what the backstage is like, and he set all this stuff on fire. Nothing scares me like fire, the whole place looked like it was going to go up like that. So I went back to get Barb; she was passed out."

He told the story well, the smoke curling up the hall, managing to heave Barbara up and get her through the back curtains onto the stage, and outside.

"Then I went back for Irv. I don't know why. The fire was too bad to get near Tito in the office. Man, you should have seen the place, ambulances and fire engines and people—I don't know where they came from. Even a reporter . . ."

Now they were getting to it. A reporter.

"He . . . um, got hold of the picture."

She fought down the desire to ask him if he had given the drawing to the reporter.

"It's no big thing. Hey, your man's a big hero. That picture don't mean a thing."

"It does when someone tries to blackmail me with it."

"You?" He laughed and winced.

"Me. What did you tell this . . . person?"

"Nothing. I talked to him for a minute, before they brought me here. He was real interested in your connections. I guess you're going to do me some good after all."

Alicia was stunned. The papers wouldn't dare print the sketch, but she couldn't yet imagine what they would print about her and Tony. And Victor had gotten his hands on a copy, using who knew what connections, and wouldn't hesitate to use it in the wake of Tony's "publicity."

"Please don't say anything more to anybody, Tony. About us. For my sake, and the school's."

"You dames are all the same," Tony said sullenly. "A guy tries to look out for the future, and you do everything you can to screw it up. The school. What do I care about the school?"

"What about me?"

"Look, sweetheart, are you going to stand by your man or not? That's your place, and don't forget it."

"I don't think I could forget," she said slowly. "You know I love you, Tony."

"Yeah. That's a good girl." He grinned complacently. As far as Tony was concerned, matters had been set straight.

"I wonder how much you care about me, Tony."

"Ain't nobody like you, Ali." He reached out and took her hand and kissed it, then closed his eyes contentedly. She leaned over and kissed him, wishing beyond all hope that this hadn't happened, feeling a rush of her old desire for Tony Spinelli.

"When do you get out of here?" she asked.

"Tomorrow." He was watching her under lowered lids, but she sensed he was seeing not her, but a member of his audience, the representative of the women who loved him and responded to him when he teased them with his body.

Alicia knew that something she had built a living fantasy upon had been irrevocably lost in the flames of the Carousel Club.

"Will you call me as soon as you're out?" She wasn't sure where they could go from here. She had too many things to think about to solve the problem of Tony here in a hospital room. "If there's anything you need . . ."

"Naw. Lina and Denise took care of everything."

"Great," she said with a tight smile. "Just great."

A sad-looking gray man shuffled in as she stood up.

"How ya doin', Spinelli?" he said.

"Sid!" Tony struggled to a sitting position. "I hear Irv's going to be okay."

"So they tell me. I came to thank you, kid. Irv, you know, he's a lousy guy, a lotta problems, always. But he's my brother. I was over at the other hospital to see Barbara. She says you're a saint."

"Sure, sure. Hey, Sid. This is my girl, Alicia. Sid Gabel, from the club."

"How do you do?" Alicia said. Sid nodded to her, but he was hardly seeing her.

"I'm going to reopen the Carousel. You won't be out of work long. The dames love you, Tony."

"Don't worry, Sid," Tony said. "I got things to do."

Alicia heard voices in the hall, and then Raoul rushed in, followed by a big, blond man.

"Tony . . . you living!" Raoul almost kissed him. He ignored Alicia.

"No sweat, Raoul. Hey, Jeff! Look who's here, Sid."

"Hiya, kid," Sid said. "Look, Jeff, I don't know why I blew up at you, back then. Irv . . . I'm a sucker for him. You doing okay?"

"Don't you worry your head," Jeff said. "I got me a real nice lady caretaker." He patted Sid on the shoulder, looking like an affectionate golden retriever.

"You are not injured?" Raoul asked Tony anxiously. "I read in the papers. . . ." His glance rested briefly on Alicia, who was now aching to depart.

"Wait till you guys hear the kind of publicity I'm going to get." Tony turned his attention entirely on the men. "They're going to be pounding on my door to come to work in Vegas. Sex and a hero! Man, there's a combination. I got to see this guy from one of the papers this afternoon, he said he'd stop by to interview me. . . ."

Alicia walked quickly out of the room.

And possibly, she thought, out of Tony Spinelli's life.

28

THE next two days were more harrowing than Alicia believed possible.

Tony made modest headlines again in a feature story about his part in the Carousel fire and, more to his delight, his work as a male stripper. Worse, from Alicia's point of view, was the fact that her name was there in black and white in the story: her "close" relationship, her connection with Commonwealth University, her background. It was the final humiliation, even though a part of her understood Tony's motivations. The good part was that Victor's implied threat of blackmail was now moot. The matter of Alicia and Tony had been taken out of his control.

She knew that if she could pull herself together, she could, with the aid of Mike's notes, do some blackmailing herself. But the turmoil distracted her.

Lenore Marks actually came to her apartment, eager to relate unversity gossip as purveyed by the secretaries and minor administrative people.

"God, Alicia, I almost died when I heard, and *I* was the one who persuaded you to go to that strip joint in the first place. What a joke. Oh, not you and this Tony," she said quickly, "that thing's no joke. But to hear people talk, it sounds like you were screwing a big porno star or something." She winced at her own words. "I guess in a way . . ."

"He's not," Alicia said passionately. "He's a nice young

255

man, he's serious about his dancing, and he's been very good to me."

"I hope he was good enough in the sack to rate that kind of defense," Lenore said, smiling wickedly. "Somebody said you'd broken up. Think he'd go for me?"

"No," Alicia said shortly. She hated to think of Tony with Lenore or anybody else. He was still hers. In a way.

Debbie was discreet, especially around the office, but Alicia had an uncomfortable sense that she looked upon her as a heroine. Elsa Morant certainly did.

"How brave of you," she twittered. "Imagine, it's like fulfilling every fantasy, first you see him on the stage, and then . . . become intimate."

Alicia smiled thinly. It was a terrible burden, she realized, for one's sexual life to become public property, which appeared to be the case if it was hinted at in the newspapers.

"I ought to tell you, though," Elsa said confidentially, "certain people are *not* pleased. I don't know if in this day and age anybody can really *say* anything. I mean, nobody's come right out and said you were . . . er . . . his . . . mistress? Is that the word they use nowadays? It smacks so much of Edwardian boudoirs or Fannie Hurst novels." She peered at Alicia, as though she were going to give her the definitive name for whatever Alicia was.

Sexual liberation, Alicia thought, lags somewhere to the rear of the media.

"Seriously, Elsa, what are they saying, and who are they?"

"The trustees, most of them out-of-towners, don't pay much attention to the local papers, but the dean has had a few calls from concerned university people. I guess a few reporters have tried to get comments." Elsa drew herself up proudly. "We can handle those people," she said. "Gossip and innuendo, that's my line. They can't get around me."

"Thanks, Elsa," Alicia said.

"I *love* it," Elsa said, and went away beaming.

Gardner Sears called, and Alicia told Debbie to say that she was in a meeting. He must have been infuriated to see the Sears name bandied about in print. Graham did not call at all.

Dean Barrow, surprisingly, seemed beyond shock. He was, if anything, rather more interested in the Victor

256

Ostrava research situation, although no names were mentioned.

"I think I've dealt with it," Alicia said, when the dean got around to the matter. "It's very sensitive. It makes my headlines . . . laughable, when you think of the hidden repercussions of scientific fraud. The person in question is going to arrange for some retractions of the validity of his data. If that doesn't happen, you'll have to take steps."

It had been a stormy meeting with Victor, who blustered and raged and threatened when she pointed out the flaws in his reports of success, when she told him she had information charging him with fiddling his data.

And when he brought up the matter of her personal life, she had made herself laugh.

"It seems to be public property, Victor. The harm, if any, has been done by cleverer minds than yours."

When she outlined the events for the dean, he said, "I want you to know that I have already taken subtle steps. A sort of investigation, acting on information received. Very discreet; he's valuable to the unversity. But," he was serious, "he is never going to forgive you. I know the man." He polished his glasses, returned them to his nose, and shuffled papers on his desk. "Discretion is to be prized highly."

"I've always tried to be discreet," Alicia said. "But events have a way of making a mockery of one's efforts."

"Well put. My dear, I sympathize entirely."

She was not sure, however, that he understood, but perhaps the enduring devotion he displayed to Mrs. Barrow indicated a passion that had once flowered in the same way hers had for Tony.

"I wonder," she said, "if this might not be an opportune time for me to make that trip to San Francisco. Get me out of the spotlight for a time. Unless you think my tattered reputation would be a disadvantage on the other side of the continent."

The dean looked amused. "I am fairly certain that no one on the western coast of the United States regularly reads Boston newspapers. I'm sure you'll have a pleasant time in San Francisco. Mrs. Madison: Lord, couldn't we use a half-million from her, and the Beck Foundation. And if you can face them, a jolly-up of the Bay Area alumni. You could put in some good work for the university as a whole, not only the medical school."

"Low profile until I depart. To think Victor was going to blackmail me! I ended up blackmailing him."

Dean Barrow stared at a nineteenth-century portrait of the first dean of Commonwealth Medical School. Alicia could never understand why he'd never had it removed from his sightline in his office. "Graham Parker is a very fine man," the dean said. Then he sighed. "We are none of us perfect."

The worst part was Tony. Or wasn't Tony, because he had become unavailable. She suspected Lina had taken him off to her house when Teresa came up from New York.

"What do you hear from the hero?" Billy asked.

"Uh . . . he's been busy. I spoke to him once after he got out of the hospital. Highly unsatisfactory."

"His condition? Or the relationship?"

"At the moment, there is no relationship to speak of. I'm going to San Francisco, by the way. End of next week."

"A strategic withdrawal. Probably a good idea. Ladies don't get noticed. Graham's mother would be the first to tell you that."

"Graham's mother, everybody's mother, has designated me a nonperson for the present. I suppose I can be grateful that nobody published the nude drawing of me on the front page."

Alicia went to Harriet's apartment after work one evening, a few days before she was scheduled to leave for California.

"It will be good to get away from Boston for a while," she said. "I haven't been anywhere for ages. I've hardly ever spent any time in San Francisco—my father took me once when I was in high school. And I was there for a couple of days when I was seeing Brett Handley; remember him?"

"Ah yes," Harriet said. "Alicia, you don't have to convince me you're going to enjoy getting away, but it sounds as though you do have to convince yourself."

Alicia bit her lip. The longer she didn't see or hear from Tony, the harder it had become. She longed for him, physically and emotionally. The flaws in his knowledge and style had become endearing. The memory of his touch, the way he looked, the way he talked, could destroy her concentration. She dreamed of him at night, and saw him every day in the distance on every street, only to discover that it was not Tony, the man didn't even resemble him.

She was tempted always to pick up the phone and call and call until she found him, but she couldn't. He had used her, he could call her.

Alicia noticed with a start that Harriet was gazing at her with the same kind of sympathy and exasperation that Dean Barrow had displayed. Joshua tottered over to her and put his hand on her knees. He looked up eagerly at her.

" 'Licia," he said.

"Hello, darling," she said, and as Harriet watched, the tears began to roll down Alicia's cheeks. One of them splashed on Josh's hand and he jerked it back, startled. He looked at the teardrop curiously and then at his mother.

"It's all right," Harriet said. Still Alicia's tears fell.

"I love him, Harriet. I don't know why. I'm furious about what's happened, the way he's used me and the fire for stupid publicity that won't achieve anything, but if we could get back to what we had . . ."

"I'm not clear on what the two of you had to begin with."

Alicia looked at Harriet, wondering if she truly didn't know. "Tony liked having a 'classy' and adoring woman, and I liked having him around to make love to me."

"I should have known. I knew it couldn't be his mind you loved him for."

Alicia felt the needle and resented it. "I suppose you think Graham's mind is a worthier object for devotion. I'll bet he and Gardner are having a grand old time gossiping about me at the Harvard Club."

"Would you take him back with open arms?"

"Who? Graham? I'm not sure he's up to dealing with a woman with such low tastes."

"Not Graham. Tony."

"Could I? I don't know. It's not as if we had a fight and could make up. It's something else. The way we used each other. And now we seem to have used each other up."

Mark burst in and swept up Josh, lifting him high in the air while he giggled delightedly.

"Watch out for that woman, kid. You think she's old Auntie Alicia, but she's really a well-known cradle robber."

"Mark Gould, shut up. Fast," Harriet said.

"It's okay," Alicia said. "Out of the mouths of babes . . ."

"And you watch who you're calling babe," Mark said. "I have a jealous wife. I thought I could recognize a scarlet woman but I was wrong. I'll never forgive myself for fixing you up with poor innocent Jerry Godwin." He winked at Alicia. "Or poor innocent Graham Parker. He must be investigating the literature on the psychology of women to figure you out."

"It must be Tony Spinelli who's the innocent one, a little boy who loves his body and bright shiny things to play with."

Like mirrors. A room full of mirrors surrounding a big, beautiful bed. Dim lights and music and Tony slowly taking off his clothes, taking off hers, hands on her body, hands on his. She felt rather than saw existence in that underground room where it was always night. She stood up quickly. How she missed him, how would she ever get through the days without him.

"I have to go now," she said.

"Come on, Alicia, stay," Mark said. "I just got here. I missed all the good stuff."

"Mark, I think Alicia wants to pack." Harriet gave him a look, a warning tone of voice.

He looked contrite. "Trying to cheer you up, Al. Isn't San Francisco where your old boyfriend lives? Aha! I see it now. It's a clever plot—"

Alicia interrupted. "I don't know if he's still living there. We haven't been in touch for a couple of years. I have a lot to accomplish on the Coast, I don't plan a social whirl. But I'll send you a postcard."

That night, of course, Tony called.

He was happy, excited, unaware (apparently) of any of her anxieties. "I've been busy, you wouldn't believe it. Ribs are okay, no scars from the burns. If there are, Sid's going to spring for plastic surgery. Barbara's okay, too. Can't do enough for me. Her family's got some connections places like Vegas and Atlantic City. I might go down to New York to stay with Terry, you could come. She likes you. Then I got to rehearse; I'm out of shape. You wouldn't want me to get fat. . . . Hey, are you still there?"

"I'm here," Alicia said. "But not for long. I'm leaving on a business trip soon. I'll be away for a couple of weeks."

There was silence from Tony. Then: "How come you didn't tell me?"

"How could I tell you? I don't see you."

"You got a telephone."

"I tried a few times," Alicia said. "You weren't around."

260

"Oh, yeah, well, I stayed with friends for a few days. You know how Lina likes to take care of me."

"How fortunate for you."

"Jesus, I hate it when you start sounding like a grand lady. What happened to the dame who liked to strip with me?"

"I'll call you the minute I get back, Tony," she said. "I might even find time to call you from San Francisco."

"Swell," he said. "Why are you doing this?"

"I'm merely doing my job, as best I can. It's been rather difficult what with the attention that's been paid to me."

"So that's what it is. You hate what I do, I know. But I do my job the best I can."

Neither said anything for what seemed like a very long time. She was hoping he'd say anything that sounded vaguely like "I love you." But love was expected to flow to him, not from him, and he didn't need to talk about it.

"Well," he said finally. "I'll be seeing you then. I'll be better than new when you get back."

If he'd only said, "Stay. I want you here. Don't leave me now. I need you." All the things she would have said yes to. He didn't. He didn't ask her to come to his place, suggest he come to hers, and she was damned if she'd ask.

So no one asked, and that was that.

Two days later she was on a noon plane from Logan Airport to San Francisco, looking down as they circled Boston. The harbor was dotted with boats of early season sailors skimming around the harbor islands in a brisk spring breeze. Cape Cod was a faint hook of land surrounded by water. Then they banked and headed west, leaving behind them an entire continent, Tony Spinelli, Victor and Mike, Graham, friends and colleagues who pitied and were puzzled.

She made a note to buy presents for Timmy and Graham Junior as well as Josh. Good old Auntie Alicia.

261

29

ALICIA had fond memories of San Francisco. It
was manageable, friendly, lovely, and sufficiently reminis-
cent of her own ocean-viewed city to be soothing rather
than strange. The hills around San Francisco Bay and the
towers of the city to the north of the airport were touched
by midafternoon sun as the plane landed.

She was staying at the Stanford Court Hotel on Nob Hill.
Apparently the school had decided that a fine hotel was
good for making a good appearance for the foundation
people and others she would be seeing. She was certain she
was not being rewarded personally. She had a day to become acclimated before her first meetings, and she spent it
driving herself around the city, up and down the terrifying
hills, which made Beacon Hill's ups and downs seem negli-
gible, along past the brightly painted Victorian houses away
from the center. She drove the roads through the trees in
the Presidio and ventured across the Golden Gate Bridge
to Marin County. She stopped in Tiburon to look at the
shops and eat a late lunch outdoors at Sam's, where she
could look at the boats in their slips directly in front of
her. At the end of the day, she drove to the edge of the
Pacific and saw the sun sinking in the distant western
ocean.

She was lonely, and thought, not for the first time, how
difficult it was to be a single woman who had advanced
beyond the carefree twenties. Billy, on the other hand, in

a city like San Francisco, would have taken himself out on the town with ease, and found any sort of congenial companionship he chose. She could call Brett, of course, assuming he was still around, but it would sound too desperate, she thought, to call her first day in town.

The problem with being anywhere unfamiliar was filling time. Gulls swooped and the ocean slithered in to the long empty beach as she got back into her car and went back to her hotel. She could go over the biographical sketch of Norma Madison the News Office had supplied her, although she knew well enough who she was and how much money she had.

Mrs. Madison was old, distinguished, wealthy. Her grandson, the last of the family, had been a graduate of Commonwealth Medical in the early sixties and had distinguished himself in whatever he had attempted in medicine through his residency. Then he had gone to Vietnam in the late sixties as a combat doctor, although with his connections he could have avoided it if he had chosen to. He had not. He had wanted to go, and he had been killed in the field in some obscure patch of jungle during the 1968 Tet offensive. He had left a widow, no children, and his grandmother. Norma Madison had been poised on the brink of endowing a chair at the medical school in his memory for some years. Dean Barrow was convinced it was only a matter of time—although time by now had reached almost a dozen years—but Mrs. Madison wavered. She was leaning toward a chair in tropical medicine, possibly because of a connection with the place where David Madison had met his death. Dean Barrow's instructions had been: "Get the money, talk her out of tropical medicine if you can. We'd rather have cardiology or immunology or anything. But get the money." Tony or not, he still trusted her.

"Get the money," Alicia muttered to herself as she parked in the driveway of the imposing Madison house on Pacific Heights. Not much of a driveway, considering that the house was built on a steep hill overlooking the bay. Alicia wondered how people had managed to negotiate the hills in the days before automobiles and trucks and cranes to raise the roofs and haul in the building materials. Or carry the groceries. Servants, of course. And nimble-footed horses and carriages for the owners.

Mrs. Madison's maid showed Alicia into a pleasant sitting room that had a superb view of the bay with its ocean-going traffic and clusters of pleasure boats around the edges. The maid brought tea, and Mrs. Madison poured from an extravagant silver teapot into fragile teacups.

Mrs. Madison was very old, but did not appear to be, as she described herself, "a sad, lonely old woman." She was sprightly and cheerful, and not the least reticent about discussing her late grandson or the disposition of her money.

"I'm delighted Commonwealth decided not to send another of their ponderous young men to sue for my favor," she said. "I always thought someone back East decided they would remind me favorably of David. Who definitely was not ponderous. A hell-raiser, although a dedicated doctor. Tell me about yourself."

Alicia was taken aback and then noticed the shrewd look with which Mrs. Madison was examining her. She wondered if someone had sent along clippings from the Boston newspapers that had featured the lady dean and the stripper. She would not be surprised to discover that Victor had done so.

"Perhaps," Alicia said slowly, "given the time scheme of things, I might have met David in Boston while I was at school, might have fallen in love with him, married him, lost him as you did." She paused. Norma Madison was listening, with a distant expression. "As it happened I married a young man from the Boston area. . . ."

"Sears, yes." Mrs. Madison spoke almost to herself.

"And in spite of pursuing him tenaciously from the time I was in my midteens, I discovered I knew him not at all, and my marriage was a mistake. I have been working at the medical school for a number of years now. Coercing anyone in range with money to share it with us."

"Yes, the money."

"I'm sure you know very well indeed how eager we are to increase our endowment. But not at the expense of your peace of mind or without your wholehearted commitment."

"Diplomatically spoken, my dear. I confess I've received none too subtle suggestions from my fellow San Franciscans that what money I possess ought to be plowed back into the city." She chuckled. "I've done far more for the city than people know. And David was greatly attached to Commonwealth and to Boston. I've examined the situation fully.

"I used to think of David out there in the swamps and jungles. He was always good about writing to me." Mrs.

Madison had a faraway look in her eyes. "I keep saying that you can't afford to look back, but at my age, there isn't a long future ahead, and what lies there in the memory —that is the way you survive the present, leaning on those good, full years. The moments you remember as if they were yesterday, they are so real. I speak of times that may seem quite distressing as they are occurring, as well as those instances of perfect joy. David's grandfather, my husband, died about the time David shipped out to Vietnam. Very sad. He and David were much alike." She put her teacup on the table and shook her head. "Listen to me ramble. You must think I dodder about this house and the city like a sad old ghost. This is not true. But a memorial to my past—to David—that is something I want very much."

"I think that whatever you decide will be the right thing for you, Mrs. Madison. I'm not here to bring pressure. Although I'd have to admit that it would make me look good in the annals of university fund raising to have persuaded you to make the endowment. Now you understand the selfish aspect to my visit."

"No more selfish and a good deal more honest than most of the petitioners who come here eyeing my checkbook." Mrs. Madison was amused. "I hope you have a young man. It's important to be attached in some fashion, otherwise you have so little to recreate a life in your mind when you get to be my age."

Mrs. Madison stood up, straight and proud, with her silky white hair coiled on the top of her head, and a sizable diamond or two twinkling on her fingers.

"If you'll telephone me on Wednesday morning, Alicia— if I may call you that—I will have made my final decision. I confess I don't know precisely what it will be, but it's time enough to commit. Wednesday won't interfere with your plans?"

Alicia stood when Mrs. Madison did, and felt very tall beside her.

"Wednesday will be fine, but we've hardly discussed—"

"My dear, for the past twelve years, since David was killed and the idea of a memorial occurred to me, I have discussed, and mulled, and mused and discussed again. I have all the information I will need, and far more than I ever wanted."

Norma Madison, Alicia decided, was a great game

player. She gave away nothing that might be stirring beneath her gracious surface.

"I hope I'll see you again before I go back East," Alicia said.

"Perhaps," Norma Madison said. She rang for the maid, and watched as Alicia was led out of the sitting room. At the doorway, Alicia looked back at her quickly, but Mrs. Madison was facing the windows that looked out on the bay.

Alicia felt that it had been a fruitless and disappointing meeting, however charming Mrs. Madison was. At least the question of the endowment would be resolved by Wednesday, but the expectation of the half-million dollars Dean Barrow had confidently predicted (and had believed in for over ten years) seemed remote. She had done her best, but Mrs. Madison had allowed her little scope for persuasion. She was a failure; she hoped she would do better with the foundation executives, with the Commonwealth alumni she was to meet at an afternoon reception a day hence, with one or two colleagues in the fund-raising game she was due to confer with.

She had Brett Handley's telephone number in Sausalito, as well as the number of the pilots' lounge at the airport. She decided it would be a feeble way to bolster her ego to call. And worse if he weren't in town or had a wife (he once had a wife, she remembered) who answered. Instead, she went to her meetings and filled up time. Twice she tried Tony, who did not answer. On Tuesday, she called Brett.

"Hey, Alicia, this is swell!" He sounded genuinely pleased and surprised to hear from her. "It's been a long time—nearly two years. I meant to call . . . I haven't been flying into Boston much. . . ."

"For heaven's sake, it doesn't matter," Alicia said. She was oddly happy to hear his voice. "I thought we might get together."

"Perfect timing, I have a few days off. Are you married? Engaged? Anything?"

"None of the above. For better or worse."

A handful of days and thousands of miles from Tony. She missed him, no question. She felt incomplete now without a man.

"Good. Dinner tomorrow night? I'll pick you up about seven. Where are you?"

"Stanford Court."

"Great. I'll have to get you to my place; I bought a house, at the end of a road on the side of a hill, with a view you wouldn't believe once the fog retreats. And it's got this deck that hangs out there in space, I don't know what holds it up."

"Fine way for a pilot to talk. I hope you don't have the same doubts about those seven-forty-sevens you fly."

"They are held up by my skill and prayers, both of which I can rely on completely. I got to run. Seven, Wednesday, Stanford Court."

"Ah . . . Brett, *you're* not married or engaged or anything?"

"Me? Free as can be, as always. You know me better than to ask that, Alicia. And that wife I once had in the dim past managed to remarry, so I don't even have alimony to pay anymore. I can promise you something better than a burger."

After she hung up, she stared at the phone beside her bed. It was one o'clock in Boston. She put out her hand. It would be so easy to connect up electronic impulses across the Rockies and the plains and the Mississippi, a right turn at Cleveland and on to Boston and Tony. To say what? She needed his arms, his mouth, his body engulfing hers. . . .

I'll call tomorrow, she thought. Or the day after. For all she knew, he'd hooked up with one of the other strip places around Boston. Or he'd be cross about being waked up, or he'd be cross because she'd disturbed him when he wasn't alone. Then she'd be hurt and unhappy, and hate herself for calling.

After the excuses she gave herself, Alicia knew that the true reason she hesitated to call was fear. She didn't want to know whether (how much) things had changed with Tony. Distance had made her easier about the Carousel situation and the newspapers. After the shock of seeing her life with Tony hinted at so broadly for all to read, after the alienation from him she had felt, Alicia had put many of her misgivings, much of her embarrassment out of her mind.

She and Tony had something wonderful, and it had to be strong enough to survive this rocky stretch of road.

She didn't like to admit that there were deeper troubles, fundamental ones, that it might not be possible to brush aside so readily.

At least, Alicia didn't have to trouble herself in that

way about Brett. There couldn't be anything less anxiety-provoking than a simple dinner with an old boyfriend from whom she had parted in distant days with no hard feelings. She did wonder if Brett would have the same appeal he once had—not sex, that was all over between them. But he had been a delight, the best of many men she had known. He had called it the curse of laid-back California, and claimed it was the only way to live.

Alicia was looking forward very much to seeing him.

She went to bed more or less content for a change. The definitive call to Norma Madison had to be made in the morning, a report to write for the dean. She would take care of her responsibilities, in some small but concrete way making up for the mess she'd left behind. The university, in spite of Dean Barrow's soothing assurances, was probably not pleased with her.

If she failed with Norma Madison, she had done her best.

If the past with Brett was over and done with, at least she would get a good dinner.

30

NOTHING turns out the way it should, the way that seems ideal when you're nestled down in an oversized and unfamiliar hotel bed in a strange city and you think you're in control of the situation. . . .

Alicia had many such random thoughts on Wednesday around about noon.

When she had called Norma Madison at eleven, a woman who identified herself as the housekeeper answered.

"Madame was called away," she said, "but she left a message for you, Mrs. Sears. Would you be good enough to join her for dinner this evening?"

"I'm afraid . . . well . . . another engagement . . ." Alicia hadn't realized that she would react so ineptly to the possibility of canceling her date with Brett. Then she got hold of her tongue—she was, after all, in San Francisco not to dally with old flames but to do the work she was well paid for.

The housekeeper said, "Madame has suggested that if you had other plans for dinner, she would be delighted to entertain your escort as well, if that would be feasible. She retires early so dinner will not be late. I assure you, the food is always excellent."

"Naturally, I'll be happy to come. But it might be an imposition to have Mr. Handley."

"Madame enjoys entertaining, Mrs. Sears. I will tell her that you and Mr. . . . ?"

"Handley, Brett Handley."

"You and Mr. Handley will be here. Seven-thirty, please. Dinner will be at eight."

Alicia felt as though she had been swept away by the whims of an old lady, but remembered that Dean Barrow had called her "strong-willed, although you wouldn't at first suspect it." And how would Brett take to having his plans for dinner rearranged behind his back? Alicia hoped that he would agree to join her but . . . she couldn't find him. He wasn't at home and the message she left at the pilots' lounge to call her she suspected he wouldn't get for several days.

Most disappointing was the fact that she would have to wait until that evening to find out about the endowment, and perhaps not then, if Norma Madison turned dinner into a purely social occasion. She called Boston to report the turn of events to Dean Barrow.

"Do what is necessary," he said and sounded resigned. "And enjoy yourself, my dear. It's an opportunity for you to . . . um . . . relax and regain . . . um . . . perspective."

Alicia felt like the delicate lass of decades past who was rushed off for a grand tour of Europe when she formed an "unsuitable connection" with a young man. Dean Barrow had clearly agreed to her Western trip in the hope that she would "forget" her misdeeds. She was both touched and amused by the dean's concern. Taking care of one of his own. She was comforted by the gesture, but not at all convinced that she was willing to surrender entirely to the demands of her class and circle. She'd definitely call Tony tonight, after dinner.

Brett Handley still looked as though he were seeing far horizons from the cockpit of a transcontinental jet. He was somewhat grayer, but he was still tall and lean, with the humorous smile that made a crinkle of fine lines around his eyes. He was still a very good-looking man. And unconcerned about the change in dinner plans.

"No problem," he said, "especially if it's something you have to do. You look terrific, Alicia. I'll be proud to sit down at anybody's table with you."

"I tried to reach you."

He laughed. "I said there's no problem. Nobody who lives around here could avoid hearing of Norma Madison, and it's an invitation you don't turn down. If she knows my name, she's probably had her secretary find out all about me. She won't let on she knows, of course."

"Do you mean to say that she knows the background of everybody she sees?" Visions of newspaper headlines danced in her head. Featuring Tony Spinelli and Alicia Sears.

"That's the rumor. She didn't get rich and old by being unprepared for what she had to deal with. You look a bit pale." He cocked his head and looked down at her. "Can you have a skeleton the good lady probably knows about?"

"I could," Alicia admitted. "And I just had a vision of half a million dollars disappearing into thin air. How could Dean Barrow not have known she'd know?"

"I think you'll probably have to tell me about it later."

"I think I probably won't. Shouldn't we be going?" They had met in the corner of the Stanford Court lobby, which was now getting crowded with people coming and going.

"I'd better make a quick call to Hans Brandt at l'Orangerie and tell him we won't be there. I like to maintain good relations with maitre d's."

She watched his tall figure, a head above everyone else in the lobby. They used to have rather good times, didn't they? He liked seeing things, doing things, he loved flying, and because he loved his work, he didn't have an underlayer of discontent to color the present moment. She remembered why they'd drifted apart, too: the very casualness about him that she liked so much hadn't satisfied her. She had wanted more, and he wasn't prepared to give it. It worked out that way in every damned one of her attachments, from Gardner to Graham to Tony, and she wondered if she were at fault, or everybody else.

"I'm almost ashamed to put you in my car," Brett said.

"As well you might be," Alicia said when she saw it. It was a shiny red and black Ferrari. "I wouldn't dream of asking how much this toy costs, but I must assume that you were paying that ex-wife a hefty alimony."

"You would be right, and suddenly that money was mine. It's a bit showy, but if I can't be at the controls in the air, I might as well be as happy as I can on the ground."

"At least we don't have very far to fall," Alicia said, looking out her window at the road, which seemed very close.

"This was a consideration," Brett said. "Now, tell me why we're having dinner with a grande dame of the city.

Other than because it's Commonwealth University's business."

"I'm not sure," Alicia said. "In theory, we're going to get half a million dollars from her. In reality . . ." She shrugged. "Maybe all we'll get is dinner. At this point, it doesn't matter much one way or the other."

"I confess I'd have preferred someplace alone with you to catch up on the past two years, but I know my duty."

They turned onto the Pacific Heights street on which the Madison house stood.

"I get the feeling, Alicia, that you're different from the girl I knew."

"You never knew me as a girl, Brett. You knew me as a child. A misguided child." She stopped. "And another misguided child made me grow up. A great many strange and wonderful things have happened in the past two years."

"Heavy talk," he said. "Let's save it for my hot tub."

Norma Madison came to the door herself when they arrived at precisely 7:30.

"How prompt," she said. "And how good of you to rearrange your plans for me."

"This is Brett Handley, Mrs. Madison," Alicia said. "He's accustomed to making landings on schedule."

"How do you do, ma'am." Brett's pilot's semi-Southern drawl surfaced.

"Come along to the living room for a cocktail, if you'd care for one," Mrs. Madison said. "May I take it that you're a pilot, Mr. Handley?"

Alicia and Brett exchanged a look behind her back that said, "She knows perfectly well . . . ," and they both smiled.

"Yes, ma'am," Brett said. "I certainly am. I fit my life around flying. Always have."

Mrs. Madison led them into a big, high-ceilinged room filled with beautiful, glossy pieces of furniture, with an exquisite blue, peach, and white Chinese oriental rug.

"Shall I call my maid, Mr. Handley, or would you care to make the drinks?" Mrs. Madison indicated the ornate table on wheels that held bottles, glasses, ice.

"I'd be delighted, ma'am," Brett said, and Alicia, close to him, whispered, "Don't overdo the good old boy, sonny." He gave her a half-wink and said to Norma Madison, "What can I get you?"

"A little sherry, please, and come join me over here, Alicia," she said. Behind her back, Brett raised a Scotch bottle to Alicia, who nodded. The chair she indicated to Alicia looked stiff and uncomfortable, but it was surprisingly pleasant. "I hope my command to dinner didn't disturb you," Mrs. Madison said. "I had thought to put you off until I could speak to you on the telephone myself, but one gets to an age where one feels entitled to make demands."

"It's perfectly all right. I'm here to see you, not Brett. He's an old friend, and he was pleased to come along. Apparently you are legendary for your hospitality. . . ."

"And a good deal more, my dear." She looked over at Brett. "An old friend . . . mmm. A very suitable-looking young man. Unattached, I presume."

"Mrs. Madison, I hope I don't detect matchmaking sounds. Because there is no match to be made."

"I understand." Mrs. Madison looked amused. Brett handed her a glass of pale golden sherry. "Were you in Vietnam, Mr. Handley? You seem to be the appropriate age, with the appropriate background."

He looked at her quickly. "Yes. I flew in Vietnam, near the end. It was safer in the air than on the ground, although not much. Certainly the surroundings were pleasanter."

Alicia shot him a warning look, but he shook his head imperceptibly. He knew absolutely what he was doing.

"Perhaps someone in your family . . . ?" he asked gently.

"My grandson, David, was a doctor there. He was killed. He was on the ground. Possibly Alicia mentioned him."

"No, ma'am, she didn't. But I must confess I knew that. No, I didn't know him, but I knew of him. He was somewhere around Hué, as I recall. A great loss, in a war with many . . . fine men lost."

Norma Madison looked at him for what seemed a long time.

"I don't know that I believe you knew of David, young man, but you do know how to say the right things."

They talked of other matters then, and dinner, when they went in to the formal dining room, was excellent, as the housekeeper had promised. Brett was charming, and Mrs. Madison was much taken with him. Alicia said little; she was rather taken with Brett herself. He fit in so easily in what might have been an awkward situation—apparently Bay Area people were so united in their fondness for their region that if conversation lagged, they could fall back on self-praise for being wise enough or lucky enough to live there. Tony would have found it rather heavy going.

In the midst of an extravagant dessert soufflé, Mrs. Madison turned to Alicia.

"I've been very cruel tonight, to have avoided the subject that I am sure has been foremost in your mind."

"Oh . . . no . . ."

Mrs. Madison laughed, a light, airy laugh as fragile as she was. "Don't deny it. Neither my cruelty nor what interests you." She put down her spoon and sat back in her chair. "I do intend to make the endowment to Commonwealth Medical." Her eyes twinkled as she looked at Brett. "I'd like you to think that Mr. Handley and his boundless charm were the moving forces in my decision, but alas, I cannot. You will discover that I was unavailable this morning because I was out seeing my lawyers and my financial people. However, I must admit that the company you keep and your own self confirm that I have made the right decision. The lawyers will want to see you in a day or two to explain some of the ramifications, answer any of your questions."

Alicia forbore to ask if the endowment was restricted; even a chair of tropical medicine would be welcome after Dean Barrow finished his mild grumbling.

"Thank you, Mrs. Madison. It's wonderful news."

Mrs. Madison merely nodded at Alicia's thanks, and led them back to the living room for brandies. "None for me," she said, "and I'm afraid I must end this delightful evening quite soon. No, no—don't rush." She sighed. "I simply can't stay up as I used to, although goodness knows, I sleep little. Yet when I want to attend the opera or the symphony, I am forced to nap and rest for two days beforehand." She looked at Alicia severely. "It is terrible to get old. See that you avoid it if possible. Stay young forever —perhaps your medical school will find a magic pill in your lifetime to solve the problem. Or else be very rich."

"Nothing is going to be solved in my lifetime," Alicia said to Brett as they walked to his car. Mrs. Madison was watching them from the doorway, she was sure. "Not for the world, not for me." She turned and waved to the straight-backed little figure backlighted by the hall lights.

"Sharp dame, Mrs. Madison," Brett said. "I'd say she doesn't hand over her money easily or to people she thinks are fools. Fact is, I've heard she was the one who controlled the old man's money; he was tending to a wastrel back in the rowdy old days, and she took the family fortune in hand before he frittered it away."

"Wine, women, et cetera?" Alicia asked.

"Something like that."

"She said her grandson was a hell-raiser, that he was like his grandfather. Maybe she thinks I'm sufficiently touched by the devil's wit to think I'm like him . . . if she really checks up on what the people she meets have on their conscience."

"You've got to be overstating your burdens of conscience," Brett said. "A nice little ole girl like you. Why, I remember . . ." Then he stopped. "Now can we catch up on the good old days? Stop someplace and talk?"

"I'd love to."

"Ah . . . why don't we do it at my place?"

Alicia cocked her head and looked at him with appraising eyes. They had paused at a stop sign, and the lights from the complicated dashboard shone up on his face. She felt a strong attraction to him, she admitted that much to herself. But because of it, because of Tony three thousand miles behind her and the unresolved entanglement, she thought it wouldn't be fair. Not to Brett who had always been so thoughtful and kind when he happened to turn up.

"Oh, Brett, I don't know. . . ."

"Hold it. I've heard that kind of coy talk too many times in my life."

"I'm not being coy!" She was almost indignant.

"Then what are you being?"

"Indecisive," she said decisively.

He laughed. "I'd really like to have you see the house. It's not far, and I have no designs on you."

Too bad, she thought. Because I think I'm getting designs on you.

But she couldn't be. She'd made mental commitments to Tony and herself.

"Why not?" she said.

"That's more like it." He accelerated and the slim, low

275

car sped along toward the Golden Gate Bridge. Alicia felt liberated by the speed and the night, and the sudden knowledge that she could do what she chose. The commitment she carried was to herself only, at least for this time, this place far from home.

31

BRETT's house in Sausalito was a strange, dark pile with jutting decks and odd, sharp corners, thrusting out from the side of a hill. He guided the Ferrari up the narrow road where the trees crowded close to the edge and overhung it so that sometimes it seemed as though they were traveling through a tunnel. There was only starlight and a thin sliver of moon, a few lights from houses along the way, mostly hidden by eucalyptus trees. It was as if she and Brett were speeding upward through a landscape that had no shape or perspective.

"I'm glad to see you've acquired a spirit of adventure," Brett said as he swooped around a turn and came to a stop in a driveway. He led her up dark steps and into a big living room. One wall consisted of glass doors that opened onto the deck. He turned on a dim light in the corner, and then drew her out to the deck to look at the bay far below them and stretching across to the city itself. The shore was marked by occasional lights, but even here it was dark and they seemed isolated from the world in the house.

When Brett stood behind her out there on the glassed-in deck, with only the one low lamp on behind them in the living room, he towered over her. He put his arms around her, and she tilted her head back to look up at him.

"It's good to be with you, Brett. Although I'm surprised to find myself here."

"Yeah," he said. "You are different, you know. I can't

277

put my finger on it—relaxed, I guess. Surer of yourself. I remember spending time with you in Boston when you were so uptight. Is that what I mean? I was almost relieved when it was time to go."

"Thanks a lot."

"Hey, I didn't mean I didn't like you. . . ."

"I understand, Brett. What happened was . . . discovery, followed by disillusionment. Hence a new perspective." She liked the feeling of his arms holding her and the feel of her body against his.

"Alicia," he said softly, "I have a strong and nearly uncontrollable desire. . . ."

She laughed. "Let me guess. Where's the bedroom . . . or the sofa . . . or the living room floor . . ."

"Come *on*," he said, grabbing her hand and leading her through the darkened house to a bedroom that also had a wall of smoky glass open to the world.

"It looks exhibitionist, except that it's one-way glass," he said as they tumbled out of their clothes. "Seeing out, nobody seeing in . . ." He picked her up suddenly and dropped her in the middle of the huge bed.

"Mmmm," he said, "different, and a lot more interesting . . ."

Alicia realized in a corner of her mind, even as Brett and she made love, that she had never been aware in the past of how appealing a lover he was. She had always missed the nuances, or perhaps it was that she hadn't before known how to take pleasure or give it. The familiarity of Brett and the strangeness of this new encounter gave a sensual delight different from . . . Tony. She pushed the thought of him out of her consciousness—and entered into the spirit of the moment, where there was no Tony, only a man who had lifted her up to unexpected peaks of passion and response.

Later, Brett said drowsily, "What have you been up to these two years? I don't recall you were ever so . . . enthusiastic."

"A little of this, a little of that." She rolled over onto her stomach and ran her hands over his body. Then she stood up and walked to the glass wall, conscious that he was watching her stand naked to look out at the points of light below them and in the distance.

"Are you sure people can't see in? I feel so exposed."

"Nope." She looked back at him over her shoulder with

278

an eyebrow raised in disbelief. "Really, they can't, Alicia. Except maybe from certain angles in certain kinds of light."

He laughed as she backed away from the windows, and then made a quick dash back to the bed.

"It's unnerving at first, I know, then you forget the feeling you're onstage for the whole world to see." He pulled her close beside him. "Look, you'll stay tonight, won't you? I could take you back to the hotel easily enough, but I want you to stay."

"Well . . ." She wanted to stay.

"I like having you here. I want you to see the place in the morning, when the fog is all around and then goes away with the sun. You can make me breakfast. Or I can make you breakfast."

"All right," she said, "except that I want more. More of you and better than ever. The whole night. And anything you want for breakfast . . ."

Alicia woke up early. Brett was sleeping deeply beside her. Outside the smoked windows, a bank of fog made it seem that they were in a cloud, but even as she watched, it lightened in the rising sun and seemed to thin and retreat. She rummaged in his closet and found a robe, then showered in a bathroom that looked more like a forest, with tall plants that almost touched the opaque skylight that was the ceiling. She was making breakfast, as promised, when Brett got up.

"Good service," he said. "I might be able to get you a job as a stewardess."

"I know all about you pilots and your flight attendants."

"Oddly enough," he said, "I date very few. They're either too young or they're married, or they're looking for the richest man in the world who happens to be on their flight—or they're looking to settle down with me, and make omelets for my breakfast and keep my windows shined."

"I like making omelets," she said, "but not on a daily basis. I don't do windows."

"Happily, I'm not around on a daily basis."

They looked at each other across the breakfast table and grinned.

"Nor am I," Alicia said. "But right now I'm thinking this was a great way to finish up a reunion of old friends."

"Think you could manage it for a couple more days? I could get you back to the city so you can go about your business, then we'll move you here for the rest of your stay."

"I shouldn't." Quickly: "I am here to work."

And it frightened her that the image of Tony had been pushed to the side of her consciousness.

"You can work as easily from this side of the Golden Gate Bridge as the other. And I'll take you about at night, we'll see some of my pals around the city, and then we'll come home and screw. I won't tell you I love you, because I don't think you expect me to anymore, but we'll have fun."

"Fun!" She burst out laughing. "Fun!"

"Not *funny*. Fun."

"I know," she said. "It's what I've always wanted."

It was fun, it was the best time Alicia had ever had, and she hated the thought it would soon be over. When she was free of commitments, they roamed the city. They drove to Carmel one day, they ate at wonderful restaurants, and joined with Brett's friends for social moments—and then fled to their glass house on the hill.

"Want to come with me when I take off for New York?" he asked one peaceful afternoon. "I'm going on Sunday."

"What are you taking off in?"

"A great big regularly scheduled airplane, along with several hundred others. How'd you like that? Flying home with me at the controls?"

"Now that I've driven with you on the ground, I wonder."

"Say yes, and we'll have a night on the town in New York."

"Yes. I'll finish everything I have to do by Sunday." She added as if it were an afterthought rather than a confession, "I could have been finished days ago, but I stretched it out so I'd have an excuse to stay on."

"Watch it. When you start rearranging your life to stick with me, you're asking for trouble."

"Don't worry, Brett," she said softly. "I'm not asking for anything beyond what I've had."

"Hey, Al." He came over and looked down at her hard. "Something worrying you?"

"Can you tell?"

"I can read you pretty well. It seems to happen when you get to like someone a lot."

"You like me a lot?"

"At least as much as you like me. Come on now, what's the problem?"

So she told him about Tony. About meeting him, and loving him, and losing her grip on him as he went off on his publicity high. She told him about the minor scandal she had been at the center of, thanks to Tony. About Victor Ostrava and the sheikhs, Gardner and Graham. But mostly about Tony.

"I guess you must think I've turned into a loose woman," she said.

"Hardly." He looked amused. "I think you're terrific. So different from when I knew you before. I like a woman who knows how to give pleasure; I like her better when she's looking out for her own pleasure too. That's not the Alicia I knew way back when, but it's the one I know now."

"And you truly like what you see?" she asked anxiously.

"And touch and smell and hold and talk to, for an indefinite length of time." She looked at him sharply. "Don't read anything into that, Al. We're on a holiday, and that makes things different."

"From real life?" She thought about how far Tony seemed from real life at the beginning, how quickly he became her real life.

"So to speak. Look, you're a strong person, with good sense and a good mind and . . . everything. I'm not going to tell you what I think you should do about this Tony."

"If there's anything left for me when I get back."

"Don't sound so bitter. We'll have fun in New York, we'll go our separate ways, and you've got to know I'll be back one of these days. But I'll understand if there's another . . ."

"Commitment? I guess I can live with that. I do like you a lot. You've been good for me."

She was damned if she was going to end this week on a negative note. After she had told Brett about Tony, he was no different than he'd been before, and Tony was not mentioned again.

She went to see Norma Madison once more before she left San Francisco.

"And how is your young man? Mr. Handley."

"He's fine. He asked me to give you his regards."

"An excellent person. A pity so many miles separate the two of you." Mrs. Madison poured out tea and handed the cup to Alicia.

281

"He gets to the East quite often," Alicia said.

"Occasional visits, yes, but it cannot be wholly satisfactory. Remember what I said about storing up memories for these old, empty years I'm living through now. You can't do that with occasional visits."

"Mrs. Madison, I ought to scold you, because now you are matchmaking."

"No, my dear. I am merely reminding you of the truth born of long experience." She wore a wise look as she watched Alicia. She probably did know all about the situation Alicia had left behind her in Boston, although she had never referred to it, even obliquely. "It's a pity, though, that you are not closer to us. I've become quite fond of you. You once mentioned that if chance and circumstances had been different, you might have met my grandson David in Boston. I must say that it would have pleased me."

Alicia laughed. "I wonder, Mrs. Madison. Then I was not the person I am now. And I'm not sure that the person I am now is exactly what you think you see."

"I see a good deal, my dear. I find you admirable in your independence, if somewhat foolhardy in your choices and the way you complicate your life."

Alicia remembered her words later, as the cab took her from Logan Airport through the tunnel into Boston. She and Brett had finally parted in New York, as Alicia boarded the shuttle flight at LaGuardia for Boston and Brett had waved good-bye before going on to Kennedy Airport for his return flight to California.

A complicated life indeed.

"Don't let this guy get to you, Al," Brett said. "None of us is worth it."

Then he said he'd be seeing her.

Alicia remembered that her mother used to say that summer romances fade with the tan. She hoped Brett wouldn't fade completely, unless she and Tony could regain what they'd had at the start. Some part of her still wanted that, and she could make it happen. She would bring Tony into her circle since he wanted it so much. She'd even harass every possible connection she had to give him a chance at what he dreamed of. The fault in Tony's ambitions was not that he was a male stripper but that he didn't have the guidance he needed.

If he could deal with Billy, he could also deal with someone like Harriet. With Mark. With Jennifer Newman.

She might take him to Paris to visit Sheila and Said, who had been settled for a month. They could go to Italy, where Tony might get a kick out of seeing where his parents came from. Goodness knows, he was fluent enough in Italian to feel right at home.

She might suggest that they try living together for a while. The time on the Cape, brief though it was, had remained a vivid memory of how beautiful it could be to be with Tony. Maybe after the experience at the Carousel, he'd be willing to find a different area of activity where he could satisfy his need to be loved.

Maybe her love would be enough.

She called Tony almost as soon as she put down her suitcase.

A recording told her that the number she had called was no longer in service.

32

"OKAY, where is he?"

"Who?" Billy was evasive. Maddening.

"Tony, goddammit. Who did you think?"

"Why would I know? Didn't you keep in touch while you were away? How was your trip, by the way?"

"Never mind my trip. I tried to call him a couple of times when I first got there," she said, "but he wasn't home. Come on, Billy. I know you know. Raoul must know."

"Raoul is no longer in residence."

"Finished him off that quick, huh?"

"I was falling in love with him. I couldn't . . . not someone like that."

"I think I must be going crazy. What's the difference between you and Raoul and me and Tony?"

"Not much, my pet. Maybe it's for the best that you stop seeing Tony. After all that's happened."

"Billy, I feel like a well-used tennis ball that's been over the net a few too many times. Exactly why shouldn't I go on seeing Tony the way I have? Harriet tells me the whole fire business has completely gone away. That kind of thing won't happen again, and that's the only thing people objected to. . . ."

"How fast you forget."

"Am I going to be able to pry Tony's whereabouts out of you?"

"No. I don't know." Billy sounded distant, as if Tony

284

and Alicia were of no interest. She couldn't figure it out. "I did happen to see him a week or so ago. He seemed rather annoyed with you, For going away. For not calling. For several things."

"He deserved it. All that cheap publicity went to his head. He needed a lesson."

"You know men, darling. Spoiled children. And don't wait around for them to grow up." Then he added softly, "Don't wait around for Tony, Al. I like him, don't misunderstand me, and I love you."

"I'm going to find him," she said stubbornly, "even if you won't or can't tell me where he is."

"Listen, Alicia. You almost ruined yourself. I don't think you quite grasp that. You and me and Graham. Dean Barrow, Harriet and Mark. We all belong to the same . . . class. It doesn't matter that I'm gay and Harriet and Mark are Jewish, and that Graham's the ultimate WASP. Those are distinctions within the group, and you belong with us. You can make mistakes, but you can't be a traitor to your class. If you are, you'll find you've gone beyond forgivable mistakes, and they'll never take you back. Is that what you want?"

"Does everybody I know believe life is a Russian novel set on the banks of the Charles River?"

"I've said my piece. I can't say more. Except that if you do find him and entangle yourself with him again, it's going to be a lot more difficult for both of you."

"I thought you of all people would be in my corner," she said.

"I am! Of course I am! That's why I'm telling you these things. Playtime is over."

"I want to see him," Alicia said. "Playtime or not."

She set out to find him, and it wasn't difficult. She tracked Lina down at the flower market, after discovering at his favorite hangouts that all people knew was that he was out of town.

Lina was reluctant to tell her at first.

"He expected more from you," she said accusingly.

"More what?"

"More attention, praise, love. I don't know how to tell you, but I understand Tony. Like he was my son."

"Lina, if he wanted more, what about me? What do I need?"

285

Lina shrugged. "Women are different. Men need to be shown how everything is centered on them."

"Is it?"

"It's what Tony expects," Lina said simply. "Take it or leave it."

"You have to give me a chance, Lina, to take it or leave it. Do you know where he is?"

"He went with Denise to some place in Atlantic City. They worked up an act together." Lina made a face. "Still stripping, but he says it's a great success. The lady he saved at the fire, Barbara, fixed it up. And Sid. One of the big casinos that has a show."

"How long is he going to be gone?" Alicia suppressed the idea of Denise.

"He didn't say. I guess he's set in this New Jersey place for a while."

"And you think I should leave him alone."

"I didn't say that, Alicia. Look, I think he liked you better than any woman I ever saw him with. He wasn't much for sticking with one girl. And I noticed he was different being around you." She chuckled. "Not smarter, but not so . . . selfish, I guess I'd have to say. That's what love does."

"I don't think Tony was ever in love with me."

"There's all kinds of ways of loving."

"I've got to see him," Alicia said. "To find out."

Alicia returned to her office feeling successful on the one hand, what with Mrs. Madison's endowment to her credit, and used up by her personal life on the other.

George was polishing the brass fixtures on the front door of the administration building when she arrived.

"Well, well, Miz Sears," he said. "Back again, and don't you look as beautiful as the day."

"You get mighty frisky in the spring, George," she said.

"Oh, spring does bring plenty of changes," he said. "Oh, yes. And you can't help hearing things, in and out of the building. Those women, they talk all the time, and such. Must be some kind of hot man, making you look so healthy."

Of course the incident of Tony would filter down to George rapidly, so she merely smiled, and went inside to the familiar, gracious hall.

"Dean Barrow wants to see you as soon as possible. He's due at nine-thirty," Debbie said. "How was your trip?

286

Pretty good, I guess, huh?" Debbie seemed excited, as though she had news, but didn't know how to begin.

"Want to tell me what's been going on?"

"I can't. I mean, I don't know, not really. But Alicia," she lowered her voice, "I've got news." She put out her left hand.

"You're engaged! Who . . . ?" Please, God, not Mike Tedesco.

"A fellow my father introduced me to. It happened fast. And Alicia, he's not one of these old guys, thank God. He's young and he's pretty good-looking. . . ."

"That's wonderful, Debbie."

"Well . . ." She shrugged philosophically. "It will get me out of the house with everybody watching me all the time. Now I'll only have one person keeping an eye on me, and he's not bad at all." Debbie was very happy, Alicia could tell. Safe in her circle and her class. How lucky she was, and Alicia remembered that not so long ago, Debbie had thought she was the lucky one.

"The big news is that Dr. Ostrava is leaving. They say he's going to work for a private company." Debbie gave her a knowing look, and Alicia wondered that she could have had the power to send Ostrava away so promptly. Then Debbie said, "From what I hear around here, he was offered so much money he couldn't refuse." She shrugged. "That's all he was ever interested in, anyhow. I never liked him."

"Nor did I." Alicia was pleased that she would not have Victor Ostrava as a constant pleader for funds or a perpetual shadow behind her private life.

Howard Barrow came through the front door, looking remarkably cheerful and brisk.

"Well, well, well. So you're back, Alicia. Come along to my office. A great deal to discuss."

Dean Barrow sat down behind his huge desk and beamed at Alicia. She thought Mrs. Barrow must be much improved.

"Excellent work. Excellent. Mrs. Madison—we were simply astounded when we heard."

"I didn't do much," Alicia said. "And after all, there's always been a good chance we'd get the money from her. It was good of her, of course."

"Good? My dear, can it be that you don't know? She tripled the original endowment we discussed, and the only

287

restriction is that some of it go toward a permanent memorial to her grandson, something that will carry his name."

Alicia sat back, stunned. "She didn't tell me. I had no idea."

"You must have made a good impression," the dean said. "Very important in this fund-raising business. Now let me see. . . ." He took a neat pile of papers from a drawer. "I assume you have heard about Victor Ostrava. Most surprising. Or is it?" He looked at her speculatively. "Is there more I should know?"

Alicia shook her head. "I believe he already had some strong connections in the private sector, Dean Barrow. He had access to money outside the university, no matter how desperate for funds he sounded. I think it would be wise to look into some of his research carefully, in order to be prepared for any challenges to our knowledge of what he was doing. We do want to avoid a scandal."

"Ah, yes. Indeed."

Alicia stood up, but Dean Barrow motioned her to sit again.

"I have one or two more things to discuss," he said. "I suppose we must consider our assault on the Arab gentlemen a failure. They were not willing to back down on their covert demands that their candidates for admission be given preferential treatment. However, we are not without hope that they will come around to our way of thinking. Especially if we guarantee certain research projects on problems that affect desert regions. Perhaps we could use some of the Madison funds as seed money. . . . Well! Enough of that for the moment." He shuffled through his papers. "Ah, yes. There's you."

Alicia couldn't imagine what was coming, but he had an almost pixie-ish smile on his face. He had avoided any mention of the Tony situation, but who knew what sort of conversations and speculations had continued to seethe through the school in her absence.

"The chancellor," Dean Barrow said slowly, "has informed me that Robert Stanforth is retiring."

"Yes?" Robert had been the head of fund-raising activities for the entire university for two decades. Alicia had worked with him from time to time, and Dorothea Stanforth, she recalled, thought that young Anthony Spinelli was a charming man. Once.

"The chancellor seems to think that you would be an

ideal replacement for him. And I have agreed, much as I would hate losing you here at the medical school."

"I don't know what to say."

"The position carries the title of vice-president. And numerous other advantages. Naturally, certain other candidates for the job are being considered, but as far as I'm concerned, this is pro forma. You are the first choice. Provided . . ."

Alicia heard a hint of something she didn't like, a suggestion that it was time for the bad news.

"You understand," he said, "in this kind of academic community we are . . . um, um . . . somewhat conservative, and we must maintain a public posture that is . . . beyond reproach." The dean seemed a bit uncomfortable now.

"If you're referring to the things in the newspapers associating me with a very close friend who happened to do something both newsworthy and courageous . . ."

"Very brave, yes, indeed, and all that will blow over soon enough if it hasn't already. What I had in mind . . . um . . ." Dean Barrow was floundering now, and Alicia decided she wasn't going to help him out of it. "I know that in this day and age, it is abhorrent to young professional women to suggest that . . . marriage . . . points in favor of . . . Don't you agree?"

"I can see many points in favor of marriage, Dean Barrow. But I certainly hope that I am not being politely coerced into considering marriage to a solid citizen, oh, someone like Graham Parker." Alicia was positive this was precisely what the dean had in mind.

"My dear, what an idea! I am merely suggesting that you might find it useful to have someone by your side who could assist you . . . emotional support . . . your home life . . ."

"I'm afraid that Dr. Parker and I are no longer as close as we once were," she said primly.

"Well, my goodness, I didn't mean to imply . . . ah . . ."

Alicia was ashamed of herself for teasing him. She knew what he meant, though she found it hard to agree. She smiled. "Unfortunately, I doubt that Dr. Parker is the type to devote himself to keeping my busy life running smoothly. I also disagree that being married has any bearing on my qualifications to raise money for Commonwealth University."

"Technically, not at all. But in more subtle ways, I think it does."

"Perhaps you're right," Alicia said slowly. "But I'm not sure I am prepared to marry because of those subtle ways. I can tell you, though, that I am not presently involved with anyone you might consider unsuitable. Does that answer doubts you might have?"

He didn't answer immediately, but busied himself rearranging his papers and returning them to the drawer.

"I hope you will think over what I've said, and let me know whether I can tell the chancellor that you want your name to be placed in consideration for the Stanforth job."

"I'll do that," she said, and stood up. "I'd better see what kind of mail has piled up while I was gone. It's been an illuminating conversation."

"You understand, Alicia," he said kindly, "I wouldn't dream of commenting on your private life if . . ."

"If it were up to you? If I didn't make my private life so public? I know."

So friends and colleagues had closed ranks behind her, the strayed lamb. Provided she proved she'd straightened up for good. Graham wasn't a real possibility anymore. Or was he? Tony—that was the bottom line. Did she still want him, or would she once she had seen him again? She was determined to find him. She couldn't simply leave well enough alone. And Brett was something else again. She couldn't see a long-distance romance with him, however much she enjoyed his company.

I want everything, she thought, everything Tony, Graham, Brett can give me. I want the job, on my terms. I want . . .

Alicia had to face the fact that she really did not know what she wanted. She supposed that the admission was some sort of progress in the direction of self-knowledge, but her confusion seemed small reward.

She postponed for a time finding Tony, although she thought about it with alternating excitement and despair. Afer several calls she found the right hotel-casino in Atlantic City and inquired how long he and Denise were booked for. She did not call him, hoping against hope that he would break down and call her first.

He did not, but Brett did, an affectionate and noncommittal call during which she tried to give nothing away about her life in Boston. Somehow, after what she had told him, it did not seem right to involve him with questions of marrying a man like Graham Parker for the sake of a job, or to weep on his distant shoulder about Tony's disappearance.

Like Mrs. Madison, she wished that they were not separated by so many miles. Brett Handley was a comfort she could use, physically and emotionally.

33

ALICIA stood outside the orange door with gold numbers and panicked. She shifted her bouquet from one arm to the other and raised her hand to knock.

And didn't knock, not for a minute.

It was stupid of her to be where she was, alone in the long corridor of the Atlantic City high-rise hotel, about to grovel to Tony Spinelli. A chambermaid pushing a cart came around a corner and gave Alicia a curious look, then continued down the hall. It was eleven in the morning, and Alicia hoped it was not too early. Tony and Denise did a very late show, as well as the earlier performance Alicia had slipped in to watch the previous evening.

When she had arrived in Atlantic City after a long drive from Boston, she had found the showroom where they were performing and then roamed around the casino until it was time for the show. She watched the crowds gamble and frolic amid glossy, somewhat vulgar surroundings. It was a long way from the shabbiness of the Carousel Club, and it was almost Tony's dream come true, a frail and inconsequential stardom in glittery sequinned trappings. She wondered if he ever noticed how deficient in that elusive quality he called "class" the place was.

She had delayed seeking Tony out. Although she had finally given in to her compulsion to come to the place where he was, she did not know whether she wished to come face to face with him.

Alicia had sat in the showroom alone and far enough away from the stage so that there was no chance Tony would notice her. The room was nearly full, a middle-class crowd of visitors and gamblers from New York, New Jersey, Connecticut. She hoped the audience would give Tony the attention and enthusiasm he craved. It was definitely not the kind of audience he was accustomed to at the Carousel, where the women had come primed for an erotic experience.

Tony and Denise came on after a singer, some dancing girls, a comedian, none of them exceptional; this was one of the lesser rooms. Alicia held her breath for Tony.

The number was elaborate, with clever costumes in satin and feathers, complicated light changes and music, and intricate choreography. It combined dancing with stripping, not the wildly sexual moves of Tony's Carousel days, but more subtly erotic combinations.

As Tony and Denise stripped, Alicia felt a pang. She recognized the moves. How often she and Tony had done the same things together in his room while the facets of glass captured the two of them in their nakedness. She wondered if it would ever happen again between them.

The audience loved Tony, and that pleased her.

It pleased her to see him and know that whatever came about between them, some part of him would always be hers. When she was an old, old lady like Norma Madison sitting alone and watching the ships in the harbor take away lives and bring them back, Tony would still be with her.

She could have located the dressing room then and gone to see him, but the idea of encountering her lover under Denise's eyes was distasteful. Who knew, in any case, what Tony's relationship with Denise was?

Who knew what Alicia's was with him?

Instead, after finding out that he and Denise both were living at the hotel themselves, she went to her room there and spent a restless night.

Seeing Tony again had stirred old desires, no question about it. She wanted him back in her arms, and so, by the time morning came, she was prepared to see him, beg him to let her back into his life as she had been in the past. She had never gotten enough of him. Their affair had been too short, their times together so random. Too few.

Yet she still hesitated to knock. Her eagerness to see

him, to begin again, was tempered by fear that it would not turn out all right.

She knocked.

It took him a while to answer. He wore a short robe and was bleary-eyed, as though she had wakened him, but to Alicia, he was the most beautiful sight she had ever seen.

"Congratulations, Tony. It's almost Vegas."

He was surprised. She thought he looked happy to see her. She handed him the flowers.

Tony glanced over his shoulder quickly. He was blocking her view of the room, but she knew he had someone there.

"Who's that?" A woman's voice thick with sleep mumbled behind him. Alicia knew her expression spoke her emotions.

"Look, it's only Denise," Tony said. "No big thing. Wait." He went over to the dresser and picked up a room key. Denise struggled to sit up on her elbows. Then her eyes opened wide at the sight of Alicia in the doorway.

"Hey, Tony . . ."

"Go back so sleep," he said. He put the flowers on a chair. "Let's go," he said to Alicia and closed the door behind them. He led her across the hall to another room. "It's Denise's," he said, opening the door. "We kind of use it to keep our costumes and stuff. She stays over with me, but it's not really . . . anything."

"You don't have to explain, Tony."

He shut the door and faced Alicia with his hands on her shoulders.

"I want to explain," he said. "Now, where the hell have you been?"

"Where the hell have *you* been?"

Suddenly she was wrapped in his arms in a moment of perfect happiness, and he was kissing her and holding her so close it took her breath away. Without releasing her he propelled her toward the bed, and she went willingly and without thinking, knowing only that she wanted him as much as he seemed to want her.

Tony swept a pile of clothes and costumes off the bed, and swept her onto it. Then he stopped, and they lay together gazing at each other, scarcely breathing, for what seemed like long minutes.

"Ali."

She was bursting with her desire. Slowly he unfastened

294

buttons, slipped off her clothing, stroked her body with a touch so delicate she felt herself grow feverish with the passion he was playing on. She reached out to him and slipped her hands under his robe. Tony's body, hers again, hard and smooth, so well remembered, so perfect. So right for her. Naked now they waited no longer, and Alicia knew that the feeling for Tony was touching depths of her being he had never reached before.

She had found what she had come searching for, and she overflowed with her love for this man. This moment was the ultimate climax of their relationship, like nothing before. Complete and exquisite, the concentrated essence of all fantasies and dreams.

Alicia thought she must faint from pure joy.

Tony felt it, too. She knew that smile. Satisfaction and subsiding ardor. They lay together in motionless tranquillity for a long time after.

"You could have waited for me for two weeks," she said finally. "Or left word where you'd gone. You could have called."

"You could have stayed home," he said.

"I couldn't, you know that. It was business." But she knew guiltily that she had chosen to go to California because of Tony and the publicity about the fire.

"Business," he said, and she thought she heard contempt for her work. She didn't want anything to spoil this time together.

"Let's not talk about it," she said.

"Pretend nothing's happening that you know is?" He sat up. "Ali, I could have waited a year, if it was me, Tony Spinelli, the way I am, you wanted. I got nothing except what I get for myself; I don't want to spend my life borrowing class from you or feeling I have to be what you want, and not who I am."

Neither said anything for a while. Alicia didn't know what to answer. He was right, and she hated the knowledge.

He got up and walked to a window and looked out through the slats of the blind.

"How did you find me?"

"Lina finally told me. I'm sure Billy knew, didn't he? But he wouldn't tell me."

"Doc's a smart guy." He faced her. "Get that look off

295

your face. He didn't advise me to go away. He just understood when I said I was going."

"I thought about coming every day for days. I couldn't decide whether it would be a good thing or a bad one."

"And now you know?"

"Wasn't it good?"

"Sweetheart, it was the best, but that ain't all there is to life. Sex ain't all."

She couldn't believe that she was hearing that from Tony Spinelli, male stripper.

"Then maybe it was a bad thing, after all," she said bitterly.

He looked at her seriously. "It *is* good, Ali. But it's the end."

"No!"

Gently he lifted up her chin. "Where are we now, then? Denise and me have got a great act. . . ."

"I know. I saw it last night. While I was getting up courage to come and find you."

"We're booked here in Atlantic City for another few weeks. There's a good chance then that we will be going to Las Vegas. Now, you want to come too?"

"I wish I could."

"No, you don't. You're saying so because it sounds good right now. What would we do? Get three rooms and make a happy trio, you and me and Denise? I got things to do, Ali, like you do. And I've had some time to think about you and me. For a long time, I wanted to be a big success to prove things to you and your friends. Now I want it for me. And . . ." He looked away from her. "I guess I don't need you to do it."

Alicia felt tears start, but she was damned if she would cry for Tony Spinelli. She slowly got dressed, trying to sort out her confusion and grief. He had learned to know himself somehow. Maybe she had given him the impetus to do so, to make what was a "classy" choice for himself.

The trouble was, he'd also made it for her, exerting his power over her one last time.

She walked to the door, but he said nothing. Didn't try to stop her. Didn't say, "Wait, I'm sorry. I'm wrong." If he had spoken so, she would have stopped, would have tried to find a way to accommodate both their lives in one.

"Ali." She stopped, and listened, breathlessly. "Don't do anything foolish, okay?"

She didn't know what he meant, but she shook her head. She couldn't bear to turn around and look at him once more.

Alicia walked out of the room and down the long corridor to the elevator. When it finally came, she stepped into it, and still did not look back, and left Tony's life.

Tony stayed for a long time in the room Alicia had left. Then he crossed the hall.

Denise was still in bed.

"Don't tell me the women are tracking you down in your room now."

"That was . . . an old friend. She happened to be in town. Brought you some flowers."

"Me? Why'd she do that?"

"She liked our act, wanted to wish us . . . success."

Denise eyed him suspiciously. "Is she that woman you were mixed up with in Boston?"

"It's none of your fucking business, Denise." He was angry. "I ain't your property. If you must know, she needed some advice."

"From you? That's a laugh, hon."

"I gave it to her anyway," he said. "Not in so many words. I hated to have to do it—she's a real classy dame. I wouldn't mind having her around. But it wouldn't work."

Denise sat up in bed and looked at him pacing restlessly.

"You still mixed up with her?"

"Shut up, Denise. God, you'll drive me crazy. I said she was just passing through."

"Okay, okay." Denise got out of bed and admired her voluptuous body in front of the mirror. "I'm hungry."

"Go get breakfast, then. And stay lost for a while."

Denise started to comb her hair slowly. "You know, Tony. I was thinking, if we're going to be here another month, we ought to find a place. I don't like living at the hotel, lousy little rooms they give us. If we had like an apartment, it would be kind of a home."

"I'm not looking for a home right now," he said, and lay down on the bed with his hands behind his head. "Move your ass, Denise. I want to be alone."

Denise shot him a hostile look but exited the room.

That was that. Alicia Sears was gone from his life.

Tony Spinelli was gone from Alicia's. She knew that as she drove back to Boston. How stupid she'd been to have made the trip to him and end up humiliated.

"I will never see Tony Spinelli again," she repeated over and over as she headed toward New York, Connecticut, Massachusetts. He was a child. Selfish. Self-centered. Uneducated. Thoughtless.

And he'd been right. About himself, about her.

She alternated between fury and depression. She allowed erotic memories of Tony to rise to consciousness, the glorious hours they had spent together that day, that time of making love such as she had never known. She felt his touch still, she felt him inside her, in her body and in her mind.

He didn't need her. She would learn not to need him.

A man like Graham Parker needed her. And perhaps, after all, she needed him. She had to give her answer to Dean Barrow and the chancellor about the new job. Gray would be an asset. Timmy certainly needed her; it might be peaceful to have a conventional marriage, home, family. She thought that if she chose to, she could win Graham back to her side. Maybe she would marry him in the end.

She would get Harriet's opinion, as soon as she got back to Boston, and had finished with her tears over Tony.

"Should you marry Graham Parker? You want a frank answer?"

"That's why I asked." Alicia had persuaded Harriet to have Mark baby-sit while the two of them went out for dinner. Alicia felt like going someplace dim and different, so they ended up at the Café Budapest.

"Well," Harriet said cautiously, "I'm not sure what your . . . present relationship is."

"Nonexistent, but he's taking me to dinner tomorrow."

"A very small beginning. But not precisely what I meant."

"Then what do you mean? Are we cordial? Could I bring him around to the point of proposing? Yes, to both."

"I think I mean, do you care about him? Love him? Like him even?"

"I like Graham."

"Oh, wow. You like Graham. It will be a marriage made in heaven."

"I told you the dean thinks a married Alicia would be better than a single one in the job at the chancellor's office, and the more I think about it, the more I want to be a vice-president. And remember, I'm thirty-four. There are fewer and fewer available men."

Alicia was taken aback by Harriet's laughter.

"Here's a woman with three men panting after her body or her mind in various degrees, Lenore should be so lucky, and she's telling me how few men are available."

"I really don't have anybody," Alicia said. "I dumped Graham, Tony dumped me, and I never had Brett at all."

"Maybe you would if you moved to San Francisco."

"Harriet!" Alicia sounded shocked. "I don't chase men!"

"Excuse me," Harriet said. "I suppose that trip to Atlantic City was just to kill time over a weekend."

"That. Dumbest thing I ever did. Eat your gulyas and give me some real advice."

"I have none to give. About Graham, though, I think you'd better remember that you've changed. I don't know your boyfriend Tony or what his influence really was, but between Gardner Sears and Graham Parker there was hardly a ripple of difference. And then this guy came along. It has to have had some effect, and I wonder if you can simply slip back into Graham's arms without . . . expecting more than he's going to give you. It's not advice, but it's what I think."

Alicia ate slowly and let Harriet's words sink in. Finally she said, "I think you're right, and I think I will marry Graham. If he wants me."

Harriet almost winced. "Alicia . . . don't be rash."

"Rashness has nothing to do with this, I assure you. No, I've decided. He's the least of many evils, and there are a lot of advantages. Even Dean Barrow will tell you that. I won't live in Weston, but I'll bet we could find a great big wonderful and incredibly expensive house in Cambridge. Brattle Street. Timmy would like living near Harvard Square. I won't have any trouble selling my apartment. Both kids will be away this summer, and Mrs. Parker will be out of my hair." Alicia was smiling, but it was a hard smile. "Funny thing. I'm right back where I was a few months ago when Graham proposed. Then it sounded awful. Now it sounds pretty good."

"I hope you're right," Harriet said. "And I'm not convinced that you could be back where you were. Too much has happened."

"You can be my matron of honor, just the way I was yours, much to the shock and disbelief of my Sears in-laws. Remember? They couldn't believe that I would dare participate in a Jewish wedding."

"And back when you married Gardner, I was sure his mother would make you send back my tainted gift."

"Hmmm. Do you think I ought to include Lenore in the wedding party for good measure? Oh, God . . . do you suppose Graham will have Gardner for his best man?"

"That's obscene!" Harriet shrieked. "I love it!" Other diners flared nostrils at the outburst.

"Of course, we'll want all the Sears family there, side by side with all the Parkers. My two mothers-in-law can commiserate while they smile and smile and smile."

"Do you suppose we can book Tony Spinelli for the entertainment? A G-string instead of a string quartet?" Then Harriet stopped in mid-laugh. "Are we serious, Al? About you and Graham? Or is it a joke?"

"I don't know, Harriet. What do you think?"

"I think it would probably be the biggest mistake of your life."

"I think you're right. But if I can get Graham to ask me, I'm going to do it."

Three weeks later, Alicia and Graham were seeing each other regularly. They were not sleeping together; Alicia could not bring herself to that, but they had returned to a pattern very much like what they had before.

Mrs. Parker was not pleased. She doubtless preferred Suzanne Benton. Timmy was delighted. Billy was not convinced that she was doing the right deed for the right reason.

"I have suffered a reversal of opinion," Billy said one day. "I know Tony had his flaws, no happy ending there, but marriage to Graham might well do more harm than good to both."

"It doesn't matter," Alicia said loftily. "I can take care of myself."

"I doubt it," Billy muttered.

"I think I'm going to persuade Graham to marry me at Dean Barrow's commencement open house. Everyone will be there, and I can leap to my feet and shout the happy news to one and all. He wouldn't dare refuse me."

"Very bad idea," Billy said.

"Nevertheless . . ."

She didn't mention her plan to Brett, who happened to call about this time.

"Wouldn't you like to come out here to San Francisco and play in my backyard?" he asked.

300

"I can't. I'm starting a new job pretty soon. Vice-president of the university, no less. One of several."

"Maybe I could come to you. I can fix it so I fly to Boston more often."

"What is all this sudden interest in poor old Alicia?"

Brett chuckled. "Must be something about a woman who can detach a million and a half dollars from a strong-willed lady like Norma Madison and who is great in bed. Too good to let slip away."

"I'm flattered. But what about my charm, my grace, my good looks?"

"All of those things, too," he said. "I'd really like to see you again, Al. A lot."

"If it works out, Brett . . ."

Perhaps, she thought, Dr. Graham Parker and his lovely new wife and two sons would pay a visit to San Francisco one day.

It bothered her quite a bit that she wasn't thrilled by the sound of that. She wondered if she was taking a wrong path with Gray. What about a continuing relationship with Brett?

Then she remembered that Brett was a nice holiday from real life. Nothing more. Not like Tony.

But Tony was gone. For the best of reasons.

Even Alicia had come to realize that.

34

"WHAT makes you think everything will be all right between you and Graham, once you're married?" Billy asked. He refused to give up prodding Alicia about her plans.

"I know it will. This is not supposed to be a grand passion. We'd be doing it for other reasons as well."

"And you'll learn to love him, later? My poor darling, that's too Victorian and entirely impractical. I know I carried on about where you belonged and how you can't betray your class, but I know this marriage is a serious mistake. Didn't you learn anything from Tony?"

"Oh, yes," she said softly. "I learned a great deal. About being selfish. About feeling for myself. I guess about love in a way I hadn't known." She sighed. "And that nobody's perfect, certainly no man, and you have to make compromises. Graham is my compromise."

She and Billy were sitting out in his garden in the late afternoon sun. The roses, orange, yellow, red, were coming into bloom, and the irises, as big as orchids, flowered in purple and white profusion along the walls.

"What about the life of the senses, my dear?" Billy said. "You will miss that. You must miss it now."

"I said, you can't have everything." Alicia spoke sharply. She did miss it. She had discovered it with Tony, and it had been fun. More than fun for a while: her whole life.

"Did you hear that a new Carousel Club is opening?" he said suddenly.

Alicia's heart stopped.

"Is . . . Tony back?"

"Don't know. Would it matter?"

"Not in the least," she said quickly. "I only wondered. Same place as the old one?"

"So I understand. Opens next week, I believe. Raoul called to tell me."

"How nice. And he didn't say anything about Tony?"

"I thought it didn't matter."

She didn't answer him. She couldn't go back, she knew. Tony had sent her away in Atlantic City, and it had been the right thing. Alicia Sears couldn't spend her life trailing after him through clubs and casino showrooms.

"I have a million things to do, Billy. The open house at the medical school is mostly my responsibility. Dean Barrow is making it a small farewell as I move up the ladder of life. And I've been working on Gray, so when I beg him to marry me, he'll be bowled over."

"And you're determined to announce your engagement?"

"Unless my feet turn to icebergs, Doc."

Billy saw her out and watched her thoughtfully as she headed down Mount Vernon Street. Then he settled down to make a telephone call.

I am lying to myself, Alicia thought, as she watched the guests for the open house trickle in to the main hall of the administration building. Today the back doors were open as well, giving out onto the fragment of lawn behind the building. Soon enough to be covered with concrete and supporting an efficient new building of many stories. This was the last year for the old one; as soon as commencement was over, the place would be demolished. The staff had already packed up most of the hundred years of files and sent them to temporary quarters until construction was completed. Alicia's successor, a brisk middle-aged woman who had a sound reputation in fund raising and would serve the medical school and Dean Barrow well, had already spent considerable time with Alicia, preparing to assume her post. She was there, making herself known to people.

Graham hovered nearby, fetching punch for his mother,

who had commandeered one of the leather armchairs and was holding court. Gardner Sears and his pregnant wife had greeted Alicia coolly, but Gardner would be delighted when she was no longer a Sears and no longer a moral responsibility and liability for him. Gardner was insufferable; too bad it had taken her so long to realize it.

Billy was there with the Goulds. They were to constitute a problem once she and Graham were married. He couldn't do much about her friendships now, but she was certain that he would not be willing to appreciate them as a couple as frequently as she did now.

She looked over at the three of them with a pang of sadness. They were all so fortunate. They gave her so much; she needed them. She didn't want to lose them.

The room was filling up: graduates and spouses and proud parents beaming over the new doctors in the family; distinguished guests from Harvard across the river, Boston University down the road, a Jesuit professor or two from Boston College; faculty and staff from Commonwealth.

I am lying to myself, she thought again, if I think what I'm doing will solve everything. And it's almost too late.

Dean Barrow was conferring with Graham. The dean was pleased about her, hopeful about her and Graham. "We've worked together a long time," he'd said. "I feel somewhat like a proud father. You've had some . . . difficult times this past year, but you've come through them well." She wasn't sure if he were referring to the Tony incident or Victor Ostrava. Likely both.

Her own father, himself heading for a marriage with Mrs. Ormond, and blissfully unaware that his daughter knew anyone named Tony Spinelli, let alone a male stripper, had not been enthusiastic when she mentioned the possibility of marriage to Graham.

"A fine man, Graham Parker. But I wonder . . ."

"Wonder what, Dad?"

"Nothing, nothing." Alicia sensed his hesitation on the other end of the line.

"He's very much like Gardner Sears," Donald Bridges finally said. "But you are not the same young girl you were when you first married. I am not in a position any longer to give you more than distant fatherly advice. I don't want you to make the same mistake twice—not that Gardner was a mistake at the time. . . ."

304

Alicia knew he was trying to warn her to think long and hard. He knew what had shattered her first marriage after its hopeful beginning. He saw the same occurring with Graham. He was right about the fact that she was different now—how different he couldn't know—but she promised herself that she was far better prepared to deal with a person like Gray than she had been with Gardner.

"I'll come East for the wedding, of course," her father said. "Unless you want to get married out here."

"I haven't even persuaded him to marry me, Dad," Alicia laughed. "Besides, you've got your own marriage to worry about."

"Yes," he said. "Vera is trying to decide when."

"Do I get to give you away?" Alicia asked. "The way you get to give me away from time to time."

"I hope you're not going to make a habit of marrying," he said.

"Nope. Graham's it." She'd hung up believing that.

As she watched the guests circulating at the open house, she began to wonder if Graham was "it" in any sense. Mrs. Parker was watching her with an icy smile and narrowed eyes, as she listened to . . .

Oh, God. Mrs. Parker was being addressed by Victor Ostrava. He had stayed at the medical school until the end of the academic year, but had given Alicia a wide berth. He had apparently undertaken to correct the distortions in his research; she had heard that much. She had also learned that his venture into the private sector after he left Commonwealh would probably make him a very wealthy man if his discoveries found commercial application. The prospect did not make him any more appealing to Alicia. She had been able to forgive Mike Tedesco for spying, but she couldn't forgive Victor for being the instigator.

What, she wondered, could he have to say to Mrs. Parker?

Then she knew, from the expression on her face.

Victor Ostrava was taking petty revenge on Alicia, one last time. He was regaling Mrs. Parker with details of Alicia's relationship with Tony that did not make the papers.

Alicia wanted to walk over to Victor and slap his smug face. How dare he? He had done enough to interfere in her life.

He had drawn a folded sheet of paper from a pocket.

305

Impossible. He could not be about to show that infamous, that lovely nude picture of her that Tony had done. The original had been destroyed under various legal threats. She had not realized that Victor might still have a copy:

"Alicia Sears does her best work lying down."

What a way to start off a marriage, with her prospective husband's mother given, she was sure, highly colored, and probably extremely prejudicial, details of her involvement with a male stripper.

Tony would haunt her forever.

I will not regret him, she thought. Never. But I will never see him again.

She saw Graham heading toward his mother and Victor Ostrava. He looked around and smiled warmly in Alicia's direction. She fairly sprinted across the floor to intercept him. If she got a commitment from him now, before he had a chance to be swayed by his mother . . .

One part of her mind was telling her that she was about to do what Tony had told her not to: something foolish. Another part told her to think of some painful, awful way to kill Victor Ostrava.

She got to Graham before he reached his mother, and linked her arm with his. Mrs. Parker flared her nostrils at the sight, but did not, Alicia noticed, actually breathe fire. Victor had stopped talking and was looking at Graham and Alicia with triumph and hatred. He believed that he had destroyed Alicia's relationship with Graham, or certainly with Graham's family. And he was glad. Perhaps he was also aware that he had been instrumental in separating her and Tony.

"Gray, I've got to talk to you about something. Right now."

"Of course, Alicia."

She looked up at the distinguished, basically kind and thoughtful man she was about to propose to. She kept repeating to herself what she and others like Billy knew: Graham cared about her a great deal. What she was about to do was foolish; true. It was also neither kind nor thoughtful.

She took a deep breath. "It's about you and me, Gray." She tried very hard to put caring and warmth into her voice. Out of the corner of her eye, she saw Billy come down the curved staircase and walk toward them. She saw

Mrs. Parker suddenly stand up, she saw Gardner Sears and his wife, and then Dean Barrow beaming at her and Graham.

"It's about marriage, Gray."

She should have done this somewhere else, alone, and not in the middle of a crowd who were waiting to hear Dean Barrow offer his and the school's congratulations on her new position in the university administration.

Billy had almost reached them. Graham was waiting expectantly. Surely he knew what she was about to say.

"Ours?" he asked gently. He looked quite happy.

"Alicia," Billy said in her ear. "You're getting one more chance. Which you don't deserve."

She opened her mouth to ask him what in hell he was talking about, please go away, when she caught sight of Debbie Koulos and Elsa Morant, who had been politely drinking punch on the fringes of the gathering.

Both of them had their mouths wide open, and were staring at a point behind her, at the front door.

Alicia spun around. George in his best suit and with the wickedest grin ever was holding the door open.

Tony walked through the door into the hall.

"Oh, God," Alicia said. "Thank God."

"The cavalry," Billy said, "has arrived."

Tony made his way through the guests toward her. She was aware of Graham behind her, and of Mrs. Parker. Victor and Billy, Gardner. She was glad Harriet and Mark were seeing this. It would appeal to Mark's sense of humor.

"Hello, sweetheart," Tony said. He looked down into her eyes and smiled. He was so beautiful. She had forgotten how beautiful he was. "You look good enough to marry. I told you you should always wear dresses that show off that nice ass."

"Excuse me," Graham said, too loudly.

"Gray, you remember Tony Spinelli, don't you?" she said, but she couldn't take her eyes off Tony. She knew she was smiling idiotically.

"I certainly do," Graham said. "I had hoped since . . . your temporary insanity, you had forgotten him."

It crossed her mind that Graham had steadfastly never referred to the Tony scandal of two months ago. Always kind and thoughtful, Graham was.

Gardner felt it necessary now to speak up. He was a

little the worse for his trips to the bar. "Young man, I'd suggest you leave."

Tony took Alicia's hand and raised it to his lips. A lovely, surprising gesture. "What do I do, Ali? Leave?"

"Be quiet, Gar," Alicia said. "Tony, that's my old husband. The person who's not allowed to call me Ali. We don't listen to him."

"I won't have this," Gardner said, as if he were in charge of Commonwealth Medical School. Whereas he was in attendance only because he was a member of a prominent local family whose name was attached to a university building.

"You're behaving very badly, Alicia," Graham said, and she heard someone, probably Mrs. Parker, harumph in the background. She looked around.

It had seemed to her that everything had stopped when Tony walked in, but except for the little group in the center of the room, everyone was behaving naturally, ignoring them, drinking punch, chatting politely.

"The party needs some livening up," Tony said. "Maybe a quick strip . . ." He seemed about to remove his jacket. Alicia recognized it as the Cardin blazer she had bought for him in March in Filene's basement, reduced from an astronomical price to a mere one hundred dollars. It seemed very long ago.

"We will have you ejected," Graham said. Tony was slipping the jacket down over his shoulders, and was rotating his hips. Shades of the Carousel indeed. George had edged over from his position at the door. He winked at Alicia.

"Alicia." Graham's voice was high-pitched and strained. "He wouldn't dare. George, if you please . . ." George made a "not me" gesture. He was enjoying this.

"Oh, I don't think he'll strip," Alicia said, not caring if Tony stripped naked. "Would you, Tony?" She was so happy to see him. "But perhaps Dr. Ostrava . . ." She looked around and saw Victor hanging back, "would like to see what all the fuss was about."

Victor melted into the crowd. More people were now paying attention to what was happening in the middle of the room. Tony wore a wry smile, as he shrugged his Cardin back over his shoulders.

"I don't think I will," Tony said. "I only stopped by to tell everybody that Alicia is going to marry me."

Above the babble of voices, Alicia heard Graham and Gardner speaking in unison: "She is *not!*"

Gardner probably believed that he would never free himself of the burden of Alicia.

"She's marrying me, of course," Graham said. "Alicia . . ."

Tony put his arm around her. Alicia's eyes met Billy's. He looked pleased with himself.

"No, I'm not going to marry you, Graham. I'm sorry."

She thought Mrs. Parker was probably as delighted as she had ever been to hear that.

"You're certainly not going to marry this—this—" Graham was sputtering.

"This very dear and special man? Who has made me happier than I believed possible?" She and Tony were standing body to body. She looked up at him. "Also unhappier, but it was worth it."

"I mean it, Ali," Tony said, and he was speaking as though they were alone in the world. "If that's what you want. We never talked about it, but I want you to be happy. You make me happy. Maybe we should give it a try. Billy says . . ."

"Billy." Alicia looked over at him and shook her head in exasperation. Billy beamed. He seldom had the opportunity to abet a public nose-thumb at society.

"Graham." Mrs. Parker's voice rose over the hum of the reception. "You do not need to subject yourself to this outrageous situation."

"Mother," Graham said sternly. "Mind your own business."

Good for Graham, Alicia thought. She was thinking several other things as well. How wonderful this gesture of Tony's was. How impossible. How wrong she had been about herself and what she wanted since their meeting in Atlantic City.

"Well," Tony said. "Will you marry me?"

"Darling," she said, "to become the third in a trio with Denise?"

"She understands, if I want to split up the act."

"You have ten seconds to make up your mind," Graham said.

"Right." Gardner was hanging in there. He'd get his ex-wife respectable if he died in the attempt.

"You will marry me," Graham said. "I forgive you and we will forget all of this. You will not consider any further contact with this . . . person."

She turned to him. "Unfortunately, Gray, 'this person' has changed me too much for him ever to be forgotten. No, I won't marry you. And there is nothing I need to be forgiven for."

Alicia took Tony's hand, and raised it to her lips.

They had that suspended moment. Their entire life together recalled in a few seconds.

"I won't, can't marry you, Tony. But thank you for asking. That was real class."

As she and Tony walked out the door arm in arm, Alicia imagined a wave of sighs of relief. Mrs. Parker, Billy, Graham, Gardner, the Goulds—all for different reasons.

Alicia felt relief, too. And her reason was one that had come to her in that electric moment when she and Tony had contemplated their past, and she had seen her future.

"Old times are gone forever, Tony."

"You can always find me, you know. If you want to."

"*When* I want to, Tony, I will."

He seemed almost shy when he said, "I'd like . . . you once more. Even if the old times are gone."

"Gone but not forgotten. I'd rather have it that way than forgotten but not gone. Tony, no one will ever love you as much as I did."

"Ali, I know. And you know . . ."

He was looking at *her*, not at a reflection of himself in her. Tony Spinelli had learned a thing or two. As much as she had.

"You and Denise are going to be big in Vegas," she said, to break the tension. "I promise I'll come to see you."

"Hurry up," Harriet called from the foyer. "Billy's double-parked."

"I'm coming," Alicia said.

Her apartment looked strange, empty of furniture, dusty already. She hated to leave it; she was glad she was leaving it. Her bags were already in Billy's car. Harriet, with whom she'd been staying while the movers had dismantled her place, had acquiesced to her desire to see the apartment one more time. And to meet Tony there, to say good-bye. She had been unable to bring herself to part at his place, where the mirrors might have had the power to call her back, draw her into the reflections and freeze her in glass.

"Thanks for coming here, Tony. Thanks for . . ." In spite of her resolve, she started to cry. "For saving my life. Graham would have—I would have died, I never would have seen the absurdity, dishonesty, until it was too late."

"Ali, please." Tony was distressed by her tears. "I'm no hero. I got forced into saving lives. I know I messed up yours some . . . because I kept thinking of me, Tony. Jesus, Alicia, please don't cry."

She wiped away her tears. "I'm *not* crying."

Tony threw back his head and laughed. "You can't learn to stop denying what's true, can you?"

He put his arm around her and walked her out the door. Harriet and Billy were standing on the sidewalk. The street, dressed in leafy trees and golden sunlight, was brimming with the loveliness of early summer.

Tony kissed Alicia one last time.

"The best," he said.

She didn't know if he meant her or himself. She thought he meant all of it, what they had, what had been hidden in them that they had discovered in themselves and each other.

We have made each other the person we are supposed to be, Alicia thought with wonder. We have made each other the best.

Billy drove her through Boston, toward the airport and the new life she had chosen to risk. She had consented to head the charitable foundation Norma Madison had decided to establish. Brett would be there to welcome her— "No strings . . . yet," he had said.

Alicia looked north over the jumbled rooftops of the North End, she saw the winding band of highway that passed by the new Carousel Club, risen from the ashes.

"Did you really love him?" Billy asked. "I don't mean to pry, but after all I contrived to do, I feel entitled."

"Did I? Billy, he was the wrongest person for me in every accepted sense. He had everything going against him; you said it yourself. I loved him, he loved me. He was . . . he is . . ."

311

She unfolded the rectangle of paper Tony had slipped into her hand as she got into the car.

A drawing of her, in that room of mirrors, naked on the bed. A hint of Tony, his face, his body, in a dozen dim reflections.

"Billy," she said, "he was . . . is the best."